SENTENCED TO TROLL 3

S.L. ROWLAND

AETHERVALE
PUBLISHING

ALSO BY S.L. ROWLAND

Sign up for S.L. Rowland's Newsletter

For signed copies and advanced chapters visit Patreon at patreon.com/slrowland

 Formatted with Vellum

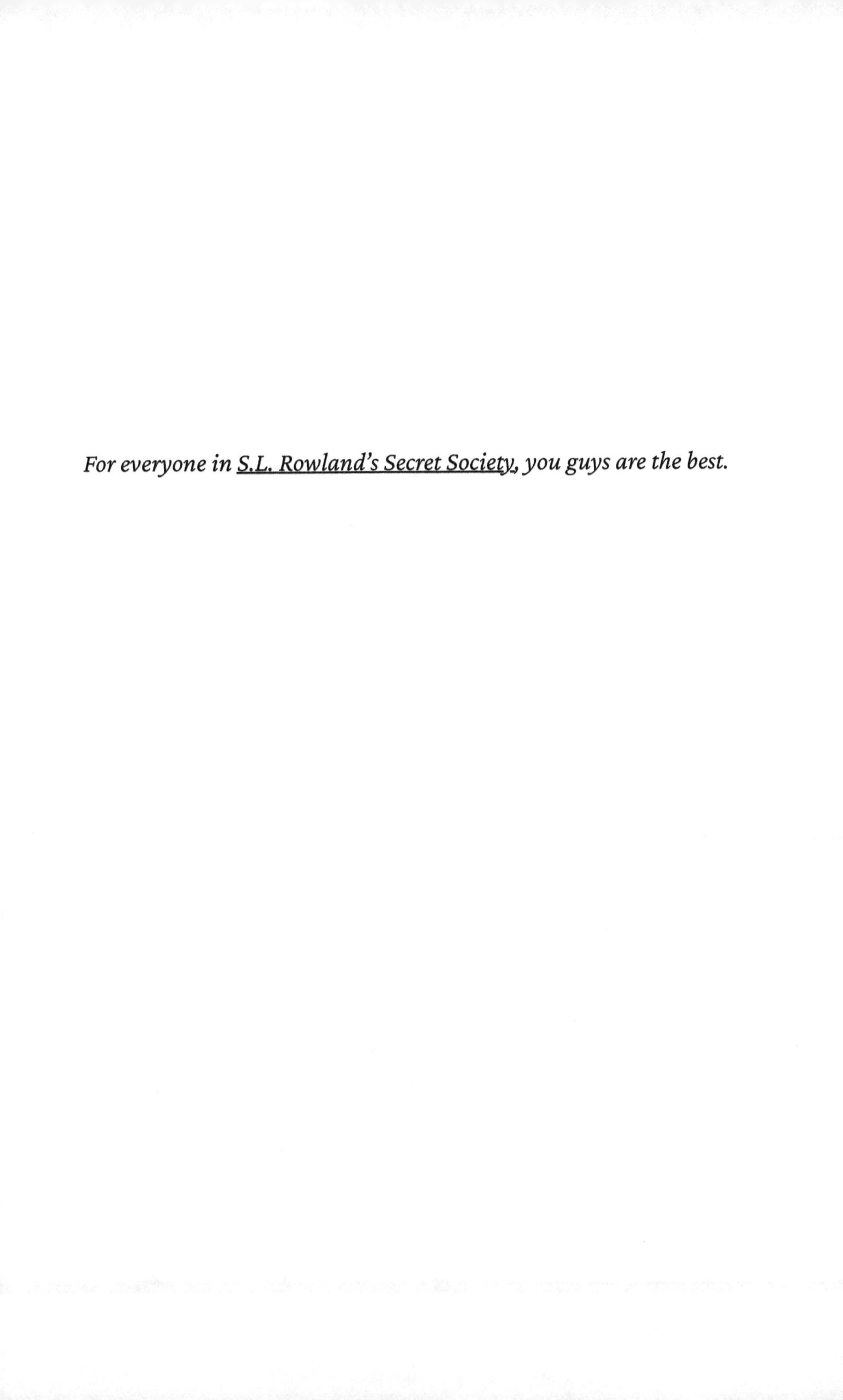

For everyone in <u>S.L. Rowland's Secret Society</u>, you guys are the best.

PROLOGUE

"Boss, you need to come see this." Thompson stared at the monitor above Chad Johnson's pod.

Valery cursed under her breath, wondering what could be happening this time. It had been weeks, but they'd made no progress in determining the connection between Chad and the AI going haywire. Tomorrow, they would be pulling him out again.

"What is it?" Valery hovered over Thompson like a hawk.

He pointed at the screen monitoring Chad's vitals. Everything looked normal.

Valery wasn't in the mood for games. She would be giving a presentation to the board in only a few short days, and while there was progress to report on the subjects' brain functions, the fact that one of the subjects was unable to log out without the system crashing would not be well-received.

Valery narrowed her eyes. "Are you going to tell me what I'm looking at, or should I find someone else who can?"

Thompson swallowed hard. "Look at this number." He

pointed to the display for Chad's body mass. "And then look at this." He handed her a tablet with Chad's initial vital statistics.

The numbers were different, which should have been impossible. The nanites were designed to keep the body in perfect stasis. They prevented muscle loss and fed the subjects with the precise amount of nutrients so that they didn't lose or gain weight.

"What does this mean? Are the nanites feeding him too much?" She compared the stats once again. It wasn't a major difference, but it was noticeable.

"I don't think so. The weight he's gained isn't fat. Look at this." He pointed to a second reading. "His muscle mass has increased."

Valery froze in place. If this were true, if the nanites were actually improving Chad's body based on what he did in the game, then this changed everything. The ability to rewire a mind was one thing—meditation had been shown to accomplish a similar feat for years—but going into a pod and coming out with a stronger body? That could change the world.

But was this an artifact of the strange connection between Chad and the game, or was it happening to everyone? Valery darted over to the next pod. Her hands shook as she called up the stats on the occupant.

CURRENT STATS

Current Stats

CHOD, *Level 21 Barbarian/Summoner Forest Troll*
HP: 4485/4485
Mana: 5000/5000
Rage: 0/100
XP: 403,625/415,000

Strength: 38
Dexterity: 24
Constitution: 39
Intelligence: 10
Wisdom: 15
Charisma: 6

+1 Strength and Constitution racial bonus per level.

2 stat points available.

0 ability points available.

Abilities:

Bite. *Using your massive tusks and powerful jaw, you take a bite out of an opponent, dealing immense damage. Cost: 10 rage Level 2.*

Claw. *You attack with sharp claws, swiping at an opponent and dealing extra damage. Cost: 5 rage. Level 2.*

Intimidation. *You stare down your opponent, confusing them so that they are unable to attack for two seconds. Cost 10 rage.*

Berserker Rage. *(Ultimate) Attacks and physical damage build your rage meter. 5 rage per attack. Rage meter deteriorates over time when out of combat at a rate of 5 rage per second. Activating Berserker Rage fills rage meter. For 30 seconds, rage meter does not decrease, deal increased damage, health regenerates at 5x the normal rate, cannot be stunned, slowed or otherwise affected. Cooldown: 10 minutes.*

I'm Always Angry *(Passive. Available at level 10). Once rage meter is at 50%, it will not deteriorate below 50% when out of combat.*

Increased Regeneration. *(Passive) Regenerate health at a faster rate. Level 2.* **Rapid Regeneration.** *(Passive) When below 10% health, regeneration is doubled.*

Nightvision. *(Passive) Increased vision in darkness and low light.*

Thick Skin. (Passive) Take 10% less damage from physical attacks.

Camouflage. (Passive) When out of combat and not moving for 20 seconds, trolls blend in with their surroundings.

Sweeping Slash. Form a sweeping arc in front of you, dealing damage and knocking your opponent off balance. Cost: 5 rage.

Conceal (Passive). Hides level from anyone who is not a guard on city grounds.

Summon horror (Passive). Ability to summon a horror. Each horror grants a unique ability. For every horror active, gain 1% increased damage and health points. Horrors decay 10% for every minute outside of combat.

Horror of Power. Summon a horror with 20% of your strength. Cost: 100 mana. Cooldown: 30 seconds. Bonus: Your next attack deals double damage.

Horror of Vitality. Summon a horror with 20% of your health points. Cost: 100 mana. Cooldown: 30 seconds. Bonus: Opponents near Horror of Vitality are slowed by 20%.

Horror of Finesse. Summon a horror with 20% of your attack speed. Cost: 100 mana. Cooldown: 30 seconds. Bonus: Your next attack heals you for damage dealt.

Sacrifice. Sacrifice X amount of horrors to receive a temporary buff. Horror of Power: +1 Strength. Horror of Vitality: +1 Constitution. Horror of Finesse: +1 Dexterity

Kamikaze. Sacrifice a horror to deal a burst of damage.

Champion. Summon a copy of the most recent enemy you have defeated. Decays 10% every minute out of combat. Cost: 50% of mana pool. Cooldown: 6 hours.

Available Abilities *(1 ability point to unlock)*:

Massive Bite. *Deals double damage. Cost: 20 rage*

Claws. *Swipe at opponent with both hands, dealing extra damage. Cost: 10 rage*

Multi Attack. *Bite and Claw at the same time. Cost: 20 rage*

Iron Will. *Immune to slows and stuns for 30 seconds. Cost: 50 rage 180 second cooldown.*

Perception. *For 10 minutes, gain increased awareness of your surroundings. Spot hidden objects, as well as unusual sounds, odors, and tastes. Cooldown: 6 hours.*

Cleave. *Your next attack causes bleed damage, dealing 1% of opponent's health per second for 5 seconds. Cost: 10 rage.*

Battle Cry. *You let out a ferocious roar, increasing rage by 20. No Cost. 60 second cooldown.*

Current Items:

Item. Phoenix Feather. 10% resistance to fire-based attacks. *A very rare item, phoenix feathers can only be gathered if they are willingly given by the host. Feathers plucked from unwilling birds turn to ash.*

Item. Tiger's Eye Pendant. Removes one debuff. Cooldown: 10 minutes. *A rare stone believed to ward off evil and bring balance to life.*

Item. Petrified Staff. An enchanted staff capable of taking on the properties of up to 3 attached stones. +3 Intelligence. +3 Wisdom. Bonus: *While holding Petrified Staff, the user can cast ranged physical attacks once every 10 seconds.*

Item. Forlorn Scepter. +5 Intelligence. _Increases the range of summoned creatures by 50%._

Item. Glouwseeker Venom. _When injected into the bloodstream, glouwseeker venom immobilizes target. Length of stun dependent on size of target, resistances, and amount injected._

Item. Sea Scorpion. +3 Strength. _An enchanted trident capable of taking on the property of 1 enchanted stone. Bonus: deals splash damage._

Legendary Item. Angel of Death Brandy. _When drinker falls below 1HP, a metaphysical event will occur, rewinding time for the user to two seconds prior to death._

CHAPTER 1

GOLDSPIRE

I ROLL MY SHOULDERS, trying to relieve some of the tension. I'm not the only one on edge, though. Dozens of guards surround the fast-travel portal located in the city square of Seascape.

They stand like statues, rigid and immovable.

Waiting.

King Orso Brightgaze looks down upon us from above the long set of stairs between the square and the castle. His kingsguard stands at the ready, their resplendent silver platemail shimmering in the midday sun.

Fast-travel has returned to *Isle of Mythos*. This should be a time for celebration, but the blood of fallen dwarves still lines the cobblestone streets.

The dwarven king towers over the dwarves surrounding him, at least a foot taller. His dull, red skin is the color of cooling magma, announcing to the world that he is one of the few blood dwarves that still exist. Bushy black hair falls to his shoulders. His black beard is intricately braided and adorned with silver clasps. He wears a black tunic and black cloak, each embroidered with silver thread. A red breastplate engraved with a silver warhammer protects his chest, and a glowing red crown rests on his head. The tines of the crown have alternating battleaxes and warhammers, emblems of his people's lineage. His face is set in stone as he watches us.

Four hours have passed since Jude and Glenn started a battle in the square that led to the deaths of many innocent dwarves. Even though both men were slain in combat, they had set their respawn points near enough that they were able to slip through the portal amid the chaos. Through a portal that had not been opened in centuries.

I worry about the havoc they may cause on the other side, wherever that may be. No one saw which rune flashed as they jumped through the portal, so the king has organized scouting parties to travel to each one, to warn the locals and search for answers and allies for what is yet to come. With a four-hour head start, even if we manage to find the correct portal, they've had plenty of time to disappear.

I still don't know if it was dumb luck or something else that caused me to open the portal. Jude tossed me against the archway, and it swallowed me in a vortex of dark energy. Somehow, the blessing that the forest trolls had bestowed upon me broke whatever dark magic had kept the portal sealed for so long.

Truthfully, I think Jude tried to kill me. Had I died, I have no doubt that he and Glenn would have killed their entire army of mind-controlled dwarf minions to try and break the seal. There was no way for him to know that I had been blessed. That portal had claimed the lives of countless men and dwarves alike who'd attempted to pass through. Only the blood dwarves were immune to the deadly effects of the dark energy, but even they received a horrible backlash from its sinister power.

I take a deep breath, trying to mentally prepare myself for

what's on the other side. The king gave us notes combed from Seascape's libraries, but so much time has passed since they were written that they may no longer be accurate. A betting man would say they aren't.

Even though dozens of us surround the portal, nobody moves. I'm sure they are all just as nervous as I am. The guards may be stoic, but the rest of us are not. An ebony dwarf constantly shuffles the butt of his spear, repositioning it with each breath. The blood dwarf paladin beside him rubs his stubby fingers against the back of his neck. None of us know what lies in wait, and if I had to guess, no one on the other side knows our portal is open either. Four hours and no one has come through. I don't know if that's good or bad.

White energy swirls inside the rune-covered archway. Hints of silver flash within the ethereal whirlpool. Half of the runes that run along the arch have a faint red glow, indicating the portal has access to a counterpart on the other side. The rest are empty engravings, their portals still blocked by dark magic, including the lands where the dark wizard vanished to centuries before.

Vanaria's portal is also among the inactive.

For now.

Isle of Mythos is about to change. For the better, I hope. Both ends of the island could use a little diversity.

While we all prepare to venture into unknown lands, Limery speeds south. First, to the forest trolls, and then to the human capital with news of how to open the portal.

King Orso was prepared to send ravens south, but I thought it would be smarter to send Limery. The imp can fly far faster than even the speediest raven, and both Chief Rizza and King Favian will trust his word.

Every second we waste is more time for Glenn and Jude to gather forces on the other side.

"Ready?" I ask Taryn.

"Not one bit." He looks at the polished marble courtyard, his dreadlocks covering his eyes. Caked blood fills in the cracks. He taps the butt of his gnarled staff against the marble tile a few times before making eye contact. His pet bear nuzzles against the druid's leg.

Taryn is still shaken up from the battle. I don't blame him. This was his first battle where he wasn't just killing monsters. When he cast Lightning Bolt, the smell of burning dwarven flesh filled the air. This may be a game, but it sure doesn't feel like it. When those dwarves died, they screamed and bled like real people. Some cried out the names of those they wished to see in their final moments. Others shit and pissed themselves with their last breaths. No, I don't blame him one bit.

White energy swirls inside the stone archway as the first group moves forward. Two blood dwarf paladins, an ivory dwarf warrior, and an ebony dwarf dressed in fine linens step up to the platform surrounding the archway.

As they approach, the active runes along the arch burst to life, glowing a fiery red that matches the skin of the blood dwarves. They look to their king for approval.

He nods before speaking. "Focus on the rune you wish to travel to." His deep voice carries like a megaphone, somehow magically amplified. "When it is the only one left glowing, step through. You will emerge in new lands. Make contact with the locals, hand them the parchment with my message, and then return home at once. If trouble arises, return to safety. Our guards will be waiting on the other side." The king raises his warhammer into the air, and the four dwarves slam a fist against their chests. The runes all fade except for one that looks like a triangle with a V passing through its center.

One by one, the dwarves step through the portal, vanishing

from sight. As soon as they are through, the next scouting party takes their place. The crowd surrounding the portal grows smaller and smaller until our group is all that remains within the circle of soldiers surrounding the perimeter.

I pull up the quest King Orso gave us.

Quest Alert. *You have been offered the quest 'First Contact: Goldspire.' Travel into the lands of Goldspire and deliver King Orso Brightgaze's message to its leaders.*

__Bonus:__ If Jude or Glenn have traveled to Goldspire, apprehend them and return to Seascape so that they may face justice.

__Reward:__ Increased favor with Seascape, potential allies in Goldspire.

Taryn and I approach the portal, his two pets following close at our heels. Berry, the umber bear with a beautiful golden coat, keeps close to Taryn. The bear guards him like a loyal dog, always obedient. Stompy brings up the rear. The mighty moulhaug with a broad, moss-covered backside and a single horn that protrudes from the center of its snout behaves more like a common housecat, if that housecat was capable of wrecking an entire building. The horn on its snout can swing with such force that it acts as a battering ram. Stompy snorts, voicing his displeasure. Despite his moodiness, Stompy has saved our asses on more than one occasion.

Further back, my small army of horrors begin to puff out of existence as their cooldowns expire. The demonic creatures won't be joining our journey through the portal for fear of what those on the other side might think. The last thing I want is to show up with a small army and start a war unintentionally. But at least they will give me an added stat boost for a few minutes before they fade away.

I hope I don't need it.

When we step on the platform surrounding the arch, I focus on the rune for Goldspire, two vertical lines with a caret symbol over the top. The rune resembles a house, or an arrow with two shafts instead of one.

The other runes dim, leaving the one for Goldspire burning a vibrant red.

As we step through, white energy surrounds our bodies, and for a moment, everything is silent. Then, just as quickly as we entered, we step into a world of chaos.

CHAPTER 2

YOU CAN'T MILK THOSE

THE WHITE SWIRL of the portal fades, and we step into a sandy arena. A rustic stone coliseum towers around us, obscuring the landscape except for blue skies overhead. The sun beams down from above, hot and dry. Clashing metal draws my attention, followed by roars, screams, and blaring trumpets that echo across the pit.

What is this place?

Wherever it is, it's far from *Isle of Mythos*. The sun was overhead when we left, but now it is closer to the horizon.

Stompy paws at the ground and releases an agitated snort. Several spots of rust-colored sand surround his hoofprint. Blood. Berry sniffs at the blood-soaked sand and curls his lips in a snarl, revealing teeth capable of snapping bones like twigs.

I feel you, buddy. How many happy endings start with a blood-covered entrance?

A packed crowd fills the stands, spectating as a half-dozen battles rage around the arena. In the blazing sun, only their outlines are visible. A dark silhouette falls to the arena floor and the crowd erupts in applause. I have no idea what we stumbled into, but I don't want to stick around to find out. I search the perimeter of the arena for an exit, but all of the tunnels are barred.

The only way out is back through the portal.

"What the hell is this place? Some kind of gladiatorial arena?" I ask.

"I don't know, but there is a giant fucking cow walking right towards us!" Taryn climbs onto Stompy's back and readies his gnarled staff to attack.

I turn to see a minotaur that's every bit as tall as I am and a little bit wider stalking in our direction. Its powerful muscles ripple with each aggressive step, and a trail of dust follows in its wake. The minotaur's broad shoulders are covered in radiant golden fur. Obsidian horns stretch the width of its body, their tips dangerous weapons capable of goring anyone unlucky enough to step within their range. A silver nose-ring dangles from its nostrils, nearly twice the size of the one Gord has. The only clothing the minotaur wears is a black leather loincloth, and the only armor, two vambraces that shield its forearms. A thick chain hangs from its waist like a belt, the end tipped with a sickle that holds the weapon in place. The minotaur's clenched fists remind me of giant sledgehammers. Sand plumes into the air with each step it takes before it comes to a stop a few yards away. Steam shoots out of its nostrils, and I take a moment to analyze it.

Dakota

Level 33

Level thirty-three. That's one badass bovine. I wish I had my horrors with me right about now. I grow weaker by the minute as they puff out of existence on the other side of the portal.

"You wish to enter the lands of Goldspire?" His voice rumbles.

"We are on a quest from King Orso to deliv—"

"Yes or no," the minotaur cuts me off.

Another silhouette falls in the distance to the cheers of the crowd.

"Yes." I force my voice to stay even, clenching my fist while sharp claws dig into my palm.

I hate being cut off mid-sentence. There are few things as disrespectful as disregarding what someone else has to say. I take a deep breath, remembering why we are here.

"Very well. Goldspire is no place for the weak. If you wish to enter our lands, then you must prove your worth on the fields of battle."

Taryn and I exchange nervous glances. This guy could probably kill Taryn in two or three hits. Hell, he could probably kill us both.

Looking around the arena, I don't see any way Jude or Glenn could have made it out of here. Then again, I wouldn't put anything past those two. This is about more than finding two murderous heroes. It's about making allies for the war to come. Something caused the portal in Seascape to come to life, and we need to prepare for the worst.

King Orso was right. We are going to need allies for what comes next, badass minotaurs included.

If our only way out of this arena is through a giant fucking cow, then so be it.

I lower my body, pointing Sea Scorpion at the minotaur. The golden trident shimmers in my hand. "Let's get this over with."

Stompy unleashes a warning call and the sound echoes across the coliseum.

"Try not to get hit." I lean in close to Taryn so Dakota can't hear me. "And if it looks like we can't win, you take Berry and Stompy and return through the portal. I have my spawn point set in the Seascape square, so that is where we will meet."

Taryn nods. His normally cheerful disposition is gone, his eyes focused on the hulking threat before us. His entire demeanor has changed since the battle at the square.

Dakota cracks his knuckles and steps forward, flexing his golden muscles.

I quickly summon three horrors and they burst to life in front of me. All pretense of peace is over. Now, all that matters is surviving so that we can deliver the king's message.

Dakota raises an eyebrow as the horrors appear.

Yeah, I'm full of surprises. I give him my best attempt at an arrogant smirk.

I step down from the platform surrounding the portal. "Spread out so that we can keep him distracted."

Taryn and his two pets go to the right and I take the left with my horrors. In response, the minotaur backs up to keep us both in his vision. He looks tough as nails, and I'm pretty sure we're going to need more than skill to get past him.

I force away the sounds of the crowd and the other battles, focusing all my attention on the threat before us. Right now, he is all that stands between us and exiting this arena.

I summon another round of horrors, but Taryn is the first to attack. He casts Lightning Bolt, and there's a crack of thunder as lightning rips through the air. Dakota is faster than he looks, side-stepping the attack just as it hits, leaving a jagged glass sculpture in the sand.

I use the distraction to lunge with my trident, putting my full weight behind the blow. The horrors follow my lead, going for the minotaur's legs. In a blur, Dakota smashes his vambrace-covered forearm against my weapon, parrying the attack. Sea Scorpion slides off the vambrace with a screech, and I stumble to my knees. There's a sickening crunch, and I feel my horrors' presence vanish behind me.

As I rise to my feet, the crack of breaking bones and a loud yelp draws my attention. Berry lies on the ground with Dakota standing over him. The bear has his teeth bared, but he doesn't move.

Dakota kneels over Berry.

"Nooo!" yells Taryn. He raises his staff and a lightning bolt plunges toward Dakota.

Dakota dodges the attack with ease, faster than I have ever seen anyone move. But Taryn doesn't give up, he's already charging, Stompy's horn swinging back and forth with each step.

I press on from the other side, summoning more horrors as I do. Maybe we can pinch him between us.

The golden minotaur raises both arms above his head, fists clenched. When we are several feet away, he slams his fists into the earth. The ground explodes, debris and rubble from the sandy floor rocketing us into the air with concussive force and taking out a chunk of health. Taryn falls from Stompy's back but uses Transform to turn into a red bird mid-flight. The small bird weaves through the chaos, narrowly dodging the raining rocks. The moulhaug falls to the ground with a thud.

Sea Scorpion flies from my hand when I hit the ground, lost somewhere among the dust and scattered earth. And just like that, three more horrors are gone. I can't summon them fast enough before they die.

I can't help but feel like I am out of my element here. He's running circles around us. But why? It's four against one. Or was Limery the linchpin that held our little band together, a small force of raw power?

When the smoke clears, Dakota stands among the rubble, a deep laugh rumbling in his gut.

"Is that all you've got?" he goads us. "I didn't expect much from the half-man, but you looked formidable." Steam shoots out of his nostrils. "I guess looks can be deceiving." He unhooks the sickle that holds the chain belt in place around his waist. "Time to send you back to whatever hole you came from. You aren't strong enough for Goldspire."

Nearby, Taryn has returned to his dwarven form and leans over Berry. Both emanate healing light as Taryn casts Restoration on his downed pet, slowly repairing his cracked bones and gored flesh.

Dakota tosses the sickled end of the chain over his head and spins it like a helicopter. The curved blade whistles in the wind as it gains momentum, eventually becoming a blur.

I have to do something, because Taryn is helpless while he tries to heal Berry. As strong as Dakota is, that weapon could rip right through him. Every second that passes feels more and more like we aren't making it out of here alive.

Three horrors appear in front of me in a puff of smoke. Before they even have a chance to move, Dakota swipes his chain with so much force that it severs all three of them in half with one motion.

I charge at him and when he swings his weapon again, I jump. It passes underneath my legs with enough power to break bone.

I'm halfway to him when the sickle whizzes back in my direction, this time a little higher. He's trying to catch me mid-jump, so instead, I duck, barely dodging the blow as it grazes my back.

Readying Claw, I launch myself at him, sinking my claws into his chest and pushing him to the ground. The chain loses its momentum, coiling like a snake through the air. I land on top of the minotaur, but he uses my momentum against me and rockets me off his knees like an acrobat.

I twist through the air and land on my feet, stirring up dust. Dakota crawls to his feet, blood streaking from the gashes on his chest, the first blood we've drawn against him.

"Ha ha," he rumbles. "You can't milk those!"

He flicks the chain and the sickle flies back into his hand.

My attack bought Taryn enough time to finish his spell. Berry scrambles up from the bloody splotch of sand, wounds healed and ready to fight once more.

For a moment, Dakota just stares at us, an amused grin on his face. His Constitution must be through the roof, because my attack barely touched his HP.

I summon three more horrors, even though I know they'll be dead in an instant. I spread them out, trying to flank Dakota, but he retreats, keeping them in view.

"We could run," I tell Taryn. We're risking a lot by staying here, and I'm almost positive Jude and Glenn aren't here.

He climbs atop Stompy once again. "A few hits and you're ready to call it a day. I thought you were a troll?" His beard twitches at the edges.

Finally, some of the Taryn I remember. Not his best joke, but I'll take it for now.

"You know, hamburgers do sound nice. Say, Dakota, are you grass-fed by chance?"

Taryn bursts into laughter. Dakota has no idea what I mean by the joke, but he can obviously sense it's at his expense because the grin fades and steam shoots out of his nostrils when he snorts.

With blazing speed, he whips his chain in my direction. The distance between us is the only reason I'm able to dodge the attack, and even then, I can hear the whir of the blade as it flies past my ear.

Before the chain retracts, my horrors are already on the offensive. Horror of Finesse is the first one on Dakota. It quickly dies, a massive hoof flattening the gangly blue creature into the sand. The Horror of Power stabs its tusks into the minotaur's calf. Blood spurts out, covering the muscled horror in dark red ichor.

Dakota flicks his wrist, recalling the sickle-tipped chain again. It recoils with blinding speed, and he catches the blade in his free hand, using it to stab my horror through the skull.

The Horror of Power puffs out of existence just as Horror of Vitality slams against a thick golden leg. The fluffy blue-and-orange horror does no damage, but a confused look on Dakota's face lets me know he's been slowed.

"Now!" I shout.

Lightning rips through the sky, followed immediately by a crash of thunder. Dakota makes to dive out of the way, but this time, he's not so fast. The Horror of Vitality's passive slows him just enough for Taryn's bolt to hit home. The attack fries my horror, but it also manages to stun Dakota in place.

Taryn casts Strong Wind, increasing my movement speed as I race toward the stunned minotaur. His eyes are red with rage. I summon more horrors as I run, tossing them ahead of me and exploding them against the stupefied cow.

Taryn casts Imbue on Stompy, making the moulhaug larger than ever. His hooves shake the ground as he charges with Taryn on his back. Berry's grunts let me know he is on the other side of the moulhaug.

We're all in. This is our chance.

Stompy collides into Dakota just as the stun wears off. Using his horn like a wrecking ball, he knocks the minotaur into the air with amazing force. I ready Bite and Claw, imbuing my next attacks with extra damage, and as soon as the minotaur hits the ground, Berry and I descend on him, dealing damage by any means available.

We kick, bite, and claw until dark red blood fills my mouth and covers my body. It's warm and satisfying.

"Enough!" shouts Dakota as he retaliates.

A powerful fist smashes into my jaw, sending stars streaming across my vision. The next thing I know, I'm flying through the air in another explosion of earth and debris.

My horrors are all dead, so I summon another round as I stagger to my feet. By the time the stars vanish from my vision, Dakota has regained his weapon. I still have no idea where Sea Scorpion is.

There's a flash of lightning, but Dakota dodges it with ease, leaving another glass sculpture buried in the sand.

Our momentary reign of terror managed to shave ten percent off Dakota's HP, but I've lost a quarter myself. Taryn still has sixty percent, but one wrong move can end him in an instant.

To my left, Berry breathes heavily. To my right, Stompy paws at the earth, readying for another charge, Taryn on his back.

I use Intimidation at the same time Dakota whips the sickle in my direction, unleashing a mighty roar and hoping it confuses Dakota long enough for Stompy to knock him down.

Taryn charges, but my ability has no effect. Is it because Dakota is a higher level than me or something else entirely?

The sickle stabs me in the chest, piercing deep and lodging in one of my bones. Sharp, hot pain flares through my body as blood spills down my midsection.

Dakota jerks the chain, but it doesn't come loose, instead pulling me forward onto my face. I fight through the pain, grabbing the chain and ripping the sickle from my chest. It leaves a gash deep enough to store items in.

Explosions and thunder echo around me, and by the time I'm on my feet, a cloud of dust fills the air. I summon my horrors, and my health continues to trickle down from the continuous blood loss. My rapid healing isn't able to keep up with such a deep wound.

Lost in the smoke, I can't spot Taryn or his pets anywhere. The grunts of battle let me know they are in there somewhere.

I roll the dice and cast Champion, my ability to summon a copy of the last enemy I defeated, but just as I suspected, a lowly ivory dwarf, probably a farmer, emerges on the battlefield. One of my horrors must have killed him during our battle with Glenn and Jude.

He rushes into the chaos and a moment later, his presence vanishes among the dust cloud.

There's a loud smash from within the dust, and Stompy soars through the air. He crashes to the ground with a thud, his body covered in bruises, cuts, and gore marks. Half his HP is gone. Slowly, he stands, ready for more.

A red bird zips out from the cloud of dust and Taryn returns to his dwarven form near the safety of the moulhaug. He places his hands on Stompy's side, casting Restoration and basking both in a splendid aura. Berry is nowhere to be found.

I summon three more horrors and send them into the chaos. The dust fades just as their presence vanishes, revealing Dakota, covered in blood, but with far more health than I would like. He's probably covered in more of our blood than his own.

Without warning, he whips his chain in Taryn's direction. I try to warn him, but the weapon is too fast. It strikes Taryn in the side, plunging the blade deep into his ribs. Taryn collapses to the ground, ninety percent of his HP gone after the attack.

The sickle is still lodged in his body, so I rush toward him, leaping for and grabbing the chain just as Dakota tries to pull it back.

I anchor my feet to the ground and activate Berserker Rage. Rage pumps into my muscles, fueling me with barbarian energy.

My vision goes red as my Strength and health regeneration increase. Dakota pulls on the chain again, but I don't budge. We're finally on equal footing. My feet sink deeper into the sand as we lock in a battle of tug-of-war.

The chain groans as we both pull with all our might. Behind me, Taryn squirms and groans.

"You have to remove the blade. I've got about thirty-seconds before he overpowers me." If he doesn't get the blade out, he's toast.

Taryn places his hands around the sickle and grimaces in pain. "I don't think I can," he pants. "It's too deep."

Careful not to let go of the chain, I summon a set of horrors and instruct them help Taryn.

Stompy places a hoof on the chain behind me, holding it in place in case I'm overpowered.

Taryn screams for a few agonizing seconds of what I can only assume are my horrors removing the sickle.

"Okay, it's out." He sounds weak, but at least he is alive.

"Alright, find Berry and then go for the portal. We'll live to fight another day."

Dakota pulls again, but my grip holds. Steam radiates from my skin as sweat evaporates from my overheating body.

Out of the corner of my eye, Taryn comes to a stop over a giant pile of sand. He bends down for a minute, and then the sand shifts and Berry shuffles to his feet. The poor bear has taken a hell of a beating today.

"Let's go!" Taryn runs past me.

"No, you take the others. I'll follow once you're through."

He cuts his eyes at me just as Dakota pulls again. Berserker Rage is almost up. "I'm not leaving you behind." He reaches into his satchel and pulls out a vial of dark purple liquid. "Infernal Darkness Potion. When I throw this, let go of the chain."

He tosses the glass vial at Dakota, and I release my grip just as Berserker Rage expires. The minotaur falls backward from the sudden slack. The vial clatters against the ground and black smoke rapidly fills the air around Dakota. A deep, dark smoke that seems to absorb the light around it.

"I forgot you had that," I say.

No matter where Dakota moves, the darkness follows.

Taryn smirks. "We've got a whole minute before it wears off."

Now that we are finally no longer in imminent danger, I take in the rest of the arena. Several bodies lay scattered on the other side. Some are still engaged in combat. Others bask in the cheers of the crowd as they toss items into the arena. The closer I look, I realize that many of the other combatants are beast-people. Like the minotaur, but with different animals. One has an elephant's head, another a tiger's. They all have stout, humanoid bodies, with furs or thick hides.

I'm more intrigued than ever, but it's time to go back to *Isle of Mythos.*

"This is one hell of a place." Taryn climbs on Stompy's back. Both of his pets look pretty ragged. "We'll have to come back some time." He winks.

The portal swirls peacefully before us. I focus on the rune for Seascape, two horizontal squiggly lines that look like waves, and it flares a bright red.

"After you." I motion for Taryn and Stompy to pass.

He's a few feet from entering the portal when I hear a grunt from behind us. I turn just in time to see Dakota, no longer covered in darkness, whipping his chain in our direction. He holds the sickle in one hand, this time tossing the weighted end of the chain. It sails through the air, passing inches from my face and wrapping around Taryn's neck. It coils down his body several times, pinning his arms to his sides. Dakota pulls, unseating Taryn from Stompy and launching him back onto the battlefield.

Stompy and Berry pass through the portal, unaware of what just happened.

Taryn soars through the air, constricted and unable to transform into his bird form, at the same time as Dakota charges. When his fist collides with Taryn, the druid's HP drops to zero. His body vanishes and his items fall into the sand.

"Ha-ha." Dakota laughs at the carnage. "If you mess with the bull, you get the horns."

Anger takes over. "You're going to pay for that!" I roar, spittle flying from my mouth as I leap from the platform.

Summoning three more horrors, I charge the arrogant minotaur. I ready Claw and Bite, not caring that he out-levels me. I know I should be grabbing Taryn's items and making a run for it, but he killed my friend, and he is going to pay. I'll mount his head on the walls of Seascape before this is over.

I bare my teeth and unleash a guttural roar. Blood pounds in my ears as my pulse races.

"Feisty. I like it." Steam shoots out of his nostrils, and he charges in my direction.

I pull Petrified Staff from my satchel and equip it, using its passive ability to fire a ranged attack at Dakota. Unsurprisingly, he dodges the attack.

Without skipping a beat, he slings the weighted end of his chain at me. It arcs in a semi-circle, decapitating both the Horror of Finesse and Horror of Vitality before wrapping around my calves. The chain pulls my legs together like a zip-tie and I fall face-first into the sand. Horror of Power's presence vanishes, and a hulking shadow stands over me.

"Anger is the enemy of strategy," Dakota huffs.

Those are the last words I hear before his giant hoof stomps my head into the ground.

CHAPTER 3

SHOP TIL YOU DROP

THE DARKNESS FADES and I come to my senses lying against the cool stone of the Seascape square. I'm on my knees wearing nothing but my loincloth.

My satchel. My items. My weapons. They're all gone. I punch the stone floor in frustration and a surge of pain runs through my knuckles.

"Dammit! Stupid, stupid, stupid!" I shout. Not only did I lose all my items, I lost Taryn's as well. We went through so much to get those items. Some were gifts from the chief. Not to mention the legendary Angel of Death Brandy we looted after defeating the dragomanders. "I'm such a fucking idiot." I let out a defeated sigh.

A small hand grabs my shoulder. "What happened?" asks Taryn.

I turn to see him wearing nothing but a simple gray tunic that falls to his knees. He doesn't look angry, though. Probably because he doesn't know what I did yet.

Give it time.

"Bro, I screwed up." I hang my head in shame.

"I think we both made some mistakes." He smiles. "We were outgunned, after all."

"No, I mean I screwed the pooch. I could have grabbed your items and ran. Instead, I got pissed and rushed into battle. Then I got my head stomped into the sand." I wait for his wrath. For him to tell me what a moron I am and how typical it is of me to lose my temper. It's what I deserve.

Instead, he cocks his head back and lets out a boisterous laugh, dreads swaying back and forth. Hand over belly, it pours out of him. Not at all what I expected.

"What's so funny? Why aren't you upset?"

He wipes tears from his eyes. "They're just items. I'm sure we'll find more. Berry and Stompy made it out alive, I consider that pretty lucky. You losing your cool, on the other hand, is hilarious." He chuckles again before patting me on the back.

"Man, you've gone off the deep end."

The portal flashes beside us and a group of three ivory dwarves and one blood dwarf step through. They make straight for the castle, at a brisk pace. The guards move out of the way, allowing them passage up the stairs.

"That looks important." I watch as the group moves with purpose, taking two steps at a time with their short dwarf legs. "What do you say we follow?"

Taryn instructs his pets to wait near the portal and we set off in pursuit of the dwarves.

As we walk, I pull up my most recent notification.

Alert! You have died. All items on your person have been lost. Items can be retrieved at the site of death in the event they have not been looted. One level and any stat points associated with it have been removed.

Fuck.

Back to level twenty. Plus I lose my newest ability, Champion.

How in the hell are we supposed to retrieve our stuff without any weapons? I can say with confidence that Dakota is now the proud owner of all our items.

"What do you think happened?" asks Taryn.

"No idea. Maybe they have news of Glenn and Jude. Whatever it is, they aren't wasting any time."

We practically run up the stairs to catch up, cardio kicking my ass by the time we reach the top. I envy Kassidy's ability to teleport up and down the castle in Vanaria right now, and wonder if the pot-bellied wizard will be joining King Favian when they meet for council.

When we arrive at the throne room, one of the ivory dwarves is already addressing the king.

"—possible that they came through. There is a land of snow and ice, where several mountain tribes still rule that do not follow the laws of the kingdom."

Sitting on his obsidian throne, the king scrunches his nose. "And what of my proclamation? My request for allies and peace?"

"They would like to meet with you in person, Your Highness." The dwarf bows his head.

"Very well. Make the arrangements. Perhaps I can convene a round table with King Favian and all of the great leaders." King Orso looks over in our direction, raising an eyebrow. "What news of Goldspire?"

Taryn steps forward and bends a knee. I do the same.

"Unfortunately, we were not able to make it out of the arena," Taryn begins. He goes on to tell King Orso of our battle and everything we saw before dying.

The king sits in silence for a moment, running his fingers

through his beard. "It is as I feared. Goldspire is an advanced zone and only those powerful enough will be allowed access to the continent. The beast-people are said to value Strength above all else. I do not wish to risk the lives of my people with times being as they are, but it is clear that Goldspire will be an asset in the wars to come should we convince them to join our cause." The dwarves surrounding the king nod in agreement. "Chod, Taryn, I know I have asked much of you already, but I would ask one more thing."

"Whatever we can do to help, Your Highness." Taryn speaks to the king with reverence.

Is that how I sound when talking to Chief Rizza?

King Orso smiles for a second. "Gather forces and return to Goldspire. We need them as allies." He leans forward, eyes boring into Taryn. "Not all allies are formed through peace. Some, like Goldspire, will be created by force. They will respond to power, because they do not want to risk their lives for those who cannot hold their own. Take the time you need to level, to make sure you will not fail again. When the time comes, show them the worth of the *Isle of Mythos*. Kurzol will show you to our troves for items and weapons. Take what you will, but before all is said and done, win Goldspire to our cause."

Quest Alert: *You have been offered the quest "Win strength with Strength." Return to Goldspire and gain access to the continent.*

Reward: *An alliance with Goldspire and increased favor with King Orso.*

Taryn bows again. "Yes, Your Highness."

I bow as well. "We will do our best, but what of Glenn and Jude?"

"For now, they will remain as outlaws on all of Mythos. Once I meet with the other leaders, I aim to make them wanted men from Pruxford to Wandermere and everywhere in between." He lifts his warhammer and points it in our direction. "Now go, there is still much to be discussed."

Kurzol takes his leave, the blood dwarf cleric ushering us into the hallway. "Follow me." He doesn't wait to see if we are coming before setting off deeper into the castle, his red robe swishing as he walks.

He takes us through several doors, down flights of stairs, and through more doors until I'm not sure I could find my way out if I tried. I don't relish the idea of returning to Goldspire, but with a few more levels and a solid team, we might be able to give them a run for their money. Having Limery around would raise the odds in our favor considerably.

Would we fight Dakota again? Or one of the other champions?

We enter a tightly-packed hallway clearly not designed with trolls in mind. I duck my head to avoid scraping it against the ancient stone. Just like the rest of the castle, the walls are adorned with engravings and ornamentation. Flickering torches hang from sconces, casting us in an eerie light and making the scenes along the wall come to life. At the end of the hallway, we stop in front of a dark and ancient wooden door crossed with iron latches. A shiny silver padlock keeps whatever secrets lie in wait on the other side hidden. It's out of place against the weathered stone and wood.

Kurzol places his hands on the padlock, and that's when I notice that it doesn't have a keyhole. He mutters something under his breath, and the lock flashes for a second. The locking mechanism unhooks with a clank and he removes it from the latch.

"That's cool," whispers Taryn. He leans around me to get a better view. "A magical lock."

With a groan, the door opens. Kurzol steps aside and ushers us in.

"Holy shit." Taryn's mouth hangs open in astonishment.

Holy shit is right. I walk past Kurzol and step into a room filled with more gold, items, and loot than we could possibly carry, even if we loaded up Stompy and Berry with saddlebags. There are enough items here to outfit every troll in the forest and then some. Everything glitters from the burning torches, reflecting sparkles along the walls and ceiling.

"What is this place?" I pick up nearby items, examining them.

"This is the king's personal treasure trove. All items have been passed through the Brightgaze family over the years. Some are gifts from foreign rulers or great families, others were won on the fields of battle, some are special items looted from dungeons or dropped from magical creatures. There is no greater vault within the kingdom." Kurzol puffs out his chest, following us inside.

"And we can take anything?" asks Taryn, picking up a golden helm with a plumed feather sticking out of the top and placing it on his head.

"By the king's orders. May I assist you in your search? I had the pleasure of conducting the most recent audit."

"Yeah, that sounds good." I place a silver chalice that transforms whatever is poured inside into mead back on a table. "Do you mind if we look around for a bit first?"

Kurzol nods and steps back against the door, giving us the freedom to explore.

"We sure hit the jackpot." Taryn lets a handful of golden coins pass through his fingers and clank against the floor.

I leave him to his wonder and step deeper into the room. Tables, cabinets, and shelves packed with items stretch forever. This is truly the hoard of generations of kings and queens. It goes beyond wealth. A dynasty, perhaps.

Picking up a golden tankard engraved with a warhammer, I examine it.

Item. Brimming Tankard. *A magical tankard that, once filled,* *will never go empty. Warning: Once filled, contents cannot be changed. Only works on beverages.*

Interesting. A never-ending mug of ale sounds nice, but even more practical would be to fill it with water. Whether it be a desert, cave, or wherever, we'd never need to find a water source again as long as we had this.

I press the lever that opens the lid and look inside. It's empty. Perfect.

"Kurzol, are there any of those expandable satchels in here?" I need something to store items in before I forget.

"Ah, yes. The cupboard to your right. Next to the green suit of armor."

I locate the suit of armor, which is quite beautiful. It has leaves etched into the breastplate and the stats are actually pretty amazing. Each individual piece has its own stats, but since the armor is equipped on a wooden manikin, I can view it as a whole.

*Item. **Verdure Armor.** Complete set. +25 Constitution. 50% reduction to earth-based attacks. Ability to blend in with surrounding trees or shrubbery when all pieces are equipped.*

The armor is the perfect size for a dwarf, but I assume it magically fits to the wearer. The stats are nice. Still, I don't think I'm ready to give up my mobility. Especially considering I have the ability to camouflage already. Any armor I choose can't affect my mobility or weigh me down. I'm going for power and speed.

The cupboard to the right of the suit of armor has clawed feet and is ornately engraved with knotted squares and triangles. Inside, dozens of leather goods line the shelves. Everything from simple knapsacks to duffels to backpacks. I rifle through them until I find a satchel that looks approximately my size.

*Item. **Expandable Satchel.** A bag capable of holding enormous content and only burdening the wearer with ten percent of its weight. Simply focus on the item inside and it will appear in your hand.*

Testing it out, I toss the tankard inside. It disappears in the vastness of the bag and when I focus on the item, its cool porcelain handle appears against my palm.

"Sweet! Taryn, take one." I grab a smaller bag that looks about his size and toss it across the room.

Taryn snatches it out of the air and looks inside. "Oh, wow! This is far better than anything I've seen in the shops."

Kurzol lets out a slight chuckle. "These are the items of royalty, made by great enchanters of days past, not your common artisan. You won't find items of this quality on the streets."

For the next few minutes, we search through the array of treasures. Some items are beyond my level, giving me no description when I focus on them.

Item. Silver Raven. ???

It's only a metal sculpture, but it must have some secret ability. The same goes for the Voodoo Doll and bright green Mysterious Egg.

There are more trinkets than I could possibly look through in the time we have. Rings, amulets, bracelets galore. Vials full of unidentifiable liquids. A bell without a clapper, which I assume isn't broken because it's in here and not in the trash somewhere.

There's not enough time for us to ask questions about every item, so I return to Kurzol. "What weapons would you recommend for us?"

A wide smile spreads across his red face. "I thought you would never ask." Clearly, he takes pride in knowing the contents of the vault. "Tell me, what is it you are looking for. What are your needs?"

"For me, Strength and Constitution are a top priority, as well as Dexterity. I want to move quick and smash hard. My horrors benefit from those stats, so there is not much need to invest in Intelligence or Wisdom." I look down and spot a red mask with a bird beak that conceals the identity of whoever wears it. "Oh, and nothing with Charisma," I quickly add at the end, noticing the plus-three Charisma associated with the mask. I'm still not ready to go down that road again.

He nods. "And what about you?" He turns toward Taryn, who is still looting items.

"Uh, I'm a druid. So, uh, things that would make me a better druid. Do you have any cool staffs?"

I raise my hand to interrupt. "If we're being honest, he could do with some better melee damage." Remembering the cooldown on Lightning Bolt, his only offensive ability. "That's one of his weaker areas."

Taryn rolls his eyes. "And you could do with some deodorant," he mumbles.

I ignore his jab, but I notice Kurzol's lip twitch as he attempts to hide a smile.

Kurzol strokes his beard. "Okay, you first." He points at me. "Follow me."

He leads me through a maze of artifacts I can't identify until we come to a corner of the room filled with weapons. So many weapons. They adorn the walls and tables, and some are littered on the floor. There are barrels filled with arrows, axes, pikes, and swords. Some are ornately designed; others are rather plain looking. One has a blue blade that pulses with energy.

How did we get so lucky?

Oh, right. I was an idiot who got his brains stomped out. If anyone asks, this was all part of the plan.

"I'll pick a few for you to choose from." Kurzol walks over to the wall and takes down several pieces. He stares at the table before grabbing another. He sets them down in front of me. "Ah, one more." He goes to one of the barrels and after a moment of clanking, comes back with a flail. "Each of these weapons are capable of taking on stones and further increasing their power. They will serve you well, whichever you choose."

Each of the weapons is truly amazing in its own right. I take my time, carefully examining them, imagining their use in battle, their strengths and weaknesses. In my short time here, I've had some truly remarkable weapons already, but I have a feeling that what I choose today will be my life and death for the foreseeable future.

The first weapon I lift is the flail Kurzol just set down. The lightweight metal staff is wrapped in dark leather, except for two settings for placing magical stones. A spiked ball dangles from the end, connected by a chain. It feels deadly in my hand, the head amplifying whatever force I swing with.

Item. Thunder's Roar. An enchanted flail capable of taking on the properties of up to 2 attached stones. +4 Strength, -1 Dexterity. *Named for the thunderous crash the weapon makes when colliding with armor.*

Pretty cool. The spiked ball attached to the end of the chain definitely has the ability for some powerful hits, but the lack of precision could be the difference between winning and losing. Dakota could probably wield this with impunity, but not me.

Next up is a long silver spear with an axe head on the end. The flat side of the axe head is etched with an array of tiny clouds.

Item. Whistler. An enchanted pike capable of taking on the properties of up to 3 enchanted stones. +4 Dexterity. *A ranged weapon capable of keeping opponents at a distance.* ***Bonus Ability: Wind Sweep.*** *Slashing attacks deal bonus air damage. Cost: 5 mana per attack.*

This would actually be a great weapon in the arena, but in a cave or dungeon, there's no guarantee I would have the freedom to swing it. I pick it up. It's lightweight and I could still stab with the spear, but it feels unwieldy in the tight quarters.

Beside the pike are two small warhammers. They look identical and when I examine them, it turns out they are a set.

Item. Twin Turbo (Set). Two one-handed warhammers, each capable of taking on the property of an enchanted stone. +2 Strength, +2 Dexterity per weapon. *A set of warhammers created for the dwarven warrior Dorfid Speedrunner, famed for his Dexterity and blurred attacks.* ***Bonus Ability: Whirlwind.*** *With one weapon in each hand, spin in a circle, unleashing random gusts of wind capable of dealing magical damage. Cost: 50 mana per second.*

Those could be useful, but they aren't really my style. I'm not a rogue or a quick-handed fighter. I'm a barbarian. I smash and look good doing it.

The final two weapons on the table are an axe and a two-handed warhammer. Right up my alley.

The axe is massive. Not a double-edged axe like Peacemaker, it has a single blade capable of splitting man or beast in two. Crafted from a dark gray metal that flirts with being black. Tiny flakes of red sparkle throughout and black leather crisscrosses down the shaft.

When I lift the weapon, it's lighter than I would have thought.

Item. Dark Fiend. An enchanted axe capable of taking on the properties of up to three stones. +3 Strength, +2 Constitution. *This ancient axe was forged in the heart of a volcano.* ***Bonus Ability: Burn.*** *Attacks deal bonus burn damage. Cost: 5 mana per attack.*

Burn damage. That sounds both painful and highly efficient. I've been burnt myself a few times, and the memories are still fresh. Lingering, excruciating pain that flared all over. Maybe it's worse because I'm a troll, but it's definitely something I would wish on my worst enemies. I almost don't even pick up the warhammer. Remembering Peacemaker and the way it felt in my hands has me ready to swing an axe all over again. The staffs were nice and added a little bit to my summoning, but truth be told, being up close and personal has always been more fun.

My horrors should be alongside me in battle, helping me to rip my enemies to shreds, not leading the front lines while I sit back and watch, wasting my Strength and Constitution. I'm a wrecking crew, not a mage. If I want to cast a horror further away, I'll pick it up and throw it. Why do I have this big strong body if I'm not going to use it?

I run my thumb along the blade of the axe. With the slightest pressure, it cuts through my thick skin and a tiny drop of blue blood trickles down.

My thoughts drift back to Peacemaker, to the trolls. It feels like a lifetime ago when I was a noob being escorted to the chief. They took me in; they believed in me. Gave me one of their most prized possessions for a shot at survival. That was one of the few rare weapons they had, and they'd entrusted it to me. Looking at the literal treasure trove before me, it paints an even greater picture of the difference between the trolls and the other races. They have nothing except for each other.

And me, their one and only hero.

I need to see them soon. With the portals reopening, everything has changed. There's a real possibility for the trolls to make a place for themselves in the world. Maybe I can help with that.

I set Dark Fiend down on the table and pick up the warhammer. As comfortable as the axe felt in my hand, comfort alone is no reason to settle.

The warhammer is similar to the axe, and despite its massive size, feels light in my hand. The two weapons must be made of the same material; red speckles gleam from within the dark metal. It could be the material or something to do with the volcanic heat that makes them so lightweight. The shaft is thick and easily four feet long, with runes and etchings running down the sides. Dark red runes run along the top half of the shaft. At the head of the weapon, there is the hammer for bludgeoning on one end, and a spike for piercing on the other. There's another spike on the tip for stabbing in close quarters. The sockets for setting stones are on the left, right, and top of the hammerhead. It's a beauty to behold. I pull up the weapon's stats.

Item. Destroyer. An enchanted warhammer capable of taking on the properties of up to three stones. +2 Strength, +3 Constitution. *This ancient warhammer was forged in the heart of a volcano.* ***Bonus Ability: Inferno.*** *With each consecutive hit, Destroyer grows hotter, allowing it to warp or pierce through even the hardest metals. Multiplier works when hits are less than five seconds apart. Cost: 10 mana per attack. Cooldown: 10 sec.*

I place the weapon back on the table, admiring it next to its twin.

Wow, I didn't expect this to be such a tough choice. Dark Fiend is amazing. With its burn damage and slashing attacks, it's just what I'm used to. But then there's Destroyer, a true brawler's weapon. With a war coming, we may be facing more armored foes. Something that could crush through skulls and armor might be just what we need.

I select Destroyer and place it in my bag.

"How is it that all of these weapons have bonus abilities? I haven't seen many weapons like this." Actually, I haven't seen many rare weapons at all outside of loot and the few that Chief Rizza gave me.

"These weapons aren't just forged; they are crafted by enchanters. Seascape had some of the finest enchanters in years past. We still have very good metal-workers, but enchanters are hard to come by these days. They make a marriage of metal and mana. A weapon of this power could take a year to create."

An entire year to make one weapon? I go back over to the

table, running my fingers along the intricately-engraved runes and symbols. So beautiful. No wonder they hide them down here.

"Now, go select your armor while I help out our dwarven hero."

Kurzol disappears among the maze of treasures, leaving me to my own devices.

There are lots of chainmail, plate mail, and other bulky items lying around, but while beautiful and undoubtedly tough, none of them fit what I'm going for. Even the lightweight armor is cumbersome. Not just in weight, but the way it fits.

That is until I spot a simple piece of shoulder armor. It reminds me of something out of ancient Rome. Something a gladiator might wear.

Item. Spaulder of Swiftness. +1 Constitution, +1 Dexterity. *Lightweight, durable leather mail designed to protect the off-hand shoulder during battle.*

It checks all the boxes for what I want, and even though it has no bonus abilities, the bonus attributes are nice. I equip it and set off to find Taryn. The leather armor covers my shoulder and arm down to the elbow, perfect for absorbing a blow with my off-hand.

Along the way, I pass a basin filled with magical stones. Some are enchanted, while others are the cores of mighty beasts. I end up taking two that modify my Dexterity, and one that allows me to walk almost silently.

Barbarian Assassin Summoner, here I fucking come!

I don't want to be greedy, so I go to find Taryn. Along the way, I toss the Mysterious Green Egg into my satchel. A loud crash of metal gives away his location no problem.

He stands holding two daggers, both blades broken off near the hilt. A pile of armor lays scattered on the floor beside him.

"Don't tell me you managed to break a pair of ancient daggers in the time I left you alone," I tease.

"Hardly. Check this out."

He grips the daggers a little tighter and what I can only describe as shadow blades appear where the metal is broken. Dark, shadowy energy pulses, distorting the light around them.

"What the hell?"

"Shadow daggers," says Kurzol. "Capable of bypassing armor and draining the victim's mana and life force. Very rare, indeed."

Taryn swipes at a helm on a nearby table. The shadowy blades pass directly through, but a moment after, it's like a magnetic energy pushes the helm off the table, clanking against the floor.

"You wanted me to be able to do more damage. I think this will do the trick. I won't have to worry about armor, just stabby-stab-stab." Taryn waves the blades through the air like a crazed lunatic. "Plus, each attack actually drains mana. Perfect for fighting other heroes."

"And there's nothing that can stop it?" I step back, not wanting to accidentally get stabbed. That could be one of the most dangerous weapons I've ever seen.

"Holy armor. They're basically useless against paladins." Kurzol moves closer to me. "But aside from that, they are very powerful items."

"What about clerics?" I remember Richard, the cleric I met in Vanaria who serves the god of chaos.

"It depends on their alignment. Most clerics don't wear armor, and shadow energy will still pierce through unarmored flesh."

"Sounds like a winner. What else did you get?"

A broad smile crosses Taryn's face. "Check this out." He puts on a gray cloak that falls to his knees and a pair of brown boots. Neither one looks spectacular by any means—in fact, they kind of look grungy—but I'm sure there has to be something special about them.

Taryn walks over to a table filled with vials and picks several up, pouring their contents onto the floor. Kurzol places his hand over his face at the wasted potion.

"Oh, it's fine," murmurs Taryn. "It's just a souped-up health potion."

The red liquid spreads across the stone floor, creating puddles in the cracks. Then, Taryn walks through them.

Red liquid splashes up with each step, but it doesn't make a sound. And when he steps out of the puddle, there are no tracks.

"How?" I ask, jaw hanging wide open.

Taryn raises both eyebrows at me. "Sexy, right? The boots hide my tracks, and the cloak conceals the sound of my movements. I figured when the time finally comes to track down those two goons, we might need the element of surprise. And there is no way in hell you are sneaking up on anyone."

"Actually." I pull out my warhammer and show him one of the enchanted stones I equipped. "This one lets me move silently."

"No shit?"

"Shit," I confirm.

Taryn tucks the daggers in his belt. "Now, all I need is a staff and I'm golden. Anything you'd recommend, Kurzol?"

"I have one that I think would be especially fitting for a druid. One moment."

Kurzol returns carrying a green branch. It still looks to be alive and covered in leaves, despite being locked in an underground vault.

Item. Sapling Staff. +3 Intelligence, +3 Wisdom. *A living staff capable of sending out whip-like vines.*

Kurzol hands the staff to Taryn and the tiny vines reach down his arm, embracing him like some toxic goo out of a superhero movie. There's a moment's hesitation where I see a slight panic in Taryn's eyes, but it quickly passes and he accepts the vines as they wrap around his forearm.

"Wow." He lifts the staff, pointing it at a nearby table. Tiny vines unravel and shoot out, entwining around a small cup and lifting it into the air. "This is so cool!" A second later, the cup falls to the ground and shatters.

Kurzol crosses him arms. "I trust that you have enough items to get you started on your journey."

Point taken. It's time to get the hell out of here.

CHAPTER 4

TREEHADEN

AFTER GATHERING BERRY AND STOMPY, we pick up provisions for the road and set foot out of Seascape. Our destination is the troll forest, but with no set timeline on when we need to reach them, we're free to go at our own pace and level up along the way. It'll be nice to see some of the smaller dwarven cities and villages.

I hope Limery will be waiting for us when we make it to the forest. Though, I have a feeling he'll be able to find us wherever we are. Imps are full of surprises. In fact, I'm interested to see if Lillith was able to gather more imps as translators for the forest trolls.

With no idea where Glenn and Jude truly are, our only goal is to grow stronger so that when we do find them, we will be ready. Not to mention the host of other threats that may be waiting on the other side of the portals. One day, we will return to Goldspire and retake what we lost.

Maybe I can convince a few heroes to join us along the way.

The roads are less crowded than when we first entered the city. Now that the portal has opened, the excitement of the king's challenge has worn off. Dwarves are returning to their homes. For most of them, they'll probably never set foot through a portal, content to live their entire lives farming, crafting, mining, or whatever their profession might be.

Even so, I'm sure they dream of it. Finding new worlds, becoming heroes, and living a life of adventure. They may be lines of code, but in every way that matters, these are real people. Artificial intelligence but intelligent, nonetheless.

With every day that passes, this feels more and more like my real world. Now that Taryn is here, it's been days since I last thought about New York, about my family. I'm not sure if that's good or bad.

My life is consumed with excitement now. Leveling, exploring, making a name for myself in this world. Or at least in this section of the world.

We haven't heard from Valery since Taryn logged in, so I'm assuming they've made no headway with the system error that's preventing me from logging out. That's fine by me. This is my home now.

For a moment, I think back to when I logged out. Back when I thought my sentence was over and I'd be going home. I remember the new pods that were lined up along the far wall. Whatever happened to that? Are they bringing in more players? Certainly not until they've solved the issue with the AI. They let Taryn in, but that was a special circumstance.

"Oh, great," mumbles Taryn. "Get out of the way, grandmas."

A wagon full of ebony dwarves takes up most of the narrow bridge that connects Seascape to the rest of the island. We follow behind them at a slow pace as they stare at Taryn and I with wide eyes. As if a dwarf riding a moulhaug wasn't strange enough, it's not every day they run into heroes, let alone a dwarven and troll hero together.

We're quite the oddball family. Even more so when Limery is around.

The bridge ends and we nod to the ebony dwarves as we pass.

"Which way do you want to go?" I ask Taryn.

The Mythroad leads straight through the desert, past Sandholde and directly through the Greystone Mountains, but there are other roads that bypass the desert, going around the edge of the island through many of the small towns.

Taryn strokes his beard, lost in thought, when a panicked ivory dwarf comes running up the road. The dwarf's eyes are set on the castle until he sees us and comes to an abrupt halt, boots skidding across the dirt road and sending a plume of dust into the air.

Sweat beads down his brow as he bends over, gasping for air. A deep gash runs along the side of his flushed face, caked with blood.

Taryn climbs down from Stompy, rushing to his countryman's aid. "What's wrong? Are you okay?"

"The village," he gasps. "It's under attack. All of our guards were in the castle for the king's event and there was no one left to protect our stores. Now the kobolds are running off with our livestock. Please help!"

Quest Alert. *You have been offered the quest 'Protect the Village.' The village of Treehaden has fallen victim to an attack of angry kobolds. Their livestock are being stolen, and their very lives threatened. Save the village before their livelihoods are destroyed.*

Reward: *Increased alliance with Treehaden.*

"Let's go!" Taryn grabs the dwarf by the arm. "Here, you ride Stompy and I'll take Berry."

The villager is nervous at first, but Taryn helps him climb onto Stompy's saddle. Stompy snorts at the unfamiliar rider, but accepts him anyway.

I pull up my map and look at the towns marked across the northern half of the island. Aside from Sandholde and Seascape, they all remain nameless.

"How far away is your town?" I ask.

"About half a day. I would have gotten here faster, but the bastards snuck our horses out in the middle of the night. Dirty monsters!" He waves his fist in the air. "They attacked when we were left unguarded like the cowards they are."

I look over the map, searching for the closest town. There's one near the road, a little south from the coast. That must be Treehaden. Taryn casts Strong Wind, increasing our movement speed, and we barrel down the road toward our next adventure while the villager fills us in on the details.

"What's your name?" Taryn glances at our new companion.

Berry and Stompy keep in stride with one another as I jog slightly behind.

"My name is Drury Hornstone. My family has been farming these lands for ages." He fumbles with Stompy's reins, clearly uncertain about riding such a massive beast, unlike Taryn who could probably sleep while riding. "Kobolds have always been a problem, but usually they skulk about in the night, stealing what they can without being caught. I've never seen them so bold before."

I think back on the few times I've faced kobolds in *Isle of Mythos*. They were always skittish creatures, behaving a lot like hyenas and roaming in small packs. The ugly, goblin-esque lizard creatures were annoying, but I could never see them attacking a village, not unless there was something greater at play.

"How many attacked you?" I increase my speed until I'm right beside Drury.

"Enough to overwhelm us." He sighs. "We tried to fight at first, but there were just too many of them. I took a claw to the face fighting them off. Once we backed off, they seemed more concerned with the animals than with us. I did my best to get everyone hidden in the cellar beneath the village temple." A pained expression crosses his face. "I hope they are okay."

Taryn and I exchange glances.

"You don't think—" He lets the words fade in the wind, scrunching his eyebrows as he puts the pieces together the same as me.

This has Glenn written all over it. A normally passive species attacking a village without fear of repercussion. Except it shouldn't be possible. We watched him go through that portal. Did he somehow manage to sneak back through?

There were dozens of guards waiting around the portal in Seascape. There's no way he made it back without being noticed.

"It can't be," I say finally. "There has to be another explanation."

We travel in silence after that, the only sounds are the pattering of feet, hoof, and paw against the dirt road. With Destroyer safely put away in my satchel, it doesn't give me the silent movement bonus until I equip it. Not that I need it right now.

Eventually, we make it to the outskirts of Treehaden. The village is small, smaller than Lynchton, and eerily quiet for the middle of the day. The farms surrounding the village remain empty, almost like a ghost town.

I equip my warhammer and the enchanted stone immediately muffles my movement.

"Psst," I call Taryn towards me. "Leave Stompy and Berry here with Drury. You and I can sneak around quietly and see what's going on."

Taryn nods before returning to the others and instructing them. The last of my horrors vanishes and I don't summon any more. Right now, I want the element of surprise, not strength in numbers.

We step through the wooden palisade that surrounds the village. The gate hangs askew from the earlier attack. Inside, it's mostly quiet except for some grunting coming from behind one of the buildings. Stray chickens run through the streets, clucking as they zig and zag. The stables to the right are empty.

A scratching noise comes from the end of a row of small houses with thatched roofs. Taryn and I run toward it—no need to move carefully since our movement is muted. At the end of the row, I peek through an open window. The place is simple and rustic. A single pot and pan hang from the ceiling and a cauldron burns over dying embers. A kobold wearing old leather rags rifles through a cupboard. A rusty shiv hangs from its belt. Everything about the creature is primitive except for a glittering ring it wears on one finger. Probably stolen. It's much too high-quality to be kobold-made.

The kobold empties the cupboard, tossing items across the floor with no regard. When it finds something it likes, a hiss that sounds almost like laughter carries out the window.

"Yes, yes." The mumbling kobold stuffs a silver goblet in its leather satchel.

Having found something of value, the kobold makes to leave.

Not if I have anything to do with it.

As soon as the creature steps out of the door, I bring Destroyer down upon its head. The force of the blow crumples the lizard like paper, smashing its frail frame into the ground. A flash of red streaks down my weapon as Inferno engages, readying the heat multiplier for my next attack.

"What the fuck!" Taryn stares at the carnage with wide eyes.

"What? No one heard anything."

Except that's not completely true because another three kobolds turn around the corner, hissing in alarm.

They are all level ten, which shouldn't be a problem unless we're overwhelmed.

"Hel—" one of the kobolds screams, but before I have a chance to move, Taryn slams the butt of his staff against the ground and three vines shoot out from the weapon, entangling the kobolds and pulling them together. Vines cinch around the three reptilian throats, quelling their cries for help. Taryn drops the staff and takes out his shadow daggers.

The kobolds struggle against their entanglements as Taryn swoops in, running the dark energy of his blades through each of their chests until their lifeforce drains completely. At level sixteen, Taryn has the clear advantage over the kobolds.

There's no blood, no wounds, but the kobolds die nonetheless. The shadowy blades fade away before he picks up his staff and the vines retreat.

"Giant oaf." He cuts his eyes at me. "I can't take you anywhere."

"Okay, fearless leader." I give him a mock salute. "What do we do now?"

He looks down at the four bodies. "We track down the rest. Try to find out where they are going, and who they are working for."

"Wait." Taryn is already leaving the scene when I spot something out of the ordinary. "Look at this. They all three have this same ring." I bend down and lift one of the slain kobold's hands. A glittering ring sparkles in the daylight. "The kobold I killed had on one, too."

With a little effort, the ring comes off and I'm able to examine it.

Item. Ring of Bliss. +1 Charisma.

I hand it to Taryn before removing the rings from the other kobolds. They are all the same.

"Why in the hell would a bunch of kobolds have Charisma rings?" He stares at the ring as if it will give him the answer.

"Here, let me see your hand."

I take his hand in mine and slide one of the rings onto his finger. It's only one Charisma, but his eyes gloss over the moment I put it on.

"Mmhm." He smiles. "This is nice." He places a second ring on, and his shoulders visibly loosen. "Man, why are we wasting time doing errands for the king? We should be running this island. Hell, we should be—"

"Alright, that's enough of that." I reach out to take the ring off and Taryn pulls away. Luckily, I'm about ten times as strong as him so I remove it no problem.

With the rings removed, Taryn returns to normal. His face is a little paler than usual.

"Holy..." His words trail off. "That was something else. I felt like a king."

"Yeah, this is a one-way ticket to bad decisions." I place the rings in my satchel, out of Taryn's sight, and he visibly relaxes. "Now, how and why would a group of kobolds end up with rings like this?"

"Someone had to give them the rings." Taryn rubs his brow.

"My thoughts exactly."

We search the rest of the town, but there are no more kobolds to be found. All the livestock are gone, minus a few stray chickens, and several of the houses have been looted.

Once we're sure that the town is safe, we find Drury. He leads us to the temple and unlocks the cellar door.

There's a gasp and several screams as I open the cellar.

"Don't worry," Drury holds his hands up as he tries to calm them. "They are here to help."

"Drury—"

"What happened?"

"Are they go—"

Dozens of voices vie for attention all at once.

"One at a time," Drury orders. "Everyone out, and I will fill you in."

The dwarves exit to the village center. Many look worried or apprehensive, their eyes darting between Drury, myself, and Taryn. Several children cling tightly to their parents' legs, their chubby, round faces unsure of what is happening as they stare openly at us newcomers.

"Our livestock is gone. Some of us may have lost items, but it doesn't seem their intent was to rob our homes, but to take our way of life." He buries his head in his hands. "It doesn't make any sense."

"What are we going to do?" a freckled-faced female dwarf asks. "We used our animals for everything. They plowed our fields, fed us, clothed us. How can we possibly replace all of that?"

"Don't worry." Taryn pats her on the shoulder. "We'll track down the kobolds and return your property. And we'll make sure that whoever is responsible pays for what they've done."

It's a great sentiment, but I have no idea how we're going to track down the kobolds. We have no way of knowing where they came from or where they went.

Drury must agree with my suspicion, because he pulls Taryn and me aside. "Do you truly believe you can return our livestock?"

Taryn puffs out his chest. "If we can't return your animals, then Chod and I will plow your fields until you can afford to buy new ones."

Seriously, what the actual fuck? My cheeks suddenly feel hot. The last thing I want to do is pull a plow from sun-up to sun-down. Taryn better have a plan, or I might punt him into the ocean.

"Then you must hurry." Drury takes Taryn by the shoulder, pointing him toward the gate. "Kobolds are fast and tricky. No doubt they will try to confuse anyone following."

Taryn flashes him a stupid grin that I want to smack away. "I don't think that'll be a problem."

We leave the villagers to repairing their broken gate and destroyed property. Once we are outside of earshot, I let go of the anger I've been holding in.

"Dude? What the hell? We're on a mission to level up. How in the hell do you think volunteering us to work on a farm is going to help that at all?"

"Bro, calm down. Finding the kobolds will be the easy part." He's still grinning like a fool. Almost like he knows he's getting under my skin.

"And how exactly is that?" I cross my arms, waiting for his response.

"Because a bear's sense of smell is about two thousand times greater than a human's." He reaches into his pouch and pulls out a piece of crude leather armor. The kobold's. "And I also have this."

CHAPTER 5
HELLA ENCHANTED

NOSE TO THE GROUND, Berry follows the scent with ease. The kobolds must not have been worried about being tracked, because we follow their trail in a straight line for several miles. Truth be told, I never thought about all the uses Taryn's pets would have outside of combat. They are so much more than just battle companions. Stompy can pull and carry anything we need. He'll complain and groan the entire time, but the moulhaug would follow Taryn into the depths of Hell, grumbling all the way. And Taryn can still tame a few more pets before they start to get unruly. From what he told me, the more he tames, the less control he has over their actions. I don't know if that means they won't behave, or if there is a chance they won't listen to him at all.

Time will tell, but I have a hard time believing Berry would ever disobey a command.

The bear leads us through a copse of trees and across a small creek. We pass through the water without missing a beat, and we're on their trail again. Every so often, Berry will turn around to make sure we are still following before bounding ahead.

"I'm sorry I got angry," I apologize to Taryn. The worst part about losing my temper is the apologizing, because there's never really an excuse for my behavior. It's just something stupid I do when things aren't going the way I want. I'm trying to get better, but old habits die hard. "I should have known you would have a plan."

Taryn winks at me. "Don't worry about it. We'll kick some kobold butt and return their livestock in no time. Then, we'll be back on the road. I'm sure there will be some awesome places to visit around the island."

That's one of the things I love most about Taryn. He never holds a grudge. I've done enough asshole things in my day to turn him away, but he never holds it against me. He sees me for who I truly am: an asshole, but one with his heart in the right place.

"You feel a connection to them, don't you?" I ask.

"Who?" He raises an eyebrow.

"The dwarves." We pass an area of upturned soil filled with reptilian footprints and hoofprints. Not that I doubted Berry, but it confirms we are going in the right direction. "I can tell. I feel the same thing when I'm around the forest trolls. It's hard to explain, but it's kind of like this sense of kinship. Like I would do anything to protect them. I know I'm not really a troll, but it doesn't stop me from feeling like I am, you know?"

"Yeah, I totally know what you mean. It's hard to believe this is a game sometimes." He holds up his hand and looks at it, staring at the back of his palm. "Most of the time, actually. Knowing what I look like in real life, it doesn't make sense that I would feel so comfortable in this skin. But I do. I feel like I've been a dwarf my entire life. I don't expect to be three feet taller or have a longer reach. This feels like who I am. Everything is so...natural. Do you think it's our minds, or do you think the AI somehow influences our perception?"

I shrug. I hope it's the first, but the second seems just as possible. How else can I explain the way Charisma affects our mental state? The nanites that keep us alive in here could be rearranging the way our bodies work, altering their chemical composition for all I know.

The hair on my neck stands on end. It's better not to think too much on those things.

Berry comes to an abrupt halt and Stompy almost runs into him, sliding to a stop so fast that Taryn nearly falls from the saddle. The umber bear stares intently at a group of boulders nearly a hundred yards away.

"What is it?" asks Taryn. I'm not sure if he's talking to Berry or me.

The more I look at the boulders, I sense that something is off about them. There's a shimmer to the air, like the horizon on a scorching hot day, only it's not hot at all. The coastal breeze is cool against my skin.

"Something's not right." I watch the fluctuating air, not quite sure what it is. "Those aren't boulders."

"Trolls?" ask Taryn.

"I don't think so. I've always been able to see other trolls when they are camouflaged." Those were forest trolls, though. Maybe these are desert or mountain trolls. Maybe it's some sort of magical area, where the mana is flowing aboveground.

I pull up my map, but there doesn't seem to be any ley lines running through the area.

"Well, this is where the trail ends." Taryn stuffs his items into his satchel. "Let's investigate."

At a hundred yards away, if it's more than just a boulder, then whoever or whatever it is has already seen us.

"Taryn, meet me behind Stompy. Out of view of the boulders."

He climbs down from the saddle and we meet behind Stompy's massive body.

"What's up?" Taryn looks up at me with questioning eyes.

"If they've already seen us, then we need you to sneak in. Turn into your bird form. If it is a troll or some other sort of monster, then they'll have no idea you left."

He smacks me on the arm. "Sneaky. I like it."

In a flash, Taryn turns into his animal form, a bright red bird, and flutters into the sky. I peek around Stompy, watching the shimmering boulders as he flies over them, landing in a nearby tree. It doesn't take long before he sends me a message.

Incoming Message (Taryn): *Chody boy, you are not going to believe this. It's some kind of an illusion.*

Message (Chod): *What do you mean? I need more details than that.*

Incoming Message (Taryn): *It could be some sort of enchantment that's cloaking the area. Whatever it is, it's not as strong when being viewed from above. I can see movement underneath, but it's kind of grainy. I'm pretty sure there are wagons, and kobolds. I definitely saw a few sheep. No idea if there is more to it than that.*

Message (Chod): *Alright, keep an eye on it and let me know. If you can get closer, go for it, just be safe. No need to be rash until we know what we're dealing with.*

Something is definitely up. The kobolds didn't just randomly walk into an enchanted area. I've never seen a kobold that could cast magic, either. Someone has to be pulling the strings.

But who?

And wagons? Are they loading them with animals, and if so, to what end? This all makes no sense.

I peek around Stompy, trying to find anything that might give me a clue as to what is going on, but all I see are the boulders. They look real enough. If I hadn't noticed the shifting air around them, I probably wouldn't have thought twice. Good thing we had Berry.

If it is an illusion, then there has to be some sort of caster nearby, probably within. With a full army of horrors, I could charge in there like a mad-man, but I'd like to plan this out for once. I've had my head stomped in the sand one time too many as it is.

As I stare at the boulders, something changes. A small green elbow protrudes from one of the rocks. Just as soon as it appears, it retracts back into the safety of the illusion. If the kobolds can move in and out of it at will, then that proves it's not an actual barrier.

There's a flash of red as Taryn swoops down from the tree and disappears behind the illusion. I wait in anticipation as a long minute passes before I hear anything from him.

Incoming Message (Taryn): *There's a guy in here. Another player. He's hiding his level and class, but his name is Jon Bailey. He looks like a dweeb. I'd put all my money that he's casting the illusion.*

Another player? That's interesting. What could he possibly want with Treehaden's livestock? My mind races with possibilities as I wait for more information alongside Berry and Stompy.

The good news, at least, is that this Jon Bailey doesn't seem bent on hurting NPCs. Not that taking their things isn't wrong, but he doesn't seem to be another Glenn.

Incoming Message (Taryn): All of the kobolds have the same rings. It's like this guy has made a little crackhead army. They're loading the animals into the wagons. I think they're planning to leave soon.

Not if we have anything to say about it.

There's so much opportunity for heroes in *Isle of Mythos*, why would he resort to stealing from poor farmers? I wouldn't be surprised if this guy was in prison for robbery.

Message (Chod): How many kobolds are there? Do they seem concerned with our presence?

Incoming Message (Taryn): About thirty, give or take. There are a few watching, but I think they assume you're just resting. No one seems alarmed.

Message (Chod): Do you think you can distract them long enough for me and the gang to make an appearance? Let's take these clowns out and get Treehaden their property back.

Incoming Message (Taryn): *When I give the signal, full speed ahead.*

Message (Chod): *What signal?*

I wait for his response, but it doesn't come. Instead, there's a crash of lightning that rips through the illusion.

"Goddammit, Taryn! I thought we were being smart this time."

I let out a stream of curses as I follow Berry and Stompy into battle. For all the talk of me losing my temper, Taryn is the one to go rogue. I summon a quick burst of three horrors as I run and equip Destroyer.

Stepping through the edge of the illusion, I'm greeted with scattered chaos. I search for Taryn, but he is nowhere to be found. A wagon sits broken and smoldering, pieces of debris littering the ground around it. Kobolds try to gather the startled livestock until they see me and Taryn's pets. They freeze in place at our sudden appearance, and I immediately sic my horrors on the closest kobolds while continuing to look for Taryn.

A man wearing a dull blue robe, and glasses with two different colored lenses, snarls at me, lifting his diamond-tipped staff into the air. It flashes white for a second and the man splits into two identical versions of himself. Each one tan and lean with shaggy brown hair, built like a runner.

Are they clones or illusions? And more importantly, are they capable of dealing damage? I focus on them, but all I see is the man's name: Jon Bailey.

Berry and Stompy stand by my side, waiting for orders. My horrors fall, but not before taking out a couple of kobolds with them. We all stand in a moment of shocked silence, waiting for someone to make the next move.

"I've heard about you." Both versions of the man speak at the same time. The words slither out of his mouth in an uneasy echo; greasy, like a used car salesman. "The troll who can't seem to mind his own business."

"Let us take the livestock and no one has to get hurt." I'm offering him a way out. More than he deserves.

"I think not. I plan to make a hefty profit selling them at the market." He smiles for a second, a cocky, devilish smile. "Minions, I'll craft a plus-two ring for whoever lands the killing blow on this one." He extends a slender finger in my direction.

The kobolds hiss in unison, making my hair stand on end. Suddenly, it all makes sense. This guy is an enchanter, capable of crafting items. Has he addicted them to Charisma? Is that why they're following him?

A bolt of lightning crashes into the left version of the man. He vanishes in a wisp of smoke, and the bolt explodes against the earth. The man steps back, raising his staff into the air once more and creating another doppelgänger.

Both versions repeat the movement and another copy appears. They raise their staffs over and over until there are at least ten of the man. He must have a hefty mana pool to cast so much so quickly.

"Kill them!" they shout in unison.

A bright glow catches my eye from under one of the wagons. Taryn hides beneath, casting Imbue on Berry and doubling his size just as a group of kobolds leap onto the bear's back. They stab and claw as Berry thrashes, eventually tossing the kobolds to the ground.

He'll be able to hold his own. Right now, it's time for me to fuck shit up.

I swing Destroyer at the closest kobold, connecting with its head and sending the lizard creature soaring across the field like a golf ball. Red flashes through my warhammer as Inferno takes effect.

Kobolds surround me, the belle of the ball, their eyes orange with greed and the promise of more Charisma.

"Sorry to disappoint, but I don't think you're going to like the outcome of this fight." I twist Destroyer against my palms, letting the head of the warhammer spin.

The first kobold leaps at me and I smash him into the ground with enough force to displace the earth. For the next thirty seconds, I play whack-a-kobold as they try to get close enough to damage me. By the time the last one falls, Destroyer is glowing molten red.

Stompy lets out a trumpet call as he smashes into a wagon, destroying Jon the Enchanter's only method of transporting his stolen goods. Berry finishes off another few kobolds while Stompy smashes the last of the wagons.

All the kobolds are gone, but there's no sign of Taryn or Jon anywhere.

Until I hear the crash of thunder in the distance and turn to see eight men in blue robes with identical movements running from a dwarf.

Taryn runs full speed, using Strong Wind to keep up with the enchanter, staff in one hand and shadow dagger in the other. Strong Wind boosts his speed long enough for him to stab one of the men. The man vanishes in a puff of smoke.

The buff from Strong Wind only works when out of combat, so as soon as he attacks, he falls behind.

As soon as the cooldown is up, he casts Strong Wind again, catching up and stabbing another clone. Down to six.

I leave the livestock and set off in pursuit. Jon has been here a lot longer than Taryn, so there is a high probability that he out-levels the dwarf. We've yet to see him cast any offensive spells, but that doesn't mean he doesn't have any. I'd rather be there to back up my friend just in case.

Sprinting at full speed, I slowly make up lost ground. Blood pounds behind my ears as my muscles fatigue, but I don't slow down. Berry is several strides ahead of me, and Stompy is a little behind. The umber bear's muscles ripple beneath his thick fur with each powerful step.

Taryn has managed to cut the illusions down to four, and I've almost caught up with him. He raises his staff to cast Strong Wind again, but nothing happens.

"Dammit!" he yells. "I'm out of mana!"

I could possibly catch the enchanter, but my own stamina is beginning to wane. If only there was a way to slow the speedy little fucker down.

An idea pops into my mind and I want to punch myself for not thinking of it sooner. I summon a Horror of Vitality in front of me and grab the chubby little furball by the horn as I run by. Planting my foot in the grass, I sling the horror with as much force as I can muster straight ahead.

It looks at me with a face of absolute betrayal as it soars through the air like an astronaut adrift in space, landing right in the middle of the group of enchanters. Their movement speed slows by twenty percent, which is more than enough for what comes next.

I explode the horror, and the three other clones disintegrate.

Berry rushes toward the lone enchanter. Jon raises his staff to cast a spell, but the bear tackles him. Using his massive paws, he pins the frail man to the ground.

"Please don't let him eat me!" Jon begs, squirming but unable to move. "Please! I'll do anything."

Berry's snout is inches from Jon's face, teeth bared and drool dripping from his exposed gums. Jon winces, as if closing his eyes will make the threat go away.

Taryn finally catches up to us, his face flushed and sweat beading down his forehead. "You mother fu—" He has his dagger drawn, but I grab him by the arm, stopping his attack on an unarmed man.

"Easy there, killer." I loosen my grip, and when Taryn doesn't immediately attack, I release. "How about we question him before you get all stabby-stabby?"

"Fine." He stares daggers at Jon. "But if you try anything sneaky, I'll gut you like a fish."

"What do you know about gutting fish?" I tease, trying to diffuse some of his anger. "You grew up in Brooklyn."

"Screw you! I know how to gut a fish."

"You're a nerd. When have you ever been in a position to gut a fish?"

"I know how to gut a fish." He crosses his arms.

"How? How could you possibly know anything about gutting fish? Worms, now, I bet you know a thing or two about worms."

Taryn makes a rude gesture at me before returning his attention to Jon. Stompy has joined us as well and has taken up a hulking position just above the enchanter's head.

"Talk." Taryn kneels next to Jon, doing a damn good job at being an intimidating mobster.

I guess that makes me the good cop.

"W-what do you want to know?" There's real fear in this guy. It probably has something to do with the fact that having one's face eaten off by a giant bear would be, at the very least, unpleasant and more than likely very painful.

"Well, for starters, why you attacked Treehaden? And then

maybe we'll get around to your little army of kobolds and the illusions."

"Can—" He gasps for air. "Can you maybe let me breathe a little?"

"Berry, off," Taryn orders. No sooner has Berry lifted his paws before Taryn has Jon fully bound using the vines from his new staff. "I don't trust you. Now, talk."

"Ugh. I'm just trying to make some gold, man. Nobody got hurt."

"You don't think that people will be hurt when they can't provide for their families, when they can't eat?" Taryn's anger is rising all over again.

Jon scrunches his face. "They aren't real, man. It's all a game."

The words hang in the air for a long moment. He's right. They aren't real, not truly. Maybe not to him. But to Taryn and I, they are. Can we really fault him for treating this as a game even if every sensation tells us that it's not?

"Have you ever sat down and talked to one of them?" The anger has vanished from Taryn's voice. "Have you spent a minute with any of them that wasn't at a shop or inn?"

"No."

"Maybe you should. Then tell me how this is just a game. Now, why steal from these people? Why not go dungeon-diving like the rest of the heroes?"

Jon sighs. "Because I fucked up. I thought it would be cool to be an enchanter. I thought I could make awesome items, sell them, and get rich. Turns out crafting is hard. You have to level that shit up. There are textbooks that are expensive if you want to learn the good stuff. I can only do the most basic enchantments right now. Nobody is willing to pay much for a plus-one Charisma ring. I don't even have a single offensive ability. Crafting and illusions. Being an enchanter is not all it's cracked up to be."

"Why the kobolds then?" asks Taryn.

"Dumb luck." Jon flashes a half-smile. "I was searching for materials in the forest and three of them ambushed me. Probably would have killed me had I not tried to bribe them. I tossed out everything I had. One of them picked up the ring and that was all it took. Their whole clan wanted some."

"Then why not take the kobolds to a dungeon to fight for you?"

Jon's eyes light up. "You know that's not a bad idea. Why did I never think of that?"

I step a little closer. "How'd you end up in prison anyways, Jon?"

"Burglary." He lets out a dry laugh. "One of the few things I was ever good at."

Taryn stands up and retracts the vines to his staff. "You couldn't have been that good."

Jon sits up, watching us with skepticism. "What's going on?"

Taryn extends a hand to Jon. "We're gonna give you a chance to make things right and maybe do some good for once."

CHAPTER 6
WALK THE WALK, TALK THE TALK

TARYN and I stand about twenty feet away from Jon the Enchanter, huddled in conversation. Jon brushes off his arms and back, trying to wipe away the dirt from his tumble in the grass.

"You want to bring this weaseling little snake with us?" I don't know what druid herbs Taryn is smoking, but this seems like a bad idea. He's a criminal. "What makes you think he won't rob us in our sleep? Or worse?"

"You're a criminal. Are you going to rob me in my sleep?" Taryn stares at me while I process the information. Technically, I am a criminal.

"It's different." I'm not a real criminal. Not like these guys.

"Is it? Look, if he wanted to run away, he could right now." He points at Jon. "No one is holding him hostage, but he's standing there. Waiting."

I can think of at least one reason he's not running away. Jon reaches out to pet Berry, but the bear snarls, flashing his dangerous canines. Jon takes a couple of steps back, holding up his hands in surrender.

"I don't know, man. It seems like a bad idea." I've had too many bad experiences with other players to want to trust one. Glenn, Jude, Richard the Cleric. Even Pressley the Death Knight and Michael the Paladin haven't been the most pleasant experiences. Everyone in this world is looking out for themselves. Now, Taryn is wanting us to sleep beside a guy who just robbed a village.

"King Orso told us to make allies. Jon can be the first. If we're not willing to take a chance on anyone, how are we going to build alliances? Don't you remember when no one would take a chance on the trolls?"

He's got me there, damn logic. I run my fingernail through the tip of my braid, trying to think of a valid argument.

"Fine. If this blows up in our faces, it's on you." I'll go along with his stupid plan, but I'm not going to be happy about it.

I sling my satchel over my shoulder. We return to Jon and prepare to get moving.

Taryn dishes out orders. "First thing on the agenda is to gather up the rest of the livestock and return them to Treehaden. We can get to know one another along the way." He climbs onto Stompy and motions for Jon to lead the way.

Surprisingly, Berry is very adept at herding animals, running to and fro and rounding up the stragglers. Maybe he's a dog trapped in a bear's body.

Jon looks uncertain at first, turning back every few seconds to see what we are doing, but eventually, his shoulders relax, and he walks more leisurely.

I walk in silence for a while, content to let Taryn mastermind this foolishness, but as they continue to talk about pointless topics, I'm forced to intervene.

"So, Jon. What level are you?" His Wisdom is obviously high enough for him to know Conceal, but that doesn't say much considering he's an enchanter. He probably had more Wisdom at level one than I do now.

"Ugh." He hangs his head before looking up with a grimace. "Level ten."

"Ten?" My mouth drops. "How in the hell have you been in here longer than both of us and you are only level ten?"

He brushes shaggy brown hair from his eyes, frowning. "I told you I don't have any offensive abilities. I've died a lot. That's part of the reason I wanted to sell the animals, so I could pay someone in the city to train me."

I can understand the toll that might take on someone, entering this world and then realizing you screwed up your character creation. Still, it's no reason for him to be a dick. "Well, what can you do?"

"I can enchant small items, and I can cast illusions. That's about it."

"Give us a little more detail than that," I snarl. "If you're level ten, you should have access to seven abilities. What are they?"

"Fine." He sighs. "I can enchant a small item with plus-one Charisma. I could have chosen any of the basic stats, but I went with the most useless one. The first time I used a Charisma item, I thought it was so cool, the way it changed how you felt, but it turns out no one is looking for them. Well, no one with coin to spend. I can also enchant a gemstone to provide light." He taps his staff on the ground and the diamond tip glows brightly. "When I managed to level up, I was stuck in a dungeon and my torch was on its last legs. Another wasted point. I can also enchant my voice so that it sounds like it's coming from several directions. It's great for misdirection but hasn't helped me kill anything. The rest of my points were put into my doppelgänger ability and Conceal Area." He stares out in the distance. "I'm a glorified distraction. That's about it."

"Hey, man." Taryn pulls Stompy up beside Jon. "Don't be so hard on yourself. I'm sure you're more powerful than that."

"Thanks." Jon gives him a half-smile before averting his eyes.

"So what if you're a distraction?" I know I've been a dick to this guy, but seeing how defeated he is in this world where I'm having the most fun in my life puts things in perspective. Not everyone is a natural at games. "If you put those abilities to use in the right circumstances, they could turn the tide of a fight. Every team needs support. You could be an invaluable part of the right team."

Jon's eyes light up. "You really think so?"

I nod. "Let's get these animals returned, and I'll show you."

I catch Taryn grinning out of the corner of my eye.

For the most part, the journey back to Treehaden is easy. Berry wrangles the livestock, with some help from my horrors to keep the wanderers in check. Only once do we lose an animal, but Taryn is able to track it down in his bird form before it truly escapes.

Jon becomes more friendly as the day goes along. The more I'm around him, the less I think he's a bad guy. Really, he just got caught in some unfortunate situations.

"How'd you end up in prison anyways? I know you said burglary, but why?" I've never had the inclination to steal something that didn't belong to me. Maybe because I've never really wanted for material goods, but even if I did, I don't think I'd have it in me.

"I don't know, man." He shrugs. It's clear that this is something he doesn't enjoy talking about. "Desperation. I was so tired of living paycheck to paycheck, you know? The never-ending grind." He rubs his forehead, as if choosing his next words carefully. "I met this girl. That's how most of the bad decisions in my life begin. Fucking women, you know? That's the real drug—a woman's love. Shit'll make you do anything. Anyways, I was in love. I wanted to buy her something nice for our anniversary, but I wasn't making shit. It's hard to show your love when you're making minimum wage."

"So what happened?" Taryn has guided Stompy right beside Jon to listen to the story.

"I thought if I couldn't buy her something nice, maybe I could take it from somebody who wouldn't miss it. I worked at a body shop, fixing cars. I've always been pretty good with my hands. One of our clients left his car with us, said he was going to be out of town for a week. It was a nice car, so I figured the house was probably even nicer. Turns out it was. I picked the lock, broke in, and the police were waiting for me by the time I was done. I tried to run and accidentally bulldozed a cop on the back steps. The pig charged me with assaulting an officer on top of it all. It wasn't my first strike, so here I am."

"Do you regret it?" I ask.

Jon laughs. "I regret getting caught. Those guys wouldn't have missed anything I took. I didn't even go for the whole stash, just a necklace and some earrings."

"You're a regular Robin Hood." The sarcasm must go over Jon's head because he smiles back at me. "Do you know much about the other players here?"

"A little bit." His smile fades. "We spent some time together during our physicals and what-not. And we all started out in the capital once we got in the game. Once they found out I was useless, nobody wanted to partner up. Been going at it alone ever since."

Damn. That's rough. I feel bad that a few hours ago, I was ready to cast this guy out. He's no saint, but he's not a murderer either.

"What do you know about the other guys?" This could be our

chance to gain an upper hand on those that we are playing with. Maybe understand how they think or at the very least, have some leverage to use against them.

"Uhm, well, some of those guys I never went around. They had a real nasty vibe about them. Three or four of them gravitated to one another and they just watched everyone. Real creepy like. You can just tell with some guys, you know. Like, it's better to just leave them alone. The docs made sure not to tell us what people were in for. So it's hard to know who was telling the truth. I heard some things, though. Most of the guys are innocent." He winks.

"What about Glenn? Do you know what he was in for?"

"Oh man, he was a strange bird. They kept him in isolation, so we only ever saw him when we were logging in. I heard he came from a crazy house. Must have been something bad. The weird thing is that he was such a nice guy the few times I met him. You'd never know there was anything wrong with him."

All in all, Jon really doesn't know shit about the other players, aside from their names and classes. Once I've milked him for all I can, I fall back, leaving him and Taryn to talk about the weather.

When we arrive at Treehaden, the villagers are more welcoming to Jon than I would have imagined. But seeing as how they have never actually seen him, only his army of kobolds, they have no reason to suspect his involvement in their recent troubles.

Taryn is treated as royalty, and once the animals are safely locked in the stables, dinner is prepared in our honor. By the time we finish eating, it's almost nightfall, so we decide to stay the night at the inn.

The Rowdy Rooster is nothing special as far as inns go, but it's a roof over our heads and ale in our bellies. With full bellies and a decent buzz, we retire for the night with a promise of adventure tomorrow.

The next morning, I wake and gather my belongings. Taryn is already waiting in the first floor of the inn, gorging on eggs and bacon. The smell of fried meat has my mouth watering.

"Morning," he gets out between bites. Speckles of egg coats his dark beard. He reminds me of Limery the way he shovels food in his mouth.

"Where's Jon?" I expected him to be down here with Taryn, but he's nowhere to be found.

"Sleeping?" Taryn shrugs.

Something feels off. I turn to the bartender, a weathered, gray-haired dwarf. "Did our companion, the human, pass through here?"

He sets the mug he was polishing on the hardwood counter. "Ah, yes. He was up with the roosters. Seemed in an awful hurry."

"Dammit!" I slam my fist on the table, causing Taryn's plate to jump. "I told you he couldn't be trusted."

Taryn picks up a piece of bacon, crunching it in his mouth.

"Why are you not upset?" I roar. "Get up, let's get Berry and track him down."

"Why?" Taryn raises an eyebrow. "If he's gone, he's gone. What do we have to gain by chasing him?"

I let out a low growl. I hate feeling like a chump. Taryn and his stupid ideas. This is the last time I let him make the decisions. "Whatever. We never should have brought him with us in the first place. I'm going to get some fresh air."

I slam the door behind me as I step out into the courtyard. I love Taryn's chill attitude most of the time, but sometimes, I just wish he would get upset about the same things I do.

To my left, I notice a crowd has gathered around one of the shops. Curious, I walk over to investigate. Nearly a dozen dwarves are huddled around the entrance. A faint glow pulses from within.

Once I'm close enough, I notice that Jon is sitting on the steps of the shop. He holds a gemstone in his hand, carving something into it. He's focused as he works and doesn't notice my approach. Once the inscription is finished, the lines glow bright for a moment before fading away. A pile of gems sit at his feet, and several dwarves hold others in their hands. They tap the stones with fascination, each touch causing the gem to burst to life with light.

I stand back and watch for a moment as Jon works. He's clearly not trying to escape, but what is he up to? Trying to swindle more dwarves out of their money?

"What's going on here?" I ask.

Jon looks up from his work and flashes me a smile. "I'm putting my skills to use. The item shop had some low-grade gemstones lying around, so I'm enchanting them for the towns-folk. So they can travel at night without needing a torch. Or, you know, read or whatever."

I guess I misjudged Jon after all. Him and Taryn. Jon's kind of like that barking dog at the pound. The one with fur on edge that's unwilling to come to the gate, but once you get him home, he's as cuddly as can be. Not that Jon and I cuddled.

Drury turns around, holding a glowing yellow stone. "He calls them flashlights." He taps the stone over and over, turning the light on and off like a kid with a new toy. "Pretty amazing."

"How long has he been at this?" The amount of enchanted stones floating about leads me to believe it's been a while.

"Since daybreak. These flashlights will do wonders for our town. We no longer have to force our schedules to the sun."

I return Jon's smile. "Meet us in the inn when you're finished here. It's time to level you up."

CHAPTER 7

SALT IN AN OPEN WOUND

WE FIND the dungeon tucked away along the coast, almost invisible from the mainland. If not for the map that Chief Rizza gave me detailing all the ley lines around the island, I doubt I would have found it at all. Yet another reason why I am better off than Jon. I've had help from the trolls since the beginning.

"That was real cool of you back there, Jon." Taryn rides atop Stompy, his dreadlocks blowing in the coastal breeze. "Bringing modern technology to a fantasy world using magic. I love it! I wonder what else we could create."

"I felt bad about what I did." Jon places his hand over his heart. "I know it doesn't make us even, but maybe it helps."

"I'd say your debt has been paid. To Treehaden, at least. They got all of their livestock back, and now they can farm late. With the lights, there's so much potential for them." I slap him on the back. "Now let's go kill some things."

Before we begin, I invite Jon to officially join our party. His location appears on my map, and we can now send one another private messages.

A hidden stairwell leads us down to the dungeon's entrance. The stairwell is made from flaky stones, unlike most dwarven architecture, which is cleanly carved. Once Stompy puts one hoof on the ancient stone, it begins to crack and dislodge, forcing him to wait at the top of the stairs. Whoever made it didn't have beasts the size of barns in mind. Or maybe they didn't want them inside the dungeon.

The stairwell itself overlooks the sea, and as we descend, salty spray from the crashing waves below gathers in droplets on my skin. The roar of waves blasts up the cliff. My horrors grumble and bump into one another on the narrow path. Stompy blows a sad trumpet once we are out of his vision. Berry, on the other hand, seems excited for some one-on-one time with Taryn. He nuzzles his nose against his master every chance he gets.

At the bottom of the stairs, a dark crevice disappears into the cliffside. It's not big enough for any of us to crawl through. Limery might fit inside, but he's not around to test it out. I'm greeted with a notification.

Salt Caves. *Would you like to enter?*

A string of runes runs along one side of the entrance, the only part that gives away that this isn't a natural formation. As soon as I accept, the runes flash and the crack widens with a groan of grating rock. I barely fit through the entrance, but once inside, I can see in the almost complete darkness. Taryn, Berry, and Jon aren't so lucky, so Jon leads the way, his staff casting light for them to see by.

The cavern is a dull white. Its jagged and abrasive formations cause Taryn's cape to snag several times on protruding salt rocks before he eventually rolls up the end and carries it in one hand. After about twenty feet, we come to a stop as the cavern empties into a polished room. Someone put a lot of time and effort into carving this cave into an actual room, making the floor and walls gleam like marble in the reflection of Jon's light. On the far side, two identical wooden doors await.

Jon eyes the doors with suspicion. Clearly, he's had a few bad experiences with dungeons. He turns around to us. "What's the plan?"

"We'll pick a door, and then we'll see this through. The three of us should be able to handle this no problem."

Taryn runs his finger across the polished salt. The residue turns his black hands a milky white before he licks it. "Salty."

Berry follows his master, pressing his tongue against the wall before recoiling and licking his lips repeatedly.

"Two peas in a very strange and misshapen pod." I shake my head at their childlike behavior and turn to Jon. "Alright, Jon. Once we go through this door, I have no idea what is on the other side. You're a part of this team, and we need you to play support. My horrors, Berry, and I will deal damage and take the brunt of the attacks. You and Taryn focus on ways to help out. Stay out of range of whatever we end up facing."

"Hey, I can deal damage!" Taryn flashes his two shadow daggers in front of my face, their illusory blades coming to life as he grips them.

"Alright, lead the way then, champ." I equip my warhammer and spin its weight against my palm. Several horrors expire and I summon new ones to replace them.

Taryn approaches the two doors and examines them. They look practically identical, both old wood with metal clasps bolted to the walls. A latch and padlock bar our entry. A gash in the wood of the door on the right is the only detail that sets them apart.

"You think that means someone tried to get into this one after exploring the other?" Taryn runs his fingers over the damaged wood. "It was definitely made by an axe."

I join him and inspect the damage. The gash is just as faded as the rest of the door. It's most likely a remnant from a very old adventurer.

Aside from the two doors, the room is entirely barren. "That's the only clue we've got. Do you think we need some kind of key to open them?"

Taryn grabs the handle of the door on the right. As soon as he touches the metal, the padlock unlocks and falls to the side. When he tries the same thing on the other door, nothing happens.

"That answers that." Taryn pulls the door and it opens. He steps behind the door, motioning for me to go. "After you."

Our fearless leader isn't so fearless after all.

There's a small passageway and then stairs that descend deeper into the cliff. Tiny claw marks run along the walls of the stairwell, carved into the salt blocks. The size of the marks doesn't alarm me, but the amount of them does. I grip Destroyer a little tighter as I follow my horrors down into the abyss.

My horrors wait for me in an empty room at the bottom of the stairs. There's a door on both sides, but nothing else aside from a single pillar in the middle of the room. Why is everything so empty? Whatever happened to having a dungeon with a few goblins here and there that we smash and move on from? Empty rooms make everything feel more dangerous.

The pillar has some weird etchings along it, but they don't look like runes or any type of language I've ever seen.

Berry sniffs at the air behind me. I wonder if the salt is having any effect on his sense of smell.

"Time to pick another door." Taryn pushes his way through my horrors and goes for the door on the right.

As he passes the pillar, it begins to crack. The rest of the room stays still while tiny pieces of salt flake off and fall to the floor. Hairline fractures creep up the pillar from floor to ceiling, making the pillar appear like it is writhing and alive.

A piece of rock breaks off, and an eye stares in my direction. With an audible crack, a six-inch piece of salt rock detaches and a small impish creature pries itself from the pillar, raining down rubble as it flexes its body for the first time in however long. It leaps from the pillar, and translucent wings emerge, lifting the ugly monster into the air.

Cracks continue to echo throughout the chamber as more and more of the tiny creatures emerge from the pillar until it is nothing more than a small pole.

Salt Fairy. *Level 17. Made of a harder substance than most fairies, salt fairies have no problem pouring salt in an open wound.*

The bone-white fairies are translucent, their organs visible beneath their brittle exterior. Their fingertips are pointy and sharp, and bat-like wings keep them aloft while menacing tails with spiked tips thrash about. They hover in the air, clicking their tongues in our direction. This is not going to be fun.

Taryn has returned to the safety of my horrors, and Jon lets out a stream of curses behind me.

I send my horrors out into the room, giving me more space to swing my warhammer. "Jon, stay behind me." I move in front of him, blocking him from view of the fairies as best I can.

The fairies dive for my horrors, stabbing and clawing at them with incredible speed. Tufts of orange and blue hair float across the floor as the Horrors of Vitality are ripped to shreds. Their passive slows seems to have no effect on the airborne creatures. One Horror of Power leaps into the air, jaws snapping on one of the fairy's tails. It pulls the fairy to the ground and paws it to dust.

One down, only about thirty more to go.

The spiked tails function like needles, stabbing my horrors in vital areas. Many of my horrors run around blind, eyes gouged out and attacking wildly, sometimes damaging other horrors.

The fairies are so quick that they dip in and out, dealing damage before the horrors have a chance to react.

I step forward, and one dives for my head. I swing my warhammer, but the creature is too quick, darting past my weapon and raking its claws across my face.

Instantly, my vision goes blurry as tears well up in my eyes. My face burns hot as salty claws rip into my skin, setting off pain receptors left and right. Even with my thick skin, it stings like a thousand papercuts.

"I can't do anything without killing your horrors!" Taryn yells as he swipes his dagger at a diving fairy. He misses and catches a spiked tail to the shoulder before the fairy buggers off.

It'd be really nice to have Limery here right about now. He'd give these fairies a run for their money.

Another fairy dives for me and this time, I lift my shoulder to cover my face. The spiked tail stabs into my spaulder, lodging inside of the leather armor. The fairy tries to pull away, but its tail is stuck. I hit it with a hard thump, and the fairy's head detaches and soars across the room, leaving a trail of pink blood.

Jon gags at the sight behind me.

I cast a few more horrors to replace the ones I've lost. They're being picked off without doing much damage, and Taryn is about as useful as nipples on a breastplate. He can't cast Lightning Bolt in such an enclosed space without killing my horrors and potentially the rest of us. He's imbued Berry, making him a mammoth bear, but the fairies are attacking his blindsides. Blood has matted his golden fur on his back and hindquarters.

All in all, this is not going well.

"How the hell are we going to get out of this!" I yell as another fairy claws my back before scurrying away.

"They're too fast!" Taryn swings at another with his shadow dagger but misses.

"Wait." Jon steps up beside me. "Everyone lie down, and quit moving."

"What? That's stupid." I turn to face him, and he stares at me with such intensity that I'm sure he has a plan.

"Just do it! Trust me." He points at the floor. "All of you, down."

I give Taryn an apprehensive glare, but I listen to Jon and instruct my horrors to quit moving and huddle against the floor. The fairies attack with free rein, tiny claws ripping horror flesh. I crouch down myself just as Jon lifts his staff. With a flourish, the diamond tip flashes blue.

The fairies quit attacking and hover in the air, looking around like they are lost.

Incoming Message (Jon): *Stay quiet. I cast Conceal Area. They can't see anything below three feet unless they go beneath the illusion.*

Incoming Message (Taryn): *That's brilliant! Now what?*

Incoming Message (Jon): *Now you kill them? I don't know. This was all I've got.*

No longer sensing a threat, the fairies begin to gather around the pillar in the center of the room. They hook their claws to the salt column and cling tight, fitting perfectly against one another. Before long, all of them have gathered on the pillar once again.

As soon as we step out of the illusion, they'll attack again. We have to find a way to defeat them before they recognize we are here.

Message (Chod): *I think I have a plan that might work, but there is no guarantee.*

Incoming Message (Taryn): *If it doesn't include hiding under an illusion and waiting for the fairies to die of old age then I say it's a lot better than what we are currently doing.*

I summon another round of horrors. If this is going to work, I'm going to need as many as I can get. Since the fairies are no longer attacking us, that means thirty is my max.

Message (Chod): *I need you guys to get away from the pillar. Up the stairs if you can manage it. Just stay under the illusion.*

Taryn crawls on all fours past me. Berry does the same, his large frame barely fitting below the illusion. His wet, matted fur brushes against my shoulder, streaking me with blood. For all the shit I give him, that is one tough and loyal companion.

As quick as I'm able, I continue to summon horrors until I have a full army. Very carefully, I send all thirty of them to gather around the pillar. Horrors of Vitality go closest to the pillar, followed by Horrors of Power, and finally Horrors of Finesse.

Once they are in position, I stand. The fairies immediately begin to stir, but before they have time to unfurl, the Horrors of

Vitality move in close together, forming the base of my plan. Next, the Horrors of Power leap onto their backs. Horrors of Finesse climb their way up until they are forming a horror pyramid around the pillar.

Just as the first salt fairy detaches, I cast Kamikaze, exploding all the horrors at once.

The force of the blast is enough to shatter the column, along with the bottommost fairies.

With the column destroyed, the ceiling begins to sag. It groans loudly now that the floor above has no support.

"Get back!" I shout, rushing toward the stairs right as the ceiling collapses, killing the rest of the fairies underneath a mountain of rubble. Dust and smoke fill the room, making it hard to see even with my night vision.

"Did it work?" asks Jon.

"I think so. It's kind of hard to s—"

"Nnggghhh." A loud, deep grunt cuts me off, followed by several more.

As the dust fades, several squat shambling bodies emerge from the rubble. They look like dwarves, but with glowing blue eyes and white, leathery skin. Their beards are coated with dust and clothing hangs in tatters around their bodies, revealing a deathly form underneath. They look like zombies, but less smelly and decaying.

Salt Draugr. *Level 19. Normally decayed, these undead dwarves were preserved by the salt of the mines, making them stronger and more powerful than their aboveground counterparts.*

I grip the handle of Destroyer a little tighter. "Preserved zombies. Great."

CHAPTER 8

FASTBALL SPECIAL

ONE OF THE undead dwarves opens its mouth and a white puff of dust spews out. The noise that follows is like nails on a chalkboard, grating against my senses. As the draugrs crawl out of the rubble, their heinous cries echo through the dilapidated room.

Milky white eyes lock on our location.

They wear tattered garments and distressed leather armor. Clothing of the common class. Alabaster skin shows through in places, their skin white as chalk. The salt of the mines has halted their decomposition, leaving the draugrs' skin and muscle intact, albeit very dehydrated. Their skin clings to muscle and bone like spandex, making the normally full-framed dwarves ghastly to look upon.

"Hey man, I didn't sign up for zombies!" Jon steps even further up the stairs. With the ceiling collapsing, his illusion has been dispersed. "I don't want to be a zombie. I might be a shitty enchanter, but at least I'm alive."

He rushes to the top of the stairs, but the door has already closed, blocking our escape. Jon beats on the door. To what end, I'm not sure. There's no one on the other side to let him out.

"Help! Somebody help!" he shouts, fist pounding frantically.

"Easy, man," Taryn tries to coax him down. "If we work together, we'll get out of this fine."

The dwarven draugrs climb across the rubble in our direction. I summon three more horrors and send them out to buy us time while we get Jon under control. The passive slow of Horror of Vitality impedes them slightly, gaining us a few more precious seconds.

"Jon!" I roar with everything I can muster, and it momentarily stops his antics. "We're in this together. If you don't want to die, then it's high time you start helping us out."

He stands at the top of the stairs breathing heavily with his shoulders slouched. He hangs his head for a moment before turning around. "Okay." He sighs. "Let's do this." It's not inspiring, but at least it's something.

The draugrs rip through my horrors with their superhuman strength. One of them steps close enough for me to attack, and I hit it with a mighty swing from Destroyer. The blow sends it stumbling backward into two other draugrs, knocking them down like bowling pins. The metal flashes red as the hammer grows hotter.

The attack doesn't do much damage. The draugrs might look brittle, but they are still dwarves with decent Constitution.

I count six draugrs amongst the debris. Six level-nineteen draugrs against a level-twenty troll, a level-ten enchanter, a level-sixteen druid, and a level-twelve umber bear. Hardly a fair fight.

The good news is that they don't appear to be reanimated warriors. Judging by their clothing and lack of chainmail or plate armor, these were worker dwarves before they turned.

Taryn casts Lightning Bolt and the resulting thunder shakes

the walls, sending even more dust and rubble raining down from above. Lightning crashes into one of the draugrs, taking out a chunk of its health and setting its clothing on fire. The draugr is unphased by the flames erupting across its body as its health trickles down. With no fluids in their bodies, the dwarves are walking tinder. Very strong walking tinder.

Despite their brittle appearance and vulnerability to fire, these monsters are still strong and tough to kill. My blow with Destroyer only took out ten percent of the draugr's health. Jon does practically no damage and Taryn does very little unless it's with his lightning. So this battle falls square on the backs of Berry and me.

Three draugrs step into my range and I use Intimidation, unleashing a roar and confusing them for two seconds. They stumble back and forth, unsure of where to go or what to do. I knock one of them to the side with Destroyer, where Berry pins it to the ground and mauls it. In the same motion, I spin around and connect my weapon with a second draugr. It flies back into the pile of rubble where the pillar once stood. Red flashes down my warhammer as Inferno gains power.

My next attack connects with the draugr's chest. I hear the crunch of breaking ribs as I send it flying into the others. Finally, a critical hit! When it stands, charred flesh and fabric still sizzle from the attack. Each hit does more damage than the last as Inferno grows hotter.

I search for my next victim, but no one is in range. Destroyer goes cold again as its timer expires.

Berry yelps as one of the two draugrs he is fighting lands a blow to the bear's ribs. Both draugrs dig their hands into Berry's fur, refusing to let go and continually kneeing and kicking as they ride him like drunks on a mechanical bull. Berry tries to claw at them over his shoulder and thrashes about in an attempt to throw them off, but it does nothing to deter their attacks. Taryn rushes to his pet's aid, stabbing a draugr with his shadow blades. It doesn't do much, but it does enough for the undead dwarf to release his grip on Berry.

With a hard swing, I send the other one sprawling into the corner.

I move away from the group in an attempt to spread out our opponents. Instead of drawing one or two my way, five of them lock on to me. Before I realize it, I'm trapped in a corner with five draugrs pressing in on me. They rush toward me with surprising speed.

I set my feet and prepare for their onslaught.

Lightning rips across the room, hitting one of the draugrs and knocking the rest of them into me. I try to toss them aside, but they weigh far more than I imagined, knocking me off balance. They claw and bite me, and I drop Destroyer as they tackle me to the floor. I summon horrors as I fall, and they attack the undead dwarves. Pain runs through my body as their hardened nails rip into my skin. The salt that coats most of their bodies only intensifies the pain, setting my flesh on fire. I hope the others are okay, because I can't hear anything over the screaming that surrounds me.

I try to fight to my feet, but the five of them have me trapped on my back. Panic flares within me as my HP continues to drop. For all my strength, I'm helpless. Trapped. It's like waking up from a nightmare only to be trapped in a blanket.

Not knowing what else to do, I activate Berserker Rage.

Bonus Strength pumps within my muscles, giving me the power I need to roll over to my side and crawl free. I kick one of the draugrs in the face and its teeth spill to the floor like marbles.

Destroyer is lying somewhere, but I don't have time to look for it. Instead, I summon more horrors, activate Bite and Claw, and rip into the throat of the closest draugr. As I tear into its throat, dust pours out. I punch the next closest one and kick out at a third, retreating toward my group just in time for Taryn to cast another lightning bolt.

It rips into the group, setting several more on fire.

"Everyone, on the stairs!" Jon orders.

Berserker Rage expires, and I do as he commands. A moment later, a half dozen of Jon's doppelgängers run past me and into the room. They spread out to all four corners. Jon cups his hands over his mouth and whispers something. Seconds later, his voice booms from every corner of the room. "Hey, dickweeds!" The draugrs that were staring into our direction begin turning rapidly, not sure which way to attack. They spread out, none of them going for the same target.

Several of the draugrs are pretty low on health. One only has a tenth of its HP, and two others are below fifty percent. A single attack is all it takes for them to dissipate one of his illusions, but as soon as they do, Jon sends out another one. His voice continues to bounce off the walls, calling them names my followers would have been proud of. Insults come from every direction, taunting our opponents.

"Douche canoe."

"Lint licker."

"Captain skinny-dick."

"Fuckass."

Thanks to Berserker Rage, I'm back to full HP myself.

"How long can you keep this up?" I ask Jon.

"I've got about five more clones left."

"Alright, keep it up as long as you can. I'm going to try to finish this. Taryn, I want you casting lightning on the opposite side of wherever I am. Have Berry stand guard in case this goes wrong and I end up dying. You'll need him to protect you."

Taryn nods gravely, taking position behind Berry.

I search the room for Destroyer and spot the glittering metal shaft protruding from the rubble across the room. There are two draugrs between me and my weapon.

I rush out to grab it with one of Jon's duplicates following alongside me into battle. We split at the last minute, drawing one of the draugrs away. Grabbing the weapon right as the other one gets to me, I swing up without looking. Destroyer connects with a crunch and explosion of dust. The one with the lowest health falls to the ground without a head.

"Come on over, you walking wounds! I've got your bag of dicks right here." Jon's voice shouts from the wall behind me.

Two draugrs turn to face me, but Taryn casts Lightning Bolt on the other side of the room, momentarily distracting them. I use the opportunity to knock them both to the ground, sweeping their legs with my warhammer. Inferno engages and I dash to the other side, where two more draugrs are chasing one of Jon's clones. The heated warhammer connects with ribs, leaving a warhammer-sized scorched indentation as the draugr flies through the air. With four stacks of Inferno, I swing the hammer for the head of the next closest, turning it to dust with one hit.

Not wasting any time, I bolt back to the other side and pummel the draugrs once again. By the time Jon sends out his last clone, all the draugrs are defeated.

I sit on the steps, letting out an exhausted breath. "I...was not prepared for that."

"A collapsing ceiling? How could we be?" Taryn takes a seat beside me, patting me on the back. A battered Berry lies on the ground in front of him. "It's just not the same without the little guy, is it?"

Limery's bulbous eyes flash in the front of my mind. I can't wait for him to be a part of the team again. "You're right about that."

"Hah! I got a level and a new ability point." Jon beams with pride.

"What are you going to use it on?" Taryn asks after healing Berry.

"I could make my current illusions stronger, or I could add a new stat to my enchantment abilities. Or there is an illusion that summons a copy of a nearby creature. What do you guys think?"

"Your doppelgängers came in pretty handy. What's the upgrade do?" Taryn stands, stretching his arms overhead.

"It makes them corporeal, whatever that means."

Taryn laughs. "It means it gives them actual bodies. They won't be just smoke and mirrors anymore. Do that one!"

"Sweet! They won't be able to do much damage, but if they can take a beating, then it'll make it harder for our opponents to pick me out."

"Exactly!" Taryn high-fives Jon.

Jon steps past and goes to loot the bodies.

"Anything good?" I ask, not ready to get up.

"Lots of salt crystals." Jon tosses a chunk of white rock to me. "Might be worth something at the market."

"Not sure I want to be seasoning my food with the remains of zombie dwarves. It's all yours." I toss it back.

Once we rest and heal up, we examine the two doors on each side of the room. It's impossible to tell which one to pick. They're similar to the ones in the first room, but both of these doors have been damaged by our recent fight.

"Do you think it matters?" asks Taryn. He's careful not to touch the door and unlock the enchantment.

"Honestly, I have no clue. I'm sure they are all connected in some way. Let's just pick one and keep moving." It's probably just a matter of the easiest route to the boss room and if we want to do a complete clear or take our levels and run.

I summon more horrors, determined to go into the next room with a full army.

While Taryn contemplates over which door to choose, Jon focuses on the collapsed ceiling.

"Maybe we should check up there?" He points to the room above us.

It's a good fifteen feet from the floor and crumbling around the edges.

"And how exactly do you propose we get up there?"

"Can you toss one of these guys up there?" He pats a Horror of Vitality on the horn and it swats him away.

"I mean I could have them look around, but I have no way of knowing what it is they are seeing in order to tell them what to do. They could accidentally trip a trap or something worse." Not a bad plan, just not very effective.

"What about Taryn?" Jon looks away as soon as he says it.

"Excuse me?" Taryn raises his eyebrows and leans forward. "I don't think I heard what I think I heard."

I fight to conceal the smile spreading across my face. "Come on, man. Let me toss you."

"No way!" He shakes his head, and the clasps in his hair jingle with the motion. "Nope. I'm a dwarf. I have my pride. Besides, I could just fly up there if I wanted."

"Come on, let me toss you. Just this once, and I'll owe you one. There could be a clue to help us navigate this maze we've gotten ourselves into." I give him my best puppy dog face, which I'm sure doesn't have nearly as an endearing effect as I hope.

"Yeah, Taryn." Jon winks at me. "Let him toss you."

Taryn stares at me for a long moment before rolling his eyes.

"Fine, but you owe me big time. And no one else hears about this ever."

I nod, keeping my jokes to myself and not pushing my luck.

Taryn is heavy, but not too heavy for me to hold him like a small child with my palm placed squarely under his bum. With a heave, I shout, "Fastball special" and toss him to the room above us.

The ceiling groans for a moment, but then everything is silent.

"Nothing up here but two doors," he says. Dust rains down as he walks around the perimeter. His footsteps are silent due to the noise-canceling properties of his boots.

"Alright, come on down then. I'll catch you." I can't hide the laughter in my voice as I say the last words.

"Wait, I've got an idea. Do you think we can open a door up here and down there?"

"I doubt it. Remember what happened in the first room? You could only open one door."

"Yeah, but maybe you can only open one door in each room. What if we can open one down there and one up here?"

"How is that going to help us?" It's not like Berry and I have any shot at getting on the second floor.

"I could lure whatever is in this next room into here, make it fall through the floor, then we don't have to fight it on the way out if we want to clear both sides."

I'll be damned. That's actually a pretty good idea. "So how are we doing this?"

"Touch one of the doors to disable the lock, but don't open it. Once you do that, I'll try the door up here."

There's no way of knowing which door is better, so I just pick one. Jon stands closely at my heels as I touch the handle and the lock falls open.

"Done," I shout.

"Okay, get ready to catch me."

There's a clank of a door opening and then dust falls from the ceiling as Taryn runs across the floor. He jumps from the room above without looking, and I catch him midair, holding him like a baby. I rock him a few times before he pinches my nipple, forcing me to let him go.

"Alright, let's get out of here." I rub my twisted nipple with a face of mock pain.

"Oh, give it a re—"

Taryn's words are cut off by a crash from above like a bowling ball on concrete. As we listen harder, the noise grows louder as it approaches our direction, like someone knocked over an entire rack of bowling balls and they are spilling down the street.

"What the hell?" asks Jon, backing up even closer behind me.

The noise grows until it is right on top of us. The ceiling shakes right before a torrent of white spheres crash through the open ceiling and smash against the floor. They crack open, shards exploding everywhere.

I'm able to focus on one right before it collides with the floor.

Salt Golem. *Level 18. These monsters can curl into a ball and travel with blazing speed, bludgeoning opponents to death.*

One by one, the golems shatter against the stone floor. They might be tough, but a fifteen-foot fall at full speed is all it takes to crack their shells. I get a nice chunk of experience for doing absolutely nothing other than being part of the team.

"Dude, that was genius." I extend my fist to Taryn and he returns the fist-bump.

"Yeah, baby." He flashes me a toothy grin. "That's what I'm talking about!"

"That's awesome!" Jon pumps his fist in the air. "I'm already halfway to level twelve."

I walk over to inspect the remains of the salt golems. Lots

more salt crystals. I'm less wary about taking these and shove a few in my satchel.

Summoning another round of horrors puts me at full capacity, so I suggest that we enter the next room. Once everyone is ready, I open the door.

The polished walls and floors that made up the last two rooms are no more. This room is reminiscent of the crevice we walked through at the entrance. Hundreds of salt stalagmites and stalactites adorn the walls, floor, and ceiling. A narrow path winds to a single door on the other side.

We wait and listen, but the only sound is the water dripping from the stalactites overhead. That doesn't mean much though, considering the pillar and the fairies that emerged once Taryn walked past. This could be exactly like that.

None of us want to take the lead, so I send my horrors in first to make sure it's safe. No sooner have they passed through the door than the nearest stalagmite explodes, sending razor-sharp shards flying like shrapnel. My oldest horrors die from the blast, but the newer ones have enough health to absorb the blow, though they lose a good amount of HP. Before they can return to me, however, another stalagmite explodes, then several more in a chain reaction that wipes out a quarter of my horrors on the spot.

"What was that?" Jon asks, wide-eyed.

"No idea. I didn't see a trap or anything." I search the path for anything that my horrors might have tripped, but there's nothing out of the ordinary.

I send another horror forward, and the next stalagmite explodes, shredding through the closest of my minions. The two stalagmites adjacent to it shatter a moment later. At this rate, if we push forward, all of my horrors will be dead before we make it halfway.

"There has to be a way through that doesn't set them off,

right?" Not knowing what is causing the explosions means we're going to be doing some trial and error.

"You would think so." Taryn strokes his beard. "Maybe the rocks are sensitive to movement or the floor responds to a certain weight limit? Try calling them back and send one in by itself."

I call my horrors back, though I don't see how Berry or I are making it across if the floor has a weight limit. I send out a single Horror of Finesse, the lightest of all my horrors. The gangly blue monster walks forward and the moment it is next to a stalagmite, the rock explodes.

"Wait a second." Jon grabs me by the arm. "Let me try something. I haven't used my ability point, so my clones are still just illusions. Let's see what happens when I send one out."

Jon lifts his staff and a duplicate of him jumps out of his body. It walks down the path silently, and when it reaches the nearest stalagmite, nothing happens. His clone walks further, past dozens more stalagmites, but it doesn't set them off.

"I don't get it. Do we have to destroy literally every single one of these things in order to cross this room?" Taryn lets out an exasperated sigh.

"Now, let's see what happens when..." Jon's voice trails off.

I look to see his eyes glaze over when, I assume, he opens a stat menu.

I'm looking across the room when another explosion rocks the cavern. Jon's clone falls to the ground, blood seeping out of hundreds of small wounds.

My heart thuds in my chest. "What the fuck was that?" I shout.

"Uh, I made him corporal," says Jon with a grimace.

"Corporeal," corrects Taryn.

"As soon as he took a step, they exploded," adds Jon.

"Wait, so it didn't set them off as soon as it changed? Only after he moved?"

Jon scrunches his eyebrows. "I-I think so."

"Hmmm." I reach in my satchel and pull out one of the salt crystals. It's light. Way too light to set off any weight enchantment.

I toss it across the room. It clatters as it lands, setting off another chain reaction.

"I think I know what's setting them off." I equip Destroyer and step out into the room. If I'm wrong, this is going to be very painful.

Cautiously, I press forward until I'm at the spot where Jon's clone died. One of the enchanted stones that I have equipped to Destroyer muffles my movements. I take one more step into the radius of the next stalagmite and close my eyes. I'm certain I could survive a single explosion, but the prospect of shrapnel ripping through my flesh makes me wince all the same.

I wait, but nothing happens. Opening my eyes, I let out a sigh of relief. The room is so quiet that I could hear a pin drop, which is a good sign. It means I'm not being sliced by a thousand tiny salt fragments.

A cold sweat erupts on my neck when I hear a soft crunch back near the entrance. New stalagmites form from the ruins of the exploded ones, trapping me in the middle of the cavern.

Still focused on my plan, I start walking back as they repopulate. With each step, nothing happens. It's just as I thought. It's not weight or movement setting off the explosions.

"It's sound," I tell my companions, but before I finish my sentence, searing pain shoots up my legs and midsection as I'm assaulted by thousands of glass-like shards. They tear through my skin, setting my body on fire and dropping my health by a third as a chain reaction of exploding stalagmites rips through me.

I fight against every urge in my body not to scream, embracing and focusing on the pain, and eventually the explosions stop. I huddle against the floor, blood seeping into a pool around my feet and knees. Every part of my lower half burns and aches. Skin hangs off my palms in tatters as blood drips to the floor.

How could I be so stupid?

Eventually, the pain fades as my increased healing takes effect, and I'm able to look up. Jon and Taryn both stare at me with concerned expressions, neither one brave enough to come to me. I crawl to my feet and return to where they are standing.

"It's sound," I finally get out. "That's what sets off the explosions."

"You couldn't have waited to tell us that?" Taryn grimaces as he looks at my wounds. "Here, take this." He reaches in his bag and pulls out a vial of red liquid.

I kneel so he can pour it in my mouth. As soon as the cinnamon-flavored liquid touches my tongue, I begin to feel better. The health potion kicks my healing into overdrive and the hundreds of cuts begin to mend themselves.

"Thanks."

"Don't mention it. So if the rocks respond to sound, how are we getting everyone through here?" He looks into the cavern. "Berry and Jon don't have sound distorting items. Not unless you can magically craft something?" He turns to Jon, but the enchanter just shakes his head.

I stand in silence for a moment, mulling over ideas in my head. I can't summon horrors quick enough for us to send them across the room. We could try throwing items ahead of us to make a path, but there's no telling if the respawn on the stalagmites are universally timed or random. One explosion is likely enough to send Jon back to wherever he set his spawn.

Brute force isn't getting us through this one, but maybe Strength will.

"We carry them. You carry Jon. I'll take Berry."

Taryn blinks at me. "He weighs like eight hundred pounds."

"Leave that to me." I flash Taryn a smile. "Saddle up, noble steed."

Jon climbs onto Taryn's shoulders like a kid trying to get a better view in a crowded room. I can't resist poking a little fun at them.

"Put on a trench coat and you might be able to get into the R-rated movies."

Taryn cuts his eyes at me. "I think you should worry more about how you plan on carrying Berry across the tunnel and less about how awesome Jon and I look."

"Awesome, right." I chuckle.

I step back into the entryway as the last of the stalagmites reform. I really hope my plan works, otherwise we are all going to be in a lot of pain.

"I need Berry to be completely silent while I carry him across. A single grunt or groan could be all it takes to set off an explosion."

Taryn nods. "I'll do my best." He sets Jon down and whispers a few words into Berry's ear. "Alright, let's do this."

Jon climbs onto Taryn's shoulders once again. Berry stands in front of me, waiting for orders.

"Alright, buddy. I need you to climb on my back. Wrap your arms around my shoulders and I'm going to hold your back legs."

I bend my knees and lower myself to make it easier for him to climb on. He wraps his massive paws around my neck and I grab his back legs, hefting him onto my back like a child. A thousand-pound child.

Immediately, my muscles burn from such a heavy weight. I

take the first step and my legs shake with the movement. If not for having Destroyer tied around my waist, each step would be thunderous. As it is, the only sounds are my heavy breathing.

Taryn takes the lead, following the narrow path that winds between the stalagmites. I follow close behind with shaky steps. Sweat beads down my forehead and my grip starts to loosen on Berry's legs.

We're nearly a quarter of the way there, but there is no way I'm going to make it at the current rate. Luckily, I thought all of this through. I send Taryn a quick message.

Message (Chod): *Time to pick up the pace.*

Taryn doesn't respond, but his speed quickens. I'm sure he could carry Jon for an hour if he needed to. The man is like a twig.

My grip falters and I know I can't wait any longer. I activate Berserker Rage and suddenly carrying Berry becomes exponentially easier. I readjust him and set off down the path.

The bear's hot breath pants against my neck, but so far, he hasn't made a sound. We pass the halfway mark and I still have twenty seconds left on my ultimate. The path is narrow, and I freeze when Berry's leg hits one of the stalagmites. Luckily, his fur muffles the sound and nothing happens. I let out a sigh and continue.

Up ahead, Taryn and Jon have finished, and pound their fists in the air in silent victory. I'm a quarter of the way when I notice the countdown on Berserker Rage is at ten seconds.

I heft Berry up higher on my back and lean forward, sprinting the rest of the way. Destroyer jostles against my waist and I'm afraid for a moment it might come loose.

I'm only a few steps from safety when my buffs expire and the full weight of Berry comes crashing back down against my body. I stumble forward, losing my footing and tumbling to the ground.

Explosions crash all around me as my face collides with the cold hard floor, and sharp pain shoots through my legs. I wait for the concussive force of an exploding stalagmite to the face, but it doesn't come. Instead there is nothing but darkness as Berry's massive body covers my upper half and absorbs all the shrapnel.

He roars in pain, crawling off my body toward Taryn. I raise my head and see Taryn rushing to his pet and casting Restoration, basking them both in a golden aura. Berry's snout is bloody, and he's covered in rubble.

Two small arms grab my shoulder and attempt to pull me forward, but I'm too heavy. I climb to my feet and very gingerly walk to the open space where I promptly collapse. My legs are tattered and bloody, but at least we made it. Berry's fur absorbed most of the damage and once Taryn is finished healing him, he looks as good as new.

Jon hands me a health potion that soothes my stinging legs. After a moment, the pain is gone entirely.

"It wasn't a bad idea." Taryn extends a hand and helps me to my feet. "Making it through there with a few cuts is about the best we could have hoped for."

"Yeah, I guess they can't always be pretty." At least we made it through.

At the end of the cavern, there is only one door waiting.

"Looks like this is our next challenge."

Jon, Taryn, and Berry stand behind me as I press my hand to the enchanted door.

CHAPTER 9

TEAMWORK MAKES THE DREAM WORK

THE DOOR GROANS as it swings open, revealing a long hallway. It's narrow and straight with polished walls and floors, no different from a passageway in most castles. The light from Jon's staff shines on an assortment of white and gray tiles that line the floor, covered in a thick layer of dust. Clearly, no one has set foot in this area of the dungeon for quite some time. From where I'm standing, I can see another door at the far end. Jon and Taryn stand behind me, waiting for me to enter.

"Seems way too easy. Jon, can you send a clone down the hallway?" I have a healthy distrust for empty hallways.

"No problem." Jon raises his staff and a duplicate of himself steps out from his body.

Five steps in, the floor shakes and stone grates together just before a scythe swings down from the ceiling, cutting the now corporeal clone in half. Blood and guts splatter the hallway as Jon watches himself die and crumple to the floor. The scythe swings back and forth a few times before coming to a stop.

Jon grimaces. "Does it really need to be that graphic?"

Taryn pats him on the back. "At least you know you have guts. Now we know what you're made of."

I imagine this hallway is full of traps. This is the exact situation where unlocking Perception over Conceal would have paid great dividends. Avoiding traps are not my favorite type of challenge. I'd much rather battle monsters with brute force than have to puzzle my way across this.

"I hope you have a strong stomach, Jon, because we are going to have to test this out a few more times." I summon three horrors and send them forward a few seconds apart from one another.

They bypass the scythe and I hear a click as one of them trips a trap. The Horror of Finesse makes it through but the other two are crushed by a massive salt block that plummets from the ceiling. The salt block is the width of the hallway, blocking our vision of the other side. A moment later, I feel the last horror's presence descend deep into the cliff before it vanishes.

My immediate thought is a vanishing tile or some kind of trap-door.

"I guess we move forward." I shrug. "Watch your step and keep an eye out for anything out of the ordinary."

I take the lead as we move down the hallway, pushing the giant scythe aside so that I can pass by. When I climb on top of the salt block, I notice a missing tile in the floor, revealing a hole that descends into complete darkness.

Jon points his staff at the hole, but the light doesn't go very far. "I do not want to find out what's down there." He takes a step back.

We're halfway down the tunnel, but who knows what traps are still waiting?

"Your turn." I nudge Jon in the arm.

He casts his clone and it barely makes it past the hole before a second scythe emerges from the wall and slashes with enough force to completely decapitate it. The head rolls along the floor before falling into the dark hole.

"You've got to be kidding me." Jon places his head in his hands. "I'm starting to regret making my illusions this realistic."

"It's for the good of the party." I climb down from the salt block and send out another horror. "Better one of your clones meets a grisly end than one of us, right? Besides, if you plan on leveling up the old-fashioned way, you're going to be seeing plenty of blood and guts."

The Horror of Vitality waddles across the marble floor, mumbling to itself when a second stone block falls from the ceiling and crushes it. If I had a drink, I'd pour it out in honor of all the horrors that have died so that we may live. Horror of Power goes next, using its powerful legs to jump up the salt block and onto the other side. It doesn't go far before I feel its presence come to a stop.

"I think that might be it." I climb the salt block and find the horror waiting at the door.

This wasn't the most difficult hallway I've experienced, but who knows how we would have fared without Jon's clones and my horrors. Not every hero comes with a set of test-dummies.

The door at the end of the hall is different from the others. There's no lock, but instead, it has a large rune carved into the wood.

"Any idea what it means?" I ask.

Taryn shakes his head.

Jon scrunches his nose. "Doesn't look like any of the runes I've encountered."

"Let me stock up on my horrors before we enter. If there is a special rune on this door, then I want to be prepared."

After taking time to summon a full army of horrors, I press my hand to the door. The rune flares a bright white and a crash rumbles from the other side. The door creaks open, revealing a circular room with a massive white turtle standing in the center. Torches line the wall, filled with blue flames that cast the room in an eerie glow.

Halite Tortoise. *Unique Monster. Level 25. Known as the Salt Turtle to the Ivory Dwarves, the Halite Tortoise is a symbol of luck and prosperity for miners.*

The turtle's skin and shell are milky white and translucent, almost like it was carved out of salt, with icy blue eyes that follow us as we enter. Its thick legs and shell are covered in murky gemstones, providing it with natural armor. My horrors spread around the room, surrounding the turtle on all sides.

I take a step back when the turtle opens its mouth and speaks.

"It has been many years since someone has trespassed into my mines. Many years since I have had a worthy opponent." The words that trickle out are raspy and deep.

The door behind us closes with a slam. The turtle clicks his beak a few times before speaking again.

"Perhaps we should make this a fair fight."

The tortoise lowers its shell to the floor and retracts its legs. Once they are inside the shell, white smoke spills out of the holes. It's thick and heavy, lingering on the ground. My horrors cough as it overwhelms them, and I feel their HP draining by the second. The horrors with the lowest HP vanish from existence.

"What is this?" Taryn asks as he backs closer to the wall.

The smoke touches my skin, but it doesn't burn or otherwise affect me. The smoke continues to pour out until a thick layer coats the bottom two feet of the room. My horrors continue to cough and die.

"I don't know, but it looks like it only affects you if you breathe it in."

Half of my horrors have died and the rest will join them soon if I don't do something. Instead of letting them go to waste, I cast Sacrifice and gain a buff for each horror as it explodes into the ether. My muscles bulge as I'm filled with bonus Strength and Constitution for the next few minutes. I even feel quicker on my feet from the influx of Dexterity.

As soon as the horrors are gone, the smoke that has coated the floor vacuums back into the turtle's shell.

"Ah." Its legs extend and lift the enormous body off the ground. "Much better." It clicks its beak a few more times.

Taryn and I exchange glances. So it looks like my horrors are a no-go this round.

"What's happening?" asks Jon.

"It seems the turtle isn't a fan of my minions. Everyone spread out. Taryn, how about you get this party started?"

We move to four separate areas around the room. The turtle doesn't move, but its eyes follow me. Does it view me as the primary threat?

Taryn raises his staff and a bolt of lightning arcs toward the turtle. At the moment before impact, the turtle retracts into its shell. A single tile on the shell opens and swallows the lightning bolt inside. The shell shakes, rumbling against the stone floor before several tiles along the edge of the shell open and four bolts of lightning shoot out.

The action is so surprising that none of us dodge the attack. The lightning bursts out with as much force as it entered with. A bolt hits me in the chest, dropping five percent of my HP and setting my hair on end.

"Ouch, ouch, ouch!" Jon screams as he jumps around, shaking as if he is having a seizure.

Berry groans, his frizzy hair making him look more like a teddy bear than the ferocious beast he is.

Taryn taps the butt of his staff against the floor. The passive from Nature's Aegis gives him immunity to elemental effects, but he still lost fifteen percent of his health. "I'm not gonna lie, that was pretty awesome. Any idea how we are supposed to beat this thing?"

I give Destroyer a few spins against my palm. "Anybody in the mood for turtle stew?"

The turtle is back standing, and I take off running toward it with my warhammer raised over my shoulder. I bring it down on the turtle's shell with as much force as I can muster. The turtle retracts its body into the shell, and when I hit it, the turtle shoots off like a rocket, ricocheting off the wall and colliding with Berry. The shell hits Berry with enough force to knock him off his feet, plowing straight through him and hitting the wall again before zooming toward Jon.

The spindly man barely moves out of the way before the shell bounces off the wall. The turtle extends its legs, flipping itself into the air and landing with a thunk near the center of the room.

Well played, turtle. Well played indeed.

It stares at me with its piercing blue eyes, and I'm almost certain it smiles.

"What the hell? This thing is unkillable!" I fight back the urge to smash my warhammer into the floor.

Taryn's lightning doesn't work. The turtle destroyed my horrors, and my own attacks turn it into a cannonball. How are we supposed to defeat this thing?

"Maybe if we flip it over, the underside will be softer," offers Taryn.

That's actually a brilliant idea. "Alright, get ready. I'm going in!"

I rush toward the turtle, intent on flipping it upside down. When I'm a few steps away, it retracts into its shell. Perfect! I can flip it over without worrying about having my hand bitten off.

I reach out to grab the bottom of the shell, but it starts spinning. In a matter of seconds, the turtle shell spins in a blur. I try to stop it, but the rough edges of the shell rip into my palm, tearing at my flesh. I recoil at the pain, and blood streaks down my arm.

Before I have a chance to complain, the turtle barrels into me like a bumper car, knocking me to the floor. It zooms toward Jon, hovering inches off the ground.

Jon tries to escape, but the shell runs him down, smashing him into the wall and dropping half of his HP in a single hit. Berry and Taryn both rush to his aid as the shell continues bouncing around the circular room.

Jon hobbles delicately, supported on one side by Taryn.

I run over to them just as the shell stops spinning and the turtle emerges once again.

"I've got a plan, but it's going to take all three of you out of the fight."

"Dude, no way." Taryn shakes his head. "That thing will kill you."

"One more hit and it's going to kill Jon." I grab Taryn by the shoulder. "Trust me on this."

He nods.

"I need you to use Transform and turn into a duplicate of Berry. Jon, I want you on Berry's back. Then I want you to make as many clones as you can. One of them is going to ride Taryn. Scatter the others around the room."

"And what are you going to be doing?" asks Jon.

"I'm getting us the hell out of this dungeon."

I stalk toward the turtle with my hammer raised, and just as I predict, the turtle retracts into its shell. Destroyer smashes into the hard exterior, sending it off like a rocket once again. The reptilian projectile crushes into the knees of one of Jon's clones, hyperextending them and launching him like a rag-doll.

I watch as the shell hits the wall and ricochets. I follow the pattern as it hits another wall and another, waiting for the perfect moment to implement my plan.

The shell soars between both versions of Berry and Jon, and I'm not quite sure which one is which. The turtle hits the wall again and comes straight in my direction.

I stand my ground as it comes barreling toward me. When it is half a dozen feet away, I summon three horrors and explode them right as the shell makes impact. The force from the explosion flips the shell end over end, and it comes to a grating halt right beside me.

Turtle legs extend and grasp at the air as it tries to flip itself over. The underbelly of the beast is slick and shiny. The first hit with Destroyer does little damage, but as Inferno builds with each hit, growing hotter, the shell eventually cracks and the turtle's struggles cease.

Notifications flash across my vision, but I ignore them for now.

The blue flames on the wall change to orange, and the door into the room clicks open. A chest made of driftwood appears next to the turtle's corpse, right beside a portal that will take us to the entrance.

"How is everyone feeling?" I ask. I'm sure this is more action than Jon has seen in a while.

Taryn returns to his dwarven form and casts Restoration on Berry.

Jon chugs a health potion as he hobbles over. "Who cares about how I'm feeling. Let's see what's in the chest."

He shuffles past me and hovers over the weathered treasure.

"Go ahead; do the honors." I point at the chest. He's earned it.

He lifts the lid and a soft white glow emanates from within. A wide smile creeps across his face. "Nice!"

"What is it?" Asks Taryn.

"Man, this is so cool! Way better than any of the items I've found on my own." He grins from ear to ear.

"Alright, let's have a look." I reach down in the chest and find an assortment of items and take a moment to inspect each one.

Item. Halite Shield. *A lightweight translucent shield capable of taking damage without reducing visibility.*

The shield looks like a replica of the tortoise's shell. Salt crystals cover the edge and center, but the majority of the shield is completely see-through. The wearer could block an attack without losing any visibility of the attacker, or hide behind it as a battering ram. Not a bad item at all.

Item. Vial of Salt Gas. *Covers an area with gas that reduces visibility and deals damage-per-second to anything that breathes it in.*

The gas wiped out my horrors in short order. I wonder if this one has the same low-hanging density, or if it will work on larger foes?

Item. Greater Salt Crystal. *A powerful mineral that can be used as a conduit to increase the range of spells.*

I could attach the salt crystal to Destroyer, but that would mean giving up one of the stones I already have. I don't think the trade-off would be worth it. It'd probably be better for Jon or Taryn.

Item. Lucky Tortoise Foot. *Increased chance of rare items and quests.*

The dried-out tortoise foot is kind of gnarly, but I can't really argue with its effects. Better loot is always welcome.

I turn to Jon. "You saved our asses back in the first room. You should take the first pick."

"Really?" His eyes are wide with surprise.

"Absolutely. Welcome to the team."

He reaches in the chest and pulls out the tortoise foot. "I think this will be worth it down the road."

"Taryn, which item do you want?"

He puts his hands up. "Nah, man. You're next. We all would have been smashed to a pulp if it wasn't for you."

I take the Halite Shield because neither of them could use it. I'll probably end up trading or selling it at the next town. Maybe I'll donate it to the forest trolls. Taryn takes the Vial of Salt Gas and then gives the salt crystal to Jon. The enchanter is practically giddy with excitement.

All in all, Jon was a pretty valuable member to the team. Once we get Limery back, I think we'll be a hell of a squad.

We all take a moment to look over our notifications.

You have defeated a unique monster: Halite Tortoise.

You have defeated Salt Caves. *Claim dungeon prize.*

Congratulations! You have reached level 21. +1 stat point to distribute. +1 Strength and Constitution racial bonus. +1 ability point to distribute.

I use the ability point to unlock Champion once again. I still have two stat points, but I'm not quite sure where I want to allocate them just yet.

Jon and Berry both gain two levels from the fight, while Taryn gains one.

"Well, do you want to go back and clear the rest of the dungeon?" I ask. There's still the entire upper level we haven't checked.

Jon shakes his head. "I don't know about you guys, but I'd rather count my blessings and stop for lunch."

Taryn laughs. "Alright, man, but you're cooking."

CHAPTER 10

CHAOS RISING

WE'RE ALL in good spirits after clearing our first dungeon as a team. Night creeps in, and we sit around a small fire beneath a copse of trees eating roasted rabbit. Taryn leans against Berry, eyes closed, and Stompy snores softly behind us.

"What are you spending your new ability point on?" I ask Jon as I take a swig of water from the Brimming Tankard I picked up in Seascape.

Jon rips into a rabbit leg. "I haven't decided. I could upgrade one of the spells I already have, or I could learn to enchant something new."

"Like what?" I ask. Enchantment and illusion abilities are fascinating to me. To think that, with enough practice, Jon could craft a warhammer like Destroyer is mind-blowing. It would take years for him to grow that powerful, but that doesn't mean it can't be done. With dwarves having such long lifespans, no wonder they have been able to craft such wondrous items.

"Well, I could make my illusions more powerful. Either making Conceal Area harder to detect for smaller areas or making it capable of concealing larger areas to the same degree it does now. Or I could make illusions of living creatures instead of just doppelgängers." He tosses the leg bone to Berry. "If I had access to the right books, I could learn all kinds of enchantments for physical objects."

"Maybe you should save it for now. By the time we get to a city, you might have enough loot to trade for one of those books."

Jon scratches his chin. "That's not a bad idea." He reaches into his satchel and pulls out a salt crystal and a feather quill.

"What are you doing?" I ask.

"Figured I might make a few more flashlights before bed so that I can sell them at the next town we go to." He holds the baseball-sized rock in his hand and presses the quill to it. "Clear crystals provide the best light."

I move over and sit beside him. "How does it work?"

He displays the salt crystal in one hand and the quill in the other. "I etch the rune for light into the crystal with my pen, then I push some of my mana into it to seal the spell." He presses the tip of the quill to the crystal and it cuts a mark into the stone.

"How is the quill able to carve into the crystal?"

He smiles. "The tip is enchanted. It makes the process faster, otherwise it would take me hours to do a single simple enchantment."

I watch as he carves the rune into the translucent crystal. When the rune is complete, he presses his fingers to it and the rune glows bright white for a moment before fading away. Then the rock emits a gentle glow like a lantern.

Jon tosses the flashlight to me. "Tap the rune to turn it on and off."

I play with it for a few minutes, watching the rock flick on and off. "Does it ever run out of light?"

"Eventually. It doesn't drain a lot of mana to make them, but it should work for a few months before it needs recharging. There are enchantments for stronger lights, self-charging lights, or even ones that can cast a stream of light in a certain direction. I haven't learned any of those yet."

"Still, it's pretty cool. I bet you'll sell out." I hand it back to him.

A droning rattle grabs my attention and I look over to see drool trickling down Taryn's beard. So much for just resting his eyes.

Jon stares at me intently, opening his mouth a few times like a fish out of water. "Hey, man, can I ask you a question?"

"What's up?"

He taps the rock repeatedly, the light flashing on and off. "You weren't in the initial group with us. What did you do to end up here?"

I sit in silence for a moment, not sure what to say. No one but Taryn knows why I'm really here. The smart thing would be to keep my secrets to myself. There's no telling how the other heroes will view me after learning I'm in here because I yelled at someone online. These are hardened criminals. Well, maybe not Jon. He accidentally ran into a cop.

"Come on, it can't be that bad."

"It's not."

"Well, then lay it on me. I told you about my stupid mistake. What's yours?"

What harm could it do? Jon is a part of our party, so I decide to trust him.

"I got in trouble for cyberbullying." I wait for laughter, but instead, he just looks confused. I can only imagine how someone who has spent time in prison would think of me being there for calling someone names.

"Cyberbullying? Never heard of it."

"I told someone on my team to go kill themselves in a broad-cast. Instead of giving me jail-time, I got sent here."

His brow furrows. "Broadcast? You some kind of celebrity or something?"

"Nah, nothing like that. I played video games online, and people watched me."

"Wait, you're just a kid?"

"I'm in college. Well, was in college."

He shakes his head in disbelief. "You're kidding me? You've got to be kidding me. They were going to send you to jail for some-thing you said on the internet?"

"Technically, this is my sentence."

"Damn. The world ain't what it used to be. We used to call each other names just for fun when I was growing up. Seems like they are policing everything these days. You can't even fart without the government sniffing it."

I laugh at his joke. He may be right, but here we are in a game, where literally every move we make is recorded and broadcast on a feed above our pods. The only privacy we have are the thoughts in our heads, and I'm not even one hundred percent sure about that.

We retire for the night and take turns keeping watch. When it's my turn, I lean against Stompy's massive backside and listen to the sounds around me. The last embers of the fire crackle away, bugs rattle, and in the distance, an owl hoots in a melody with the howls of some untamed beast.

The sky overhead is full of millions of twinkling stars. As I watch them, I can't help but wonder how this could be a game. The work it must have taken for this much depth. It feels more real than anything I've ever experienced in the real world.

I don't care if I ever go back. My parents will be fine without me. In here, there are people relying on me, and for once in my life, it feels like I have a part to play in the fate of the world around me. It's like—

Something stirs behind me, interrupting my thoughts. I grab Destroyer and turn to find Taryn wiping the sleep from his eyes.

"Is it your turn already?" I ask.

He comes and sits behind me. "Not sure. I was having this terrible nightmare about the draugrs from the salt mines. I was trapped underneath a mountain of them while they ripped me apart." He shudders.

"Those things were pretty creepy." I laugh. "You were right, though. About Jon. He saved our asses in there. And I think he might view this game a lot differently going forward."

Taryn smiles, and his teeth catch the glow of the moon. "You brought it out of him. I know you don't see it, but when you really invest in someone, you have a way of getting the best out of them."

I'm surprised by his statement. I might have helped open Jon's eyes, but it was Taryn who believed in him, who wanted to give him a chance.

"He's only one guy, though." I pick up a twig and toss it into the fire. "We're going to need a lot more for what's coming. Hell, we're going to need a lot more just to get into Goldspire."

Taryn strokes his beard, the golden clasps jingling as they touch. "It will all work out. Now, go get some sleep. I can take it from here."

I wake to the smell of fried eggs and find Taryn cooking with a small iron pan over the fire. Jon sits beside him, enchanting more flashlights.

"I hope those aren't *your* eggs." I squint an eyelid at Taryn.

There's no way I'm ready to eat something that came out of him while he was in bird form.

He shakes his head as he flips the eggs over. "First off, I transform into a male bird. Secondly, even if I could lay an egg, it would hardly be enough to eat." He places an egg on a small metal plate and shoves it toward me. "How about you be thankful that I scoured the trees for our breakfast while you were still snoring your life away."

He gives me a rude gesture as I take the plate. Point taken.

"Where'd you get all the cooking supplies?" I devour the egg in one bite.

"I picked them up before we left Treehaden. Thought it might be nice to try cooking something besides roasted meat for a change."

"Thanks for breakfast. Are you all about ready to get on the road?"

"I'm excited." Jon places his newest enchanted object in his bag and stands up. "Where are we going first? More dungeons?"

I pull up my map. There's a town between where we are and the next cluster of ley lines. "There's a town we can hit up to resupply. It might be a good spot to sell off some of your items as well."

We gather our things and set off for the next town. We make good time, thanks to Taryn casting Strong Wind while we travel. It doesn't allow for me to level my herbalism or other skills, but those aren't a priority right now. We stop in front of a wooden sign that displays the town's name, Narthensted, outside of the palisade.

Even though it is still daylight when we arrive, the entry is barred. I rap my fist against the wooden gate a few times before someone answers.

"What's yer business in Narthensted?" a gruff voice asks from the other side.

"We were hoping to buy and sell, maybe stay at your inn for the night." I spot a brown eye peeking through a slit in the wood. Something is definitely up with this place.

There's movement and shuffling as a board is removed from the other side of the gate. A bushy-bearded ivory dwarf pushes the door open a few feet and motions for us to come in. He wears a plain gray tunic and weathered boots, and his eyes look past us suspiciously as he ushers us in. He breathes heavily as he opens the door further for Berry and Stompy to enter.

"Hurry up, hurry up," he mumbles. Once we are all inside, he boards the gate again.

"Everything okay here?" I ask.

"These be dangerous times. All of our guards have not returned from Seascape, and there is word of undead roaming the Glossop Forest."

"Oh, great," moans Jon. "More zombies."

"So, it is true?" the dwarf asks with wide eyes.

"Calm down, brother." Taryn places a hand on the dwarf's shoulder. "We were in a dungeon. I can't speak for your forest, but if you would like, we can check it out for you."

"You'd do that? I know a lot of the women and children would sleep a lot more soundly if they knew we had heroes dealing with the threat."

The women and children, sure. "We'd be happy to help once we've finished our business here."

"Speak for yourself," says Jon.

"Come on, Jon. You're part of the team." I slap him on the back, and he stumbles forward.

Taryn takes Berry and Stompy to the stables, and we split up to handle our business.

Narthensted is a small town, but it has a few shops where we are able to sell our loot and resupply on food and health potions. Most of the buildings are either stone or wood, with thatched roofs. Their supply is limited after the massive influx of people to Seascape for the king's announcement, but we're able to grab the basics. I hold off on selling any of the more valuable items for when we come to a larger city.

While digging through my bag, I come across the Mysterious Green Egg I found in the castle. I'm still not sure what it does and when I try to analyze it further, all I see is a series of question marks. I drop it back in and go search for the others.

I find them both waiting outside of the Stedfast Inn

Jon jingles a bag of coins. "Not a bad haul. I should have been selling flashlights from the start instead of tricking kobolds into doing my dirty work."

"You don't say," mumbles Taryn before turning to me. "Want to grab a drink and see what we can find out about this haunted forest?"

We bypass the inn for now and go to a tavern called The Spotless Toad. After stepping inside, I think it should be called The Grimy Toad. The floors and tables are stained with a layer of dirt and grease. A thick fog of smoke coats the ceiling thanks to an ebony dwarf intensely smoking a hookah pipe. An ivory dwarf with a patchy beard and a boil on his nose stands behind the counter. He smiles, revealing a mouth full of yellow, crooked teeth.

"How can I help yous?" he asks.

"Three ales, please. We'll take a table in the corner." I drop a few coins on the bar, and we head to the back.

A group of dwarves sit at one table with dirt-stained clothing. They look like farmers. Taryn nods to them as we pass.

"This reminds me of some of the places I used to hang out back in the day." Jon winks.

I come to an abrupt halt when I spot a cloaked figure sitting in the corner, hood drawn over his eyes.

Jon runs into my back, splashing some of his ale on the floor. "Chod, what the heck?"

The cloaked figure wears red robes with a giant gash in the middle. A black chain hangs from his neck. I've seen this man before.

Richard Hummel
    Level 17
    Cleric
    Human

He's a level lower than the last time I saw him, when he was partied up with Pressley the Knight as they attempted to open the portal in Seascape. When their plan backfired, it created the chaos that allowed Jude and Glenn to march on the portal.

They are the reason Jude and Glenn escaped *Isle of Mythos*.

My heart pounds, and I grip Destroyer tight against my palm.

"There's no need for that." Richard sits forward and points to his chest. The spot where Pressley stabbed him. "I've paid my dues."

I step forward until I'm towering over his table. The other dwarves have stopped talking and I'm sure they are watching every move I make.

"Maybe you paid your dues to Pressley, but what about all of the innocent dwarves that died because of your actions?"

I'm surprised when he lifts his hood and two vibrant blue eyes stare back at me. The man has a chiseled jawline and short blond hair. "My actions? Did I brainwash them and force them to march into a heavily-guarded regional event? Did I summon the monsters or cast the spells that sent them to their graves?" He leans back against his chair. "I'd watch where I were throwing stones if I were you, Mr. Troll."

I lift Destroyer, ready to bring it down on his weaseling little head.

"Chod," Taryn calls to me.

"What?" I whip my head around, spitting out the word with more ferocity than I mean to, and Taryn takes a step back.

He cuts his eyes at me. "It's not his fault. Jude and Glenn are the enemy."

I lower my weapon.

Richard points to the chair next to him. "Have a seat."

I take a deep breath, knowing that if I don't, I'll smash my hammer through the table. My heartbeat lowers and I try to rationally view the situation. Whatever Richard and Pressley had planned, it was separate from Jude and Glenn.

I take a seat at the table. "So what happened?"

He lets out a low chuckle. "Chaos happened."

That's right; he serves the god of chaos. "What exactly does that mean?"

"Buy a down-on-his-luck cleric a drink and I'll give you all the details."

I wave over the bartender and order another ale. A moment later, he sets it on the table and Richard takes a long swig.

He sets his mug on the table. "You don't know much about clerics, do you?"

"No, not really." I don't know much outside of what I was offered to play as a troll. I'm aware that there are multitudes of classes and races still waiting to be unlocked.

"What about you two?" He glances between Jon and Taryn and they both shake their heads. "Figures. Why choose the path of religion in a game like this?"

He twists from side to side, cracking his back, before continuing. "Allow me to enlighten you. Different classes have various ways of leveling up and gaining experience. For most classes, it's raiding dungeons and killing monsters. Clerics are primarily a quest-based class. We can level the other way, but we very rarely have offensive abilities for ourselves. We do make great supports, however. Each cleric has a primary deity that they serve, and when an opportunity presents itself to please the deity, a quest appears. Experience is given upon completion of the quest."

He takes another long draw of his ale and snaps his fingers for another.

"And that's why you were with Pressley?" I tilt up my glass, finishing my own drink. My mood has lightened, and my head has started to buzz around the edges.

"More or less. We were in the same town when the regional event occurred. I received a quest to help him and I took it."

"Did you know your spell would backfire when he attacked the portal?" asks Taryn.

"I had no idea, but I've learned to expect the unexpected."

"Any idea where he is?" I ask.

"Pressley? Your guess is as good as mine. I've heard the rumors of undead in the forest, but I don't really have a desire to get stabbed in the chest again." His fingers run across the slit of exposed flesh in his torn robe.

If he's not looking to party up with Pressley again, maybe I can at least convince him to join our cause. We're going to need all the heroes we can get. I don't trust him one hundred percent, especially considering who he serves, but I didn't trust Jon in the beginning either.

"You know the portal in Seascape was reopened?"

His mouth curls at the edge. "I received the notification."

"Jude and Glenn escaped into one. We're not sure which, but I'm gathering forces to go through and warn the other leaders. King Orso believes that the dark wizard is still alive after all these years, hiding behind a closed portal somewhere. He fears an attack is imminent and we need to be prepared. Will you join us?"

Richard drains the rest of his ale in one gulp. "Oh, I wish I could, but unfortunately, I have prior commitments." He gets up and heads to the door. Hand on the door, he turns back in our direction. "Thanks for the drinks."

The door slams behind him as he leaves.

I have no idea where he's heading, but I'm certain trouble won't be far behind.

GLOSSOP FOREST

Jon looks me in the eye, arms crossed. "Let me get this straight. You want us to go into a haunted forest at sunset?"

"What's the big deal? Taryn and I can both see at night, and you have your light. We'll be fine. Plus, there's no proof it's haunted. It could have been Pressley that scared them." If there's a chance I can find the death knight before he moves on, I want to try. It's very rare to run into another hero, so if he's here, I can't squander the opportunity.

"I'm leaning with Jon on this one." Taryn stands beside the enchanter. "Who knows what kind of monsters and creepy crawlies come out at night in there?"

"Bro, you're a druid. You're supposed to be one with the forest. Don't think of them as monsters. Think of them as potential pets."

A devious grin spreads across his face. "You know, that's not a half-bad—"

"Oh, come on!" Jon puts his fists over his eyes, and for a moment, I think he's going to scream. "Not you, too."

"Two against one, let's go." I give him my best smile.

Jon crouches down, covers his face, and groans. "Fine, both of you owe me one."

We stop by the stables for Berry and Stompy and set off toward Glossop Forest. It's rife with ley lines, so either there is a dungeon or it's full of magical activity like the troll village. Either way, I'm excited to see what happens. If Pressley is there, then it has to be worth it. All he cares about is gold.

Thanks to Strong Wind, we travel the few miles to the forest quick enough. The road bypasses the forest entirely, so we are forced to make our own path once we enter the woods.

The sun dips closer to the horizon, casting the world in shades of lilac and tangerine, but as soon as we step into the trees, it's all grays and blacks.

With my night vision, I can see in complete darkness. Dwarves have darkvision, allowing them to see in dimly-lit areas like the forest, but not complete blackness like a cave or tunnel. With Jon around, there's no need for either. He activates his staff, the diamond tip glowing like a lantern and reflecting off the eyes of silent watchers in the trees.

Jon keeps close to me. So close that he steps on the back of my heel several times before I tell him to back off. My horrors lead the way, grumbly little minions that will take the brunt of any surprise attacks.

The forest is creepy at night, I'll give them that. Branches snap in the distance and animals scurry in the trees. Weird noises echo from the forest's depths, and due to Jon's light, I have a hard time seeing past twenty yards.

I've spent time in the forest ever since arriving on the island, so I know the biggest fears are the ones that linger inside the mind.

"How do you suppose we find this guy anyhow?" Jon pushes a low branch out of the way.

I shrug. "Follow the sounds of chaos and destruction?"

"I'll have Berry keep his nose alert for any unusual smells." Taryn rides on the back of his beloved bear.

Stompy tramples through the forest, making enough noise to alert anything nearby.

I come to a stop when I see a pair of glowing eyes in the distance. The green dots focus on me for a moment before disappearing.

"What is it?" Jon steps a little closer.

"Some wild animal. I think we scared it off." I pull up my map. Ley lines run throughout the forest, one right beneath us.

I freeze in place as several of my horrors vanish instantly. I'm not sure why since they had more health than some of the others that remain.

"Guys, something just killed three of my horrors." I search the vicinity for signs of a threat but see nothing.

Stompy unleashes a bellowing trumpet, and I turn to see his back leg vanishing into a pool of complete darkness beneath the earth. He struggles to pull himself free as tendrils of dark energy wrap around his leg.

Lightning crashes into the darkness and it recoils back into the earth. Several more of my horrors vanish.

"Run!" shouts Taryn. "It's darksand. Get moving or it will devour us whole."

I don't waste any time, running deeper into the forest. Something cold wraps around my leg, stopping me in my tracks. I fall forward and my tusks smash into the ground.

A dark black substance creeps up my leg. I smash it with Destroyer, but it does nothing. My mana and health both begin to drain, and I struggle for my freedom. I focus on the darksand, hoping for any knowledge that might help me escape.

Darksand. *Level 18. This sentient, carnivorous sand thrives in* *darkness, absorbing the life force and mana of anything unlucky enough to be caught in its grasp.*

Jon rushes to my aid, pointing the tip of his staff at the black goo. It recoils from the light, releasing me.

"Get up!" he yells.

We stampede through the forest like a herd of buffalo until we empty into a small clearing.

"Holy shit! What was that?" I gasp.

Jon has his hands on his knees as he pants for air. "That's why you don't go into the forest at night."

Taryn examines Stompy's leg, making sure he's okay. "It's called darksand. It's like quicksand, except it's sentient and eats you alive, draining your life force. This place must be crawling with magical energy for it to be here."

"Weird. I've never heard mention of it in the troll forest."

"It's pretty rare, from what I've read. And it needs a mana source to survive, so it's likely any that was in the troll forest died off when the ley lines were blocked." Taryn pets Stompy on the shoulder, trying to calm the startled beast.

I know how he's feeling. "We'll need to keep an eye out going forward. How do we kill it?"

Taryn scratches his head. "I'm not sure how to kill it completely. I think they only die when their mana and health are completely depleted. For something that can separate like sand, that's easier said than done. I know it recoils from light and heat."

"It'd be nice to have Limery right about now." I wonder where the little guy is.

Jon stands up, finally breathing normally again. "What the hell is a Limery? You keep saying that word, but I have no idea what it means."

Taryn and I both burst out laughing.

"Limery is an imp. He's small and red and powerful as hell.

He's one of my best friends, and he's gotten us out of some sticky situations." I smile. I really do miss the little guy.

Jon cocks an eyebrow. "One of your best friends is an NPC?"

I know it sounds crazy to say that one of the beings I am closest to in the entire world is a string of code I've known for a couple of months, but it's true. Is it really any different than someone bonding with a plant or pet? Just because he was artificially created doesn't mean he doesn't have thoughts and a personality.

Instead of telling Jon all of this, I just say, "Wait until you meet him."

I summon more horrors, and we go deeper into the forest. Jon leads the way this time, using his light to make sure we don't step into any darksand again. My horrors flank him on both sides.

He comes to a stop underneath a massive oak tree and steps back a few paces. "Guys, the trees are moving." He points above to branches that bend and move like appendages.

"It's okay. They're infused with mana. As long as you don't try to harm them, we should be fi—"

A limb smacks me on the side of the head and stars dance across my vision. I stumble forward and hear Taryn grunt behind me.

"The forest is trying to kill us!" yells Jon.

Another limb swings at me, its branches curled into a fist. I duck at the last second, leaving it swiping at air. A group of horrors get smashed into the ground by another limb. Something has to be causing the trees to behave so violently, but what?

"Let's get out of here!" I turn to find Taryn dangling in the air, held around the midsection by a large branch.

The branch lifts him higher, and then thrusts him toward the ground. His dreadlocks whip as he's rocketed toward the forest floor. I equip Destroyer and jump in the air, smashing my warhammer into the branch. It connects, breaking the branch in half and raining down splintered wood as Taryn falls to the ground with a thud.

I pick him up and toss him onto Stompy's back. "Get out of here!" I yell, smacking the moulhaug on the backside.

Jon has used his ultimate ability, and a half-dozen versions of him lay scattered on the ground broken and bleeding. They all grimace and clutch at wounded body parts. I have no idea which one is the real Jon.

Next to me, branches continue to smash into my horrors. A group of horrors band together and pin one branch to the ground.

"Jon!" I call out, trying to find the real enchanter.

"Over here," a weak voice replies.

Jon is pinned to the ground by a collection of smaller branches. I rush to his aid, narrowly dodging swinging limbs like a blue-skinned acrobat. Destroyer smashes the limbs that pin him to the ground, and I toss Jon over my shoulder, running in the direction of Taryn and Stompy.

I find them in another clearing. Stompy is covered in scrapes and gashes. Taryn has a knot on his forehead seeping blood. I sit Jon down beside them and search my bag for health potions to hand out.

"Where's Berry?" Taryn clutches his forehead.

"I thought he was with you." I look around, but there is no sign of the bear. He must be back at the trees. "Stay here and heal. I'll go find him."

My head still throbs from the blow to the back of the head. I bound through the forest, scanning every tree I pass for signs of movement. I can't help but think I may have made a mistake coming here at night. Jon isn't prepared for this. I keep thinking we can do things like we did with Limery around, but the truth is that we can't. His value can't just be replaced. Without his quick speed and fire magic, things are a hell of a lot more difficult.

I come to the spot where we were attacked. There are broken branches and upturned soil everywhere. It looks like a warzone. Several of the branches clench in my direction, daring me to come near. All my horrors are gone, and there is no sign of Berry anywhere.

There's so much debris from the fight that it's hard to make any sense of the situation. The upturned soil makes it impossible to search for tracks.

I stand back, careful to not get too close to the swinging limbs. It appears that only the trees within a small circle are mana-infused. Their roots must go directly into the ley line.

I'm about to go back to Taryn and the others when I hear a roar nearby, a roar I've heard hundreds of times.

Bolting through the trees, I cast more horrors and ready Destroyer for what might be waiting. The roars grow louder and more vicious, and I can't help but wonder what foul creature Berry is fighting. I come upon a ravine, and the roars echo around me louder than ever, but there is no sign of the bear anywhere.

The roars fade and a shrill laugh cuts through the silence. Atop the ravine, a shriveled old lady looks down on me with dirty yellow eyes. She has green skin, long gray hair, and a hooked nose. Her robes are tattered and covered in dirt and moss. Her laugh reveals a set of crooked brown teeth.

I focus on her and realize what a mistake I've made.

Green Hag. *Level 21. Although appearing as frail and weak, hags are anything but. They have ravenous appetites and use their powers of mimicry and illusions to lure unsuspecting adventurers to their doom. Three or more hags in one location becomes a covey, unlocking spells a single hag cannot perform alone.*

I should never have split the party.

CHAPTER 12

NEVER SPLIT THE PARTY

THE HAG LEAPS from the top of the ravine with amazing finesse for such a withered old lady. She lands right in front of me, grabbing me around the biceps with her gnarled fingers. I'm surprised by how much it hurts. I try to sling her off, but her grip is powerful. Blackened nails dig into my skin, drawing blood, and rancid breath assaults me as she cackles madly.

"It was foolish to enter the forest at night. Something might try to eat you." She licks her lips, and there's malevolence in her black eyes.

"I'm not afraid of monsters," I snarl. "I am one."

I activate Bite and sink my tusks into her shoulder. The hag cries out, releasing me from her grip. Sour blood fills my mouth and I fight back the urge to gag. When I spit it out, it's as black as her soulless eyes.

I use Intimidation, staring her down and momentarily confusing her. I need to get away and back to the others. At level twenty-one, she's just as deadly as I am. I turn to run, and her shrill voice cuts through the air.

"Spirits of the earth, I summon thee. Capture the interloper!"

Come on, lady, I'm just trying to find a missing bear. No need to bring in backup.

The ground shakes on both sides of the ravine. Dirt breaks away from the embankment, crumbling to the ground and revealing two stone golems buried within. The golems pry themselves free, and more dirt collapses into the imprints they leave behind.

Rock Golem. *Level 18. Unintelligent elemental power, golems tend to the wishes of those who control them.*

Great, just what I needed—a hag and her minions. I summon a few minions of my own.

The golem to my right swings at me with its boulder of a fist, but I'm fast enough to dodge the attack. It stumbles forward and I smash Destroyer into its backside. A chunk of rock flakes off from the blow.

Good to know that I can break them down—another reason I'm glad I took the warhammer over the axe.

I look for the hag, but she is nowhere to be seen. The second golem charges me, and I attempt to climb out of the ravine. My feet slip in the soil, and I slide back down just as it tackles me to the ground.

The monster is solid rock, and I struggle to free myself underneath its weight. There's a crash, and then I sink deeper into the earth as the other golem dogpiles on top of me.

Their combined weight is too much for me to lift. They crush my ribs, making it hard for me to breathe.

I summon three horrors to my right and explode them, creating a crater beside me. When the cooldown is up, I repeat the process, making the hole deeper and deeper.

After the third round of explosions, I activate Berserker Rage. The added stats give me just enough strength to roll the golems off me. With a heaving push, they fall into the crater I created. They try to climb out, but they weigh too much. The soil crumbles around them as they attempt to scale the embankment.

The hag cackles behind me, and I turn just as a blast of green energy hits me in the chest, taking out fifteen percent of my health. Destroyer falls from my grip, and I tumble into the crater with the trapped golems.

The golems clobber me with their powerful arms, dropping my HP with each hit. I do my best to fight back, but it's a losing battle. Claw scrapes against their tough bodies, barely doing any damage. Using Bite means risking a broken tusk, and Berserker Rage is on cooldown.

I summon horrors and explode them against the golems. They do damage, but the cooldown is too long for me to destroy the golems with my horrors alone. That's when I remember I have Champion.

Champion. *Summon a copy of the most recent enemy you have defeated. Decays 10% every minute out of combat. Cost: 50% of mana pool. Cooldown: 6 hours.*

It will deplete half my mana pool, but I have enough mana that it shouldn't be a problem. The bigger issue is the six-hour cooldown, but it won't matter if I die in this hole.

I cast Champion and a copy of the Halite Tortoise appears in front of me along with a list of notifications. I don't have time to check them in the chaos, so I push them aside.

The tortoise is indistinguishable from the real thing, all the way down to its piercing blue eyes.

The golems switch their focus to the turtle. One of the golems smashes his fist into the translucent shell just as the turtle retracts into the safety of its carapace. The golem's fist connects with the jagged exterior and a crack shoots up the golem's arm. If Destroyer couldn't crack the shell, what luck would stone have?

That's when I remember my new shield that I looted from the salt mines.

I equip the Halite Shield from my expandable bag, and the see-through shell allows me to keep complete view of the golems while remaining behind its safety.

The golem punches the turtle again and its fist splits in two. The second golem charges me, and I use the shield to deflect its attack. As it punches my shield, flakes of rock explode into the air. The golems continue to clobber my shield and the turtle's shell until their arms crumble up to the elbow.

"Imbeciles!" the hag screeches. "Must I do everything myself?"

She lifts her hand and a green aura surrounds it. She thrusts her hand forward, sending out a beam of energy. It heads straight for me. I cower behind my shield when I hear a click from the turtle behind me.

My mana drops suddenly. One of the tiles on the turtle's shell opens and draws the green energy toward it, suctioning it inside. The tile closes and the shell shakes for a moment, glowing a bright green, then three tiles around the base open, shooting three beams at my opponents.

A beam blasts into each of the golems, and their stone bodies return to the earth. A third beam hits the hag, stunning her in place.

I take the opportunity to use the golems' bodies as a ladder to climb out of the hole. I don't waste time searching for Destroyer, instead jumping on the downed hag. I activate Claw and Bite, ripping into her rotten flesh. By the time the stun wears off, she's already dead.

I fall to my knees, visibly shaking as adrenaline pumps through my veins.

Holy shit, that was close.

The Halite Tortoise attempts to climb out of the crater with no luck. I have no choice but to leave it there as its health decays by the minute.

"You saved my life. Too bad I'll never be able to summon you again." Now that I defeated the hag, she's next up once the cooldown for Champion resets.

Something whimpers not too far from where I am, and I go to inspect. I find Berry pinned to the ground by a massive network of vines. He looks at me with panicked eyes, unable to move.

"Don't worry, buddy. I'll set you free."

I use my claws to cut through the vines. They've dug so deep into his skin that he is bleeding in several places. Once I've removed enough vines, he's able to break free. Half his health is gone, but he seems to be okay as he licks my knuckles.

"Did the mean old hag trap you in these vines?" I ask him, scratching behind his ears, but he just licks at his wounds. "Taryn will get you fixed up once we find him."

Berry's ears perk up at the sound of his master's name.

I take a moment to look over the notifications from during and after the fight.

*You have summoned **Halite Tortoise**. You have summoned a copy of a unique monster.*

The following abilities will drain directly from your mana pool.

***Salt Fog.** Halite Tortoise releases a dense, unbreathable gas that deals damage per second to its victims.*

***Consume and Destroy.** The shell of the Halite Tortoise will open, consuming magical energy and dispersing it back at enemies.*

***Spiral.** The Halite Tortoise retracts into its shell, spinning in a circle and making it impossible to grab.*

I receive a fair amount of experience from my encounter with the hag. Not enough for a new level, but it moves me much closer than if I had tackled it with the others. Surprisingly, there's not a single item to loot aside from her tattered clothing, so I track down Destroyer and head to find the others.

***

Berry and I hobble into the clearing where Jon, Taryn, and Stompy are still recovering from the first encounter.

"What the hell happened to you two?" Taryn jumps to his feet and rushes over. He immediately begins casting Restoration on Berry.

"I ran into a hag. She'd trapped Berry, and I think she was planning on eating him." I go on to tell the rest of the story about the golems and how I was able to defeat them.

"I told you it was a bad idea coming here at night." Jon throws his hands up in the air. "But what do I know?"

"Alright, alright. You were right. Happy?" I walk over to a tree stump and take a seat. "We're here now, though, so we might as well see it out. Pressley has got to be around here somewhere."

Jon picks at a rip in his robe. "Is this guy really worth it? Is having him on our side worth possibly dying?" He shakes his head and sits beside me. "I mean, I just started leveling up. I don't want to lose all my progress."

I understand his frustration. Jon has spent the majority of his time here being an under-leveled loner. At least I had Limery around even when everyone was trying to kill me.

"Listen, I don't want to die. I don't want any of you to die either, but this is the path we are going down if you choose to stay with our party. I've made promises that I intend to keep. Something big is coming to Mythos. Something we need to be prepared for. I know you haven't had a chance to see these people like we do, but if we don't gather forces for when the time comes, they could all die. And they won't respawn." I sit there for a moment, letting the words hang in the air. "Do you really want to be stuck in a game where all hope is lost, where darkness wins? If so, is this place any better than prison?"

No one speaks for a long moment, and the only sound is the voice of the forest.

Jon nods. "Alright, we'll do it your way."

Time to go find us a death knight.

CHAPTER 13

THE DEATH KNIGHT RISES

AFTER HEALING UP, we prepare to journey deeper into the forest. Everyone is on edge after our first battle, and every shadow looms as a potential threat. We walk cautiously, inspecting the forest before moving along. We're here to find Pressley, not to level up or engage in battles with the local flora and fauna.

Truth be told, I'll be happy if I never see another hag again.

The deeper we go, the more difficult it becomes to avoid the forest's monsters. We're forced to fight a group of spiders that refuse to leave us be, and we almost run into a minefield of darksand trying to escape the ravenous pincers of the spiders.

We're following a well-worn path when suddenly a streak of green light ignites the sky. A gust of wind hits us head-on like a tidal wave before the forest sits in a stunned silence.

"What the hell was that?" Taryn gazes at the streak of light high above the trees.

"No idea, but it can't be good." I grip Destroyer and strengthen my resolve. "So, naturally, that's where we need to go."

Jon sighs audibly beside me, but he doesn't complain.

We follow the glowing green beam like a guiding light. The closer we get, the more the aura seeps out into the forest, casting everything in its eerie glow. Grunts and explosions grow louder until we come upon the source of the chaos.

Three hags stand near one another, and the giant green aura makes perfect sense. I remember part of the description for the hag I defeated. *Three or more hags in one location become a covey, unlocking spells a single hag cannot perform alone.* This can't be good.

A forcefield of energy surrounds the covey as they cackle madly. Pressley the Death Knight stands across from them in all his glory.

Pressley Allen
  Level 25
  Death Knight
  Human

He's a far cry from the gallant knight I saw at the jewelry shop in Lynchton, but he is stronger than ever and looks like a total badass. He's already gained another level since Seascape, making him the highest-level hero I've seen. His silver armor is now a dark gray, with chainmail as black as night underneath. Dark energy radiates from his body, and the slits in his helm are full of darkness. Deep purple sparks trail up and down his glimmering obsidian sword.

He's surrounded by a group of skeleton warriors. One of them runs at the hags, but when it hits the green barrier, its bones disassemble and fall to the ground in a clatter. Pressley grunts, raising his hand as another skeleton charges. This one carries a rusty dagger. It swipes at the shield, and a blast of green energy explodes, sending more bones rattling to the ground.

As I look around, I realize what a dire situation we've stumbled upon. Two massive ogres stand inside the shielded area with the hags. They wear armor made from bones, and each one has a glowing medallion around its neck. The bones look like they belonged to dwarves or humans. There are also several huts in the area, constructed from a mixture of mud and bones. The entire area looks like a graveyard.

Pressley lifts his left hand and a black aura surrounds it. The aura grows larger as his health ticks down. He must be powering the spell with blood magic! The ball of infernal energy swirls in his palm like a fireball composed of pure darkness. His health drops to ninety percent and he unleashes the blast of energy. It hurls at the shield, exploding like thunder against its surface. A tiny crack forms at the site of impact.

"Holy shit!" gasps Jon.

I couldn't have said it better myself. He's even stronger than I thought.

The hags inside the shield raise their arms in unison. The forcefield pulses for a moment, and another gust of air rips through the forest.

Dozens of angry eyes appear in the darkness surrounding us, reflecting the green light. They grow bigger as their hosts approach.

"He's going to die." Taryn steps beside me. "There's no way he can handle all of them."

Taryn is right. The three hags are each level twenty-one. The two ogres are level eighteen. Not to mention whatever they just called in as reinforcement. I don't care how strong Pressley is, he can't defeat them all. And there's no telling where he set his spawn point. If he dies, it's possible I'll never see him again.

A mangy wolf steps into the light of the forcefield and lunges at Pressley. The death knight spins like a dancer, with speed no one that size should have, and slashes his sword at the beast. There's a brief yelp before the wolf's head falls to the forest floor.

The ogres step through the forcefield wielding clubs made from the bones of some great beast. The skeleton warriors charge the ogres, bones rattling as they run. Wolves, warthogs, and giant spiders leap from the darkness, their glowing eyes set on Pressley.

"We need to help him!" I shout as I run into battle.

"What the hell am I supposed to do?" yells Jon.

"Be useful!" I don't have time to hold his hand. Not for this. We're already massively out-leveled, even with Pressley, and Jon needs to figure this out by himself. The time for coddling is over.

The hags hide behind the safety of their forcefield while the minions of the forest do their dirty work. Well, two can play at that game. My horrors rush into battle by my side while I unleash devastation. A giant snake slithers along the ground and I smash it into the earth. Its skull crushes beneath my warhammer. Horrors swarm the lower-level monsters that emerge from the forest, and I summon more as quickly as I am able.

Pressley turns in my direction as a Horror of Power gores a spider's abdomen with its tusk. Green ichor drips from the open wound.

"What are you doing?" His voice is deep and distorted, like he's calling from the end of a cave.

"We're here to help. We can talk later, but first, what is it you're after?"

A bolt of lightning rips through the trees, stunning a wolf and setting a bush on fire. The forest is pure chaos as skeletons, horrors, and wild beasts fight it out.

"I'm here for the hags. They use a magical gem called a hag eye to control the ogres and other creatures. Help me retrieve it, and I will hear you out." He stabs a spider between the pincers and a streak of green goo spurts into the air.

"How do we get through the forcefield?" Destroyer hits a warthog in the ribs, sending it tumbling across the battlefield.

"I'm not sure." His sword glows purple, and when he stabs a wolf, his health shoots up a few ticks.

One of the ogres grunts as it swings its bone club. The strike rips through my horrors, sending many of them soaring through the trees.

Berry's muzzle is coated with blood as he fights with a pack of wolves. They have him surrounded, but Taryn charges in riding Stompy, and the moulhaug uses his massive horn like a sledge-hammer, knocking them aside.

This gives me an idea. "Taryn, try to charge the forcefield with Stompy!"

Pressley looks over in my direction, a spider speared on the end of his sword. "Stompy?" His sinister voice is full of disbelief.

"Don't ask."

Jon's clones run around like headless chickens, while his voice echoes from every corner of the battlefield. I have no idea where the real Jon is, but he's causing a lot of chaos.

Stompy paws at the earth, and his massive horn swings from side to side. He lets out an angry snort, and Taryn lifts his staff in the air. Stompy builds up speed as he runs, until the trees are shaking with each step. He lowers his horn and collides with the hag's forcefield.

The shield bounces Stompy straight back and Taryn flies from his saddle, smashing headfirst into the forcefield. He looks shaken up as he crawls to his feet.

A spider descends from a tree above him, dangling by its

thread. Its pincers click as it reaches for the dwarf. Taryn has no idea he's about to become arachnid food.

I lift a Horror of Vitality by the horn and prepare to toss it, but a streak of purple energy shoots across the forest, hitting the spider and draining its HP. It falls to the ground and its legs curl up in its final embrace.

"Are you going to watch or are you going to fight?" Pressley's voice draws me back to task at hand.

His health is down to seventy-five percent. Did he just blow a quarter of his HP to save Taryn?

The ogre unleashes a mighty roar, and the bone armor it wears rattles. I ready my warhammer to fight, when Pressley steps up beside me.

"I'll handle him. You focus on the others." He lifts his sword above his shoulder, ready to attack.

This is his show, so I leave him to it. I jump in the fray with my horrors, crushing skulls and taking names. As the battle rages on, I start to have fun. It all becomes a beautiful dance of devastation.

I summon a Horror of Power, and it doubles the damage of my next attack. I swing, crushing warthog ribs and adding a stack of Inferno to Destroyer. Then I summon Horror of Vitality on my nearest enemy. The passive slow buys me time to get in position before summoning Horror of Finesse. The bonus from summoning it grants me healing on my next attack, repairing any glancing damage I may have taken in the fracas.

I repeat this process until Destroyer is glowing a vibrant red. Every swing I take cooks flesh and singes hair. Berry and I fight back to back, bringing pain and suffering on everything around us. I lose myself in the glory of battle and for the first time in a while, I let go of the thoughts of protecting Jon and Taryn. They are perfectly capable of taking care of themselves. I let the barbarian in me take control.

A guttural cry captures my attention. I turn around to find Pressley standing over the ogre as he drives his sword through its chest. The second ogre has retreated behind the safety of the forcefield.

Taryn sits atop Stompy, using his staff's special ability like a whip and cutting the thread of any spiders that try to sneak down on the battlefield. When the spiders fall, my horrors and Pressley's skeletons swarm them like ants on a fallen ice cream cone.

The last of the green-eyed monsters falls and the forest is quiet. The only sound is the buzzing of the forcefield. The hags are no longer laughing. Instead, they look upon us with hatred in their black, soulless eyes.

Not only are the hags quiet, but so is Jon. His bodies lay strewn across the ground. Some are missing limbs, others are gored or covered in bite marks. One has his head completely caved in.

I search for the real Jon. I expect him to step out from behind a tree, complaining about how scary and dangerous this all was, but he's nowhere to be found.

"What are you looking for?" asks Pressley.

"The enchanter, Jon, I don't see him."

Taryn jumps down from Stompy and starts checking the bodies. "I don't know how to tell if one of them is really him."

"You don't think he..." I don't finish the sentence, letting the words trail off into the ether.

I promised Jon I would take care of him. I told him that he was part of the team, then I left him alone in the fight. I thought he could take care of himself, but I was wrong. He'd only just learned to fight as a team. This was too soon.

"I'm sorry," I whisper.

I should have done better. If he never joins up with us again, I won't blame him. Some kind of leader I turned out to be.

"Guys." Jon's voice echoes around us. "Can one of you help me get down from here?"

I look around, but there's still no sign of him. "Where are you?"

"Oh, sorry. Look up."

I do as he says, but there are only trees. I search the branches for signs of him, but there's nothing. Am I imagining his voice?

Suddenly, there's a shimmer in the trees and Jon appears on one of the branches, clinging to the trunk. "I cast Conceal so that none of the monsters could see me, but I'm kind of afraid of heights."

Laughter runs through me. Deep from in my belly, it pours out, echoing off the trees. Taryn joins in, and I'm sure Pressley thinks we're insane.

I was right after all. My instincts were right. The little thief can take care of himself.

I climb up the tree, and he wraps his arms around my neck. A moment later, we land safely on the ground.

Pressley grunts. "Now, if you all are done, I'd like to return to the objective at hand."

He sheathes his sword and lifts both hands slowly into the air. A black aura surrounds his hands; it pulses as tendrils of dark energy whip at the air. The tendrils grasp for one another.

Pressley's health trickles down as the energy grows. The tendrils coil together, forming a ball of darkness between the death knight's hands. It continues to grow until it takes up the majority of his chest.

With a flourish, Pressley sends the energy hurling at the dead ogre lying on the ground. It penetrates the ogre's body and the energy disperses within.

What in the hell did I just watch?

A moment later, the dead ogre stirs. It opens its eyes, and they are void of all recognition. Pressley bends over and rips the medallion that hangs from its neck, and the ogre rises to its feet.

Pressley's health has fallen to fifty percent after summoning the monster.

"Are you okay to fight?" I ask.

"I'll be fine." He clenches his fist. "Let's finish this."

I nod. The sooner we settle this, the better.

CHAPTER 14

AN EYE FOR AN AYE

MY HANDS TINGLE as I hold my warhammer. The green forcefield shimmers in front of me, while on the other side, three hags and an ogre stare at us with hatred.

These hags are less talkative than the one I met earlier. I don't know if it is because they are focused on maintaining the force-field, or if there is more at play. From where I'm standing, it looks like they are in some sort of demented Halloween snow-globe. The ogre smacks his bone club against his hand, as if telling us to come get some.

All in due time. We have our own ogre, freshly resurrected by the death knight to my side. Pressley used half of his health to summon the creature, so I hope it was worth it. If Champion wasn't on cooldown, I could have landed the killing blow and summoned a second ogre, but we're not that lucky. Pressley still has a handful of skeleton warriors, and I have a half dozen horrors. With Jon, Taryn, Stompy, and Berry, we have the numbers advantage, but I have no idea what these hags have up their sleeves. Three of them makes it a covey, unlocking special powers, like the forcefield that's keeping us from going in there right now and ending this.

Pressley unsheathes his sword and steps in front of the glowing green shield. "Let's tear this bitch down."

One of the hags turns her head toward Pressley. "Leave now and we will grant you safe passage. No one need die."

Hmmm, that's odd. Taryn must agree because he furrows his brow. I've never seen a monster offer to let someone go before. Do they have a sense of self-preservation? In a game like this, why wouldn't they?

"You know I can't do that." Pressley's demonic voice sends a shiver down my spine. He raises his sword overhead.

I've got a feeling his endgame here is bigger than just loot and glory.

I ready Destroyer. There's a brief moment where no one is breathing or talking, where my horrors aren't grumbling, and the buzz from the forcefield is like sitting too close to an old television. Then our weapons fall.

I summon a Horror of Power and my attack hits for double. The warhammer crashes against the forcefield and recoils hard against my hand. I quickly swing again, gaining stack after stack of Inferno until the hammerhead is glowing a vibrant red.

Lightning crashes into the forcefield from the other side. The zombie ogre's bone club rattles with each hit. We attack the barrier with everything we've got, but still it holds.

Destroyer glows bright red as I hammer repeatedly. I summon horrors when I'm able, and each one claws and rams against the forcefield. I hit the dome again and a crack shoots out like a spider vein.

The hags raise their hands and a fresh gust of wind rips into us. My horrors and some of the skeletons are blown away. The crack spreads as I continue to bludgeon the forcefield.

"Not much longer!" Pressley's sword hits with an explosion and a crack shoots from the point of impact and connects with my own.

"Everyone, get back!" I order.

They step back and I send all my horrors to the forcefield. They climb upon one another, forming a horror wall from Pressley's crack to mine.

"You want to fire up one of those black balls of doom?" I ask Pressley. I've got a plan but could use some added insurance.

He grunts and sheathes his sword, placing his hands together as a ball of dark energy forms between them. His health trickles down as the orb gains power. Once it is big enough, he launches it at the forcefield.

I activate Kamikaze seconds before his attack hits, detonating my horrors. Dozens of cracks spread across the forcefield and when Pressley's attack hits, the dome shatters into the ether.

Their ogre lifts his club and charges out.

The hags chant faster than ever, and my communication stone allows me to decipher what they are saying.

"Spirits of the forest, I summon thee. Spirits of the forest, I summon thee. Return to your vessels and protect us."

The earth shakes and the dead monsters groan all around us. The broken bodies of the slain rise to their feet, fueled by magical power.

"You have got to be kidding me." Jon backs closer to Stompy with his staff raised. "What is it with you people and zombies?"

"Maybe you should climb back in that tree." I point overhead. "I have a feeling things are about to get real uncomfortable."

Before the undead minions are fully on their feet, I start playing whack-a-mole with Destroyer, crushing anything and everything I can. If I can limit our opponents before they've done any damage, all the better.

The hags' ogre crosses the threshold where the barrier once stood. He raises his club and swings. Pressley's undead ogre answers the call. The two clubs connect with a crash, and both bone weapons shatter. The two monsters maul at one another, clawing and biting. It's primal. Blood and spittle fly from their mouths as they go at it with everything they've got. No magic, no spells, just raw nitwit power.

A bolt of lightning zips across the forest, electrifying a group of reanimated wolves. Jon's voice echoes around us, adding to the chaos as he calls the hags a slew of inappropriate names.

A second lightning bolt rips through the canopy, crashing into my three recently-summoned horrors.

"Easy there, Taryn. Watch the friendly fire."

"That wasn't me," he shouts as he uses his staff's special ability to wrangle a warthog within its vines. He jumps on the tangled beast and stabs it in the head with his shadow dagger.

A third bolt of lightning arcs straight for me, and I barely dodge it at the last second. Thunder rumbles overhead and then the heavens pour out. Thick drops of rain rattle in the trees above.

The strings of energy that connect the three hags have changed to yellow. They must have called in a lightning storm. What have I gotten us into?

Lightning strikes through the trees again and again, sometimes hitting our minions, sometimes our opponent's. Pure chaos. Other times, it crashes into the trees, sending scorched and burning limbs raining from above.

"Ouch! Hot, hot, hot!" Jon's voice echoes around us, but when I look up, there's no sign of him.

"We must get to the hags!" Pressley slices a zombie spider in two, spraying black ichor across a group of nearby horrors. "If we kill one, this madness will stop."

Just ahead of us, the two ogres are covered in blood and open wounds. Both of their HP are nearly depleted. The zombie ogre has a broken leg and has fallen to one knee. The living ogre picks up a boulder and lifts it overhead.

Pressley shoots a beam of black energy at the ogre, and its health drops to zero. The ogre collapses to the ground, and the boulder falls on top of its pea-brained head. Pressley's own health jumps up by a tick. He reaches down and snatches the medallion from the ogre's neck.

The attack reminds me of some of the blood magic champions I used to play while streaming. I would bait low-health opponents into thinking I was weak and then drain their life force, turning the battle in my favor.

"Charge!" Pressley points his sword toward the hags.

Lightning crashes behind him, spraying dirt and cooking the flesh of dead monsters. Rain continues to pour through the trees, creating puddles and slippery mud.

Taryn jumps on Stompy's back, and we press forward with what few horrors and skeleton warriors remain. A skeleton wielding a bow sits on Berry's back, firing arrows at the hags. The arrows pass through the hag like she's some kind of apparition.

"They're illusions." Jon's voice echoes over my shoulder. "The real hags must be somewhere near."

Have they been illusions the entire time, or did they disappear when we weren't looking?

Pressley rushes into the clearing where the hags stand. He stabs one in the face, but the apparition doesn't flinch.

Rain patters off his armor. "Dammit!" he shouts as he stabs the other two. "Where did they go?"

A cacophony of mad cackling answers.

"Jon, do you see anything?" I ask.

"No," his voice echoes.

"Taryn, what about Berry? Can he track them down?"

Taryn shakes his head. "Their stench is all over this place. Unless they took off running, he won't be able to fin—"

A streak of bright green light shoots out from the darkness and hits Taryn in the face. His lips fuse together, sewn shut. He mumbles, but nothing is audible.

"They've got us surround—"

Another flash of green hits Pressley and his words fall short. Thunder continues to roll in the sky above.

I search for the source of the magic, but see nothing. Nothing but empty forest that surrounds us. I send my horrors out into the depths of the forest to inspect. Before they've even made it a few feet away, I'm hit with a blinding green light and my mouth locks in place.

Alert! *You have been hit with a silencing curse. You will be unable to talk until the spell wears off or the caster is defeated. Timer: 2 hours.*

You've got to be kidding me! How many tricks do these hags have up their sleeves? How are we supposed to fight them without being able to communicate?

"Guys? What's going on down there? You're awfully quiet." Jon's voice echoes all around us.

At least they don't know where he is. Maybe I can use that to our advantage. I send him a quick message.

Message (Chod): *We've been cursed. This is the only way we can communicate. And since Pressley isn't a part of our party, you need to talk to him for us. And whatever you do, don't let the hags find you.*

Incoming Message (Jon): *I'm on it.*

"Hey, Pressley. I'm sure you know this, but you're cursed. So are the other guys. They can't chat with you since you're not in our party. Do you want to join us?"

Pressley shakes his head as he stalks the perimeter searching for the hags. Water splashes around his massive boots. What possible reason could he have for not joining us?

"You had your chance to leave," a shrill voice calls from the depths, but when I turn, nothing is there.

"We will very much enjoy our new playthings," a second voice echoes.

"Very much, indeed," a third voice joins in. "They should stay for a while. I'd love to have them for dinner."

The ground shakes and roots reach up from the earth. They swirl around my legs, locking me in place. I rip at them with my claws, but for every root I cut, another takes its place.

All around me, the others are suffering a similar fate. Many of my horrors die from the roots that strangle them, and Pressley's skeleton warriors have their bones pulled apart. Stompy unleashes a bellowing trumpet as he struggles to free his hooves.

A long tendril of a root reaches for Taryn, attempting to pull him from the moulhaug's back, but he transforms into his bird form and disappears into the trees.

At least one of us got away.

"Oh, yes. You are a special one. You and your friend here," a voice whispers in my ear, and I almost jump out of my skin.

I reach out behind me, attempting to grab whoever is there, but I'm left grasping at air.

"Yes, indeed. These will do very nicely."

I can feel the hag's icy breath on my skin. Goosebumps erupt all over my body. She's there, she has to be.

I close my eyes and listen.

"This one is full of more mana than any troll I've ever seen. Quite the specimen, indeed."

I listen as rain pours down all around us. Thunder rolls. Berry and Stompy struggle for their freedom. A twig crunches beside me, and I hear the soft suction of a footstep.

"And this one. It has been quite some time since we have seen such dark energy."

The footsteps move from my right to left, closer to Pressley. I open my eyes and see the smallest of indentations in the muddy soil.

They're invisible! I try to shout, but the words lodge inside my mouth. The hag is just out of my reach. I wave for Pressley's attention, but he's focused on something else. I send Taryn and Jon a message instead.

Message (Chod): *The hags are invisible. I'm not sure how it works, but I can hear their footsteps and see their footprints once I locate them.*

A red bird lands on the tree limb next to me. It winks at me, and I know it's Taryn.

I extend a finger, pointing in the direction of the invisible hag. The bird tilts its beak in affirmation.

The spot of sunken earth moves, and a tiny track trails toward Pressley before the rain washes it away. He thrashes about, swinging at an invisible object. I assume the hag is whispering in his ear the same as she did me.

Mad laughter fills the air. "You can't catch what you can't see."

Taryn's pets continue to grunt as they struggle to free themselves from the roots that hold them in place. The good news is that the roots don't seem to be getting any tighter.

In my brief distraction, I lose the positioning of the hag. Curse it all!

My body erupts with pain as lightning strikes my shoulder. My entire body stiffens from the jolt of electricity and every nerve in my body screams at me. Rain steams off my skin.

I lose a quarter of my health from the strike. We're all sitting ducks. If we don't do something soon, we're done for.

Another lightning strike hits Pressley and for a brief moment, the man beneath the darkness glows inside of his helm. His face contorts in anguish and his body seizes.

"Don't cook them too much," one of the hags laughs. "I like mine on the rare side."

Taryn flies down from his branch. Mid-flight, he transforms back into his dwarven form and extends the vines from his staff. They wrap around the hag a few yards in front of me, disrupting her invisibility spell. Taryn hits the ground and slides through the mud, toppling the hag. The vines continue to pour out from the staff, wrapping around her until she is entombed in foliage.

She screams, "Release me!"

Taryn pulls his shadow blade and buries it into her skull. The rain suddenly stops, and the roots that bind us in place release.

Hell yeah! Way to go, Taryn. Swinging in like an acrobatic dwarf!

Even though Taryn freed us, the curse that binds our lips is still in effect. It must have been a product of an individual hag and not the covey.

I search for signs of the other two hags.

"Behind you!" Jon's voice bounces off the forest.

I turn around to see two glowing green hands pointed in our direction. The limb above me shakes and Jon jumps down from the tree, tackling one of the hags to the ground. Both hags become visible, and the second hag blasts Pressley in the chest with a bolt of green energy.

The death knight stumbles back, rights himself, then charges.

The first hag grabs Jon by the robe and tosses him across the forest like a ragdoll. He slams into a tree and falls to the ground.

Noooo! I scream inside my head.

Anger floods my veins and I activate Berserker Rage without thinking. The silencing spell disappears, and my vision goes red as I leap on the hag. Her spindly fingers and long nails dig into my arm, but it doesn't deter me. She's absurdly strong to be so small.

Right now, all I can think about is revenge. Jon risked himself to save us, and this bitch is going to pay for hurting a member of my party. I activate Claw and drag my nails across her shriveled old chest. Black blood oozes from the wounds.

Screams and explosions echo behind me, but my focus is lasered in. The hag's hands begin to glow again, and I smash my forehead into her nose. The attack does enough to cancel her spell. She pushes me off with barbaric strength.

I roll to my feet and equip Destroyer. She turns to run, and I swipe at her legs. She falls down and looks up at me with a snarl. I swing Destroyer with all my might, but she rolls out of the way at the last second and it smashes into the ground.

Vines zip past me and grab the hag by the legs. She trips and falls, finally trapped. I bring down Destroyer on her head, ending her torment.

A notification flashes across my vision, and there's a sharp intake of breath beside me as her silencing spell lifts on the others. I push the notifications away for now.

With her out of the way, only one hag remains. I turn to find Pressley kneeling over the downed hag, his gauntlet is wrapped around her neck. Black energy radiates from his hand. Her health depletes and what color she has drains from her face. Pressley's own health recovers bit by bit.

She tries to speak, but Pressley presses harder, cutting off her words. Her body convulses a few times before she falls limp against the forest floor.

Pressley pulls out a dagger and sticks it into the hag's eye socket. He rocks the dagger back and forth before there's a pop and a jewel comes loose.

Taryn gags at the sight. I'm taken aback myself. What the hell just happened?

Pressley moves to the hag I killed and rifles through her brain matter before pulling out another jewel. He then walks over to the body of the third hag without saying a word.

I'll get answers later, for now, I need to check on Jon.

I roll him over and he stirs.

"Ugh. What happened? Did we win?" His head sways back and forth.

"Yeah, man, you came in pretty clutch." I help him sit up, then search through my bag for a health potion. "Here, take this."

He downs the potion and I return to the others. Taryn is using Restoration to bring Berry and Stompy back to full health. Pressley searches the remaining corpses for loot.

He kneels next to a dead spider and breaks off one of its pincers, stuffing it in his bag.

"Find everything you needed?" I ask.

He grunts in affirmation. I guess he's not offering up information unless I probe him for it.

"What's the deal? Clearly this wasn't a dungeon, or we wouldn't have been able to gain access." I look over the corpses of the fallen monsters, but don't see anything worth taking. I wouldn't trust any of the meat, not after it has been reanimated.

"There were certain...items I needed." He reaches in his pouch and tosses me a plum-colored gem.

***Item. Hag's Eye.** The jewel from the eye of a hag. This enchanted jewel is created when a hag joins a covey. It replaces one of their eyeballs. The original eyeball is then worn by a minion, sealing the pact between them. The minion then functions as a summon, controllable by the hag.*

Interesting. "What do you plan on doing with these?" I toss the gem back to him.

"My new class allows me to use them for certain spells. This is one of the few forests on the island where hags still dwell." He goes back to searching the bodies.

Pressley is being incredibly vague and mysterious. If I'd been sabotaged and turned into an undead warrior, I'm sure I would be hesitant to give out too many details, too. For now, he can keep his secrets.

"Whoa!" Jon kneels over the hag I killed. "You missed something."

He displays a vial of glowing pink liquid.

"What is it?" I ask.

He walks over to me and carefully hands me the vial.

***Legendary Item. Potion of Reincarnation. (Only usable by heroes.)** User gains increased size and doubles all stats for the duration of the potion. Health drains with each step. When user's health reaches zero, their character is randomly re-rolled to level 1.*

"Wow," I whisper as I reread the description for the fourth time. "It's a do-over."

"Yeah, but you lose all progress and have no choice over the character you get." Jon shakes his head. "You'd have to be in one hell of a bind to use something like that. I'd rather be a shitty enchanter than a shitty halfling farmer. Who knows, there could be something worse."

He's got a point. I can't imagine anyone willing to risk the rest of their in-game existence being stuck as something they hate. Especially after spending months leveling. Remembering all the options I wasn't able to pick in character creation, the likelihood of getting a race and class that I would want is slim. Still, it is a legendary item. My pulse quickens when I remember my own legendary item that I lost in Goldspire.

"Let me see." Pressley extends his hand.

I hand it to him, and he looks over the potion. He turns it in his hand, watching the thick liquid run down the sides of the vial. "Interesting."

"Take it. It's yours," I offer. "We don't want any of the loot. This was your battle, and we helped in good faith. All that I ask is that you hear us out."

He stuffs the vial in his bag and takes a seat. "Alright, let's hear it."

Jon mumbles something about loot, but I pay him no mind.

I take a deep breath and sit across from Pressley on the ground. If I weren't so scared of what might happen, this would be a great opportunity to use a few of Jon's Charisma rings.

I look deep into Pressley's helm, searching for eyes, but all I see is swirling darkness. He looks downright sinister. But if anyone should know that looks don't determine the worth of the individual, it's me. I sit up straight. "Pressley, we need your help."

CHAPTER 15

SOMETHING DOESN'T FEEL RIGHT

"So what do you say?" I ask Pressley. I've filled him in on everything I know about the new portals, Goldspire, and the potential to travel to other locations.

He places both armored hands together and they clink softly. "You saw how they looked at me in Seascape. After I turned into this—this monster. They'll try to kill me before I ever set foot in the city."

"They were frightened," Taryn interjects. "This entire island has a fear of the undead because of what happened long ago. If you join our cause, then we can make sure you have safe passage through the city."

Remembering the tower and walls in Vanaria that were designed to keep out the undead, Pressley would likely not even be able to set foot on city ground. "He's right. The king himself has sent us to gather forces. You're the strongest hero I've seen. We need you." I stand up and pace. I need to convince him that teaming up with us is better for him than going at it alone. "Besides, you need tougher opponents. You won't be able to grind here forever without wasting your time. You want power, right? Gold and power? Then this is how you get it. We don't know what's on the other side of the closed portals, but if you wait around to find out, then there's a chance you'll lose everything."

He grunts in response. It's difficult to get a read on the man since we can't see his eyes or facial features. That's part of the reason people wearing masks always creep me out. It's hard to gauge a person when you can't see their eyes.

Pressley stands up, his armor clanking as he does so. "I will help you, but I have certain conditions."

My heart jumps with joy, but I try to conceal my excitement and keep from smiling. "What are the conditions?"

"I want no part in your dealings with other heroes. My business with the Cleric is mine, and your business with Glenn and the others is your problem. I don't need any more targets on my back."

I nod. "That seems reasonable. What else?"

"I will not be joining your party. I still have business to attend to, and I don't wish for my whereabouts to be known. I will see you to the edge of the forest, but then we will be going our separate ways. When the time comes to move on Goldspire, I will reconvene with you in Seascape."

"How will we find you when the time comes?"

"I'll be in the city before you return. You can find me at the Brown Boar Inn."

It's not an ideal situation, but if it means having him on our side, then I'll take it. I extend my hand.

"Deal."

He grasps my forearm and I feel a tingly sensation. I wonder if it's the dark energy that turned him into a death knight.

Jon claps his hands together. "Alright, great. We're all friends. Now, can we get out of the creepy forest?"

I pat him on the shoulder. "Sorry, man. We need to rest before exhaustion kicks in. The worst is behind us, though."

He rolls his eyes. "Pfft. I'll believe that when I see it."

Taryn takes first watch, and we all settle down for the night. The forest is surprisingly quiet without the hags. The only noise is the gentle hoot of an owl. After everything that happened today, my body is exhausted. I fall asleep as soon as I close my eyes.

I wake to the sound of something breaking. It's morning, and streaks of sunlight filter through the canopy overhead. Another crash comes from inside one of the hag's huts.

Pressley and Taryn both sit up. Taryn's beard is matted from how he slept on it.

"Whasgoinon?" he mumbles.

I grab Destroyer and stealthily walk to the hut. Through the window, I see Jon inside smashing clay pots with his staff.

"What in the hell are you doing?" I ask.

He jumps, and a squeak escapes his lips. He turns around, startled. "I was looking for loot."

"By breaking pots?"

He shrugs. "You never know."

I shake my head. "You couldn't have just turned it upside-down?"

He looks back at the wreckage he has caused. "You know, I'll be honest, that did not occur to me until just now."

I sigh. "Come on, let's get going."

Jon walks across the broken mess, shards of clay cracking with every step. "Wasn't anything worth taking anyways."

We gather our belongings and set off toward the edge of the forest. In the daylight, everything is less haunting. We're able to spot mana-infused trees and darksand long before they are a threat. It might have been a mistake entering the forest at night, but it all worked out in the end.

Pressley and Jon lead the way, followed by me. Taryn pulls up the rear riding Stompy, and Berry trails right beside him. I feel like we have enough of us that I don't bother summoning any horrors. We don't plan on engaging in any battles until we're out of the forest anyway.

I suddenly remember that I never checked my notifications from the fight with the hags. I was so caught up with talking to Pressley that it slipped my mind. I quickly pull them up.

You have defeated Glossop Forest Covey. *Due to the death of a member, this covey has been disbanded. All related skills and abilities have been lost. To form a new covey, a new member must be recruited and rites performed.*

Congratulations! You have reached level 22. +1 stat point to distribute. +1 Strength and Constitution racial bonus.

Nice! One more level and I'll get another ability point. I've still got three stat points to distribute, but I'm not entirely sure where to allocate them. I could go with Dexterity, and build on my barbarian fighting style. Or I could put them in Intelligence or Wisdom and maybe help with my summoning skills. The one thing I know is that I have zero desire to add them to Charisma. My low Charisma has had zero effect on people liking me, which makes me believe that it truly only affects how the individual perceives the world, not the other way around.

I focus on the others. Both Taryn and Jon managed to gain a level, making them levels fourteen and eighteen respectively. Both are even levels like me, so they won't have any new abilities.

Jon leans in toward Pressley. "So, big guy. What are you in for? I remember seeing you at the physicals, but you always kept to yourself."

For the longest time, Pressley doesn't respond, then he lets out a deep breath that sounds more malevolent than any sigh I've ever heard. "I made some bad decisions. Got caught up with the wrong people, and I paid for it."

Jon laughs. "Oh, come on, Mr. Secretive. Give us more than that."

Pressley grunts, and I wonder if it's a side effect of his new class.

"I used to be a bouncer at a club. A damn good one, too. One night, this guy comes in, real rich type. Thousand-dollar suit, Bentley, the whole nine yards. He asks me if I want to make a little money on the side. I'm young and I'm hungry, plus I've got a daughter to provide for, so I say, 'Why not?'" He clenches his fist, as if he's reliving the memory. "They wanted me to be an enforcer, to go around and collect outstanding debts. I figure maybe I scare a few guys, rough up someone every now and then. You know, not much different from a night at the club. Turns out it wasn't that simple."

"It never is." Jon shakes his head. "So what happened?"

"For the first few months, it was easy money. Then they said that they needed to send a message. That I needed to round up this guy and meet them at the docks. I figure it's just some extra scary shit to get the guy to pay, but when I get there, they hand me a gun. I tell them there's no way I'm killing anybody. They say to do it or I'll never work for them again. I refuse, and they kill the guy anyway. When the police find the gun, it has my prints on it and no one else's."

Damn. I glance at Taryn, and he has the same wide eyes that I'm sure I do. I wonder how much of that is true. Jon did say that everyone in prison was innocent. Is it possible Pressley really killed a man? He has such a calm demeanor and is always strictly business. He doesn't seem like a murderer. Not that I would be a good judge of who seems like a murderer.

Regardless of what he did in the past, he's on our side now.

I speed up until I'm right behind them. "So, how'd you end up working with Richard?"

He balls his hand into a fist. Clearly, he still has some issues with the cleric. "We were staying at the same inn when the announcement went out about the king's challenge. He told me that his god had a plan for me. That he had a spell that could grant me holy energy and allow me to open the portal." He clears his throat. "He didn't mention that his god was a trickster, that I would be turned into this." He extends his arms, displaying his dark armor.

"What's it like?" Taryn shouts from behind us.

"What is what like?" asks Pressley.

"Being a death knight."

Pressley stops walking, and we all gather around him.

"It's...different. I feel different. More...hollow might be the right word, but it doesn't fully describe it." He lifts his hand in front of his face, as if he can see right down to the bones. "Everything changed when I hit the portal. All of my abilities, my appearance. For a moment, all I felt was overwhelming anger and sadness. Is that grief? I ran away as fast as I could until I could make sense of it all."

"Have you?" asks Taryn.

"It's a process. But I'm on the path to understanding."

Listening to his story has the hairs on my neck standing on end. I've personally experienced the way this game can change how someone feels. If he's feeling all of that constantly because of a decision he made in the game, I wonder if there is more at play. Could it be part of the rehabilitation or is it as simple as an effect of switching classes?

We're all in the same pods being fed and cleaned by the nanites. There's really no telling what other chemicals they might be putting in our bodies. I push the thoughts away. I'm just being paranoid.

Time passes quickly and before I know it, we reach the edge of the forest. We say our good-byes and Pressley heads back toward Narthensted while we take off for the Greystone Mountains.

CHAPTER 16

NEVER HAVE I EVER

"That was pretty weird, right?" I ask Taryn as we travel down the desolate dirt road.

He shrugs. "What, Pressley? Not much different than anything else we've experienced in here."

I suppose he's right. I'm a troll; he's a dwarf. We've done things we could never possibly do in real life, and it all seems so natural. He's a regular Snow White when it comes to pets, and I can go into a barbaric rage and not end up in jail for it. Why wouldn't a supposed death knight have emotional problems and mood swings? Maybe that's why it's such a rare class.

We pass the last of the major towns surrounding Seascape, and for the next two days, we only encounter small villages. More often than not, village is overstating it, and they're just a couple of farmhouses that offer a room to weary travelers.

Not many people take the eastern road to the mountains. The Mythroad is the safer and more populous route that cuts straight across the island. I'm sure once the portal is opened in Vanaria, it will be used less and less.

It's unfortunate for those that depend on travelers and tourism, but such is the price of progress.

We're about a day's ride from the base of the mountain, even with Taryn using Strong Wind to speed up our travels. The journey is long and boring. What I wouldn't give for some in-game music to help pass the time.

I check every tab of my user interface, but there's no such luck. Instead, we're forced to rely our own devices, playing "I Spy" and "Never Have I Ever."

Jon taps his finger against his chin. "Never have I ever...flown on an airplane."

I put down one of my fingers, leaving two up. Taryn still has all three of his.

"No shit?" Jon tilts his head. "I thought I was one of the few people to have never flown. I've got a terrible fear of heights. Can't even imagine looking down from the inside of a plane."

I'm surprised I'm the only one who has flown in a plane. "It's not so bad. When you're up that high, it doesn't even look real. It's like staring down at some kid's playset. The trees, the cars, they all look like models. Taryn, have you really never flown?"

He gives me an incredulous look. "To where? My family never had money for vacations. My vacation was a long walk through Central Park." He laughs. "Or a weekend at your place."

I smile. "We had a lot of those."

Thinking back on all the times I flew in a plane, there were too many to count. There was a time when we would take vacations as a family. I remember playing on the beach in Mexico with Maria, my first nanny. Dad was on the phone practically all day. Maria took me down to the beach and we built sandcastles.

Or the time we flew to Colorado to ski. I ended up building a snowman outside of our cabin with Rosa because Mom had a meeting and couldn't go to our skiing lessons.

So many trips spent with people who weren't my family. By the time I was a teenager, I didn't even bother going anymore. They were nothing more than glorified business trips. Staying home and playing games was more fun. At least there I had people I could count on. People who noticed me.

"Your turn, Chod." Taryn's voice pulls me from my own head.

"Hmm. Let me think." I search my brain for something that I think both of them have done that I haven't. "Never have I ever..." I pause. "Had a girlfriend."

Jon laughs before he realizes I'm serious. He and Taryn both put a finger down.

Jon's mouth hangs open. "You're a rich streamer guy and you've never had a girlfriend?"

"No, it just never happened. All the girls I liked never liked me."

"Don't give me that." Taryn mocks shoving me away. "You never tried. You don't get to be a popular streamer without a few girls throwing themselves at you. Be honest. You just weren't interested."

Jon stops in his tracks and puts both hands up. "No offense, but are you..." He whispers the word, "gay? Not that there is anything wrong with that."

I can't help but laugh. "No, not at all. I like girls. I guess I've just never had that desire that most guys have. I like girls, but they don't consume my thoughts. Maybe I'm just waiting on the right one."

"Maybe you're just afraid of rejection." Taryn crosses his arms.

Maybe he's right. I went on a date once. I was so nervous that I spilled my water across the table. I had spent so much time babbling about myself to try and fill the awkward silence. I got a hug at the end of the meal, the kind of hug where their crotch is far away from you and they just pat you on the back a lot. It was not my best moment, not by a long shot.

That's enough time delving into my personal life. "How about a new game?"

"What'd you have in mind?" asks Taryn. He sits atop Stompy, his dreads swaying in the gentle breeze. He looks very regal on top of the moulhaug. Give him a crown and some brightly-colored fabric to drape down Stompy's side and he'd pass for royalty.

"Give me a few minutes." I close my eyes to see what I can come up with. Anything to avoid more personal conversations.

I take the next few minutes to summon a few Horrors of Finesse. The blue gangly creatures are perfect for what I have in mind.

"Alright, each of you pick a horror and adorn it with something so that we can tell them apart."

Jon gives his horror a Ring of Bliss. I'm actually surprised when I see the +1 Charisma take effect on the small horror. Its body loosens and it walks with a new swagger, smoothly wrapping an arm around one of the other horrors.

Taryn takes a piece of leather and ties it around his horror's neck like a necklace.

"Good, mine will be the one with no items." I stop walking for a moment to explain the rules for the game I've created. "We're going to have a race. We'll leave the horrors here." I draw a line in the dirt. "Once we are far enough away, the horrors will take off. Whoever's horror reaches us first will be the winner."

"Can we try to slow them down?" asks Taryn.

I nod. "Yes, but only using abilities. We all have to stay put."

Once we are about a quarter of a mile away, I lift my hand in the air. "On three. One. Two. Three!"

I instruct the horrors to run to our location and wait to see what happens.

Jon makes the first move, sending out two doppelgängers. They leap out of his body and charge toward the horrors.

"Hey, not fair!" shouts Taryn.

"What?" Jon raises his hands up as he shrugs. "It's an ability."

"Not cool." Taryn lifts his staff and a bolt of lightning crashes into one of the doppelgängers.

"Oh, come on." Jon frowns, then he sends out a third clone.

The three horrors are neck-and-neck. I wait on taking any action, biding my time. Jon's horror waves at us as it runs, its Charisma in full effect. They are halfway to us when Jon's doppelgänger tackles my horror to the ground.

My horror quickly disengages but is now way behind the other two. I summon a Horror of Vitality and grab it by the horn. Taryn and Jon are bickering as I toss the horror as far as I can. It lands with a thud, losing a chunk of health from the impact, before running toward the other two.

The two Horrors of Finesse run past the Horror of Vitality without slowing down at all. That's when I realize my mistake. Its passive slow doesn't work on my own summons. I instruct the Horror of Vitality to chase the others, but they are too fast.

Since that failed, I summon a Horror of Power and send it out.

Taryn casts Strong Wind on his horror, but since it effects any party members surrounding the spell, both his and Jon's horrors speed up. My own horror falls even further behind.

Horror of Power launches itself into Taryn's horror, tackling it to the ground. They tumble in the dirt for a moment, giving just enough time for my Horror of Vitality to catch up. Together, the two horrors pin Taryn's to the ground and my own Horror of Finesse passes it by.

Jon's horror is in the lead by a good margin, when a lightning bolt crashes into it. The horror loses all but ten percent of its health. A moment later, the passive health loss due to being out of combat vanishes it into thin air, leaving only mine and Taryn's horrors remaining.

"Suck it, Jon." Taryn laughs.

My own horror is about to cross the finish line when Stompy steps forward and crushes it underneath his massive hoof.

"Last one standing. I win!" Taryn tosses his arms up in victory.

"Not if you don't cross the finish line." I cast Kamikaze on the two horrors pinning Taryn's to the ground, and they all three explode. The game is a draw.

Jon bursts out laughing. "No, you suck it, Taryn." He howls with laughter, clutching his stomach.

And that is how we pass the next five hours.

CHAPTER 17

RUBIES ARE RED

THE GREYSTONE MOUNTAINS tower above us, a watchful boundary that separates the kingdoms of Seascape and Vanaria. Home to goblins, mountain trolls, and who knows what else.

Clouds cover the highest peaks, hiding the mountains' best-kept secrets. Before we pass through, I intend to uncover some of those secrets. My map shows various locations with ley lines. The only problem is that the map is two-dimensional, while the mountains are not. A cluster of ley lines under a single mountain could mean a lot of searching. Who knows how many crevices and cave entrances we might need to check?

Still, we need to continue to level up. What good is it if we gather more heroes, but none of us are strong enough when the time comes? Finding a dungeon seems a lot smarter than aimlessly leveling as we travel.

There has to be a dungeon here somewhere. I can feel it in my bones.

As we ascend the mountain, I spot a cluster of snowy moss that glitters in the fading light. It's been a while since I have invested in my herbalism or potion-making skills, but I remember that snowy moss is one of the ingredients in perception potions. If I could make one, then it would help us notice anything out of the ordinary.

I think back to my training with Yashi, the potions master of the forest trolls, trying to recall the other ingredient. It mixed with the snowy moss and turned it pink. Jackal's blood!

Climbing up a few branches on the tree, I cut away the snowy moss with my claw.

"What are you doing?" asks Taryn.

"I'm going to make us some perception potions, but I'm going to need your help."

Jon walks over and examines the snowy moss. "What's it do?"

I open my hand, showing him the bright white moss. "By itself, nothing. But when you mix it with jackal's blood, it heightens your senses. Kind of like the Perception ability. This isn't as strong as Perception, but it lasts for two hours instead of ten minutes."

Taryn climbs down from Stompy. "Let me guess, you want me to fly around and see if I can find a jackal?"

I flash him a smile. "You don't even need the potion to be perceptive."

He rolls his eyes. "Did you come up with that all by yourself? What is it I'm looking for?"

"They're like a cross between a fox and a wolf. I saw a lot of them in the troll forest, but I'm hoping they might roam here too. They usually travel in packs, but one should be enough. We just need enough blood to grind the snowy moss into a drinkable liquid."

"Alright, I'll see what I can do." He turns to his pets. "Berry, Stompy, behave until I get back."

Berry shakes his stump of a tail, but Stompy just snorts. Typical.

Taryn transforms into a red bird and disappears amongst the trees.

We continue with our journey up the mountain. There's no point in lounging about while Taryn searches for a jackal. In his bird form, he'll be able to find us wherever we are. Stompy's massive frame takes up most of the path. Hopefully, we don't run into any other travelers.

After an hour passes, I send Taryn a message.

Message (Chod): *You've been gone a while. Any luck?*

Incoming Message (Taryn): *I've found a pack of them. I've got an idea. Let me handle this on my own.*

Message (Chod): *Try not to get yourself killed.*

Not that I don't think he can survive a run-in with a pack of jackals, but he doesn't have Stompy or Berry to protect him. I have no idea what he's up to, but Taryn is smart, so I don't argue.

A few minutes later, I hear thunder on the other side of the mountain. I'm not sure if it's Taryn or an actual storm we're heading into. I fight the urge to check in on him again. If he's in trouble, he'll let us know.

Jon hurries up beside me, his blue robe swishing as he walks. "Hey, man. I just wanted to say thanks. It means a lot that you took me under your wing. I've done more in the past few days than I did in the first two months of being here. Whatever happens, I won't forget that."

Wow. His words catch me by surprise. I'm not really sure how to respond, but I do my best. "You're a good guy, Jon. No matter what you did to get you here, I think your heart is in the right place. You're not a villain." I slap him on the shoulder. "You're a valuable member of our team now."

I must have said something right, because I've never seen Jon smile so wide. We continue up the mountain until Berry stops. He sniffs at the air, then takes off at a full sprint.

Jon and I exchange glances. What the hell is going on?

"Stay with Stompy!" I order and take off after Berry.

Jon protests, but I leave him anyways. Berry has a connection to Taryn, so if he is running, then something is up.

Running at full speed, I turn the corner and plow into the backside of the umber bear. After narrowly avoiding tumbling off the side of the mountain, I notice the reason why Berry stopped.

Taryn scratches the bear on the chin with one hand and pets a jackal with the other.

He winks at me. "What do you think?"

"Another pet?" I ask.

He flashes me a brilliant smile. "Yep, meet Ruby."

Ruby looks up at me and yawns. She has a slender snout and wide-set golden eyes. Her fur is a beautiful straw color, with a streak of black that goes down her back. She's smaller than the jackals I saw in the troll forest. Her ears are long and pointy, like a fox, and her big bushy tail curls around her left leg as she sits.

I extend my hand and let her sniff the back of it. "She's beautiful. I know I'm going to regret this, but why the name Ruby?"

Taryn's lip curls up at the edge like he's holding back laughter. "Rubies are red. So is blood. And since she is going to be donating her blood to help us..."

I shouldn't have asked. I don't even acknowledge Taryn's comment. "Welcome to the team, Ruby."

The small jackal walks over and licks at my fingers.

"She's a great judge of character it seems." Taryn runs his fingers down her back. "Plus, she comes with some nice perks."

"What do you mean?"

"Having pets is different than having something you summon. Your horrors have abilities that you are able to control when you cast them. Pets have their own skills, but I can't control them. Take Berry, for instance. He's a great tracker with an excellent sense of smell, but I can't tell him to follow a smell and automatically know where he's leading us. It's up to him to decide if he wants to listen to me. Stompy can pull a barn down, but he will only do it if he's in the mood. Ruby here, she has an excellent sense of perception on her own. She's able to see, smell, and hear things you and I never will, but it's up to her to let me know what she finds." He scratches her ear. "She's a good girl, though. Aren't you, girl?"

Ruby nuzzles her head against his hand. Berry steps in between them and licks the jackal on the head.

"Someone is jealous." I laugh. "Now that you have three pets, what does that mean for your ability to control them?"

"It drops to eighty-five percent. If I had to guess, I imagine Stompy will be the rebellious one. It doesn't mean that they will actively betray me, more so that they won't do things exactly to the letter each time. Maybe I'll tell them to attack one enemy, and they go after the one next to him. Things like that."

Or maybe you'll tell Stompy to go and he'll sit down instead.

I pet Berry a few times so he doesn't feel left out. "Well, now that you're keeping her as a pet, how are we supposed to get her blood?" It feels kind of wrong bleeding a living animal, let alone a pet.

"She'll be fine. We'll make a little cut and then once we have enough blood, I'll use Restoration and heal her." Taryn climbs on Berry and Ruby jumps in his lap.

She's really taken to Taryn quite quickly.

"If you say so—"

"Hey, what's going on over here?" Jon turns the corner, followed by Stompy.

Taryn waves at the enchanter. "Hey, Jon. Just introducing Chod to my new pet. Meet Ruby."

Jon's mouth drops open. "Wow. She's pretty. Can I pet her?"

While Jon is enamored with Ruby, Stompy turns his head away from us and snorts.

"Oh, don't be like that," Taryn scolds. "I love you all the same."

Stompy paws at the earth and huffs again.

"Meh, he'll get over it. You guys ready to get moving?" Taryn maneuvers Berry until they are facing up the mountain.

"Aren't you forgetting something?" I ask.

Taryn stares at me blankly.

"The potion?"

"Ah, yes." He climbs down from Berry and strokes Ruby on the head a few times. "I'm sorry about this, girl, but it's for the good of the party."

He rummages through his pack before pulling out a small knife and an empty vial.

"You sure this is okay?" I ask. I'm hesitant to draw blood if it's going to hurt Ruby. She seems so sweet and innocent as she rubs her head against Taryn.

"It'll be fine. A quick cut and it's all over. It's not like we're going to torture her. I don't think it's much different than a veterinarian drawing blood." He takes the knife in one hand and the vial in the other. "Now, I need you to hold her."

I feel slightly queasy as I hold the small jackal in my arms. She nuzzles against my chest, unaware of what is about to happen.

Quicker than I expect, Taryn makes a small incision in her foot. She flinches for a moment, but she remains calm. Taryn places the vial underneath, catching the blood as it drips.

Taryn gently caresses Ruby's leg. "I'm going to fill this vial up. I'd rather make extra than have to do this constantly."

When the vial is full, Taryn hands it to me and takes Ruby. He casts Restoration, and a few moments later, she is as good as new.

I pull my mortar and pestle from my satchel and take a seat against the mountain. Remembering what Yashi taught me, I place the snowy moss in the mortar and grind it with the pestle. Next, I add a small amount of the jackal's blood until it forms into a light pink paste. I add a little more until the mixture swirls around in the mortar.

Item. Perception Potion. *+2 Wisdom. This potion heightens awareness of details and that which might normally go unnoticed. Duration: 2 hours.*

I take a sip and pass it to Taryn and Jon. Immediately, my senses feel sharper. I can hear better, see better, and even smell better. I pack away the remaining potion and extra ingredients, and we continue on our journey.

As we walk, I scan everything we come across. I'm able to notice things that would normally pass me by, such as bird nests, animal burrows, and areas where the stone is loose on the mountainside. Plants that I know appear from farther away. It's like the world is a puzzle and I'm able to see all the pieces.

Taryn rides atop Stompy in an attempt to calm the grumpy moulhaug. Berry follows behind his master while Ruby prances along at the front of the group. Due to the narrow path, I have no horrors summoned currently.

We travel for hours, until the sun begins to dip behind the

peaks. A notification pops up, telling me that the potion has expired.

"Dammit. I really hoped we might find something useful from all that." I pick up a rock and toss it off the side of the mountain in frustration.

Taryn brings Stompy to a halt. "Give it time. There's a lot of mountain here. Who knows what we might come upon?"

We travel a little further, searching for a place to make camp for the night. Suddenly, Ruby lets out a low bark and runs ahead. When we don't immediately follow, she turns around and howls.

Taryn and I look at each other.

"What's that all about?" I ask.

He scrunches his nose. "No idea. I think she might have found something."

He climbs down from Stompy and we follow Ruby on foot. She's stopped in the middle of the trail, staring at the mountainside.

"What is it, girl?" Taryn kneels beside her. "What do you see?"

She takes a few steps closer to the mountain, until her nose is an inch from the stone surface. She barks again and paws at the mountainside.

I'm shocked when her paw passes through and the surface ripples.

I'll be damned. A hidden entrance!

CHAPTER 18

BURNING HEART OF THE MOUNTAIN

I REACH for the mountainside and my fingers pass through the illusion. I feel my way around until I touch solid rock. After careful examination, I determine the hidden entrance is big enough to walk through.

Jon moves his fingers in and out of the illusion. "Whoever made this has some real skill. It looks like a permanent enchantment. You can't even tell that it's here. If you look at mine long enough, you can see a sort of shimmer in the air. This is high quality, and I bet it has been here for a while."

Taryn scratches Ruby behind the ears. "Look at you, Ruby. You're so smart and perceptive." He turns to me and Jon. "We gonna stand around all day, or are we gonna check this thing out?"

"Lead the way." I step aside and gesture for him to enter.

Taryn puts his hands out in front of him and slowly steps through the hidden entrance. After a few seconds, I follow.

We enter a massive cave that grows larger the farther in we go. It's big enough that even Stompy can fit inside. The air is hot and stifling, like a sauna between two hairy men. Several lit torches hang along the cave walls. Their fires burn, but they emit no heat. When I reach out and touch one, my fingers pass through them no differently than the entrance to the cave.

"More enchantments." Jon picks up a torch and examines it.

A notification pops up across my vision.

Burning Heart of the Mountain. *Would you like to enter?*

I pause for a moment before continuing. The hot temperature and name of this dungeon are giving me second thoughts. Trolls are especially susceptible to fire, and I no longer have my phoenix feather to help mitigate the damage.

Jon and Taryn are already making their way down the corridor, so I summon a few horrors and follow along. We walk for a ways until we come across a massive door with three latches keeping it shut. I try to open them, but they don't budge.

"Wait." Taryn pushes me aside. "There are words engraved into the metal."

They're hard to see, but eventually, I make out the words on the first latch. *What can bring back the dead; make us cry; make us laugh; make us young; born in an instant; yet lasts a lifetime.* They sound like nonsense to me. "Are they riddles?"

Taryn traces underneath the words with his finger. "Looks like it. Maybe you have to answer them to open the door?"

"What's it say?" asks Jon.

Taryn clears his throat and reads the first riddle.

Jon raises his hands and takes a step back. "I swear, if there are zombies involved, then I'm out."

I grab his shoulder. "It's not zombies. You answer the question and then the door opens. Well, there might be zombies if you get it wrong." I turn to Taryn. "What do the other ones say?"

"The second riddle says, 'Mountains will crumble to it, temples will fall, and no man can survive its endless call.'"

Oh boy. We are in for a long night. "And the last one?"

"I was carried into a dark room and set on fire. I wept, and then my head was cut off. What am I?"

I scratch my chin. "I don't know, a burn victim?"

The cavern shakes and then one of the torches extinguishes, casting the tunnel behind us in shadow.

Stompy snorts, and Jon clutches his staff to his chest. "Chod, what the hell? Now is not the time for jokes!"

"Sorry, guys. I didn't know it would take me seriously. I've never been in a dungeon like this."

Taryn takes a step back. "Okay, so we know that it has the ability to understand our answers. So it's probably best to discuss in our party chat before we try again. Losing the torches won't cripple us, but we have no idea what else might happen if we get it wrong."

"Sounds good to me." I move close to the engravings and read them again. "So, either of you have any ideas about these? Puzzles aren't my strong suit."

I read the first riddle out loud again. We stand in silence as our brains try to decipher its hidden meaning.

Incoming Message (Taryn): *This is tough.*

Message (Chod): *No kidding. I hate riddles. The answer is always so simple, too.*

Jon taps his fingers against his lips, and then suddenly, his eyes light up.

Incoming Message (Jon): _I think I know what it is. A photograph!_

Taryn claps his hands together. "Holy shit! I think that's it. Chod, do you agree?"

I read over the riddle again. It all fits, but something tells me it's not right. "Something is off. This is a fantasy world. They don't have photographs here. They have paintings and tapestries, but those aren't born in an instant. And if it lasts a lifetime, it has to be something that can't be destroyed."

The excitement fades from Jon's eyes. "Damn, I thought that was it."

"It was a good guess," I reassure him. "I think you're on the right track. What is similar to a photograph but can't be destroyed?"

"A memory." Jon covers his mouth with his hand. "Shit, I'm sorry guys."

The cavern shakes, and I raise Destroyer, ready for whatever is about to happen. There's a loud groan as the latch slides open. I release a sigh of relief.

"Ha! Nice work, Jon." I raise my hand, and he gives me a high five.

"Yeah, man. Good thinking." Taryn gives him a fist-bump.

Jon beams with pride. "You can thank my mom for that. When I was little, a house fire destroyed everything we owned. One of mom's favorite things were her photo albums. They had pictures of me and my brothers from when we were babies. She was so sad to have lost them. I remember her wiping away the tears, and she said, 'It's going to be okay. At least we have the memories.'"

I give him a smile. "It was your memories that solved the riddle. I'm sure your mom would appreciate that. Let's see if we can solve the second riddle."

I read the second riddle over and over. "Mountains will crumble to it, temples will fall, and no man can survive its endless call."

Earthquake is the first thing that comes to mind, but I've never felt called to by an earthquake. Erosion could crumble a mountain, but that would take so much time. Time, that's it. No man can survive time!

"Guys, I got it! The answer is time."

Another loud groan and the second latch slides open.

We hoot and holler in celebration. Even Berry and Ruby get excited.

"Only one more." I read it aloud for the others. "'I was carried into a dark room and set on fire. I wept, and then my head was cut off.' Any ideas?"

Incoming Message (Jon): *I was thinking torch, but that doesn't make any sense for the second part.*

Message (Chod): *What about a match? It has a head. But what does weep mean?*

Taryn jumps up and down, and the clasps in his beard clink together. "I know it! It's a candle."

The third latch slides open, and the torch that had burnt out behind us rekindles.

"How did you know that?" I ask.

He grins. "My mom loves candles. She would trim the wicks every so often so that the flames would burn evenly. She always had a joke about taking a little bit off the top."

I find it interesting how both of their personal relationships with their mothers led them to solving the riddles. But now is not the time for an internal debate on our various upbringings. I'm sure the grass is always greener on the other side. I'd rather focus on the dungeon we're trying to defeat.

With the third latch unlocked, I grab the handle and heave the massive door open. It's wide enough for Stompy to fit through.

On the other side is another long cavern. At the end of the cavern, there's a mirror the same size as the door we just entered. There's no door handle, no locks or latches, just our reflections in the giant mirror.

"That's weird." Taryn presses his hand against the mirrored surface. When his hand touches his reflection, he jerks back and shivers.

"What is it?" I ask.

"Touch the mirror."

I cast him an untrusting glance.

"It's not going to hurt you. Just touch it."

What could possibly have Taryn so shaken up? I do as he instructs, reaching out for the mirror. I expect to feel the cool sensation of glass, but when I touch my reflection, I feel the warm rough calluses that coat my fingers and palms. I immediately retract my hand.

"Whoa, that is weird. What do you think it means?" It's clearly not just a reflection. It's like we're staring into a mirror universe.

Taryn stares at the reflection as it mimics his every movement perfectly. "I think it means we have to get past our reflections to move to the next room."

Jon steps between us and places his hand to the mirror, immediately jerking it back. "Yep, that's creepy as hell."

He takes a step back and casts a doppelgänger. The cloned

enchanter walks straight into the mirror, continuously bouncing off the reflection. Their foreheads redden from running into one another until Jon calls it off.

"Any better ideas?" he asks.

I have a sneaking suspicion it won't work, but I try anyways. I equip Destroyer and swing at the mirrored surface. My warhammer collides with the reflection and the recoil reverberates all the way up my arms. The pain rattles in my bones so much that I have to sit the weapon on the floor and shake my hands out.

We spend the next half-hour trying various ways of getting past the door. My horrors bounce off one another. When I stack them and create a wall in order to cast Kamikaze, it has no effect. Taryn's lightning bolts smash into one another and we nearly go deaf from the explosion.

"There's got to be something we are missing." Taryn slouches against the wall in exasperation.

I don't know why I didn't think of it before, but I grab the perception potion and take a swig.

I pass it to the others. "If we can't get past it with brute force, then it has to be some kind of puzzle like in the other room."

Sitting next to Taryn, I wait for the potion to kick in. When it does, I scour the room, looking for hidden coves, cracks in the wall, anything that might give us some sort of clue as to what is happening.

No luck. We're in an empty cavern. There's nothing special about it aside from the mirror barrier.

Jon sighs. "Maybe this one is out of our league."

It might be, but I refuse to give up. I walk over to the mirror and stare at my reflection. As I stand there, I'm reminded of the character creation screen when I first logged in—the only time I've been able to observe myself in the third person.

I've grown accustomed to this body, so much so that it feels as natural to me as my actual body ever did. I take a moment to appreciate what I am, what I've become. My once forest green skin has a soft blue glow to it thanks to the mana I absorbed. A flat face with two gigantic tusks stares back at me. Deep blue freckles accent my wide nose. Pointy ears jut upward from both sides of my head, where two long, black braids dangle and drape over my powerful shoulders. Each shoulder has patches of rough walnut skin, almost rock-like in appearance. My muscles bulge as I hold onto Destroyer.

I am a complete and total badass, and I refuse to be defeated by a mirror. I've faced a lot worse than my own reflection.

As I stare into the mirror, I notice something out of the ordinary. There are torches hanging from the walls in the reflection, but not on our side. They have a faint aura about them from the perception potion.

"Did you guys notice this?" I point to the torches in our reflection. "They are only on the other side."

Taryn strokes his beard. "Hmmm, that is strange. Maybe we have to use them somehow."

This dungeon just about has me at my wits' end. "How could we possibly use them? We can't get past our reflections to do anything."

Jon scrunches his eyes, as if he's deep in thought. "What if our reflections can pick them up? Maybe that's the key."

Taryn nods in agreement. "That's not a half-bad idea."

Taryn takes a few steps back until his reflection is at the same depth as one of the torches. He moves closer to the wall and reaches out his hand. It takes a few tries, but the druid in the reflection eventually wraps his hand around the torch. Taryn squeezes his fingers and raises his arm higher.

The torch in the reflection comes loose of its sconce.

"Nice!" shouts Jon.

Holding his hand out in front of him, Taryn attempts to pass through the mirror while his reflection holds the torch. When he reaches the barrier, his fist bumps against his reflection.

"Dammit!" Taryn flings his hands down to his side, and his reflection drops the torch.

The flame extinguishes when it hits the ground and the cavern grows a little dimmer. It gives me an inkling of an idea.

There are still three more torches burning in the mirror. I wonder if we extinguished them, would our reflections remain? I'd be able to see in the complete darkness, but the others wouldn't.

I move with my reflection until I am standing next to a torch. With some trial and error, I'm able to remove it from the wall. I immediately toss it to the floor and watch the flame go out.

"Chod, what are you doing?" asks Jon.

"I had an idea. What if the torches are the reason we can't pass through?"

Taryn's expression changes from one of frustration to curiosity. "What do you mean?"

"If a tree falls in the forest and no one is around to hear it, does it make a sound?" I quote the age-old question of existence.

Taryn cuts his eyes at me. "Chod, I love you, but if I have to answer another riddle, I'm going to break something."

I chuckle before continuing. "It's the same principle. If no one can see the mirror, does it have a reflection?"

Their eyes light up with realization.

"You think that if we remove the light source, then we can just walk through?" Taryn asks.

"It's worth a shot. But since none of you can see in complete darkness, I'll need to lead you through if it works. So group up and hold hands or something."

I extinguish another torch while they gather themselves in the middle of the cavern. Jon takes the lead. Taryn stands behind him and uses the vines on his staff to make temporary leashes for his pets. I bet that Ruby has night vision, but I'm not so sure about the other two.

I take my position by the final torch. "Ready?"

Taryn places his hand on Jon's hip. "Ready."

Reaching out, I wrap my hand around where the final torch would be. My reflection mimics my every movement. I lift the torch and drop it to the ground. The cavern goes dark and my night vision quickly adjusts.

Just as I expected, our reflections vanish from the mirror. I move in front of the others and take Jon by the hand.

As soon as we step through where the mirror once was, I'm hit with a gust of stifling heat. It's like we walked into a sauna. There's a bright flash of light that temporarily blinds me, and when my eyes adjust, I take a step back.

A magnificent phoenix hovers in the air over a pit of bubbling lava. In the center, an imp sits on a narrow platform.

What in the hell did we just stumble upon?

CHAPTER 19

BREAKER OF CHAINS

FLAMES SHOOT out from imp's small hands directly into the moat of molten lava.

"Holy..." Jon's words trail off as he stares at the magnificent creature hovering above us.

Phoenix. Unique monster. Level ??? One of the rarest creatures in all of Mythos. A feather willingly given from a phoenix can guard against fire. Tears of the phoenix heal better than any potion. The life-cycle of the phoenix stretches beyond the lifetimes of many mortal races. When a phoenix fully matures, it will burst into flames, rising from the ashes to start the process anew. Only the most blazing of locations can temper the phoenix's maturation. Many phoenixes will retreat to volcanoes to prolong their matured forms.

I'm just as awestruck myself, but the fact that we can't see its level is a little daunting. The phoenix flaps its wings, sending a fresh gust of hot air across the room. Its orange and red feathers shimmer like dancing flames.

There's a clink of metal, and I notice a chain that stretches from the phoenix's leg to the floor. A gigantic spike holds the chain in place. Good to know we will have a range where it can't reach.

The phoenix is nothing less than living fire. Dark crimson feathers cover its underside and the topmost feathers on its wings. They gradually fade to tangerine and marigold, with streaks of bronze mixed in. Amber eyes look down at us, but it doesn't attack.

I take a moment to inspect our surroundings. The room we're in is a massive dome with jagged walls cut from the mountain. A moat of lava sits in the center, surrounding the imp on the small platform. The imp must be a full-grown male, because he's about twice the size of Limery. He has the same large yellow eyes, long spindly limbs, and forked tail. His dull, reddish skin matches the lava surrounding him, and his wings remain tucked behind his back.

Something feels off about this. I wait for the phoenix to engage or taunt us, anything that initiates a boss fight, but it never comes. It just hovers in the air, a watchful guardian, occasionally flapping its vibrant wings.

The imp finally notices us, and he appears shocked as he looks at us with bloodshot yellow eyes. "How did you get in here?"

I step forward and answer. "We solved the riddles and opened the doors. What is this place?"

The imp shakes his head, scowling at us. "You should not be here."

This got real ominous, real quick. "What do you mean? Why shouldn't we be here?"

He looks at me, but it feels like he's looking past me. "If Thyrim returns, you may find yourself trapped in here the same as us."

Wait, what? "Did you say trapped? Who is Thyrim, and why does he have you trapped here? Can't you just fly away?"

A fresh burst of fire shoots out from the imp's hands into the lava. "I have been here many years, locked away against my will and forced to keep the lava hot enough so that the phoenix doesn't age."

Jon moves closer. "You're a prisoner?"

The imp nods. "I am."

"We know how that goes." Jon straightens his back. "Can we help you escape?"

The imp goes silent for a moment. "I wish it were so. I am the only reason that the lava does not cool. The mountain is full of enchantments designed to keep me here and keep others out. If the lava cools, then the ceiling will cave in. If I move off of my island, then the lava will rise up and devour me. I am trapped for eternity."

Jon looks between me and Taryn. "There has to be something we can do to help him."

I understand Jon's desire to help the imp, but the last thing I want to do is end up an enemy of some powerful mage. If Thyrim is the one who enchanted this cave, then he's definitely out of our league. He has a pet phoenix for crying out loud.

But what if it were Limery in this situation? Wouldn't I do everything in my power to get that little guy home safely?

The imp's bulbous yellow eyes lock with my own. Fuck.

"What's your name?" I ask.

His face softens. "You can call me Bazel."

"That's a nice name, Bazel. What can you tell us about Thyrim?"

Bazel's eyes narrow. "He is powerful and cunning, capable of changing his appearance at will."

"So, he's an enchanter." Jon taps the butt of his staff against the floor. "How long before he returns?"

"There is no way of knowing." Bazel shrugs. "He comes and goes as he wishes. It has been many moons since I last saw him."

Taryn walks to the edge of the moat and looks down. I join him, watching the molten lava as it bubbles and splashes.

"Have you ever tried to let it cool?" I ask.

"I have not." Bazel sighs. "I do not wish to die just yet. I hold out hope that one day, Thyrim will return and call the phoenix into battle. Only then will I be free."

I strengthen my resolve. We'll find a way for him to escape; we just need time. "And what happens if you leave your platform?"

In answer to my question, Bazel unfurls his wings and takes flight a few feet off the ground. Instantly, the lava shoots up from the moat like a geyser, barring his exit and nearly melting my face off. Jon and Taryn jump back, and Taryn's pets scatter toward the door.

Bazel lands on the platform and the lava returns to its normal state. He hits it with a fresh burst of fire.

"What happens to the phoenix if we are able to get you out of here?" asks Taryn.

Of course the druid is concerned with the safety of the magical beast.

"It will age normally. Eventually, it will burn out and be reborn from the ashes as a chick, continuing its cycle."

Taryn nods. "That's not so bad."

"Were you really questioning if it was worth it for Bazel to be trapped in here?" I shoot Taryn a questioning look.

"I just want to know all the facts before we take action." He gestures toward the lava and the phoenix. "If you hadn't noticed, this is sort of a delicate situation, and the last thing we need is an angry guardian phoenix trying to kill us. We don't even know what level this thing is, but I'm pretty sure it could probably wipe us all off the map."

Point taken. I hadn't even thought about the possibility of the phoenix attacking us. "What if we could replace Bazel's weight on the platform?"

Jon laughs. "The old bait and switch."

Taryn kneels and inspects the moat. "I don't know how we could do that. It would have to be fast, and there's at least ten yards of lava between us and him."

That is the main problem, getting something out there quickly that weighs the same as Bazel. With the risks involved, we'll only get one shot at this. Failure means Taryn, Jon, and I respawn. Everyone else doesn't come back.

"Do you think you could fly up there and see if there's something we're missing?"

Taryn transforms into his bird form and flutters high into the cavern. The phoenix's eye follows Taryn as he flies. It gives me an idea.

Message (Chod): *Hey, you can talk to animals, right?*

Incoming Message (Taryn): *In a manner of speaking. I can communicate with them, but it's not like I can understand what they are saying.*

Message (Chod): *You could try talking to the phoenix. They're supposed to be noble birds. Maybe it knows something we don't.*

Taryn flutters down until he is right in front of the phoenix. In his bird form, Taryn is barely bigger than the phoenix's eye. He chirps several times and erratically zooms left and right.

An ear-splitting shrill answers him as the phoenix caws. It flaps its wings a few times, and hot air beats down upon us. The chain bound to the creature's leg clanks against the stone floor.

A moment later, Taryn returns to his dwarven form beside me.

"Well?" I ask.

"I think she wants out."

"She?"

"Yep, she's a female phoenix. She's not a pet, either. Well, not a willing pet, at least."

I walk around the edge of the room until I find the chain that is holding the phoenix in place. It's thick. Each of the links are thicker than my fingers. The phoenix must be incredibly strong to stay aloft with something that heavy weighing her down.

I give it a hard tug, but it doesn't budge.

The beginning of an idea starts to form for how to free the phoenix, but I'm still not any closer to freeing Bazel.

"I think a Horror of Finesse could take his place on the pedestal, but I don't know how to get it there." I summon one and compare it to Bazel. They look about the same size.

"Could you throw it? Like you did with Taryn?" asks Jon.

Taryn rolls his eyes at the memory.

"Too bad you can't make a bridge with your vines out to the platform." That would make things so much easier.

Taryn raises an eyebrow. "Why couldn't I?"

"If the enchantment is calibrated to Bazel's weight, then anything using it as a bridge would set it off."

"But what if I didn't attach the vines to the center? What if they went all the way across?" Taryn equips his staff and steps to the edge of the moat.

The vines on his staff begin to extend. Taryn grips the staff and slightly squats as the vines grow longer, reaching across the moat. They bypass the center island and extend until they grip the other side. The tiny leaves and flowers that grow on the vines wilt in the blazing heat. The vines themselves begin to harden as the lava dries them out.

Taryn quickly retracts them back into his staff. "Okay, good to know it works. We'll have the horror walk across. He can step onto the platform the second Bazel takes off."

I really hope this works. If it doesn't, we're all in trouble.

"Do you think the phoenix can understand me?" I ask Taryn.

He nods. "They are one of the most intelligent creatures in all of Mythos."

I walk around until I am directly in front of the phoenix. It flaps its wings and a fresh burst of hot air consumes me.

"Hey!" I yell.

The phoenix tilts its head in my direction.

"We want to get you and Bazel both out of here. I'm going to try to break the chain bound to your leg. Please don't attack me."

The phoenix doesn't acknowledge that I spoke, so I just have to take it on faith that she won't burn me alive. I equip Destroyer and take my position at the base of the chain. Taryn stands near the moat, staff in hand. Jon waits near the exit with Taryn's pets.

Taryn turns to Jon. "If this looks like it's going downhill, you take them and you get the hell out of here. We'll meet up with you later."

Jon shakes his head. "Don't talk like that. This is going to work out."

"Alright, everyone. Get ready. Bazel, you know what to do, right?"

Bazel blasts fresh fire into the moat. "I do."

I lift Destroyer overhead and bring it down with a smash on the chain. The clash of metal on metal rings throughout the cavern, and the tip of the warhammer flashes red as the first stack of Inferno takes effect.

I swing again and again, until my ears are constantly ringing. My arms grow fatigued from the effort, and Destroyer's head glows a vibrant red, matching the chain links. The chain is blazing, but the metal refuses to give.

Why the hell isn't this working?

My swings grow more labored and my speed slows as my stamina wanes. I activate Berserker Rage to keep from tiring out. Fresh adrenaline pumps into my muscles and I swing faster and harder than ever, but the chain still doesn't give. Maybe it's enchanted too.

I glance at Taryn, and he knows something is wrong. He says something, but I can't hear over the ringing in my ears.

He lifts his staff, proceeding with the plan. I hammer even harder. When I look back over my shoulder, the vines are nearly across the moat, forming a bridge.

I summon a Horror of Finesse and send it toward Taryn. I don't stop hammering. The heat from Inferno has traveled up the chain, and now several links glow red.

The horror walks across the bridge of vines and steps onto the platform. Bazel flies upward.

Lava erupts from the moat, shooting straight into the sky, and my horror dies immediately from the heat. Taryn takes off running for the door, and I hit the chain one last time before bolting away.

I curse our luck. The platform must not have been monitoring Bazel's weight. And now Bazel is going to die because we fucked this up.

A wall of lava continues to shoot up from the moat, concealing Bazel inside of it. I wish that there was something, anything, that I could do.

A violent caw cuts through the chaos, so loud that I hear it over the ringing in my ears. I look up to see the phoenix diving toward the wall of lava. She opens her wings, and her feathers turn black. She tilts her head back and absorbs the heat from the lava into her body. I can literally see the trail of heat as it escapes the molten lava. Color returns to her feathers and a shimmer surrounds her body. The chain melts away from her leg and coils to the ground.

Where there was once a wall of molten lava, now, there is only hardened rock. I use Destroyer to break a hole and crawl through. Inside, I find Bazel curled into a ball, his small body covered in sweat. He's worse for the wear, but he's alive. I lift him off the ground and carry him to the others.

His body burns against my skin. The hairs on my arms melt away and I do my best to ignore the pain as his body blisters my skin.

Gently, I lay him on the floor. "Someone hand me a potion."

Jon digs through his bag and hands me a vial of red liquid. I pour it in Bazel's mouth. His body begins to cool, and eventually, he stirs. My own burns will heal in time due to my natural regeneration.

His eyes flutter open, and he grabs my arm. "Thank you."

Above us, the phoenix circles the cavern. She flaps her wings, sending gust after gust rushing past.

"We need to get out of here," says Taryn.

"What about the phoenix?" I ask.

"I think she'll be able to take care of herself. We need to get far from here before Thyrim discovers what we have done."

I pick up Bazel and carry him in my arms like a small child. We hurry out through tunnels until we emerge back onto the mountainside. We step into the night, and I relish the cool, fresh air of the mountains.

There's a rumble inside the cavern, right before a gust of dirt and debris explodes from the entrance. The tunnel collapses, and the phoenix bursts from the cavern in a dazzling display of fire and color. Her caws echo through the mountains as she rises high, a brilliant meteor against the night sky.

I can't explain it, but a sense of peace washes over me as I watch her fly. I follow her flight until she disappears among the clouds. Enjoy your freedom, girl.

CHAPTER 20
KING OF THE MOUNTAIN

After hiking several miles from the hidden cave, we make camp on the side of the mountain. I hunt down a mountain goat, and we roast it over the campfire. I hand a piece of roasted meat to Bazel and he devours it.

"Feeling better?" I ask.

He looks much better now that the potion has taken full effect. He's less shaky, and no longer sweating. I didn't even think that imps could sweat. I was definitely worried about him for a minute there.

Bazel smiles, showing us his demonic teeth in the firelight. "This is the first time I have breathed fresh air in many years. It feels good."

"How did you end up there anyhow?" I take a bite of goat leg and the delicious juices trickle down my chin. The light char on the skin offers a crisp bite.

Bazel's eyes droop for a moment, like he's reliving some distant memory. "Thyrim is a man of great trickery. He promised to help me in exchange for my services, but once I was in the cave, he trapped me there. He took advantage of my situation and used it to his own ends. I'm sure I'm not the first one to fall prey to his wicked motives. And I don't even know..." His voice trails off before he sits back in silence.

I pat him softly on the knee. He leaves me with more questions than answers, but after what Bazel has been through, I don't want to pressure him to talk about it if he's not ready.

Jon cuts himself a slice of meat and sits on a log beside Bazel. "What do you plan to do now that you're free?"

"I'll return to my home. I'd like a life without adventure for a while." He cracks off a bone with his teeth and sucks at the marrow.

"Spoken like a true prisoner." Jon laughs.

Bazel tilts his head. "You have been a prisoner, too?"

Jon stares at his feet. "Unfortunately, yes."

The imp reaches out and pats Jon on the arm. "Then I am glad you found your freedom, too."

If he only knew the truth behind us being here. I may have served my sentence, but the others are still prisoners, even if it may not feel like it at times.

"You're more than welcome to travel with us," Taryn finally chimes in. "We are heading to the troll forest. They have formed an alliance with many of the imps, so you may find your family there."

"That is most interesting. It seems a great deal has changed since I've been gone. I don't remember a time when the trolls roamed free anywhere, and now I see one with a dwarf and a human." Bazel stands and scratches his belly. "I will accompany you through the mountains for the assistance you have given me, but then I am afraid I must make my own way. If my home is empty, then perhaps I shall venture to the troll forest. But for now, it has been too long since I last slept."

We take turns keeping watch for the rest of the night, nestled in a crevice with Stompy blocking the entrance. Today was an amazing and unbelievable experience that I can't stop thinking about it.

I'm still in awe of the phoenix. The image of her soaring through cave with wings of fire will forever be burned into my mind. She saved Bazel's life. Who knows where she is flying to now? Hopefully somewhere that she can roam freely, to eventually burn out and start over.

A new beginning. Something I know all too well.

As great as it is that the phoenix is free, I still have my worries. My main concern lies with Thyrim. In order to capture a phoenix, he must be pretty powerful. Unless he somehow managed to trick her the same way he did Bazel. I will have to enquire about him with King Orso once we return to Seascape. If anyone will have knowledge of this man, it would be the dwarven king.

I watch Bazel as he sleeps. Little bubbles of snot rise and fall with his breath, reminding me of Limery. I've learned to never be surprised by an imp. I'm not sure any other creature could have survived being trapped in a mountain for so long under those circumstances. I pray that he finds his family and has a very safe life for years to come.

Eventually, Jon taps me on the shoulder, relieving my watch, and I quickly drift off to sleep.

***

A beautiful clear day awaits us as we journey up the mountain. Bazel sits atop Stompy's horn, swinging back and forth with each step, but the moulhaug doesn't seem to mind. Jon rides Stompy's back, while Taryn rides Berry and Ruby sits in his lap. I'm the unlucky one who has to hoof it.

Most of the day is spent traveling in silence. I try to enjoy the moment as much as I can. Here I am, in a beautiful fantasy world with a view of magnificent mountains, attempting to save the world from some dark force that hides in the shadows. It's almost unbelievable, but it is my life now.

There's so much opportunity here in Mythos. Someone like me can build themselves up from nothing, making friends, going on adventures, and really finding a purpose for their life. I wonder, how many of the other heroes can say that? I want to make this world a better place, for me and for others.

"What do you say we stop by the home of the mountain trolls?" I ask.

Taryn stops in his tracks. "Do you have a death wish? Don't you remember what happened last time you were there? We all nearly died."

"Yes, I remember. But I gave Kronan the option for a better life for his people. Maybe he took it." He might have been a brute, but I think deep down, he cared for his people and their well-being.

"Who's Kronan?" asks Jon.

"He's the leader of the mountain trolls. Big brute of a troll."

Jon shrugs. "I wasn't there, but it sounds like a bad idea to me."

I shrug. Maybe they're right. But what good am I doing if I don't follow up on my actions?

"Screw it, we're going."

I know that if it comes down to it, I can win a fight with Kronan, but I've got a feeling I won't need to.

Everyone looks at me like I'm crazy, except for Ruby, who swishes her tail from side to side.

"We'll be fine. He might need our help," I plead.

Jon glances at me with suspicion. "Well, if I die, you're retrieving my items."

"Deal." I shake his small human hand.

I search for the location of the caves where we encountered the mountain trolls and plot our destination. It'll take at least an extra day to get there but it'll be worth it. King Orso might have tasked me with uniting the heroes, but I have a feeling that when the times comes, we'll need every able-bodied fighter we can get.

At such a high altitude, the air is cool against my skin. Every breath is like inhaling after eating a peppermint and I love it. It's truly refreshing. I'm admiring the beauty around me when a screech cuts through the air above us.

I look up to see a griffin descending below the ring of clouds that hide the peak from view. It flaps its powerful wings and dives straight for us.

"Everyone, get your weapons!" I rally the others and summon a round of horrors. This was the last thing I was expecting to happen today. Griffins are deadly, intelligent beasts.

As soon as I equip Destroyer, I notice there's a rider on the griffin's back. The rider wears boiled leather with a griffin emblem branded on the chest. A pair of large goggles conceal his face, and his short brown hair whips in the wind as they dive.

I lower my guard and laugh. What are the chances?

I raise my hand, signaling the others to stand down. "It's okay. I know this man. It's King Favian from Vanaria."

"What the hell is he doing all the way up here?" asks Taryn.

The griffin comes to a sliding stop several meters ahead of us. Its beak clicks at the air, and Favian climbs from the saddle. He removes his goggles and offers me a warm smile.

"Chod, I didn't expect to run into you here." His blue eyes sparkle with adventure.

"That makes two of us. You're a little far from home." A long ways from home, actually.

"Truth be told, I'm here on business. Searching for a mate for Grimclaw. There are very few griffins on the island, but the ones that are here live high in these mountains." He strokes Grimclaw on the neck. "What brings you here?"

"Have you not heard? The fast-travel portal has opened in Seascape. I sent Limery south to instruct you on how to open yours. King Orso wishes to call a meeting."

The king's eyes go wide. "I'm afraid I've been away for a few days. If what you say is true, I must return at once."

"Wait!" Bazel grabs me by the arm, and his sharp nails dig into my skin. "Did you say Limery?"

I pull away, but the imp doesn't loosen his grip. What's gotten into him? "Yes, he has been my companion for some time. Do you know him?"

Bazel grips me harder. "He's my son! Does that mean... Did Leo—" The words get stuck in his mouth.

It all comes flooding back to me. Limery said that his father had been tricked. That when Leo was sick, a healer promised to help in exchange for his father's service. Is that how he ended up in that cave?

"Leo is fine. I saw him recently. Lillith, too."

Bazel releases me, overcome with emotion. I pat him on the back as his body shakes underneath his heaving sobs.

"I was afraid I lost them." He sighs. "I'm afraid I must go."

I understand completely. Were I in his position, I would do the same thing. "Go to the forest. Lillith is leading the alliance between the imps and the trolls. They will know where to find her."

Bazel moves from one of us to the other, hugging us. "Thank you for freeing me. I will not forget it."

The imp takes to the air, and in a flash, he is gone.

King Favian looks at us in disbelief. "I feel there is a story there, but first, tell me about the portals."

"When King Orso announced the challenge to reward anyone who could unlock the portal, thousands of people flooded the capital, even a few heroes. Many people attempted. Some even lost their lives from the dark energy that surrounded it. Then, Glenn and Jude showed up with a small army of mind-controlled dwarves."

King Favian scowls at the mention of Jude's name.

I continue. "There was a fight, and I was thrown into the portal. The dark energy surrounded me and for a moment, I thought I would die, but then a blessing that had been bestowed on me by the forest trolls saved me. It did something to the energy too, because when I got up, the portal was accessible."

The king places his finger on his lip for a moment before speaking. "And you think this can be replicated?"

"We believe so. We sent Limery to the forest to gather a few trolls to march south."

"That is most interesting." He turns to the griffin. "I'm sorry, Grimclaw, but it looks like your search for love will have to wait."

The griffin huffs in response.

"But before we leave, introduce me to your friends. I'd also love to hear the story behind the imp. It sounds most fascinating." He raises his eyebrows.

I motion to Taryn. "This is Taryn. He's a druid."

Taryn nods his head. "Pleasure to meet you, Your Highness."

"And this is Jon. He's an enchanter."

Jon drops to one knee and lowers his head. "Your Highness."

The king smirks. "An enchanter, you say? We don't see many of those nowadays. How is your training coming along?"

Jon stands. "It has been a slow start, but since meeting Chod, I've seen some real progress."

King Favian winks at me. "There is no doubt that you have. Where this one goes, greatness follows. I may be able to offer you an opportunity to advance your skills far quicker than traveling from dungeon to dungeon."

Jon straightens his back. "I'd love to hear more."

"Vanaria has one of the greatest libraries on the island. We haven't produced as many master enchanters as the dwarves, but we do have great scholars. And I happen to have one enchanter who could help teach you at an extraordinary rate. You'll learn in days at our library what would take weeks on your own. If you would like to return to Vanaria with me, I will make sure you push your limits like no other."

Jon's mouth hangs wide open, practically dragging the floor. His eyes dart between me and Taryn before answering. "Are you serious? That, uh, would be amazing."

"What is your enchanter's name?" I ask. I have a sneaking suspicion that he might be the one who locked Bazel away.

"Her name is Sirina. She has served us faithfully for many years."

A woman. So it wasn't Thyrim. Still, Favian might know of him. "Do you know an enchanter by the name of Thyrim?"

The king furrows his brow. "How do you know that name? Thyrim is Kassidy's brother. He holds a small keep outside of Vanaria."

Ah, Kassidy. The teleportation mage who always has food in his beard. Power must run in their family. "He's the one who trapped Bazel in the mountain."

King Favian places his hands together and brings them to his chin. "Trapped, you say? This grows more curious by the minute. Please enlighten me."

I tell him the story of the hidden entrance, of the puzzles, and then the phoenix and Bazel trapped inside. Then I inform him of how Bazel was tricked in the first place.

The mirth has vanished from the king's face. "I am sorry for the imp's troubles. I will make sure to have a talk with Thyrim the next time I see him. While I cannot justify his actions, I can understand them to a degree. Phoenixes have a natural predisposition toward darkness and the undead. They are very rare, but exceptionally powerful. There is a long history of fear of all things of a dark nature on the island, especially the undead. If what you say is true and the dark wizard is afoot, then a phoenix would have been a great weapon in the wars to come." He gazes off into the direction of Seascape. "I don't agree with his methods, but what is one imp in exchange for one of the most powerful creatures on our side when that day comes?"

I'm surprised when Taryn answers. His face is set, and I don't know if I have ever seen him so serious. "It's the difference between us and them. We don't sacrifice our own without their permission. We don't take the lives of those we should protect just because it might give us an advantage or make things easier. Every life matters, and Bazel deserves the chance to live his own life and make his own decisions just as much as any of us."

Chills run down my spine. I couldn't agree more.

Favian lifts his hands, palms up. "I can't argue with your reasoning. Many a king has kept himself up at night pondering over this very question. For you, it is simple. You live for yourself and use your abilities to protect others. For me, I have an entire kingdom to rule over. Thousands of lives that I need to value. Do I tend to the needs of a hero like yourself, who could possibly turn the tide of a battle, over an infantryman when the time comes? Or do I make the tough decision when the time comes, losing one man but saving thousands. Nothing is black and white, not even good and evil."

Taryn sits speechless atop Berry. I understand the feeling. I couldn't possibly imagine having to look out for so many people. One thing I'm certain of is that Favian is a good king. Many leaders only look after themselves and expect their subjects to fall into place. He cares about his people and wants what is best for them.

"Perhaps one day we can discuss this in more depth, but for now, I must return to see what new adventures await my kingdom." He turns to Jon. "Will you be joining me?"

Jon turns to me like a small child waiting for their parent's permission to go play at the park.

I smile. In the small time we've been together, I've watched Jon grow from someone who was selfish and just looking for a way to get by to an actual caring teammate, and dare I say, maybe even a friend. "Go ahead. You'll be a great enchanter. I'm sure we will see each other again."

I extend my hand, but he bypasses it and wraps his arms around me. "Thank you, for everything." When he releases me, there's a glisten to his eyes. "And you were right. After talking to Bazel and hearing his story, I know what you mean now. This place is the real deal."

I slap him on the back a little too hard, knocking his glasses askew. "And that is exactly why we need to protect it."

CHAPTER 21
GIANT PROBLEMS

"Looks like it's just you and me again." I duck under a low branch from a tree that grows on the side of the mountain.

We're traveling toward the mountain troll caves, and I have no idea what to expect. After our last encounter, there's no telling if they are friend or foe.

Stompy refuses to duck and powers through the branch with his horn until it snaps. Debris falls on Taryn as they pass.

He picks pieces of broken bark from his beard and flicks them away. "I know. We were just starting to be a formidable group, and now I only have you to watch my back."

"I'm sure we'll see them again. I can't wait for Limery to see his father. I bet he'll be so happy." I still can't believe he was trapped in a cave for years on end. I get bored sitting alone with my own thoughts for more than five minutes. I can't imagine spending years with no one to talk to.

"You know, I have missed his antics." Taryn grins. "And what about Jon? His luck turned around pretty fast."

One of my horrors slips and falls off the mountain. I feel its presence as it tumbles down the mountainside, losing bits of HP with every hit until it disappears altogether.

Now, that it's just me and Taryn, I keep as many horrors on hand as I can. I want to be prepared in the event we come upon anything dangerous.

"Yeah, good for him, though. It's an amazing opportunity." Jon's a good guy, and it's about time he caught a break.

By early afternoon, we near the mountain troll lands. Around the next corner is where I first found them tucked away in a massive crag. I keep an eye out for goblin scouts, but so far, all is quiet. I equip Destroyer, both for the added protection and its ability to muffle my movements. Unfortunately for Taryn, his boots' abilities don't transfer to his pets. Berry and Ruby walk quietly, but there is no mistaking Stompy's footsteps.

The crag is filled with many full-grown trees in its opening. A well-trodden path winds between them until we find ourselves in a clearing surrounded by mountain on three sides. There are remnants of the fire pit and chairs carved out of stone, but there's no sign of the trolls or the goblins. Where could they have possibly gone?

Taryn and I search the premises. There's nothing to give the impression of a struggle or fight, so they must have willingly moved.

"Maybe he did take your advice." Taryn stands in front of the entrance to the largest cave. "Want to check it out?"

I shake my head. I've had enough cave adventures for the time being. "It's a little too soon for me."

He laughs. "I feel you on that. I guess it's back to the trail then. Were you wanting to take the route to Smalltown or go a different way this time?"

Ah, Smalltown, the best place to have your items smuggled from one kingdom to the other. I wonder how their business will be affected once the portals between Seascape and Vanaria are both open?

I don't imagine many people will be venturing through the mountain unless they have something to hide. And if there is one thing I know, it's that if you deal with unsavory characters, you'll get unsavory results.

Pulling up my map, I see that there is a more direct route to the forest. Our last time through, we strayed into the marshes to level Taryn up, and it took us a bit out of the way.

"Let's take a new route. There's no use exploring the same old places when there are plenty of opportunities for new adventure. Lead the way."

As soon as Stompy turns away from the cave, a loud rumble echoes from within. I've had enough experience in this world to know that's not a good sign.

Taryn and I exchange glances, and I can tell he's thinking the same thing as me. Fight or flight?

The rumble fades, replaced by a light patter reminiscent of a heavy rain on a roof.

"What the hell?" Taryn stares at the cave. "Is that rain?"

While I wouldn't say it's impossible for there to be rain inside the mountain, I highly doubt it.

I've seen enough movies to know what's coming. "No, that's a bunch of small creatures running down the cave toward us."

Just as I say it, a speckling of tiny orange dots appears in the depths of the cave. They grow bigger as the sound increases. I grip Destroyer tight, ready for whatever comes next.

Fifty or sixty goblins emerge from the tunnel. Green-skinned, with lanky arms and pointy ears, some carry torches, others wield spears and beat them against their crude wooden shields. They're clad in rags and scraps of leather. Their orange eyes stare at us with intrigue. There's no sign of any mountain trolls among their ranks, and the metal collars they wore around their necks are gone.

I take a step forward. "Where is Kronan?"

One of the taller goblins shoves his way through the crowd on the back of a mangy looking wolf. His bright orange eyes stare at us with menace. "Kronan go. Now you go." His voice is high pitched and shrill.

"Where did he go?" I ask. Would the mountain trolls really leave the goblins behind?

The goblin points past us, repeating himself. "Kronan go. Now, you go."

Whispers snake through the group, growing louder until the entire group is chanting "go, go, go," and pointing their fingers or weapons at us.

"I think we might should go." Taryn slowly backs Stompy away.

I think he has a point. Maybe we could take the entire group at once, but I don't like the odds. Even if they aren't as strong as us, there is strength in numbers.

I raise my hands. "Okay, we're going."

Another thunderous rumble echoes from the cave, and the hair on my neck stands on end. There's still something inside.

The goblins move aside and fall silent, creating a path down the center.

"Chod, I've got a bad feeling about this." Taryn backs Stompy away a few more steps.

I know we should run, but there's also that part of me that wonders what might be coming. What new challenge awaits?

I stand my ground. A loud groan escapes the cave, and the goblins all gasp. Two massive gray legs appear from the darkness. Each step thunders as more of the creature becomes visible. Each leg is as big as I am. When it fully emerges, the monster is twice as tall as me, and it carries a stone club that could potentially end me with one hit.

Giant. *Level 22. As tough as the mountains from which they spring, giants' bodies regenerate at such a rapid rate that the only way to kill them is to remove the head.*

Oh, fuck.

I thought all the giants had left the island with the dark wizard. This one must have taken up residence in the cave after Kronan left.

I take in the grotesque creature. Skin as gray as the mountain itself. Two bulging eyes the color of pus and teeth that look like wood. Stringy gray hair mixed among the bald patches stick to its sickly face. Boils cover its hawk-like nose. By far, this is the ugliest creature I have ever come upon. It's so ugly that I can't help but stare. But underneath the flaky skin and disgusting appearance is the body of a warrior. Muscles bulge and contract with every movement until it stops between the two groups of goblins.

The only reason I can imagine as to why the giant and goblins are living in the cave together is because the goblins flock to creatures with power. They take a bit of abuse for the solace of protection.

To each their own, but I can already smell the garbage bin that resides in its mouth and can only imagine the smell inside that cave.

I slowly back away. "Sorry to disturb you. We mean you no harm, so we're just gonna turn around and be on our way."

The giant shakes his head. "No," his voice rumbles.

"Look, I can see your time is precious. And you're a man of few words, which I can appreciate, so just let us be on our way and no one has to get hurt." I turn to leave when something warm and squishy hits me in the back.

I look over my shoulder to find a goblin laying dazed and confused on the ground.

"No way. You did not just—"

Before I even finish my sentence, the giant picks up another goblin and throws it at me. I step out of the way and it goes sailing into the trees, screaming the whole way.

"So, that's how it's going to be? Two can play at that game." I grab a Horror of Vitality by the horn.

"Chod, don't—" Taryn tries to stop me, but I've already committed.

I hurl the horror at the giant with all my might. The fluffy horror looks at me with betrayal as it soars through the air and bounces off the giant's chest without doing so much as a trickle of damage. The giant grunts and smashes the horror with its rock-like foot before lifting his club overhead and unleashing a mighty roar. Spittle and drool fly past his rotting teeth.

I roll my shoulders and answer his call, roaring with all the defiance I can muster.

"Bro, this is not going to end well." Taryn's face is full of worry.

"Dude, he threw a goblin at me." I toss my hands in the air. "I can't let that stand."

The giant charges, and for the briefest moment, I think about running. Then I remember I'm a goddamn troll and I take off to meet him head-on. Taryn jumps off Stompy, but I don't wait around to see what he does.

"Keep the goblins off me, and I'll handle the giant."

Me and Mr. Giant are the same level. Time to find out what happens when an unstoppable force meets an immovable object.

Time seems to slow down as we approach one another. He swings his club and I duck, sliding through the giant's legs and feeling the displaced air as it barely misses rearranging my face.

As I'm sliding, I summon a horror and explode it right on his nut-sack.

The giant howls in pain. Even though it didn't do more than a sliver of damage, there's no way that didn't hurt.

He yells at the goblins to attack, and Taryn finally makes his move. I send all my horrors with Taryn and his pets to handle the goblin horde. Lightning crashes into the group of goblins, and all hell breaks loose.

While I'm still on the ground, the giant swings his club at me like a sledgehammer. I roll to the side, and the club caves in the stone ground, exploding rubble into the side of my face. I quickly scamper to my feet and back away.

He's actually pretty fast to be so big. I may not be as strong, but I know I'm faster, so I'll need to use that to my advantage.

The next time he swings, I meet the blow with Destroyer. A chunk of stone breaks off from the giant's club, but I take the brunt of the attack as its recoil reverberates through my forearms. The giant laughs at me and kicks out, planting his foot into the center of my chest and knocking me back several feet before I land on my back.

I gasp for air like an asthmatic. Damn, that hurt. Luckily, I don't think he broke anything. The giant stalks over me with the slow pride of someone who thinks they have won the fight. Bad news for you, buddy, because I don't fold that easily.

I summon another horror and toss it at the giant. A half second later, I do it again. He swings his club like a baseball bat at the first horror and it dissipates in a puff of smoke. The second horror strikes home on the giant's family jewels before he has time to react.

The giant falls to his knees, grabbing his groin. Two for two.

"Hey, man. You started it. Play dirty, you get the dirt."

His booger-colored eyes look at me with disgust, but I don't care. I jump to my feet and smash Destroyer into his side. The giant grimaces in pain before stumbling to his feet.

"Troll not nice!" he roars.

I check on Taryn, and he's managed to back all the goblins into the mouth of the cave. The horrors and his pets have formed a barrier, blocking the goblins from getting out.

Alright, so it's just me and the big guy. No problem.

The giant rushes me again, club raised over his head. I'll give him this, he really goes all out. The club crashes into the earth as I sidestep out of the way. While he's still lifting his weapon, I hit him in the side of the kneecap with my warhammer. Something crunches, and he falls to one knee.

The giant grunts as he attempts to stand, eventually using his club as a crutch.

"Bad troll," he grunts.

I feel the presence of most of my horrors behind me and call them to my aid. The giant reaches down, attempting to grab me, and I barely escape his reach.

I send my horrors after the giant, and they rush him, biting and clawing at his legs. He steps on several horrors, and I summon more. Their attacks do almost no damage to his hardened skin. Every time I hurt him, his regeneration kicks into gear. Currently, he still has ninety-five percent of his health.

There's no way I'm going to be able to whittle him down at this rate. I'll need a killing blow—something he can't recover from.

I keep a healthy distance from the giant while I try to formulate a plan. He crushes my horrors with ease, but at least they are keeping him distracted.

"Taryn, I need your help."

A moment later, he's beside me. "What's up?"

"If I create a distraction, do you think you can tie his feet together with your staff?"

He frowns. "I don't want to get anywhere near that thing."

"Come on, dude," I plead. "It's the only way I see us beating him."

He raises his eyebrows. "Maybe you should have thought of that before you got us into this situation." He sighs. "Fine. I'll do it."

"Alright, get ready." I really hope this works. The giant is strong, but he's not the brightest. If I overwhelm him with too many things at once, I think we've got a real chance.

I summon another round of horrors. The Horror of Power and Horror of Finesse rush in to join the others. I take the Horror of Vitality by the horn and chuck him at the giant's face.

As the horror flies, I wind up Destroyer and let it fly. The giant grabs the horror out of the air, and I explode it against his hands. At the same time, I cast Kamikaze on the rest of the horrors attacking his feet and legs.

It distracts him enough that he doesn't see my warhammer coming straight for his face. It hits him in the chin, and he stumbles backwards. His eyes cross for a minute as he regains his senses.

"Special delivery, air mail." I chuckle at my own joke.

Taryn is already on the move, vines extending from his staff and wrapping around the giant's legs. They keep pouring out until they cover him completely from ankle to calf.

Now is the time for the finishing touch. I run for my warhammer, and the giant focuses on me. He tries to step in front of me, but his legs are tied. He wobbles back and forth, trying to regain his balance, but it's too late. He tumbles to the ground just as I grab Destroyer.

He reaches for me, but I smash his hand into the ground.

When he recoils, I land a blow to his rock-hard head. His eyes droop from the blow. The tip of Destroyer flashes red with each hit. The giant's head bobbles like a fighter about to fall. It takes several hits before the skin breaks, several more before bones crack, but eventually, the giant lies lifeless on the floor.

I sit down on the remnants of Kronan's throne, thoroughly exhausted. The goblins stare at us from the cave, but they take no action.

"Nice going. Couldn't have done it without you." I reach out and fist-bump Taryn.

I check my stats. After the fight, I'm not too far off from level twenty-three.

"Sweet, new level!" Taryn pumps his fist.

When I focus on him, I see he is now level nineteen. We've bridged the gap pretty nicely and now he is only three levels below me.

"Nice! Any new abilities?" I ask.

His eyes glaze over. "Let me take a look."

He goes quiet for a moment.

"Dude, I've got three new options! One is Barkskin. It allows me to buff anyone in my party with tougher skin, as if they were wearing wooden armor. The second is Summon Fungus. It summons mushrooms that release poisonous gases, but they are poisonous to us as well. The third is Stonewall. It summons a stone barrier wherever I want."

All of those seem pretty handy. "Which one are you going to choose?"

He strokes his beard. "I'm not sure. I could also further buff my current abilities. A level-three Lightning Bolt would be nice, too."

"Your call." I set Destroyer on the ground and stretch my arms over my head.

Taryn paces, tapping his staff on the ground. "I think a new ability would serve us better, especially since it's just the two of us for now. You've already got pretty tough skin, and I'm not much of a brawler, so I think Barkskin is out for now. Summon Fungus and Stonewall both seem pretty good options. It'd be nice to summon a wall if we're retreating or need to keep someone out, but I think Summon Fungus could accomplish the same thing, but it could also be used offensively as well. What do you think?" He looks at me for approval.

"Sounds good to me. It'd be nice to have some more crowd control abilities aside from Horror of Vitality's passive slow." I go back over to the giant's body to look for loot, but aside from the giant club, there's not really anything there.

It makes me wonder even more how he and the goblins found themselves together.

"Ready to get out of here?" I ask.

Taryn glances at me out of the corner of his eye. "Sure you don't want to start another fight beforehand?"

I laugh off his comment. "I know, I know. I let my temper get the best of me again. What can I say? I just don't like being disrespected."

Taryn calls his pets back from the cave entrance. The goblins just stand there, watching us. They truly are strange creatures.

"Enjoy having the place to yourself." I give them a two-finger salute and turn toward our next destination.

We've still got a few more hours before sunset, so we should be able to make some good progress. I imagine we have at least a couple of days before we're out of the mountains, even with Taryn using Strong Wind to increase our speed.

As we make our way down the mountain, I hear something behind us. I turn around with Destroyer at the ready.

An army of green descends the mountain, stirring up dust and gravel as they come. Taryn steps up beside me, his staff raised.

"These guys don't learn, do they?" His staff glows brown for a moment, and a cluster of mushrooms spring up across the path. Light brown mushrooms with purple spots and bulbous caps. There's no way anyone is passing through them without taking some damage.

The goblins come to a halt, sending a dust cloud wafting in our direction.

"Are you looking to die?" I raise my hammer. "Go back home."

The larger goblin comes forward, still riding his mangy wolf. "You strong. We follow."

Taryn and I look at each other, confused.

"You have got to be shitting me."

CHAPTER 22

BRIDGE OVER TROUBLED WATER

Taryn bursts out laughing. "You killed their new leader, now they're all looking to you. It's like they're lost ducklings and you're the first thing they saw." He wipes a tear from his eye.

After I used my horrors to disable the mushroom traps, the goblins have been following us ever since. They hunt for themselves. They don't bother us, but they won't take no for an answer. Sometimes, I look over my shoulder and they are just staring at me. It's so creepy.

"Let this be a lesson to you. You don't have to fight everyone who wants to fight you." Taryn holds his stomach as a deep belly laugh takes over.

I roll my eyes. As if my grumbling horrors weren't enough of a responsibility, now I have fifty goblins following my every move.

As we journey through a narrow pass of the mountain, the line of goblins and horrors stretch behind us for a great distance. It's like we're some banished group on a pilgrimage to a new land. With such a large troop, at least we don't have to worry about being attacked unaware. However, we'll have a harder time being inconspicuous, and I'm sure enemies will spot us from further away.

Unfortunately, Strong Wind doesn't work on a group this large, so we are forced to travel at a more moderate pace. We could just cast it on ourselves and leave the goblins in our dust, but Taryn is having so much fun watching them follow me around that he won't use it.

Who knows, maybe I can pawn them off on the forest trolls once we finally arrive at the forest.

As we make camp for the night, howls fill the air in the direction of the grasslands below the mountains. Usually, we hear one or two creatures howling at the moon, but this is different. Dozens, maybe more, howl in unison. The sound sends a chill down my spine.

Ruby sits up, ears pointed and head cocked, as she stares in the direction of the howling.

I turn to Taryn. "That's odd. I've never heard anything quite like that. Any idea what it is?"

He closes his eyes, attempting to listen. When he opens them, a frown paints his face. "No idea. They aren't wolves, coyotes, or jackals. Whatever it is, it sounds like a bunch of them."

The next night, the howls sound even closer, and I can't help but wonder what we might be walking into.

The mountain path widens the lower we descend, allowing us to spread out as we walk. When we make camp, the goblins form a circle around myself, Taryn, and his pets.

The largest goblin approaches me. "You sleep. We watch." His orange eyes are piercing as he stares at me over his hooked nose.

I nod. For whatever reason, I'm strangely comforted by the gesture. In an alternating order, half the goblins sleep, while every other goblin faces away from the group, watching for threats. For the first time since staying at the inn, Taryn and I both sleep through the entire night.

When I wake up, I feel refreshed and ready to take on the world. A new notification flashes in the top of my vision.

Regional Alert! *The portal to Vanaria has been reopened. Fast-travel is now permitted to Vanaria.*

Awesome! It looks like the troll blessing worked after all. And at this rate, we'll probably arrive at the forest around the same time as the others return.

Taryn wipes the sleep from his eyes. "Things are changing fast. I can't imagine what the island will be like now that both portals are open."

I know what he means. The world just got a whole lot more interesting.

I summon horrors as we descend the final stretch of mountain and empty into the lush grasslands below.

Berry stuffs his nose in the grass, sniffing as we go along. Stompy rips a bunch of wildflowers from the ground and eats them. I think he and Stompy are both glad to be back on flat ground.

A few hours in, we come upon a river blocking our path. As far as I can see, there are no bridges or methods of crossing. I wade in a few steps, but the bottom quickly falls out. There's no way we're crossing with the goblins, and it's too far for me to throw them across.

"Let me take to the air. I'll see where the closest crossing is." Taryn doesn't wait for a response before transforming into his bird form and disappearing into the sky.

I soak my feet in the cool water while I wait for him to return. Several goblins use their spears to fish in the shallow parts of the river. They offer me food, but I decline. I watch them roast fish over a small fire when a red bird lands on my shoulder.

I jump, startled by the sudden appearance.

Taryn transforms back into his dwarven form. He looks at me with a devious smirk. "Got you."

"Ha-ha." I scowl at him. "Very funny. Did you find anything?"

"It looks like we have two options. There is a ferry several miles east. I imagine it would be pretty costly to get all of us across."

I nod. "And what's the other option?"

"A few miles west, there's an abandoned bridge. It looks a little worse for the wear, but if Stompy can swim across, then I think the rest of us could take the bridge."

I pull my feet from the water and return to the goblins. "Alright, troops, time to get moving."

The goblins rush to action, extinguishing the fire and gathering their belongings. They are truly devoted to me and follow every command I give. Stompy could take a few notes.

When we arrive at the bridge, "worse for the wear" is an understatement. The thing looks like it could fall apart at any moment. Several planks are missing and many more look rotten and dilapidated. The first step creaks as I put my weight on it, and there's a section in the middle with a three-foot gap we'll need to cross.

I'm sure the goblins are lightweight enough to cross, but for Berry and me, we might want to take our chances in the water.

"You think this will hold up? It doesn't look like it's been used in ages." I place my hand on the railing and it wiggles back and forth.

"It probably hasn't been. We're quite a ways from the main roads. This thing looks like a relic from the past, but I don't see many other options. I can fly further downstream and see if there's another crossing."

I shake my head. There's no point in wasting more time. I'm anxious to get back to the troll forest and see what's happening.

To make matters worse, the current is a lot rougher here than in other spots. Rapids bubble on both sides of the bridge. If anyone falls in, they'll be taking a long ride downstream.

Standing around all day staring at the bridge isn't going to get us anywhere, so I call everyone to action.

"Goblins, you're up first. One at a time, please." I step aside so that they can cross.

The head goblin steps up first, riding on the back of his mangy wolf. "I go." He flashes me his teeth in what I assume is a smile.

Before he leaves, I stop him. "What is your name?"

He tilts his head to the side before answering. "This one is called Cheevus."

"Okay, Cheevus, show them how it's done."

Carefully, the wolf steps onto the rickety bridge. Since he's the heaviest of the goblins, this will be a good test. The wolf meticulously chooses its steps, placing each paw delicately on the aged timber before moving forward. A few times, it changes its foot placement mid-step.

When they arrive at the section where all the boards are gone, the wolf lowers itself, and I can see the muscles rippling just before it launches across the divide. They land and the bridge wobbles for a moment. Cheevus tenses up, gripping the wolf's fur. A minute later, they step off the bridge onto the other side.

"Awesome!" I turn to the rest of the goblins. "Form a line and cross one at a time."

It's a lengthy process, waiting for each goblin as they slowly make their way across. A few of them struggle to jump the gap in the center. One almost misses the leap entirely and dangles precariously with his feet dipping in the water before a second goblin comes out and helps him up.

Eventually, they all wait on the other side. Ruby crosses with no problem, and then it's just me, Taryn, Stompy, and Berry left.

"How are you planning to get Stompy across? I'm pretty sure the water is deeper than he is tall, and the current is moving pretty fast." Not to mention he has to weigh a couple of tons. Honestly, I'm not even sure if he can swim.

Taryn winks. "I've got it covered."

He climbs on the moulhaug's back and Stompy steps toward the riverbank. Taryn raises his staff. It glows for a moment and then Stompy trumpets as his body suddenly doubles in size.

After casting Imbue, Stompy is larger than an elephant. I'm still not sure if he's big enough to withstand the current, but it'll be close.

Stompy steps on the edge of the riverbank and the earth collapses into the river. Taryn holds steady as they slowly enter the tumultuous water. Stompy leans into the current, battling nature with his massive frame.

On the other side, Ruby paces on the river's edge.

"I guess it's time for you and me to get moving." I scratch Berry behind the ear and step onto the bridge. "I'll go first."

As I move across, I have the uneasy feeling that the entire thing could collapse at any time. I'm halfway across when I hear Taryn curse to my right. I turn just in time to see Stompy sliding closer to the bridge in the raging current. He tries to push forward, but each step drags him closer to me.

His head is only inches above the water, and Taryn is holding on for dear life as the river covers him up to his waist. He could easily transform and fly away, but there's no way he's leaving Stompy to fight through this alone.

"Easy, boy." Taryn tries to comfort the struggling moulhaug. "It's going to be okay. Just one step at a time."

Stompy slips, and both he and Taryn disappear beneath the

surface. The bridge shakes and I think they've smashed into it, but a second later, both Stompy and Taryn break the surface gasping for air. I can't do anything but watch in horror.

I think about retreating until they make it across, but when I turn around, Berry is already halfway to me.

"Berry, go back!" I shout. "The bridge can't support both of us."

The umber bear's eyes are focused on Taryn. He grunts and groans as he watches his master struggle.

"Berry! Go back."

I'm so focused on getting Berry off the bridge that I don't notice when Stompy loses his footing and collides into the bridge. Wood splinters and the bridge cracks in half from the weight of the moulhaug.

The impact knocks me into the water, and I sink underneath the rapids. I fight to swim to the surface, but the current pulls me under. My back hits the silty bottom of the riverbed, and I tumble in the river's violent grip before it releases its hold on my body.

My head breaks water and I gasp for air. Up ahead, Berry and Stompy are both bobbing in the current, but Taryn is nowhere to be seen. The goblins run along the riverbank, following us as the current carries us away.

I fight to keep my head above water. In the raging river, that's all I can do. Any attempt to move to the shore is useless. We're forced to take the whims of the river until it decides to release us.

Suddenly, a tight pressure cinches around my wrist. A vine trails from my wrist to the side of the river, where Taryn stands with his staff pointed at me.

"Grab the others!" he yells.

I fight against the current, and my muscles burn until I reach Berry. The vine extends and wraps around his paw. I grab Berry's other paw and swim toward Stompy as best I can. He bobbles up and down as his hind quarters flirt with riverbed. I grab hold of his saddle and yell for Taryn to pull us over.

Water rushes into my open mouth. With one hand on Berry and the other on Stompy, I'm like a buoy at sea. There's a slight pressure as we begin moving toward the eastern side of the river.

My head bobs above water and I see Taryn surrounded by fifty goblins as they all pull on the staff like a giant game of tug-o-war. Inch by inch, we move closer until the current releases us and I feel muddy earth beneath my feet.

I crawl to the bank and collapse in the grass. Closing my eyes, I let the sweet relief of fresh air fill my lungs.

When I open my eyes, dozens of orange eyes look down on me.

"Chod okay?" asks Cheevus.

"Yeah, I'm good." I cough a few more times before finally sitting up.

Beside me, Berry shakes the water from his coat, drenching us in a heavy mist. Stompy sulks a few feet away as Taryn tries to calm him.

I take a deep breath and try to calm my racing heart. At least we made it across.

CHAPTER 23

OH GNOLL YOU DIDN'T

I FIND myself looking at the goblins in a new light. Without being asked, they rushed to Taryn's aid, not only saving me but Berry and Stompy as well. I'd always viewed them as unintelligent monsters, nothing more than lackeys for the trolls or giants or whoever they were following at the time, but they are much more than that.

They might not follow those that appear weak, but they are blindly devoted to those they do follow. They respect power above all else. So I decide that going forward, I'll treat them with more respect.

Something I doubt they have ever experienced.

We're about a day's march from the edge of the forest. That still leaves us with another day of travel through the woods before we make it to the troll village.

Looking at my map, I don't foresee any major obstacles on the way.

When we camp for the night, the goblins take their positions around me and Taryn, forming a protective circle. I nod to

Cheevus before lying down and letting the sound of chirping crickets pull me into slumber.

A loud howl wakes me. As I wipe the sleep from my eyes, I notice the goblins are on their feet with their spears, pickaxes, and rusty swords pointed into the darkness. I nudge Taryn and get to my feet.

Something is up, but I'm not sure what.

Another howl pierces the night, followed in quick succession by several more. Whatever creatures we heard howling when we were in the mountains, we've stumbled right on top of them.

"What's going on?" I ask Cheevus.

The leader of the goblins turns to me. "Gnolls coming."

I search the perimeter, but see nothing. My night vision only allows me to see for so far. After that, it's up to the moonlight, which is currently hiding behind the clouds.

I equip Destroyer, not sure what to expect but wanting to be prepared. Quickly, I summon three horrors.

Berry lets out a low growl, and Stompy paws at the earth. Clearly, they can sense something is amiss. Ruby stares out in one direction, rigid as a statue.

"She sees something." Taryn squints, though if I can't see it, then he definitely won't be able to.

Something howls behind us. All I hear is a loud swish as we all turn at once. A second howl echoes from my left, and then another from my right. They pour out of the darkness until we don't know which way to face.

"Everyone, stay calm and hold your positions." I do my best to keep an air of authority. "If you see anything, call it out."

The howling continues to the point where I can't tell where one howl ends and the other begins.

I continuously summon horrors since there is not much else I can do.

One of the goblins screams and points into the darkness. I'm able to make out the shape of some bipedal dog-like creature. A second later, another becomes visible.

As they get closer, I begin to make out their features. They look like hyenas, with stubby snouts, spotted fur, and short dumpy ears. Taller than most humans, their bodies are lean and muscular with thick necks. Their eyes are solid black and devoid of emotion, and their lips curl up in a permanent sneer. They wear leather armor and wield rustic spears. Some appear to have damaged armor or dented metal weapons. All in all, they look like scavengers.

More and more approach from the darkness, until we're surrounded by a pack of at least twenty. Finally, they get close enough that I'm able to focus on their stats.

Gnoll. *Level 15. Nomadic scavengers, gnolls wander the country-side looking for victims to rob and towns to pillage. Gnolls often travel in packs, submitting to the will of the pack lord.*

Before I even have time to question what a pack lord is, he appears before me. Similar to the other gnolls but bigger and wielding a massive sword he no doubt stole.

Gnoll Pack Lord. *Level 20. Leader of the gnoll tribe, the pack lord is able to bind the lesser gnolls to a common cause. A pack lord can also rally his pack with Rampage.*

Great. Us and a bunch of goblins against a pack of hungry killers. We outnumber them two to one, but I don't see the goblins offering much help in this situation.

"What do you want to do?" asks Taryn.

The gnolls continue to stalk toward us, like predators preparing for the hunt. After saving my life, I don't want to put the goblins at risk, but I don't see any way out of this besides fighting.

"We're gonna have to fight. Or at least scare them enough that they run off." I've summoned twelve horrors since the gnolls appeared, putting the numbers slightly more in our favor. "Maybe if we swarm them, they'll run."

"Honestly, I don't have a better plan. Let's do it." Taryn climbs atop Stompy.

"Goblins, group up. I want at least four goblins to a group. Run out to the closest gnoll and hit it with everything you've got. It's time to raise hell!" I lift my warhammer into the air.

Cheevus does the same with his spear, and the goblins join in. Their high-pitched yelling fills the air, causing the gnolls to stop in their tracks.

"Attack!" I roar.

Like an explosion, we disperse on our attackers. Several of the gnolls exchange glances, uncertain of what is happening. I rush toward the pack lord, and several goblins and horrors follow me.

He slashes his sword at the same time I swing Destroyer. The two weapons clash, and it rings through the night. The sword flies from his grip and sticks point-down in the nearby grass.

The pack lord roars, and two gnolls rush to his aid. Goblins jump on them, biting, clawing, and stabbing at any exposed areas. Lightning crashes somewhere behind me as Taryn joins the fight.

I catch a glimpse of Stompy bulldozing one of the gnolls into the ground. His hoof caves in the creature's chest as he runs him over.

Everywhere I look, goblins and horrors overwhelm the gnolls. They cling to them like spiderwebs in a dark attic. Clearly, gnolls aren't the smartest creatures.

Destroyer crushes the ribs of the nearest gnoll and the tip flashes red. A second gnoll stabs a spear at me, but I parry the wooden weapon with ease. The pack lord retrieves his sword and comes back for more. He charges at me, but stumbles forward as Cheevus's wolf pounces on him from behind, sending him stumbling to the ground.

I step on his sword as he tries to stand. He jerks at the weapon, but I weigh too much for him to pull it free.

"You picked the wrong group." I smash my warhammer into his ribs and he flies several feet.

He snarls at me as he crawls to his feet. All around him, his men are bruised and bleeding. Some have already turned and ran, freeing up the goblins to overwhelm the others.

Cheevus lifts his spear and points it at the gnoll. "You go!"

For a moment, I think the gnolls might actually retreat, but they all group together around the pack lord.

The pack lord tilts his head back and howls. The others follow his lead. A red aura forms around them, then I notice that their black eyes are now bright yellow. Their bodies twitch as muscles grow and expand. Claws lengthen and teeth extend, and suddenly, their health bars replenish completely.

The pack lord smirks at me. "I think we'll stay." His voice drips with venom.

They charge at us. With those teeth and claws, they don't even need weapons.

Taryn casts Lightning Bolt, but the gnolls move aside. Lightning explodes into the earth like a grenade.

I step in front of the goblins and take a deep breath. I'll do my best to protect them. I call my remaining horrors and summon a few more. Then I remember I have an ace up my sleeve.

I cast Champion, and a fifteen-foot giant appears out of thin air. He bends down and picks up the pack lord's sword. The mighty weapon looks like a dagger in the giant's hand.

The giant meets the gnolls head on. He swings the sword with raw power, severing two gnolls in half with a single blow.

The goblins cheer at the devastation.

Taryn casts another bolt and we all rush into battle. The giant has turned the odds heavily in our favor. Stompy charges through the group of gnolls, head swinging like a battering ram. They fly to the side, and horrors and goblins swarm them like ants on candy.

For the second time today, I watch the pack lord lose his cool as the giant lifts a gnoll with his free hand and crushes its skull like a rotten apple.

He slings the body aside, and it collapses like a ragdoll.

The gnolls turn to retreat, and we chase them for a few hundred meters before they disappear into the night.

When I return to our camp, many of the goblins stand in a circle. I push my way through to see what's going on.

Cheevus kneels next to a small green goblin with a wooden spear sticking out from his throat. The goblin's lifeless orange eyes gaze up at the heavens. Cheevus reaches down and closes them.

He died protecting us.

"What was his name?" I ask.

Cheevus strokes the goblin's cheek. "This one is called Doren. Very brave."

"Very brave, indeed. We will give him a proper funeral." The goblins should be given the opportunity to mourn their fallen.

Cheevus stares at me for a long moment. I can't tell what he's thinking.

"Thank you." He kneels beside Doren, removing the spear and crossing Doren's arms over his chest.

I use the spiked end of Destroyer to break apart the ground, then dig the upturned soil with my hands. Doren is so small that I don't have to dig far to make a suitable grave.

No one talks as I work. Even Taryn stands stoic next to the goblins. When the hole is big enough, I pick up Doren. He feels like a small doll in my hands, and memories of holding Limery come flooding back. I find myself fighting back tears as I place the small goblin in the grave.

I stand there, looking at his frail body, wondering how a game could ever feel this real. Not just the sensations and experiences, but the emotions that come with it.

The goblins gather around the grave, silently watching their fallen brother. I take a step back to give them the opportunity to mourn however they see fit.

Cheevus reaches down and picks up a handful of dirt. He squeezes it in his fist, closing his eyes. When he opens them, his grip loosens and the dirt falls into the grave grain by grain, like sand through an hourglass.

"Good-bye, Doren." Cheevus tilts his head, and once the dirt has emptied from his hand, he steps back.

The words are simple, as is the gesture, but it pays respect to the fallen in a way only the goblins know how. Each goblin takes their turn, saying good-bye and placing a handful of dirt in the grave. When they are finished, Cheevus drops to his knees and begins shoveling the rest of the dirt while the others return to their duties.

I kneel beside him and help. We don't talk; we just shovel. And when the grave is filled, Cheevus places Doren's sword point down at the head of the gravesite.

Wherever you are, I hope you rest easy.

CHAPTER 24
NEW FRIENDS
IN OLD PLACES

The journey to the edge of the forest is somber and uneventful, which is good. After losing Doren to the gnolls, I'd feel sorry for anyone or anything unlucky enough to come across us right now. There's a lot of hurt and anger flowing through the group.

"That was really nice of you back there." Taryn strolls up beside me, riding Berry. "I'm sure it meant a lot to them."

I give him a half-smile. "Thanks. I just did what I thought was right. It's a delicate balance, the urge to play this like a game, but also taking into account that everyone here has the ability to react like real living creatures. It's a mindfuck, sometimes."

"I totally get it. We kill to level up, but at the same time, seeing a group of goblins mourn their fallen is a sobering experience." He takes a deep breath. "It's a fine line, indeed."

A familiar comfort washes over me as we step into the forest. Is this what returning home feels like? The magnificent trees that tower overhead, the lush vegetation, birds and bugs that fill the forest with their orchestra. My shoulders relax and the tension I've been carrying lessens.

"So this is it?" Taryn looks around, taking it all in.

I forgot that he has never been here before. I ran into him while on the quest for the mayor in Lynchton. He never got the chance to see the troll village.

I shake my head. "This is the forest. Once upon a time, the forest trolls ruled over all of it, but now, their numbers are so small that they all reside in a single village."

"Well, maybe now that they aren't being hunted, their population can grow and expand."

Wouldn't that be nice.

Stompy comes to a stop and rubs his backside on a massive tree, scratching some unknown itch. The tree shakes with the movement, sending nuts raining down from above. The goblins scatter out of the way to avoid being hit.

Taryn just laughs at the moulhaug's antics.

We prepare to make camp for the night. By this time tomorrow, we should arrive at the village. We find a clearing where all of us can sleep safely, when something catches my eye. A few hundred meters away, I spot the translucent outline of a forest troll.

I do a double-take to make sure I'm not imagining it. Why would a guardian troll be this far out? He's way outside of the tribal boundaries.

"Taryn, do you see that?" I point in the direction of the troll.

When he shakes his head, I realize my mistake. Only other trolls or creatures with high perception can see the outline of a troll using camouflage.

"There's a guardian troll over there. He's awfully far from the village. Stay here while I go check it out."

"You sure?" He raises an eyebrow.

I nod. The trolls all know me.

"Be careful. Scream like a little girl if you need us." He pretends to punch me in the arm, pulling back at the last second.

I equip Destroyer and use its ability to muffle my movements to my advantage. If it's Malak or Jojin, maybe I can give them a good scare. As I get closer, I realize that this is a troll I don't recognize. He must have been gone last time I was at the forest.

When I realize why I don't recognize him, I freeze in place. It's because he's not a forest troll, he's a mountain troll. What in the hell is he doing all the way out here? And alone, at that?

The mountain troll has some stark differences from the forest trolls. His skin is a light plum-color, dotted with speckles of gray. His hair grows in a short gray mohawk. He has a long hawk nose that nearly touches his lips, and his tusks are shorter but more girthy than mine. Mountain trolls are stockier than forest trolls, built for strength and not speed. And they're really great at tossing boulders down the mountain.

I put away Destroyer, so that I don't alarm him when I reveal myself.

"Hey, you're a long way from the mountains." I put my hands up so that he knows I mean him no harm.

The translucent sheen fades and his color returns as the mountain troll stands, ending his camouflage.

He eyes me warily before speaking. "Ah, you. Our devoted hero."

I can't tell if he is mocking me or not. My experiences with the mountain trolls have been far from pleasant.

"I passed through the mountains. There were no other trolls there. What happened?"

He steps closer. His body language is tense, but not hostile. "I'm afraid that is not my story to tell. Kronan will fill you in."

"Kronan is here, too? Are all of the mountain trolls in the forest?"

He sighs. "You do ask a lot of questions, even for a forest troll."

"Fair enough. What's your name?"

He stands up straight, puffing out his chiseled chest. "I am Ekon."

Time to extend a little hospitality. "Welcome to the forest, Ekon. I'm traveling with a group of goblins and a dwarf. Would you like to join us for dinner?"

I can see the internal debate raging behind his eyes. Eventually, he nods.

Good, at least he doesn't completely hate me.

Several goblins have already started a fire by the time I return, and a few others set out to hunt.

Ekon looks at the goblins with suspicion. "The goblins follow you now?"

"Yeah, after I defeated the giant, they wouldn't take no for an answer."

His eyes squint even further. "You defeated a giant?"

I laugh. "Look who's the one with all the questions now."

Ekon grunts but remains quiet.

"This is my friend, Taryn. We're on our way to the troll village."

"Nice to meet you." Taryn extends his hand and smiles.

Ekon nods in return but doesn't move his hand. Maybe I got in his head with my comment.

It doesn't take long before the goblins come back carrying a wild boar over their heads. The beast greatly outweighs the small goblins, but eight of them manage to keep it from dragging the ground. They skin it and remove the entrails, and soon enough, it is roasting over a spit. The savory aroma drifts to my nostrils, and I have to wipe away a bit of drool.

We all sit around the fire, and I take another crack at getting some information out of Ekon.

"So, you can't tell me why you left the mountains. What can you tell me?"

He scowls at me. "Why must you know everything?"

Taryn burst out laughing. "I like this guy."

Ruby crawls into Taryn's lap and curls up.

I feel myself getting angry, so I take a deep breath. "Fine. Let's just eat."

The goblins slice up the boar and give both Ekon and I an entire leg. Ekon rips into the meat, and the juices stream down his face.

"Mmhm. Good." He manages between bites.

I pass my brimming tankard around and we wash down our boar with a never-ending supply of fresh cool water. Whatever the enchantment is that allows it to replenish itself is fascinating. It only refills when the tankard is in an upright position. When turned upside down, the water stays inside. I imagine this is to keep people from accidentally flooding areas by knocking the tankard over.

The goblins pick the boar to the bone, leaving nothing for the scavengers that may come after we're gone.

Once he's finished, Ekon stands. "Thank you for the food. Now, I must return to my post."

"Anytime." I wave at him as he leaves.

He starts walking, then turns around. "We are here to make the trolls great again. We are tired of hiding."

Before I have a chance to respond, he leaves.

Taryn nudges my shoulder. "You did it, man. You really did it."

It feels good to know I had some part in it, but I can't take all the credit. "Whatever it is they are doing, Kronan made the decision. I may have helped open his eyes, but that's it."

Taryn rolls his eyes. "Whatever you say. Time for me to get

some sleep, I'm looking forward to meeting all of the trolls you've been blabbing about."

Truth be told, so am I.

—

A soft tickle moves up my arm, and I reach down to scratch it. Sharp pain flares through my finger, pulling me from sleep, and I wake up to find a small red lizard with its mouth wrapped around my knuckle. A hard shake sends the creature flying into the bushes.

I curse loudly, waking the others. They all look at me like I'm crazy.

"A lizard bit me." I hold up my finger to show them, but the wound has already healed.

We pack up everything and set off for the village. I instruct the goblins to stay behind me. If there are more guardian trolls this far out, then I want me to be the first thing that they see. It's more likely to be peaceful that way. The forest trolls will welcome me with open arms, but if there are more mountain trolls, I'm not sure how privy they are to my relationship with the forest trolls.

As we travel through the forest, the effects of the ley lines become gradually clearer. Trees and vines that move of their own accord, flowers that bloom as we pass or curl up in defense. One plant mimics the look of a tropical bird almost perfectly, going so far as fluttering its leaves so that they look like wings moving. I smile fondly at the memory of the glowing flowers that would light a path through the village at night.

Taryn's mouth hangs open. "Dude, this is amazing."

We pass another mountain troll, cloaked in camouflage. He watches me, but he doesn't move as we walk by. Ruby is the only one aside from me who notices him.

I see a few more trolls in the distance as we continue onward. When we're only an hour from the village, I spot a familiar face.

"Malak! What are you doing up here? I thought you guarded the southern border?"

Malak runs to me and embraces his hand around my forearm. Several goblins are startled by his sudden appearance as he decloaks.

"Chod! It is good to see you! Much has changed since you left. We are trading with Lynchton, the mountain trolls now help us protect the forest, and the chief has left for Vanaria to help the human king." The words spill out of his mouth.

Good to see he is as easily excitable as ever.

"Easy there." I pat him on the shoulder. "One thing at a time."

He smiles wide. "Now is a good time to be a troll. For the first time in a long time, we feel like we are a part of the world." He claps me on the shoulder in return, his green eyes gazing intently into mine. "And it is all thanks to you."

I introduce Malak to Taryn and the two shake hands.

"Any friend of Chod's is a friend of the forest trolls." He smiles.

"Likewise." Taryn grips the troll's massive hand with both of his own.

I move right into business. "Are any of the council members around? There are things I would like to discuss."

"Tormara is still in Vanaria as part of the alliance. Chief Rizza, Gord, and Jira left to help the king, along with a few other trolls. Kronan is holding a seat on the council in their absence."

Kronan has a seat on the council. That is very interesting. I can't wait to find out how that came to happen.

Malak decides to accompany us as we head to the village. As we go, he fills us in on what has changed since I left. Lynchton has become a bustling town, where humans and trolls trade. People travel from all over to buy troll potions. Humans are now allowed to hunt in the forest as long as they stay away from the village, and now that the mountain trolls have moved to the forest, they are able to send scouts to farther areas.

We bypass several more trolls along the way. Some wave from the distance. The ones that do not I assume are mountain trolls.

I'm so caught up in conversation that I'm startled when we pass the barrier into the village. The illusion that keeps the village hidden from outsiders is fueled by the rich flow of mana beneath the soil. No doubt Jon would be amazed to see it. One minute, we're looking at an expanse of lush forest, and the next, I'm walking down a path with the village visible in the distance.

The thorns and vines that form a wall around the perimeter unravel and create an opening for us to pass through. As soon as we are inside, the hole closes, forming a barrier once more.

My mouth waters as Kea's famous stew wafts in our direction. A giant pot is always boiling, providing nourishment to anyone who is hungry.

My heart warms as I spot the young trolls running between the huts, swinging clubs carved out of wood. Like all the architecture in the village, the huts are formed from living trees.

"Chod!" A familiar voice calls my name, and I turn to see Ismora carrying a small troll on her hip.

She sets the troll down and sends him off with the others. I'm surprised when she wraps me in a hug. I return the gesture, giving her a hearty squeeze. It's so nice to be around familiar faces.

"Everyone, this is Ismora. Weapons master and a great fighter." Her face is covered in scars from her many battles over the years. Nowadays, she trains the children in the ways of troll weaponry and fighting. Limery's handprint is seared into the side of her neck from our first adventure together, one where she almost lost her life.

"Yashi will be thrilled to see you! Right now, she is out gathering herbs for potions. We've been selling them to the humans at the market." She beams with pride.

"That's great to hear. Are any of the imps around? I'd love to speak to Lillith. I hear she might have found out some exciting news."

Ismora shakes her head. "No, they are all at the market. Their help with translating has been invaluable. Come, have a rest. I'm sure you are tired from your travels. We can have accommodations for all of your party by nightfall."

"By nightfall? We don't mind sleeping on the ground. How are you going to have something ready in such a short amount of time?" asks Taryn.

Ismora winks. "The forest provides. If you want to show your friends the village, we'll get started right away."

"That would be great." I embrace Ismora again, and she disappears into the village.

Taryn gives me a questioning look.

"Mana infusion. Trolls can infuse mana directly into living objects. Our skin is tough enough that raw mana doesn't burn us. You see how the huts are formed out of living trees? The roofs are made from the leaves. Mana infusion allows the plants to understand our will, and they do as we say."

He looks confused. "So all of this, the moving plants, the blossoming flowers, it's all because of mana?"

I nod. "Yep. Trolls are one with the forest."

The village hasn't changed much since my last visit. Leather boils under a giant pergola while one of the female trolls stirs it with a long stick. A wide assortment of hides lay draped across a section of vines. Under another, the many weapons the trolls have looted over the years are organized by type. I know from experience that they keep the best weapons in Jira's hut, but I'm sure these are great for trading with the townspeople.

Just as always, the village is home to mostly females. The male trolls take turns guarding the boundaries. I'm honestly surprised that the mountain trolls had no problem with it. Almost all village business is handled by the women. I would imagine they handle the majority of the trading as well.

A female mountain troll and forest troll are engaged in conversation. They stare at us as me and my goblin troop make our way to the village center. When we arrive, a fire burns in the fire pit. Its embers are low, but it will be blazing come nightfall.

"Chod!" A deep, cavernous voice calls my name.

Kronan. The plum-colored troll, larger than any of the forest trolls, myself included, glares in my direction. A fur shawl covers his broad shoulders, despite no longer being in the mountains. One of his tusks is cracked at the tip, and he wears his hair in a braided mohawk with the braid hanging over his shoulder. At level twenty-five, I'm still surprised I defeated him.

"Kronan. Long time, no see."

He looks past me, observing the goblins. Cheevus steps up to my side, his chin held high.

"I see you've gained some new companions." He clenches his fist, and for a moment, I worry that he wants to fight. It has to be a blow to his pride to see the goblins following the troll who bested him in front of his own tribe.

He reaches in a pouch that hangs from his side and pulls out a vial of frothy yellow liquid. He hands it to me. "I pray they serve you well."

I examine the vial. It's sweetwater, a specialty of the forest trolls. It's deliciously sweet, but burns like hell going down.

Is this a gesture of peace?

I uncork it, take a swig, and pass it to Taryn. The familiar burn trails into the pit of my stomach.

"What made you come here?" I ask.

He stares at me for a moment. "Follow me."

I instruct the goblins to stay in the village center with Taryn's pets while Taryn and I walk with Kronan. We follow him until we come upon the council area. Chief Rizza's throne, along with the chairs for the council, are all empty. They are constructed in the same way as all troll architecture—bent into shape out of living plants. Beautiful white flowers blossom while they remain empty. Kronan takes a seat near the end and the flowers retract everywhere except around his head.

It says a lot that he doesn't take Rizza's seat even though she's not here.

He motions to the chairs across from him. "Go ahead, have a seat."

I do as he says. It wasn't that long ago that I was a member of the council, until I vacated my seat to Gord before setting off to find my own path.

Kronan raps his fingers against the armrests of the chair. He stares at his feet, as if wondering where to begin.

He clears his throat. "After our battle, I was furious. More angry than I had ever been in my life. My hatred for you was so hot that I could feel it sizzling in my very veins. For days, I hid away in the caves, unwilling to show my face to anyone. I lost my purpose. If I wasn't the greatest warrior, then what was I? The goblins abandoned us in defeat, and the mountain trolls were at a point of decision." His claws dig into the bark of the chair. "We could continue down our ways, and eventually, there would be no more mountain trolls. Or we could embrace the ways of our ancestors and take what was ours."

His eyes bore into me. "Through it all, I saw your face. As I slept, as I woke, it was always there, looking down on me, judging me. I would wake in the night and see you with my own warhammer raised above my head. Your words cycled through my mind." He sits back and laughs. "And then one day, I reached up and I took the warhammer back. The visions stopped, and I marched my people here. Chief Rizza was not what I expected. She is no weakling as I had thought. She has a strong mind. We have formed an alliance, and we aim to bring more troll societies to our cause."

He stands up. "I have been to the nearby village. I've seen with my own eyes that men do not attack us like they once did, and I am told that you are to thank for that. I would rather use my weapons on the beasts of the forest than on fighting for survival. My people deserve peace and safety, a chance to raise their families." He walks over and extends a hand. "So, thank you, Chod, hero of the forest and mountain trolls, for showing me the way."

I take his hand in mine, but the words get stuck in my mouth. I'm truly and utterly speechless. My eyes are suddenly wet, and I blink rapidly to fight back the tears.

I'm glad his people have found peace, but the fighting is far from over.

"Uh..." My first attempt at talking is a croak. "That is wonderful to hear, but I'm afraid we may need your warhammer before you find true peace."

His face turns to stone. "What do you mean?"

"Call a council meeting. I will fill in everyone on the details."

***

It takes a while for Kronan to gather everyone, but eventually, the council takes their seats while Taryn and I stand before them.

Kina sits to my left, one of the few trolls who doesn't wear her hair in a braid. Her bluish-black hair would make even the most confident supermodel green with envy. Next to her sits Guilda, Gord's mother, and one of the elders of the village. A long gray braid drapes over her shoulder and into her lap. On the other side, Kronan is to my right. He stares at me with intrigue. Next to him sits Sonji. There's nothing remarkable about her. She wears her hair in a black braid, and her clothing is the typical leather of the average troll. You'd never know she held a seat of power just by looking at her.

Four members is the smallest council I have seen, but they govern the forest in Chief Rizza's absence, and I must inform them of what is coming.

"What is it you would have us know?" Guilda doesn't look annoyed, but rather ready for me to get to the point.

I take a deep breath, thinking of the best way to put this. "As you know, the fast-travel portal has opened in Seascape. And now, the portal in Vanaria has been opened as well. In many ways, this is great. It will open up trade between the dwarves and humans. Everyone, trolls included, will benefit from the races mixing more openly."

They all watch me intently, and I try to make eye contact with each of them as I continue.

"There are other continents out there, as well. And the portals will have access to many of them. I believe the majority of them will trade with us. Some will probably send their own warriors or adventurers to *Isle of Mythos* in time. For heroes like me and Taryn, there is a whole wide world of opportunity for us to grow and level. But the truth of the matter is that not all of the portals are opened."

The council members exchange glances, and Kronan sits on the edge of his seat.

"The dark energy that kept ours closed for so long still keeps several portals closed and their secrets hidden. We don't have the ability to open portals from our side. They can only be opened from the destination. King Orso believes that the dark wizard who wreaked havoc long ago is still out there, and that one day, he will open his portal again. We don't know if the other closed portals are allies or enemies, and we have no timeline for when they might open, but when they do, we need to be ready."

"What are you proposing?" asks Guilda.

I wait before answering, because I know what I am about to say will not be taken well. The trolls finally have peace. They are finally rebuilding from everything they have lost over the years. Even the mountain trolls have fallen into a better way of thinking. I wish desperately that they could hide away in the forest and that all of this would pass them by. But in my gut, I know that is not the case. Every troll is worth at least five men, and they will be integral in what's to come.

I straighten my back and strengthen my resolve. "It is time for the trolls to prepare for war."

For the first time since I've known her, Kina loses her cool. She stands to her feet, snarling. "This is preposterous! We are finally safe again and you want us to march to war? Do you have so little respect for us?"

Guilda counters. "Easy, Kina. Chod has always been a friend of the forest trolls. He is the reason we have risen to where we are."

Kina shakes her head, and her beautiful hair shimmers in the fading sunlight. "This is not our fight. Let the humans and dwarves go with their massive armies. Let the heroes fight the darkness. I will not see our children become orphans of war."

Sonji nods. "I agree with Kina. We have come too far to lose it all now. Let someone else fight this war, we have fought for long enough."

Kronan makes to speak, but as he opens his mouth, Taryn steps in front of me.

He raises his hand, asking without words for them to listen. To my surprise, they do.

"You're not wrong to fear losing what you have worked so hard to attain. In my own life, I've had to work for everything I have. Some people are given things. They wake up in the morning, and they have what most of us dream of. Things that they take for granted." He shakes his head and the clasps in his beard jingle. "This isn't about losing what you have. It's about standing idle while everything is taken away from you. If the men and dwarves and all the heroes go to face this threat and we lose, what will happen to you then? Who will stand up for the trolls when we have all fallen? Who will protect the little ones that run through the streets of your village? If you sit by while we go into the unknown, you may find yourself standing alone if we fall."

I try not to take his comments personally, but I know he's referencing me and my life outside of the game. I never took Taryn as the jealous type, and maybe he's not, maybe he's just trying to relate to the trolls, but it still stings. I didn't choose the life I had any more than he did.

A smirk spreads across Kronan's face. "The half-man speaks the truth."

Taryn spins on his heel, pointing at Kronan. "I'm a dwarf, asshole!"

Kronan tilts his head back, laughing. "Right you are." He turns to the others. "The dwarf speaks the truth. My people have sat idle for too long, afraid of dying out and in turn slowly fading into nothing. While I cannot determine the fate of the forest trolls, for the mountain trolls, we will relish the opportunity to go to war among allies. For if we fade from this world, it will be with a weapon in our hands and a roar in our throats."

The others sit in contemplation. Sonji twiddles her thumbs, Kina silently shakes her head, and Guilda stares off into the forest.

Finally, Kina speaks. "We will discuss this matter with the chief once she returns. Her guidance has not led us astray yet. I am sorry for my coarseness, Chod. You have always done well by us. Though this news is not welcome, it is not your doing, and I should not have lashed out at you."

I smile. "I won't take it personally. I've lost my temper on occasion."

Guilda shuffles in her seat. "If there is nothing more to discuss, then the council meeting is over."

***

"Good speech." I have a hard time hiding the disappointment in my voice. Maybe I'm just being sensitive, but I still can't stop thinking about what Taryn said about those born with things that others want.

Taryn steps closer until he's looking up at me. "Hey, man. It wasn't personal, and it wasn't aimed at you. I just know what it's like to want to hold on to what you have."

"What, and you don't think I do? Just because I had more than you doesn't mean I wasn't afraid of losing it. It doesn't make me a bad person because I grew up in a wealthy family. Those are the cards I was dealt. I didn't choose them."

Taryn shakes his head. "You don't get it. I mean, how could you?"

My hands get jittery, and I feel my breathing quicken. "So it's like that? I shared everything with you. Every new game, I bought you a copy. Whenever we hung out, I paid for everything. And not because I felt sorry for you, it was because you were my friend."

Taryn throws his hands up and turns away. "See, you're missing the point. It's not about you! It's not about what you had or didn't have, what you were afraid of losing or not. It's not about how generous you are. It's about me. My experiences! I can never understand what it is like to be wealthy, but you also can't understand what it's like to come from nothing. It's not your fault; it's just the way it is. Every time I mention my situation, it's not a reflection of yours. And as long as you carry a chip on your shoulder because you resent where you came from, you'll never see it any other way."

He storms off and I start to follow.

He turns around, cutting his eyes at me. "Chod, just leave me be for a bit."

I stand there in the empty council area and watch as Taryn disappears into the woods.

When he's gone, I take a seat on one of the empty council chairs. A fresh bout of anger flows through me and I pound my fist into the armrest. The flowers retract into the safety of the vines. How could he be so rude? I've never flaunted my wealth in front of him. I've always tried to make Taryn feel like an equal when around me.

I sit there for a long time lost in my thoughts. As much as I try, I just can't put it behind me. Was Taryn right? Do I resent where I came from?

When I think on it, all the bitterness and anger in my life is aimed at one thing: my parents. That they cared more about money and lifestyle than they ever did about me. And no matter how many presents or new games they got me, it never filled the void that I was missing from them.

I let out a deep sigh. I am ashamed of where I came from. Because everyone looks at me like I have it all, when in reality, I have nothing. Nothing but a best friend who I just yelled at.

I find Taryn sitting on the bank of the village lake. He skips stones across the water. The goblins have joined him and several swim in the crystal blue water. Berry lays sprawled out in the fading sun while Stompy eats leaves from the tree branches. Ruby turns in my direction as I approach.

Taryn tosses another stone. He looks in my direction, but he doesn't say anything.

"Hey, man. I'm sorry. I shouldn't have taken that so personally. I know you didn't mean anything by it. I just get upset sometimes when people think I have this great life just because I have money. It's like that's all they see when they look at me."

He tosses another stone, but it sinks straight into the pond. "I'm sorry, too. I was a little hard on you." He smiles. "That speech got me all kinds of emotional."

"It was a good speech." I laugh. "And when you called Kronan an asshole, that was priceless."

Taryn joins my laughter and his dreadlocks swing back and forth. "If they ever make a movie of my life, that better be in there."

I put my arm around him. "We good?"

His hand pats me on my lower back. "Yeah, we're good."

"Cool, let's get back to the village then."

Back in the village center, several guardian trolls have returned for the evening. I spot Kronan talking to another mountain troll. They both glance in our direction as we enter, and a scowl immediately forms on the second troll's face.

Brutus. The last time we met, I had my trident pointed at his throat. He looks at me with contempt. His plum-colored skin is scarred in many places, with a pronounced lilac scar that runs diagonally down his chest. His shoulders and arms are dotted with speckles of gray, perfect for blending in with the mountains. He has the same long nose and short, thick tusks that are common among mountain trolls. His hair is braided into a long mohawk that runs down his back.

"What is he doing here?" asks Brutus.

Kronan laughs. "Come now, Brutus. Jealousy doesn't look good on you."

I approach the two, and Brutus continues to stare daggers at me.

"Kronan, may I have a word?" I ask.

We step to the side.

"He'll come around in time." Kronan smirks. "Brutus is a great warrior, but he lacks vision. What is it you want?"

I glance over my shoulder. "It's about the goblins."

Kronan raises an eyebrow. "What about them?"

"Taryn and I have a long road ahead of us. We will be traveling to the other continents as we level and gather others to our cause. I'm glad that the goblins have chosen to follow me, but there's no place for them on this journey. You know as well as I do that they are valuable companions, and we will have need of them in the wars to come, but for now, I would have them stay in the forest to train and learn to fight alongside the trolls."

Kronan grunts. "They will not be happy. Goblins are incredibly loyal to those they choose to serve."

I shrug. "Then they should have no problem following my orders."

"We could always go for round two." He winks.

"I'll keep that in mind as a backup plan." I'm not entirely sure that the outcome would be the same if we fought again.

I return to the goblins, who have gathered around the fire pit. "Alright, goblins, I need to talk to you all."

Over a hundred orange eyes stare in my direction.

"I'm glad you all chose to follow me, but unfortunately, we will have to part ways for a while. I want you to stay here and train with the trolls. A battle is coming, and I will need you ready to fight."

Cheevus stands up. "No. We follow Chod. We ready to fight."

Of course, this is going to be difficult. "I know you are, but where I'm going, I can't take all of you with me. Train here, grow stronger, and we will meet up again, I promise."

Taryn looks at me with amusement as the goblins grow visibly agitated.

"Look, this is not open for discussion. I need you to—"

All the goblins gasp in unison and stare over my shoulder.

I turn to see a massive wyrm slithering between the trees. The wingless, legless dragon glows a faint blue from the toxic gel that coats its scales. Bright blue eyes stare at me. Its snout looks like a beak, perfect for burrowing underground, and it has grown even larger since the last time I was here. It rises like a cobra, nearly doubling my height.

Yashi's small hand waves at me from atop its back. Then she jumps down like an acrobat, landing softly on the ground. The diminutive potion master is as agile as I remember.

"Chod!" she squeals as she runs and jumps into my arms, wrapping me in a hug.

"It's good to see you too." I look up at the wyrm. "What have you been feeding these things?"

She flashes me a sneaky smile. "The forest provides."

"So I hear." I laugh and we end our embrace.

"What brings you to the forest?" She looks past me, finally noticing the goblins. "Your party has grown larger since we last saw one another."

The goblins gaze upon the wyrm with greedy eyes.

"I was actually hoping to leave the goblins here to train with you. The council members will fill you in on the details. I was also hoping to see Chief Rizza before I left. Do you have any idea when they will be returning?" I don't have time to just wait around for them to show, but we need to talk.

"It should be any day now."

I sigh. I suppose we could always go to Lynchton to check on the progress they've made with trading while we wait.

Yashi's wyrm lowers itself to our level. Yashi strokes its hardened snout and its eyes close slightly.

"We should have a celebration tonight." She beams. "To celebrate your return and our alliance with the mountain trolls."

"That sounds nice, but first, I need to have a talk with these guys." I motion to the small army of goblins over my shoulder.

They continue to stare at the wyrm, following its every move.

I walk over to Cheevus and kneel beside him. "Cheevus, I need you to understand. It's not that—"

"We stay." He's still fixated on the wyrm.

I can't help but chuckle. "You know, there's actually two more."

His eyes turn to slits and his lips curl up into a devious smile. I have a feeling the goblins will be just fine without me. I can already picture them riding giant wyrms into battle.

The last beams of daylight fall beyond the trees, casting the forest in darkness. The wyrm's glow seems more pronounced in the firelight.

Ismora emerges between a row of huts and embraces Yashi in a massive hug before coming to us. "Your shelter is ready."

"Alright, troops, let's get you settled in and we will all meetup afterward. I'm sure Yashi will tell you all about her pet wyrm." I wink at Yashi.

As we walk to our new accommodations, I receive a message notification. I expect it to be some snarky comment from Taryn, but I stop in my tracks when I notice it's from Valery.

Incoming Message (Admin): *You've made quite the name for yourself since we last spoke. Our developers have been hard at work on* *the backend, trying to fix the system error that is keeping you logged in. We may have found a solution, but we'll only know once you log out. I recommend finding an inn and setting your spawn point there. The time has also come for Taryn's scheduled break, so we will be pulling you both out at the same time. You have until tomorrow evening. - Valery*

Taryn stands still right beside me, but his expression is unreadable. "Did you get a message too?" he asks.

"Yeah, looks like we're heading to Lynchton tomorrow." I can't explain why, but there's a knot in my stomach. If they've found a fix, what happens to me? Will they still want me to log back in?

My chest is suddenly tight. I'm not ready to go back.

CHAPTER 25

LIVE AND LET LIVE

AFTER MOVING the goblins into their freshly-constructed barracks, we all meet up in the village center for a celebration. This is the most crowded I've seen the village as mountain and forest trolls join in the camaraderie. Sweetwater flows all around as trolls let loose with displays of strength and tribal dancing.

Through it all, I can't get Valery's message out of my mind. Part of me secretly hopes that they haven't found the answer. I know it's their job, but too much is riding on me being here. I will do everything in my power to stay in this world for as long as I can.

Taryn comes and sits beside me, his eyes slightly glazed over from the sweetwater. "I thought the dwarves knew how to party, but this is something else."

We watch as Brutus and Malak face one another, surrounded by dozens of trolls. Drums echo through the night, and the two trolls compete in a ceremonial display. They mimic one another's moves, stomping and clapping in the same fashion as their ancestors. They continue the display until one of them misses a movement, then they embrace to the cheers of the crowd.

Nearby, drunken goblins pile on top of Stompy and ride him through the forest. For such a grumpy animal, the moulhaug doesn't seem to mind.

"How are you feeling about everything?" I ask.

Taryn tilts his head, and his dreads cover part of his face. "You mean logging out?"

I nod.

"It'll be nice to call my mom, but truth be told, I'm already excited to get back here." He takes another swig of sweetwater. "Besides, you can't find this stuff out there?"

I take a sip of my own, letting the burn trail down my insides. "Ain't that the truth."

The more that I drink, the less I dwell on Valery's message. Eventually, I get up and actually enjoy the celebration.

A drunk Kronan approaches me. "There's our hero!" He slaps me on the back and some of my drink spills on the ground.

In my buzzed state, I wrap my arm around his shoulders. He's much more affable after a few drinks.

"Kronan. Good to see you enjoying yourself."

"I can't remember the last time we had reason to celebrate." His face goes suddenly serious. "What do you say you join me in a mountain troll tradition?"

Sounds intriguing. "I'm in."

Kronan gathers everyone's attention. "Follow me! We will finally settle who is stronger—me or Chod!"

I follow him past the huts and into the forest. Kronan comes to a stop, and I have no idea what is about to happen. The area looks like a normal section of forest to me.

He points to two different trees. Each one is over a foot in diameter. "Take your pick."

I examine the two trees, not sure what I'm looking for. "Uhm, what exactly am I picking?"

He grins. "First one to uproot the tree is the victor. Normally, we would toss the tree off the mountain when we're done, but since we are running low on firewood, we can use it for that."

I follow the tree from the base to the canopy. It has to be at least fifty or sixty feet tall. How the hell am I supposed to uproot a tree that large?

I glance around at the others. They all watch like this is perfectly normal.

"You seriously think we can pull a tree this big from the ground?" I ask.

Kronan laughs. "Some of us can."

There's that mountain troll bravado.

"Alright, let's do this." I move in front of the tree to the right.

Kronan takes his position in front of the tree to the left and wraps his arms around it in a bearhug. I do the same. Kronan's muscles bulge as he clasps his hands together. I may have beaten him in a fight, but he still has two levels on me. Plus, he's a mountain troll, the naturally stronger sub-race.

Several feet stomp behind us. A moment later, they stomp again, but more join in. It continues until all the trolls are participating and their stomps thunder through the forest. Then, they add a clap at the end. Stomp, stomp, clap. Stomp, stomp, clap.

As their bodies beat like drums, something stirs inside of me, and I feel confident that I can rip the tree from the earth.

"Begin!" Kronan shouts above the noise.

I squeeze my hands together and lift, but the tree doesn't budge. My muscles tense with the effort, and I expect the ground to at least give a little, but nothing. I heave again to the point where I think I might shit my pants. Still nothing.

Beside me, Kronan's tree rocks gently as he pulls. His normally light purple face is flushed like a dark grape.

I pull again, pushing against the earth with my feet. The tree doesn't budge, but my toes sink into the earth.

"Come on, Chod!" Taryn cheers from over my shoulder.

The trolls continue to stomp and clap, the rhythm slowly increasing. Something crunches beside me, and I glance over to see the roots of Kronan's tree starting to break free from the earth.

Oh, come on. I can't let him pull out an entire tree without at least getting mine to move. It's time to use the advantages that come with being a hero. I summon a round of horrors on the other side of the tree. With their passive stat boost, I feel a little stronger, but the tree still isn't budging. When I hear another crack as a piece of root snaps free beside me, I activate Berserker Rage.

Strength floods my body, and the tree creaks slightly as I pull. I cast Sacrifice on the three horrors, granting me a temporary buff to my stats. I lift again, and this time, I feel the roots give against the pressure. I pull with all my might until I'm certain my body is going to rip in half. Steam rises off my skin as sweat evaporates from my overheating body.

I close my eyes and pull with everything I have. Roots snap and the tree comes loose. I lift it from the earth and sway back and forth for a moment before letting it fall to the ground. Trolls and goblins scatter out of the way as the tree breaks branches as it crashes into the ground in an explosion of dirt and leaves.

I turn around, hands raised over my head and ready to celebrate. My excitement quickly vanishes when I see Kronan sitting on his own downed tree and cleaning his fingernails.

Dammit! I thought I beat him. At least now I know who to call if I ever find myself in need of brute strength.

"Nice try, hero." He laughs. "Kronan has never been bested in a tree pull."

I hate losing, but in this case, I think it's well deserved.

I walk over and grip Kronan on the shoulder. "I'm glad you're on our side."

There's still no sign of Chief Rizza or the others when we say our good-byes. I thought that at least Limery would be here by now. We travel alongside those heading to Lynchton to restock potions and other items.

There are four female trolls who I haven't spent much time with. Feylin, Tezzi, Azra, and Nel carry satchels loaded with items. Their satchels are a much higher quality than anything I've been able to construct myself, but now that I have one with an expandable inside, I doubt I'll ever have need of that skill. I offer to help carry the items, but they turn me down.

"Perhaps you have spent too much time with the human women." Feylin laughs. "We have no need of a gallant hero to ease our burdens."

The others join her in laughter. One thing I can say about the female trolls is that they don't take shit from anyone.

"Hey, Chod. You can carry my things if you want." Taryn holds out his bag and satchel as he rides Stompy.

I pretend to reach for his items, and then shove him off Stompy's back. He falls to the ground, and the trolls laugh even harder.

Thanks to Strong Wind, we make it to the edge of the forest much faster than normal, cutting our time in half. When we step past the tree line, I'm amazed by how busy the road is. Lynchton is far busier than I have ever seen, and people wait to get in.

We make our way to the gate and take our place in line as people enter. We get a few looks, but they seem more curious than hateful.

A familiar face inspects travelers as they pass through.

"Jameson!" I wave at the soldier on gate duty. I hope he's not still pissed about the moulhaug head I left outside the gate the last time I was here.

His old dented armor has been replaced with shimmering new plate mail. He looks up in my direction and does a double-take. After saying something to his partner, he comes out to greet me.

"Chod." He extends a hand, and we shake. "I don't know whether to love you or hate you."

I cock an eyebrow, unsure of what he means. "Why's that?"

"Lynchton has been bustling since we partnered up with the trolls. The inn is packed every night. The market is always full. People come from all over to buy and trade. Things have been so good that the mayor bought us new armor." He flaunts his new armor like a peacock.

"Those sound like good things. What's the problem?"

"What's the problem?" He shakes his head. "The problem is I've never been busier in my life. But what's good for the town is good for me, I suppose. Come on, I'll move you to the front of the line. Bring your friends too. We don't want the trolls selling out of items."

Jameson escorts us to the gate, bypassing the other travelers. We catch a few glares, but no one says anything.

Inside, the market is packed. There are more vendors than ever before. The stables are crowded with horses. The inn is bustling. If I didn't know any better, I'd say we were at the market in Vanaria.

"I'm going to check Stompy and Berry into the stables. Want to meet up at the inn afterward?" asks Taryn.

"Actually, I have a friend I want to say hi to." The stable-boy, Luka, was one of the first friendly faces I met in Lynchton. He lost his brother to one of Glenn's battles with the forest trolls.

I tell Feylin and the others that I will be by shortly, and Taryn and I make our way through the crowd. As people bump into me, I no longer feel like the pariah I was before. I'm just another body in a busy town. Stompy barrels his way through the crowd, and Berry and I follow in his wake. Ruby sits in Taryn's lap, enjoying the view from high up.

At the stable, I find Luka handing the reins of a beautiful black stallion to its owner. He smiles when he sees me.

"Chod, good to see you." He runs his fingers through his curly brown hair.

"You too. We were hoping you had room for Taryn's mounts."

Luka looks up at Stompy and then over to Berry. "You want me to put a moulhaug and a bear in with the horses? Is that safe?"

Taryn offers up a sheepish smile. "They're very well-behaved. Well, most of the time."

Luka ponders for a moment before finally agreeing. "Only because it's you." He looks me in the eye as he opens the gate, and Taryn guides his pets inside.

I pull Luka aside. "Glenn and Jude are still at large. They escaped through the portal that opened in Seascape. I know it's not perfect, and it won't bring your brother back, but they're somebody else's problem for now."

Luka sighs. "Not the news I wanted, but at least they are far away from my friends and family."

"I'm sorry. I just wanted to let you know." I place my hand on his shoulder and offer what consolation I can.

After leaving Stompy and Berry, we head back toward the market. Ruby weaves in and out between people's legs. Every time

I think she may get stepped on, she moves out of the way at the last second, always seemingly one step ahead.

"What was that about?" asks Taryn.

"He lost his brother in one of Glenn's battles." I clench my fist, still angry when I think about it. "An entire family heartbroken because of one asshole's grudge against the trolls."

Taryn glances back over his shoulder. "I'll drop him a little extra tip when I pick them up."

My heart leaps when we finally arrive at the troll tables. Dozens of people wait in line for a chance to buy potions and other items. A small army of imps hover in the air, translating between the humans and trolls.

Lillith, Limery's mother, takes a coin and hands a potion to a woman. The woman walks away with a smile.

I push my way through the crowd until I reach her. When she spots me, she flies over and gives me a hug.

"I was right about you, Chod. You are a curious troll. One that is destined to be a part of my family's affairs." She sits on my shoulder and crosses one leg over the other. "Bazel told me what you did. I'll never be able to repay you for giving me my partner back."

"Don't mention it. Where is he anyhow?"

"Spending some long overdue quality time with Leo. The two are adventuring through some of the lower-level dungeons. Leo has dreams of being a hero, you know." She gives me a knowing look.

"I didn't know that. Have you heard anything from Limery?" If anyone is to know where he's gotten off to, it's Lillith.

"Not since he first passed through the forest. If I'm being honest, I would have expected them back by now. But he's a smart boy, and he's with some of the strongest trolls around. I wouldn't worry too much. Limmy has always been an adventurous spirit." She smiles in the way only a mother can.

"It looks like you are all doing pretty well. Most popular vendor in the market." Even though it's afternoon, the line shows no signs of slowing down.

"This was a truly great idea, Chod. I never would have expected it to be so popular, but now there's talk of expanding to other towns." She gestures out over the crowd. "If you would have told me a few months ago that trolls, imps, and humans would all be in the same place, I'd have been certain it was on a battlefield. But here we are, trading. I have more imp volunteers by the day, more than I can possibly use, and we can't stock Yashi's potions fast enough. It might be time for her to train a few more potion masters."

The success of this venture has me elated. Three societies working together, and all benefitting. I couldn't have imagined my little idea would transform into this.

"Well, I won't keep you. There are plenty of customers waiting to buy your items." I reach in my satchel and pull out the rest of the perception potions I have on hand. "Here, add these to the cause."

She gives me a final hug and returns to the table. "Oh, Chod, you're too good to us. And I wouldn't worry about Limmy. He'll find you."

I nod. I'm sure he will.

Taryn looks around at the chaos surrounding us. He's like a small child lost at the airport, and everyone towers over him. "Dude, this is insane. It's like a completely different town from the last time I was here."

It truly is. And not only are the trolls benefitting, the shops and taverns are thriving as well. It makes me wonder how

Tormara is doing in Vanaria. The hotheaded troll is part of a diplomatic exchange with Vanaria.

I turn back to Taryn. "What do you say we check into the inn? I'm starving and could use a drink."

Taryn's eyes light up. "You beautiful blue monster, you truly know the way to a dwarf's heart."

The porch of The Dancing Donkey is as lively as ever. People sit around drinking and singing. A woman wearing a red tunic plays a guitar and leads the revelers in an ancient song about a griffin that fights against an army of skeletons.

Inside is even busier, and not a single table is empty. The delicious aroma of smoked meat fills the air, and a thick layer of smoke coats the ceiling. We must have arrived just in time for the dinner rush.

I fight my way to the bartender and ask for a room for myself and Taryn.

He frowns. "I'm 'fraid we're nearly full. Only one room left, but if you don't mind sharing a bed, it's all yours."

One of the drunk patrons turns to me. "I bet the little one can sleep between your legs."

Several more people laugh, but I pay them no mind.

Taryn doesn't find it amusing, however. "Actually, I'll reserve it for you since I'll be staying with your wife tonight."

"Why you little—" The man stands up, ready for a drunken brawl, but when I place my massive blue hand on his chest, he thinks twice about it.

"We'll take the room." I slide a few coins across the bar, and he gives me a key.

Inside the room, I'm greeted with a notification.

Welcome to The Dancing Donkey! *You may set your respawn point in your room for as long as you are staying here. Once your stay is*

*over, your respawn point will be reset to its previous location. Would
you like to bind here?*

I agree, doing as Valery told me. I'm not entirely sure when
we'll be pulled from the game, but I imagine we still have a few
hours before it happens.

Ruby curls up in a ball on the bed, making herself at home.

I set my bags down in the corner. "I know you could kick his
ass, but do you really want to start a barfight in here of all places?"

Taryn shrugs. "In the words of my father, 'If you don't start
none, won't be none.'"

"Yeah, yeah, yeah. Let's go see if we can get a bite to eat
among all this madness."

Back downstairs, there's still nowhere to sit. I scan the room,
looking for a friendly face that might share their table with us. I'm
surprised when I spot two tables with heroes sitting at them. Two
of them I recognize from my first days in Mythos. They passed me
while I was camouflaged in the fields outside of Lynchton, back
when my reputation had me targeted on sight. They've leveled up
quite a bit since then.

Randy Billson
Level 26
Rogue
Human

The dark-haired rogue has upgraded his items and clothing as
well. He still wears boiled leather, but his chest is emblazoned
with a silver wolf. His gauntlets have silver accents as well, and he
wears a sword with a red gemstone in the pommel. On his other
hip, he wears a dagger with a silver wolf engraved in the pommel.

He also has several glimmering rings on his fingers. Next to him sits a gray-haired wizard.

Don Othello

>*Level 27*
>*Mage*
>*Human*

The mage wears a dark purple robe. A long gray beard falls across his chest, and I can't help but wonder if the man behind the avatar has one as well. His hands glitter from all the jewelry adorning his fingers.

Clearly, these two have been busy.

Three men sit at a table in the back of the room. One of them points in our direction, and the other two laugh. I focus on the man pointing.

Otis Wiggins

>*Level 27*
>*Barbarian*
>*Human*

Another barbarian! That'll be a nice icebreaker. I wonder if his skills are similar to my own.

The man is clothed in a variety of leathers and furs. A thick, bushy brown beard covers most of his face, while his head is shaved bald. He's a stark contrast to the two men sitting next to him.

Ethan French
> *Level ???*
> *Warlock*
> *Human*

Kevin Harris
> *Level ???*
> *Sorcerer*
> *Human*

Both men have their levels concealed, which isn't surprising considering they are magic users. I'd imagine they are around a similar level to the others, making them more powerful than me and Taryn. It's good to see that most of the other heroes are out actually leveling up instead of being murder hobos like Glenn and Jude.

The warlock has dark skin and sports dreadlocks pulled up into a bun. His face is covered in what resembles tribal tattoos, but I imagine they are somehow part of his chosen class. From what I recall, warlocks are given their power from some other-worldly entity. Not a god, but something similar in power. He wears a black robe, but aside from the amulet around his neck, I can't see any other weapons or items. That doesn't mean they aren't concealed beneath the flowing robe.

Next to him, the sorcerer watches us with amusement. He wears a light gray tunic and a blue cloak. A variety of straps with holsters for potions run across his chest. He wears his hair in a short afro that matches the length of his beard.

"Mind if we join you?" I ask no one in particular, hoping that at least one of the groups will offer us a seat.

The warlock stands up. "I suppose you're the one we have to thank for the mobs running the streets around here."

His voice is so even that I have no idea if he's joking or angry. I decide to be straightforward.

"Yeah, I had a part in it." I suddenly realize that the entire tavern is quiet, watching our exchange.

The warlock stares at me, and I notice his eyes are an eerie red. He bangs his fist on the table. "Well, then let me buy you an ale. The perception potions I've bought from the trolls have saved my life on more than one occasion."

His two partners burst into laughter, and the rest of the tavern returns to a dull roar. Ethan waves to the barmaid and orders a round of drinks.

"Mind if we pull our tables together?" asks Randy the Rogue.

"The more, the merrier." Otis the Barbarian removes his fur coat, revealing a sleeveless leather tunic underneath. His arm muscles are hairy and massive, and they bulge as he lifts the solid wooden table and moves it next to his own.

Taryn and I pull up a seat.

I wave at the group. "Nice to meet you all. This is the most heroes I've seen in one place."

Kevin the Sorcerer leans forward with his elbows on the table. "Ah, yes. You were late to the party." He looks me up and down. "Looks like you've done pretty well for yourself, all things considered."

I shrug. "It was a rough start to begin with. Everyone wanted me dead. I actually hid from these two—" I motion to Randy and Don. "—during my first few days. It wasn't that far from here, actually."

Randy punches Don in the arm. "See, you son of a bitch, I told you I saw a troll that day."

Don raises his hands in defense. "So it seems you did."

"What brings you all to Lynchton?" I ask.

Ethan the Warlock answers. "Same reason as you, I suppose. We're doing our scheduled logout tonight."

That's interesting. I didn't expect them to pull everyone all at once. Maybe they are wanting to test the system with everyone out to see what happens.

The barmaid returns with our drinks and sets them on the table.

Otis the Barbarian lifts his glass. "To Mythos, the best damn punishment I've ever had to endure."

"Cheers to that." I clink my glass against each of them in turn. The ale goes down smooth; it's sweet and malty, reminding me of honey and bananas.

Ethan the Warlock takes a hearty gulp, then focuses back on me. "What I really want to know—" He points a finger and moves it between Taryn and me "—is how the two of you got to be different races?"

I find myself staring at the amulet hanging from his neck. It's made of some black metal with flakes of purple. It's hard to make out, but I'm pretty sure there is a skull engraved into it, with pieces of obsidian for the eye sockets.

The silence draws me back, and I realize they are all staring at me. I'm not ready to tell them what it was that landed me here. I don't know these guys, and even though they may seem nice, I don't trust them just yet. Luckily, Taryn answers before I can.

"Must be because we logged in later. I hear there are even more races available on the other continents."

The group gets excited by that, and I welcome the attention going elsewhere.

"Oh, man, I can't wait to explore some new lands." Randy the Rogue licks his lips at the thought.

Don nods in agreement. "Yep, we're heading to the portal first thing in the morning."

Ethan the Warlock laughs. "I hear Jude and Glenn made it through the portal before they could be caught."

Kevin the Sorcerer slaps his knee. "That's an odd pair if I've ever seen one. Didn't Jude hate Glenn's guts?"

Don shrugs. "I thought Jude hated everyone's guts. Well, except for that paladin he was always with."

Ethan locks eyes with me. "You've got a real way of getting under people's skin, don't you?"

Great, the focus is back on me again. "I like to think I'm a pretty nice guy."

Otis shakes his head. "If you were a nice guy, you wouldn't be here."

Another reminder of what led us all to be here. Well, all of us except Taryn.

We order our dinner and make small talk for the rest of the meal.

Before we go our separate ways for the night, I take the opportunity to try and win them to King Orso's cause.

"We think that a war is coming. That eventually, more portals will open, ones that are not so welcoming. The dark wizard that nearly destroyed this world is still out there. When the time comes, we need you on our side."

Otis flexes his muscles. "What's in it for me?"

Of course he'd ask that. I'm sure that "the safety of innocents" is not a compelling enough answer.

"I'd think that an army of darkness controlled by the most powerful wizard this world has ever seen would have a pretty good loot drop."

A devious smile spreads across the barbarian's face. "Not bad at all." He stands and pushes in his chair. "Catch you guys on the other side."

Eventually, they all leave, until it's just me and Taryn. Most of the room has cleared out now that dinner is over.

"Strange bunch, don't you think?" I ask.

"Yeah, the rogue and the mage seem okay, but those other three, I've got a bad feeling about them." He scrunches his eyebrows.

We can't exactly be beggars and choosers when it comes to getting help. "I mean, they aren't Boy Scouts, but if they can help us when the time comes, I'll take it."

He turns around, watching the warlock as he turns the corner to go upstairs. "Just so long as they don't stab us in the back."

I stand up. "Well, you ready to do this?"

Taryn nods. The time has finally come to be me again.

CHAPTER 26

BACK TO REALITY

I OPEN my eyes to a blue haze. The door to the pod opens above, and the nanite gel level around me decreases. As I sit up, the blue gel drips effortlessly from my body. I don't feel hot or cold, since the nanites are capable of matching the surrounding air perfectly. I cough a few times, expelling the last bit of nanites from my lungs, and then everything feels normal.

I can't explain it, but when I look at my hand as it grips the edge of my pod, it feels different. Maybe I'm expecting to see my massive blue troll arm, or maybe it's because I've been under for so long, but it feels weird. Weak.

"How are you feeling?" Valery's sensual voice calls from beside the pod. She holds a tablet in her hand, tapping it repeatedly. For once, she wears a labcoat over her tight-fitting dress. Several technicians stand behind her, either watching my feed, or with their noses buried in tablets.

"Off," I answer honestly.

She taps the screen again. "That's to be expected. The longer you're in, the more your mind embraces your digital avatar.

277

Everything will feel normal within a few minutes." She looks up from her tablet and her violet eyes pierce into me. "Thanks again. For staying in while we work this out."

"No problem. I'd be lying if I said I haven't grown attached to everyone I've met in there."

She turns to one of the technicians. "Thompson, how is everything looking?"

He swipes at the screen on his tablet. "So far, so good."

"Chad, do you want to get out and stretch your legs?" she asks.

I almost tell her to call me Chod, but then I look down at my body. This isn't the body of a Chod.

I don't really feel like I need to stretch. The nanites have kept my body in great condition, probably better than I'd do on my own. I don't fully understand the science behind it, but they clean and feed, plus they prevent my muscles from atrophying. If I didn't know any better, I'd say I've put on a little muscle mass since I've been under. But that's impossible, right?

Still, I'd like to look around, so I accept her offer. She extends me a hand, helping me out of the pod. I'm wearing nothing but the spandex style underwear, but I've spent so much time wearing a loincloth that it doesn't bother me like it used to.

I look around, expecting to see the other heroes going through the same motions, but they're all in their pods. The room is the same pristine white and gleaming metal that I remember. I bet I could spot a speck of dust if there were any.

"Where is everyone? I thought they were all being pulled tonight?"

"We're doing it in cycles since we don't need as much staff when we do it that way. These are still violent criminals after all." She winks. "Not to mention, you're a special case."

The black pods against the far wall remain empty, all except for one.

"Is that Taryn?" I point at the one black pod filled with nanite gel.

"It is. Want to take a look?"

We walk over to his pod. The feed on the screen shows Taryn sleeping at The Dancing Donkey. I'm lying on the floor next to him. It's weird seeing the digital version of me still in the game. Ruby curls up on the pillow next to Taryn's head.

Looking at Taryn's real body lying in the pod, it's funny to me how the roles are reversed. He's the massive one. Without his shirt on, he could pass for a football player.

"We'll be pulling the rest of them out in batches of two or three, but we wanted to pull you alone after everything that happened last time."

"Do you mind if I look at the others?" I'm curious how some of the players look in real life.

"Be my guest. I'll be over here if you need me. We'll be logging you back in in fifteen." She walks over to the technicians and quickly engages in conversation.

I smile when I look at the pod to my right. Jon the Enchanter lies in a four-poster bed at the castle in Vanaria. He certainly is doing well for himself. He looks remarkably similar to his avatar.

The next two I don't recognize, nor do the rooms look familiar. It makes me wonder how many towns I still have left to explore in *Isle of Mythos*, not to mention all the inns in Vanaria and Seascape. They could be anywhere.

Next, I stop in front of Ethan the Warlock. The tribal tattoos that adorn his avatar are gone, but he does have a small teardrop on one cheek. I always thought that those were just something they added to movies to make characters look tougher. I wonder what he is in for.

Next to him lies Jude. In the pod, Jude is clean shaven and has an athletic body. His chest and arms are covered in a variety of poorly-designed tattoos. Dice on the back of his right hand. A skull on his forearm. There's a woman tattooed over his heart that looks like a child drew it.

On his feed, however, it's a different story. Jude lies on the floor of what looks like a cave, covered in furs. His beard is long and scraggly.

Next to him lies Glenn. They're either still on the run, or they haven't made enough money to afford an inn. They went through the portal in nothing but their starter rags with no weapons and no money.

I'd sympathize with how difficult it must be if not for the fact that they brought it upon themselves.

I call for Valery and she comes over.

"Where are they?" I ask.

She gives me a devious smile. "You know I can't tell you that."

"Isn't it counterproductive to let them go around the game behaving like this? I thought this was all about rehabilitation." It seems to me like they are reinforcing bad behaviors by letting them go free.

"It is. But we aren't the ones who decide what is right or wrong for them. Our psychiatrists come in every day and monitor what is happening, but it is the AI that guides you all. Who am I to say what works and what doesn't? Not every path is straightforward. Sometimes it zigs and zags. Sometimes it goes backward." She looks up at the monitor, focusing on Glenn. "And sometimes it is about the lesser of two evils."

"What about Taryn then? If he's not being rehabilitated, what is the AI doing to him?"

She grins. "That's a good que—"

"Valery, come look at this!" Thompson calls urgently.

I follow her over, eager to know what's going on.

"What is it?" she asks.

"The system, it's acting up again. I don't know why. I thought we had everything in order this time, but it's going haywire. Respawn timers are off again, and it looks like something is going on with the portals."

I almost feel bad that the news offers me relief. This is their job, and yet I'm secretly hoping it fails just so I can stay in the world they created. But it's not just their world anymore. It's mine. It's the other heroes. And more important than anything, it belongs to the people who live there.

"Dammit, Thompson, I thought you had this figured out." Her words have a bite to them that I haven't witnessed before.

"I thought we did, but we need to get him back in there before something irreversible happens."

"Looks like the tour is over, kid." She gestures toward my pod. "We'll pull you again when we've figured this out."

This time, I give her a wink. "Don't rush it. I'm quite enjoying myself."

She laughs. "I'll make sure to put that on the recruitment posters."

I climb into the pod, and she closes the lid. There's a slight whir as the pod fills up with nanites. When the blue gel covers my face, I take a deep breath, and everything goes black.

CHAPTER 27
PLAYERS REVEALED

I'M the first one to wake up the next morning. I wipe the sleep from my eyes and am flooded with relief when I see my blue troll hands.

Ruby looks down at me from atop the bed with her small paws curled over the edge and her snout buried between them. I quickly get up and shake Taryn. I'm eager to know what his experience logging out was like.

He wipes the sleep from his eyes. "Just five more minutes, mom."

I shake him again. "Dude, wake up! Tell me what happened."

His eyes go wide. "Oh, right, we logged out. Everything was normal for me. I called my family, though they weren't happy it was this middle of the night. Since I'm here of my own free will and can leave at any time, I don't think it's the same as if I were in prison. How'd it go for you?"

"It was fine for a few minutes, then the system crashed again. I have no idea why."

He sits up and swings his legs over the side of the bed, but they don't touch the ground. "Man, that's weird. You think it has something to do with why you're blue?"

I shrug. I am the only one who jumped directly into an open mana source. It's possible that the mana that fuels all the magic on the island is also integral to coding. "I don't have the faintest idea. It has to be something I did if it's not happening to anyone else. Did you feel different when you logged out at all? Like your body felt weird?"

Taryn looks down at his hands like he's examining them. "Yeah, for a bit, but Valery said it was normal."

I sit beside him on the bed, and it creaks under my weight. "Something felt off for me too. I kept expecting to be my troll self. And maybe I'm crazy, but it felt like my body was in better shape than when I logged in."

Taryn laughs. "Well, that's probably because it's not being fed soda, chips, and candy bars for three meals a day."

I roll my eyes. "I don't mean like that. It felt like my body had put on muscle. I've never been one to go to the gym, but it felt like I had some definition to my body. Not a lot, but more than I've had before."

Taryn climbs down from the bed and starts getting dressed. "I don't know. I wouldn't put anything past those nanites. If they can make us experience this, why can't they improve our bodies?"

It's a sobering thought. I close my eyes and try to push it from my mind.

"Speaking of bodies..." Taryn rubs his stomach. "I'm hungry. Let's go grab a bite to eat."

We gather our things and head downstairs. The inn is already full, but we take a seat with Don the Mage and Randy the Rogue. We order breakfast from the barmaid and catch up with the others.

"Morning, fellas. Where are you off to today?" I ask.

Randy bites into a sausage and the juices trickle down his chin. It smells delicious as it wafts across the table. "I think we're heading to Vanaria. We're interested in the new portals. It's time to explore what else Mythos has to offer. Besides, we need to level up if we're going to help you with the big bad wizard." He winks.

"What about you?" asks Don.

"Same, but we're taking the portal to Seascape. We need to meet with the king, then we have some unfinished business in Goldspire. Have you seen the others?" I ask, referring to the three heroes we met the night before.

Randy wipes the sausage grease from his face. "They were out of here early. Looked to be in a pretty big hurry." He leans forward. "If I'm being honest, I don't trust those three. They've got a weird way about them. They aren't as reckless as Glenn or Jude, but I'd never turn my back to them if I could help it."

I wonder if there's any truth to his statement, or if it's just paranoia because he knows them outside of the game.

Our breakfast arrives, and the conversation comes to a halt as we stuff our faces. Before Taryn and I are finished eating, Randy and Don get up and leave, wishing us luck on our travels.

We finish our breakfast and head outside. Before leaving Lynchton, I stop by the troll table at the market. Bazel and Leo are there this time, helping Lillith translate for the trolls.

"Chod, fancy seeing you here!" Bazel offers a big smile, displaying all his sharp teeth.

"Glad to see you're doing well. Good to see you again, too, Leo."

The small red imp with a tuft of black hair flies over and wraps his arms around me. "Thank you for freeing my father."

"No thanks needed." I turn to Bazel and Lillith. "Still no word from Limery?"

"That boy always had a will of his own," laughs Bazel. "He'll be around when he's good and ready."

I'm certain I'll see him again, but that does little for the pocket of imp-shaped emptiness I feel when I think about him. "Well, let him know we are heading back to Seascape. We're going to pass through Vanaria, since it's shorter. So who knows, maybe we'll run into him on the way."

I say good-bye to the trolls, and we pick up Stompy and Berry from the stables. And just like that, we're back on the road again.

While I'm sad I didn't get to see Chief Rizza and the others, I can take solace in the fact that Lynchton is thriving. Things are looking up for the trolls. Maybe they'll be lucky and King Orso's prediction will be wrong. Maybe there won't be a war at all.

I wave at Jameson as we pass through the gate.

"Take care, Chod." He waves back.

We travel in silence for the first few miles. Eventually, the thoughts in my head are too much to manage.

"Do you think I should be worried?" I ask.

Taryn looks at me, confused. "About what?"

"Limery. I know he can take care of himself, but after what happened to his father, it makes me nervous."

Taryn nods. "I know you care for him, so it makes sense to worry, but that little guy has more spunk than the rest of his family combined. And from what you've told me about the others, good luck to anyone who tries to take them on."

That makes me feel a little better. With Taryn using Strong Wind, we make fantastic time. We camp for the night underneath a bridge.

As I settle in for the night, Taryn can't stop grinning.

I don't engage with him, because I already know what he's going to say.

"Oh, come on." He shoves me in the shoulder. "You have to see the humor in this. You're a troll sleeping under a bridge, for crying out loud. There have been stories written about this for ages."

I decide to shut him up. "Remember that time I tossed you to the second floor of that dungeon? That was humorous."

As I fall asleep, I hear him muttering something about paying the troll toll.

"Chod!"

Taryn's screams wake me before they are abruptly cut off. I open my eyes to see him bound by a glowing purple chain. It wraps around his body several times, pinning his arms to his sides. Three figures shrouded in a dark aura stand behind him. The aura conceals their features, but the center figure's eyes radiate a fiery crimson.

Berry stands back a few feet, snarling, while Stompy huffs and puffs beside him.

I make to stand, but the center figure moves forward.

"I wouldn't do that if I were you." The voice is distorted, but it sounds vaguely familiar.

It's still night out, so whoever this is must have waited until we made camp. But what do they want? Did they follow us from Lynchton, or just happen to see us on the road? The fact that Taryn is still alive means that they want more than just our items.

I try to focus on the figures, but whatever darkness it is that conceals their identities is also blocking me from analyzing them.

"What do you want?" I stare at them with defiance, refusing to let them rattle me.

Taryn's eyes are wide as he stares at me. The more I look at the chain, the clearer it becomes that it's magical. It's possible that the spell binding him in place is keeping him from communicating as well.

"It's not about what I want. There are bigger pieces in play here." The figure steps closer. "Stop your foolish attempts to unite the heroes. Nothing but death and destruction will come of it, for you and for all those you hold dear. Go and explore. Become rich and powerful and stay in the forest where you belong."

How do they know about my plans?

I can't shake the feeling that I know this person. I focus on them, looking for anything that might reveal their identities. Even with the shrouds, the figures still maintain their body types. The figure on the left is stocky, with broad shoulders and a wide neck. The center figure is taller than the other two. When I gaze into those flaming red eyes, I realize where I've heard that voice before. He's Ethan French, the warlock. That would make the figure to the right Kevin Harris, the sorcerer, and the stocky one is Otis Wiggins, the barbarian.

So Randy was right about these three. I take a deep breath, hoping that this isn't as bad as it looks. I don't know why they have an issue with me uniting the heroes, but I aim to find out.

"You can cut it with the smoke and mirrors. I know who you are." I keep my voice steady. Calm.

The shroud fades, revealing the three heroes I shared dinner with the night before.

Ethan steps toward me. The fire has faded from his red eyes. "Well, you're not as dumb as you look."

I grunt. "Why do you have a problem with me uniting the heroes?"

He turns his back to me, and I have the urge to attack him. That would be bad, though. Taryn is bound, and the three of them greatly out-level me. I have to play along and hope I can talk my way out of this.

"I don't have a problem with it." He turns back around. "Unfortunately, the being that gives me my powers does. So either you can call off this whole charade, or we can do the same thing to you that you did to Glenn. Then we'll see what kind of an army a level-one troll can raise."

Otis tilts his head back and laughs. Stupid barbarian.

Taryn struggles against his chains. Kevin the Sorcerer squeezes his fist, and they cinch tighter. Taryn grimaces, and I have to fight the urge to engage. Okay, so the sorcerer has the binding spell, and the warlock has the shroud. Good to know.

"There's no need to do this. Just let us go, and no one has to know." I'll try bargaining for my first attempt.

He shakes his head. "It's not that easy. If I piss off my patron, I lose my abilities. Without my abilities, what am I doing here?"

The familiar tightness in my forehead right before I lose my cool makes an appearance. "So, what, you're going to ruin the lives of thousands of people just so you can get what you want?"

"Thousands of people?" He laughs darkly. "You act like they are real. If I'm going to be here, then I'm going to have fun while I'm doing it."

"And how exactly do you plan to enforce this demand of yours?" I ask.

He kneels, smirking at me. "That's not my role. I'm here to deliver the message. We're going to kill you, take your items, and make sure you remember the consequences of your actions. If you keep it up, maybe you see us again, maybe you don't, but you'll always be looking over your shoulder."

It takes everything in me not to punch him in the face. "Looks like I don't have much of a choice."

He stands up, smiling. "Now you're getting it."

"So what now?"

"Now, we get out from under this bridge and you take your

punishment in the open like a man. I have a new ability I've been dying to try. You and your friend here will both die, and we will all learn a valuable lesson." He motions for me to stand. "Don't try anything stupid."

I glance at Berry and Stompy. Ruby must have found somewhere to hide.

"What about Taryn's pets?"

Ethan shrugs. "Not my call. The boss wants this message to stick."

My vision goes red. It's one thing to harm me or Taryn over this, but to kill his pets. That's over the line. They won't come back.

As quick as I can, I equip Destroyer and swing for his head. Before the warhammer is even halfway to him, he blasts me in the chest with a bolt of black energy. It takes out a chunk of my health and knocks me off my feet.

Otis and Kevin both burst into laughter.

I clench my throbbing chest. Whatever he hit me with burned through my skin.

Ethan stands over me. "You don't have to make this hard. But if you want to, we can make this very difficult for you."

I crawl to my feet. "Bring it on."

I charge at him with my weapon raised. His eyes flare a bright red, and he lifts one hand, shooting another bolt of energy into me. It knocks me back, taking out another huge chunk of health and dropping me to seventy percent HP. I stand again just as a streak of purple energy shoots out from his other hand.

The purple beam hits me, but nothing happens. A second later, pain flares through my entire body as my health drops another fifteen percent. A bulb of energy shoots from my body and trails back to the warlock.

As Ethan absorbs the energy, his face softens for a fraction of a second. He just stole my health!

I summon a horror and toss it at Ethan, exploding it right in front of his face. The warlock's health drops by a fraction.

He looks over his shoulder at Kevin. "Don't let that happen again."

I summon another horror and repeat the action. This time, the sorcerer raises his free hand and a forcefield emerges in front of Ethan, absorbing the explosion.

"Much better." Ethan cracks his knuckles.

Three attacks and I've lost almost half my health. There's no way I'm making it out of this alive. I'm sure Taryn knows it too. If I'm going to die, then I'm going to do my best to make sure Taryn's pets escape.

"Stompy, Berry, I need you to run! We'll find you when this is over." I don't wait to see if they listen. Right now, I need to become the biggest distraction possible.

I cast Champion, and the Gnoll Pack Lord appears in front of me. I also summon a round of horrors. I can't best Ethan with melee, but maybe my summons can do better.

The pack lord equips his bow and fires an arrow at the warlock. It bounces off of Kevin's forcefield.

"Is that the best you've got?" His eyes flare red again.

I notice his hand glow purple right before the energy shoots out, giving me just enough time to equip the Halite Shield. Its translucent material allows me to block the attack without losing visibility. The beam of energy ricochets off the shield and crashes into the embankment.

The warlock curses. "Dammit, the pets are gone. Otis, handle this while I go chase them down."

Suddenly, shadowy wings sprout from the warlock's back, and he takes to the air. Otis walks toward me with a giant shit-eating grin. He swings a massive axe a few times, and the sharp blade whistles in the air.

"This is going to be fun." He kisses the head of his axe and charges me.

The gnoll shoots another arrow, but the sorcerer blocks it again. My horrors charge, and Otis cuts through them without slowing.

I toss the shield away and equip Destroyer. I'll come back for the shield later. We run at each other, and our weapons clash together in an explosion of sparks.

Otis furrows his brow, clearly confused as to why he didn't just demolish me. He might out-level me, but considering my racial bonuses per level, I'd say we're on a pretty even playing field. If I can handle Kronan, I can handle this piece of shit.

He swings again, and again I meet his blow, only this time I have a stack of Inferno on my weapon. A few more and it might actually make a difference.

The pack lord switches to his spear and stabs Otis in the leg. The barbarian falls to one knee, but still manages to parry my attack.

"A little help here," he calls to the sorcerer.

Kevin grunts. "Useless barbarian."

The sorcerer leaves Taryn, but the chain that binds him stays attached to the sorcerer as he walks. He makes a motion with his hands, and then green gas rises from the ground around me. It obstructs my vision, and then my lungs burn and my eyes sting. My health ticks down each second. It must be some sort of poisonous gas.

I turn to run, but something wraps around my feet, and I fall to the ground.

A moment later, a sharp pain flares through my side. When I

touch the wound, all I feel is wetness. My health drops even further.

The poison gas fades, and I witness the massive gash that runs along my side from an axe blade. Blood pours freely from the wound.

I've failed again. And this time, everyone pays.

I activate Berserker Rage to stop the blood loss, and the chains release from my feet—I can't be slowed or stunned by spells while it's active. Still, it won't be enough. Otis raises his battle-axe overhead, and I accept my fate.

A ball of fire shoots through the darkness and smashes Otis into the embankment.

"You no hurts Chods!" Limery's skin is molten lava as he wraps his tiny hands around Otis's neck. He bares his teeth, and pure violence emanates from his small frame. The air shimmers around his scorching body.

Even in such dire circumstances, my heart jumps at the sight of the small imp.

The barbarian's health ticks down second by second as Limery burns him alive.

There's a loud roar to my right as a massive wyrm descends into the ravine. Chief Rizza rides on its back, her braid whipping behind her as blue flames pour from the wyrm's mouth. The sorcerer abandons his chains on Taryn and focuses all his energy into a forcefield to block the flames. Fire pours around the forcefield, scorching the earth to both sides.

Otis goes into a rage and rips Limery from his throat. He tosses the imp away, but Limery rights himself mid-air and conjures fireballs in both hands.

"I am so fucking glad to see you! Let's finish this asshole."

Limery smiles at me, and I feel like I can take on the world. "Limmy's on it!" He hurls both fireballs at Otis.

The barbarian absorbs the attack as his rage rapidly heals him, but the fire burns all the hair off his face. Something rattles to my left, and I turn to see Gord as he jumps down with the dwarven axe, Peacemaker, slung over his shoulder. He looks like a being straight out of hell wearing his bone armor that rattles with his every movement.

"Help with the sorcerer. Limery and I have this one," I call.

Gord nods and rushes into battle alongside the chief.

Taryn scrambles past me in a panic. "I need to save my pets."

A second later, the forest troll shaman, Jira, arrives and sets off in pursuit of Taryn.

"We'll be right behind you." I turn to Limery. "Flame wall!"

The imp erupts a wall of flame on both sides of Otis, leaving him no escape. I pick up Destroyer and march towards him. The flames lick at both of us, but I ignore the burn. It's nothing compared to the rage inside of me.

Otis snarls at me and charges. Our weapons clash, and sparks fly. On his next attack, I duck, leaving him swinging at air. The momentum sends him spinning, and I kick him hard in the back. He falls forward and I bring Destroyer down on his head.

He wobbles back and forth, dazed from the blow. A blazing heat presses against my back, and I turn to see Limery with a mega fireball raised above his head. I step out of the way and let him unleash hell.

When the fire dissipates, all that remains are Otis's clothing and items.

I find Gord standing over the sorcerer's body, pulling his axe from his back. A moment later, the body vanishes, but there's no time for a reunion.

"We need to help Taryn! The warlock is trying to kill his pets."

They don't question who Taryn is or why they should help him. Instead, they rush into battle by my side, because that is what family does. When you're desperate for help, they help—no questions asked.

We climb the embankment and sprint down the road. I hear Stompy's trumpet carrying across the night. A bolt of lightning crashes in the distance.

"That's where we need to go!" I point.

Chief Rizza takes off ahead of us on her wyrm.

"Limery, go ahead. We'll catch up."

The imp zooms off like a bat out of hell.

My lungs burn as Gord and I sprint to catch up. We arrive just in time to see Ethan facing off against Taryn, Jira, Limery, and Chief Rizza. Stompy and Berry both lay on the ground, neither one of them moving.

"It's over, Ethan." I step up beside my friends. "Your buddies are dead. Just leave and let us heal his pets."

The warlock's eyes blaze a vibrant red. "I can't do that."

"You can. No one else has to get hurt."

He laughs maniacally. "You don't understand."

Berry groans in pain, and Taryn rushes forward. Ethan shoots a blast of dark energy at the dwarf, stopping him in his tracks.

"I said no!" The warlock hovers in the air on wings of shadow. "They will die, and my message will be delivered."

I take a step closer. "That's not going to happen."

His lips curl up in disgust. "And who's going to stop me?"

"I will." Chief Rizza moves her wyrm closer, and a stream of smoke shoots out of its nostrils.

"And me." Gord lifts his axe in the air.

"As will I." Jira steps forward calmly, his white-tipped dreads swaying.

"Mees, too." A fireball crackles to life in Limery's palms.

"Then so be it." The warlock's eyes blaze brighter than I have ever seen.

He presses his hands together, and two massive balls of shadow form between him and us. They pulse with dark energy. The shadow is so black that it seems to swallow the light around it. A black clawed hand emerges from within the darkness. Then another. They grip at the edge of the shadow until a demonic face pokes through. A demonic being with a head that resembles a horse's skull peeks through. The demon climbs from the shadow and stands on long hoofed feet. It unfurls the same shadowy wings that keep Ethan aloft, and its eye sockets burst to life with blue fire.

An identical creature emerges from the second shadow.

Shadow Demon. *Level ???*

Chief Rizza gasps beside me, and I instinctively take a step back. What the hell are those things? They have no level, and no description, and I'm pretty sure they're not from this plane of existence.

Tears stream down Taryn's face as he looks at his pets, helpless to save them. I know this is tearing him apart.

I need to rally them, but is it worth losing Rizza or Limery for this? What am I even saying? Of course it is. Taryn cares for his pets just as much as I care for the trolls.

"We have to fight, or his pets don't have a chance." I summon a horror and toss it at one of the flying demons. A foot from hitting the one on the right, the horror explodes into smoke, only I didn't cast Kamikaze.

Taryn summons a lightning bolt. It comes crashing from the sky, but it explodes before reaching the demon. It's like they have some kind of shadowy forcefield protecting them.

"It's over," says Ethan.

Chief Rizza's wyrm unleashes a stream of fire, but it never makes contact. The blue flames curl around this invisible barrier, lighting the night sky. Even Limery's fireballs have no effect.

The demons raise their arms, and shadow blades form in their hands. They swipe them, and I feel a chill through my body. The next thing I know, half my health is gone.

"They're shadow blades." Taryn grimaces. "The same as mine."

Weapons that can't be blocked by armor or magic. We're screwed. My instincts tell me to run, but there's no way I could live with myself if I left Taryn's pets to die like this.

I equip Destroyer and prepare to go out in a blaze of glory, but the chanting next to me stays my attack. Jira stands with his eyes closed, repeating the same phrase over and over. I don't know what he's up to, but the shaman's health is almost completely depleted from the attack.

Ethan looks at him and laughs. "Give it up, old man. No one can stand against the shadows."

Jira's eyes open, and he spreads his arms wide. A red aura surrounds them, and he brings his hands together in a clap. As his hands meet, a fiery phoenix explodes from his palms and takes off toward the shadow demons.

I've seen this ability before, back in the forest the first time I fought Glenn. The phoenix absorbed all the flames from the burning forest, growing stronger with each one. But there's no fire here. At least he tried. At least we all tried.

The phoenix soars toward the demons, a fraction of the attack I witnessed before. It opens its beak and caws. I wince as a shrill shriek cuts through the air from above. The demons flinch at the sound, and their focus moves upward. A second later, the air grows stifling, and I'm reminded of the cave where I found Limery's dad.

The demons raise their swords, but not at Jira's phoenix. They point them overhead.

My night vision fades as the area around me is showered in

light. I look up to see fire made flesh as a real, live phoenix barrels down from the sky. Her wings are tucked as she dives like a falcon, and streams of red, orange, yellow, and blue fire trail behind her.

She screeches again, and fire consumes the phoenix as she engulfs the shadow demons. The demons howl in distorted tones as the fire consumes them, and Ethan cries out as he is burned alive.

In an instant, it's over, and we're all covered in ash. I don't know what the hell just happened, and right now, I don't care. Taryn rushes to Berry and casts Restoration. I go to Stompy and gently pet him until Taryn is done. He breathes heavily beneath my touch.

Nobody talks until both pets are fully healed. Once they are both back on their feet, Ruby emerges from the darkness and nuzzles against Taryn's leg. She has a real knack for getting out of dangerous situations. Taryn presses his head to Stompy's jaw, and I give them their space. I can't even imagine what he is feeling right now.

I turn to Jira. "Jira, what in the actual hell was that? That was a real phoenix you called into battle."

He looks at me intently, and I remember how unsettling his red pupils are. "The phoenix is my totem. For the longest time, I felt her dwelling in the mountains, but recently, she has been on the move. The phoenix is the enemy of darkness, and when she felt their presence, she was compelled to assist us."

Chief Rizza climbs down from her wyrm. "She did far more than assist. She is likely the only reason we are all still alive. I have never seen such creatures on the island."

Something stirs beneath the ashes, and Gord raises his axe in alarm. A patch the size of a baseball shakes until a tiny, hairless head pokes through. It opens its beak and squawks.

A tiny reborn phoenix. She sacrificed herself to save us.

Limery flies down to the creature and cups it against his chest. "Look, Chods. Its is a baby."

The small phoenix nuzzles into Limery, no doubt feeling the natural heat that radiates from his body.

"What should we do with it?" asks Chief Rizza.

Jira steps forward and takes the phoenix from Limery. "I will see that she is taken care of."

I can't help but notice the trace of a smile on the wizened shaman's face.

Taryn finally joins us. When he speaks, his eyes glisten. "Thank you all. I would have lost them if not for you. That is something that I can never repay, but I will do my best."

Chief Rizza gives him a loving smile. "You owe us nothing. We will always go to battle for our own and the causes that are important to them."

Taryn just nods. I can tell that he's fighting back tears. I don't blame him. Just because the trolls are monstrous doesn't mean they aren't loving, caring, and willing to fight for each other.

I introduce Taryn to everyone, and then I ask the question I've been dying to know. "Where the hell were you all? I went to the forest expecting to see you days ago. There's no way it should have taken you that long to get back from Vanaria."

She laughs, lightening the mood. "I'm sorry to have inconvenienced you. There was a festival in the city. Once Gord opened the portal, we spent time enjoying the celebrations. Now tell me, how did this come to pass?" She gestures to the devastation surrounding us.

I tell them about the meeting with other heroes at the inn, and how we were attacked at night. To give them more context, I tell them about King Orso's prediction, what he believes waits on the other side of the portals, and how Ethan's patron is likely a part of it.

"King Orso wants to call a meeting with Favian and the other leaders from the lands across the opened portals." I look Chief Rizza in the eye. "You should come."

She shakes her head. "I'm no king."

"No, but you're the leader of two tribes of trolls. If you don't speak for them, who will?"

"He is right." Gord nods, and his nose ring catches the moonlight. "It is time to claim our place at the table."

"Spoken like a true councilman." I say it just to tease Gord, and sure enough, his cheeks flush.

Deep down, I know he is proud to have a seat on the council. "Oh, and I almost forgot! Limery, we found your father. He's waiting for you in Lynchton."

The imp's bulbous yellow eyes go even wider. "You dids? You found Daddy?"

I smile. "We did. I underst—"

Limery plows into me, wrapping his arms around my neck. "Oh, Chods!"

"I understand if you need to go see him. I'm sure he will be glad to see you after so long, but Taryn and I have to go to Seascape. You can come find us when you're done."

Limery shakes his head. "No, Limmy goes with Chods. Limmy will see Daddy later."

"Are you sure? I promise I won't mind."

"Limmy is sure. Chods needs Limmy." He takes a seat on my shoulder.

That might be the truest thing I've ever heard.

"It's settled then. We'll leave for Vanaria in the morning."

CHAPTER 28
VALMAR WORREN

We take turns keeping watch for the remainder of the night, and at daybreak, we hit the road. Chief Rizza talks to me about the progress with Lynchton, while her wyrm scouts ahead. The pride is evident in her voice as she details her plans for the future, which include trading with other towns. No wonder Kronan follows her. She's a natural leader in every way.

Jira and Limery take turns feeding the baby phoenix, and it plucks worms as they dangle them from their fingers. Tiny orange feathers have already sprouted on her small bobblehead.

Taryn keeps to himself for most of the journey. I think for the first time, he realizes there is a real chance he could lose his pets. Last night was terrifying for us all, but I think it shocked him to his core. As long as I've known him, I've never seen Taryn panic like that.

We see the towering castle of Vanaria long before the rest of the city. The keep in the center shimmers with a pearlescent sheen—the blessed stone is the one place on the island where the undead cannot set foot. The spires of the castle rise high into the sky and disappear among the clouds. Eventually, we crest a hill and the rest of the city comes into view with its obsidian walls that gleam with a dark fervor, daring anyone to challenge their protective power. Atop them, the city watch patrols in their silver-and-blue armor.

I still remember the first time we came here, back when our only goal was acceptance. Now we strive for something greater. Unity.

The captain of the city watch greets us as we cross the bridge and enter the city. "Back so soon?" he asks Rizza.

"We're traveling to Seascape. It's of great importance."

He nods. "Very well. I'll have some of my men escort you."

Four guards with gleaming plate mail and billowing cloaks usher us through the city streets. Their weapons are pristine, and the spear tips are sharpened to a razor's edge. I wonder how many of them have seen actual combat.

We pass through the dirty cobblestone of Rat Row and into the inner bailey. My thoughts drift briefly to Hawkin and the Underground Circus. Where could they possibly be right now?

The market bustles with activity. Guards surround the portal, questioning everyone before they enter. I watch as a wealthy couple steps into the portal and disappears. A moment later, an ivory dwarf appears out of nowhere and vanishes into the crowd.

Our guard detail speaks to those around the portal and they motion for us to step forward.

"Focus on the rune for Seascape, and then step through one at a time."

Chief Rizza takes the lead. The rune for Seascape glows a bright red, and then she steps into the portal. In the blink of an eye, her body vanishes. One by one, we follow. Taryn rides through on Stompy, leaving me and Limery as the last two.

I step into the swirling white portal with Limery on my shoulder, and the next thing I know, I'm in the Seascape square. Dozens of armed guards patrol the square. The vibe here is vastly different from Vanaria. In Vanaria, the city bustles with opportunity and adventure. Here, the air feels restless. After what happened with Glenn and Jude, I don't blame them for being on alert.

When the guards see me, they offer to take our pets to the stables and allow us access to the stairs leading to the castle. Chief Rizza is reluctant to leave her wyrm, but I assure her it is in good hands. At the top of the stairs, one of the kingsguard waits to escort us inside.

The massive twin doors to the castle open, and Kurzol, the blood dwarf cleric, waits on the other side.

"You're late." He frowns. "Follow me."

Late? I scratch my chin. I didn't know we had a standing appointment.

Kurzol leads us into the throne room, where King Orso is talking to his advisors. He looks in our direction as we enter.

Taryn drops to a knee, and I follow suit in a gesture of respect, but the others remain standing. He's not their king, after all.

"Chod, Taryn, I see you've brought guests." The king's face gives nothing away.

I stand. "This is Chief Rizza, leader of the forest and mountain trolls; Jira, the village shaman; and Gord, a member of the troll council. They have come to aid Seascape, and discuss plans for what is to come."

King Orso's lips curl at the edges. "Very well. You have arrived just in time then. Several other great leaders wait for me in my private council chamber. Kurzol will escort you there, and I will be along shortly."

We follow the cleric down a long hallway and up several sets of stairs until we come upon an old wooden door. Aside from the fact that guards from several different races wait in the hallway, nothing would give away that this is where the king has his most important meetings.

The guards move aside as Kurzol escorts us into the room. Down the hall, I spot Warwick, the captain of King Favian's kingsguard, with his hand on his sword. Always the watchful guardian.

Inside, there's a round table filled with leaders and their councils. King Favian nods at us from across the table, dressed in his most stately attire. He wears a blue tunic with a silver griffin embroidered into the chest. Next to him sits Kassidy, munching on an apple.

"Don't be shy, take a seat." Kassidy motions to a row of empty chairs next to him. Chief Rizza and Jira take a seat, while Gord, Taryn, and myself stand. Limery sits perched on my shoulder.

As we wait for King Orso, I use the opportunity to take in the other leaders. Their levels are all concealed, and I wonder if King Orso can see them since it is his castle.

Next to King Favian, two gnomes lean in close together, deep in conversation. They look like tiny humans, but with big noses, and a short limb-to-body ratio. They are clad in vibrant greens and wear jeweled rings on every finger.

Beside them, a centaur anxiously paces back and forth, his hooves clopping against the stone floor. The human half of his body wears brilliant golden armor. A second centaur gazes out the far window overlooking the ocean.

Next to them, a group of catfolk wearing fine silk rap their claws against the wooden table.

There are also lizardfolk, merpeople, and halflings, but my observations are cut short when King Orso enters the room followed by two blood dwarves, an ivory dwarf, and Lady Brollen, the ebony dwarf from Sandholde.

The other leaders all stand as he enters. King Orso nods to

them and takes a seat next to Chief Rizza. Everyone else follows suit.

"Thank you all for coming. It is good to know that Seascape still has allies after all these years. We may not know one another, but our ancestors fought together in ages past. It is an honor to have you in Seascape."

The centaur's feet clop in agitation. "Get on with it. Why is it you have called us all here?"

King Orso pauses for a second. "Right, it is best to get to the point. After all, much is at stake." He takes a deep breath. "The short of it is that I fear for our safety, not only of my people but for all of Mythos. How long will it be before the other portals open? And what monstrosities wait on the other side? The majority of the portals that remain closed were conquered by the dark wizard when he last sought to bring the world under his rule. The day will come when he attacks again, and we should all be ready."

One of the catfolk leans forward. When she speaks, her voice has a very sensual quality to it. It reminds of Valery, actually.

"While Seascape's portal has only recently opened, the portal in Antadale has been open for many years. We have witnessed the other portals opening and the world expanding. Every time a new portal opens, there are the same fears, the same worries. But the dark wizard is dead. His army was defeated. There is no point in preparing for a war that will never come."

"How do you know he is dead?" asks one of the gnomes in a high-pitched voice. "None of us were there. Most of the histories have been lost to time, and the ones that remain are glorified tales that cannot be trusted as fact. Only the elves have the lifespans to remember those days, and they all hide behind the portal to Mosstar."

The feline cuts her eyes at the gnome. "If he were there, he would not have waited this long to attack. What possible reason would he have to wait?"

King Favian responds. "The last time the dark wizard was seen was in the Age of Heroes. After he was defeated and sealed off all the portals, there were no more heroes within Mythos. But now, here they are again. If he has word that the heroes have returned, he will attack before they grow too strong. Are you willing to bet the lives of your people on your own arrogance?"

The catfolk hisses at Favian, and the entire room goes into an uproar. King Orso beats his fist on the table to regain order.

"Enough! We are here as allies to discuss the future of our kingdoms. The least we can do is treat one another with respect." He motions to Kurzol, and the cleric brings a massive tome, placing it on the table in front of Orso. "Most recountings of the last great battle with the dark wizard have been lost to history, it is true, but after scouring our ancient libraries, I found this."

He flips the book open and turns to a page near the end. "The rise and fall of Valmar Worren, the dark elf necromancer of Mosstar." King Orso clears his throat, reading from the ancient book. "We are not sure when the rise of Valmar first began. The elves always were an isolated people, and by the time that Valmar rose to power, it was already too late to save the elves from one of their own. After conquering Mosstar, Valmar set his sights on Blacktide, home of the seafaring orcs. Whether through magic or brute force, we do not know, but he won the orcs to his cause. Next, he conquered Grimsbay and the werepeople joined his ranks. With those powerful societies on his side, he ventured to the Shadowlands, and that is where he found the demons and shadowpeople that gave him the confidence to invade the mainland.

"Those were the last kingdoms he allied with, but that was

not the end of his reign. Word of his conquest spread far and wide, and the dark races flocked to his cause. The giants and ogres rallied on foreign shores, eagerly awaiting Valmar when he arrived. When he tricked the imps into joining his service, all was feared to be lost."

The entire table glances in Limery's direction. I scowl back at them, knowing all too well what it's like to be judged just for your race.

King Orso continues, "As his army grew, so did his power. One by one, he conquered kingdoms and nations, driving race after race from their ancestral homes. He raised the corpses of the defeated, adding them to his own ranks. Before anyone could stop him, he had conquered half of Mythos. And while many of us banded together, Vanaria clung to itself. The most powerful cleric in Mythos resided in Vanaria, and the Vanarian king commissioned him to create a blessed tower where no undead could set foot in its shadow.

"The dwarves left the island to fight, but the humans remained. The Vanarian king wanted to protect his people, and almost cost us everything. Countless lives were lost as the living battled the dark and the dead on the plains of Wandermere. When hope was nearly lost, the Vanarians arrived, and the king flew in on the back of a griffin. The Vanarian army helped to turn the tide. The heroic cleric rained holy light down on the battlefield, destroying the undead and forcing Valmar to retreat to Mosstar. As we set off in pursuit, the portals closed, blocking our chase. Over the coming days, the portals of Isle of Mythos closed, barring our contact with the outside world. Great creatures have risen in the depths of the sea, making sea travel impossible. I cannot begin to speculate on the fates of those across the sea."

King Orso closes the book. "That is the only recounting we have found of the actual events. We almost lost everything to the darkness because the Vanarian king waited behind the safety of his walls."

King Favian shifts uncomfortably in his seat.

"We cannot afford to let that happen again. We must present a united front and destroy this evil once and for all."

The outspoken catfolk shakes her head. "That was hundreds of years ago. It was a terrible time, that much is true, but those days are long gone. We have prospered for many years. What evidence do you have that there is anything out there that wishes us harm?"

King Orso opens his mouth, but I cut him off.

"I've seen it." I gesture toward Chief Rizza and the others. "We have all seen that there is more at play."

"And who are you?" asks the catfolk.

I stand up straight and speak with all the authority I can muster. "I am Chod, hero of the forest trolls. And I have witnessed first-hand the dark powers that you believe no longer exist. I witnessed a warlock, bound to a hidden patron, summon shadow demons on the island. He demanded I stop my attempts to unite the heroes. This Valmar, if he doesn't know already, will know soon that heroes have returned to Mythos. And he will do everything in his power to destroy us before we can destroy him."

One of the lizardfolk raises his hand to speak. "There are heroes again? This is the first I have heard of this."

King Orso nods. "Heroes have returned to Isle of Mythos. One for the dwarves, one for the trolls, and many for the humans."

"Most strange." He hisses the words.

King Favian stands. "Which is all the more reason we must band—"

Regional Alert! *The portal to Blackspire has been reopened. Fast-travel is now permitted to Blackspire.*

An alarm horn blares from outside the castle. Its deep tone resonates through the room, blaring long and loud.

King Orso jumps to his feet, eyes wide. "Seascape is under attack!"

CHAPTER 29
BEHEMOTH

Kurzol tries to stop him, but King Orso rushes out of the room with his warhammer in hand. Everyone else follows in quick pursuit.

In the hallways, the guards from the other lands are full of questions.

"Follow the king!" I roar above the chaos. "Seascape is under attack."

We rush down the hallways as the horns of war continue to blare. No one talks as we run, and tension practically radiates from the beautiful carved stone walls.

A bestial roar unlike anything I have ever heard echoes above the sirens. Limery groans on my shoulder, and his claws dig into me.

King Orso pushes the castle doors open with such force that they slam against the walls. I'm surprised they don't break off the hinges. As we step out onto the balcony overlooking Seascape, a knot forms in my stomach. A massive beast, nearly two stories tall, wreaks destruction below. Dozens of guards lay dead, and more try to keep the beast at bay. They point their spears at the monster, but it marches forward, unafraid.

Behemoth. *Unique Monster. Level 40. A monster from the Shadowlands with one purpose: destruction.*

The behemoth is the creature of nightmares. Solid black scales cover the majority of its body and thick, sharp spikes run down its back. A spiked tail swings like a torturous wrecking ball, colliding with the shield of a paladin and sending the blood dwarf flying. Two long tusks hang from its jaw, and four dark eyes look at the world with ill intent. Its maw is full of jagged teeth. Each massive paw has four large claws, and I witness it crush a guard like he's nothing. It opens its mouth and an acidic spray shoots out, rapidly depleting the guard's health.

The catfolk curse loudly as we all stand helplessly by.

I try to swallow, but my throat is so tight that I can't. I've never seen a monster this powerful. Is this what waits on the other side of the blocked portals? My heart pounds in my chest. This is so not good.

King Orso lifts his warhammer in the air, and his entire body glows in a golden aura. When he speaks, his amplified words travel across the city. "Warriors of Seascape, your kingdom needs you!"

The guards in the square shimmer for a moment as the king's ability takes effect, boosting them with some unknown power. Orso rushes down the stairs, and Kurzol follows in pursuit.

The cleric grabs the king by the arm. "Your Highness, you can't. What if something happens to you?"

King Orso jerks his arm free. "Then I will die protecting my people."

King Favian puts his fingers to his mouth, and his whistle slices through the air. A moment later, his griffin lands on the balcony. Favian climbs on its back and joins the fray, diving straight for the behemoth.

I turn to the others. "We have to help them."

"That thing is level forty!" protests one of the merpeople.

"Yeah, and there's only one of it. Look at how many of us there are." I take off down the stairs, summoning horrors as I go, and to my surprise, most of the others follow. I turn to Gord and Rizza. "Help get the wounded to safety. Those of us with range will take on the behemoth."

King Orso still has about three flights of stairs left to go when I witness his true power for the first time. He leaps from the stairs and soars through the air like he was shot from a rocket. His warhammer connects with the behemoth's head, and the resounding crack sounds like a cannon firing. The level forty behemoth loses five percent health from the attack.

The monster stumbles from the blow, and when King Orso lands, he stares up at it defiantly. His kingsguard and what soldiers are left rally behind him. I continue to summon horrors as I descend the stairs.

King Orso's warhammer glows a fiery red as he smashes the behemoth's legs. "It's time to send this beast back to Hell."

The behemoth stomps, and the king rolls out of the way. The earth shakes, knocking several guards off their feet. A centaur gallops past me, bow raised, and fires an imbued arrow at the monster. It strikes the behemoth's scales in a display of fireworks.

We finally reach the square and spill out in every direction, surrounding the creature. Limery takes to the air, and launches a barrage of fireballs. King Favian rides his griffin, attacking the behemoth with his sword every time it faces away from him. A lightning bolt crashes into its back.

One of the gnomes raises his staff, and a giant bubble forms around the behemoth's head, obstructing its view. All the warriors run in, hacking and stabbing until the effect wears off. I send my horrors in with them. The behemoth swings its head and its long tusks nearly kill two of the lower-level guards.

The catfolk who refused to believe we were in danger must be some sort of healer; she tends to the wounded behind me. Gord runs with a dwarf tossed over both shoulders, carrying them to safety. He's a great warrior, but he's out of his element here.

Another jet of acidic spray shoots out, but it disappears into a portal before hitting anyone. The acid exits a second portal and burns through the wall of one of the buildings. Thank God for Kassidy, wherever he is.

I continue to summon horrors and send them into battle. Taryn sprouts a colony of poisonous mushrooms underneath the monster. They explode, covering the area in toxic gas. Jira sends a burning phoenix, but it dissipates against the behemoth's scales. The monster takes a beating as arrows and spells assault its body, but even with a host of high-level warriors attacking it, we've only whittled it down to fifty percent. Many more will die before we kill this thing.

The behemoth stomps again, knocking us all back, and follows up with another acid spray. For a second time, the acid is teleported before hitting us.

I search for Kassidy, but the teleportation mage is nowhere to be found.

"Kassidy!" I call out.

A second later, he appears beside me. "I'm a little busy here. What do you need?"

"Can you teleport something that big?" I point at the behemoth.

He frowns. "Yes, but not very far."

"Can you teleport it over that wall?" I point to the wall that runs along the side of the road, separating Seascape from the cliff-side towering above the ocean.

"I can try, but I need the monster to stay in one place long enough for the portal to open."

I nod. "Leave that to me. Just be ready when the time comes."

King Orso charges the behemoth, but he takes a hit from the monster's spiked tail. It sends him flying like a ragdoll. He crashes into a wall and immediately stands up, rushing back into battle.

I call to him as he rushes past me. "If we can keep the behemoth in one spot, then Kassidy can teleport it over the wall!"

"Brilliant! Where is Kurzol?" King Orso scans the battlefield for his cleric.

A host of skeleton warriors runs past, and I turn to see Pressley the Death Knight rushing toward us. Several dwarven warriors turn on him, spears raised, but I rush between them

"He's on our side! He's a hero."

The warriors cast me an uncertain glance, but King Orso nods to them, and they return to the behemoth. Pressley joins the ranks of dwarven warriors and shoots a beam of purple energy into the behemoth's side.

Limery and King Favian zoom through the air, constantly distracting the behemoth. I cast Champion, and a shadow demon joins the aerial attack.

"Kurzol!" King Orso's amplified voice rings out above everything. "Bind the creature."

An out-of-breath Kurzol joins us. "On a creature that big, it will only hold for a few seconds at most."

Kassidy claps him on the shoulder. "That is all we need."

"Very well. It shall be done." Kurzol equips a pearlescent staff and raises it into the air. The ground around the behemoth glows in a white circle. Kurzol thrusts his staff forward and ropes of white energy reach up from the ground, entangling the behemoth and rooting it in place.

At the same time, a second circle forms within the first one, this one a brilliant blue. Kassidy's face strains as the circle shimmers like a staticky TV. For a moment, I don't think the portal will take, but the static fades and a swirling vortex engulfs the behemoth. It falls through the portal and we all rush to the wall overlooking the sea.

I make it to the wall just in time to see the behemoth splash into the ocean. There's a dark splotch in the water that slowly fades as the monster sinks into the ocean's depths.

As the chaos of battle fades, all that is left are the groans of the wounded and the silence of the dead. King Orso looks out over the wreckage of Seascape square. The beautiful buildings that line the courtyard are in shambles. The marble tiles that formed a beautiful mosaic are crushed. The only structure undamaged is the portal itself.

I gain just enough XP to level up from the fight, but that is the least of my concerns. A crowd of dwarves has formed around the edges of the square, where the people of Seascape look on in horror.

King Orso shakes his head. "The buildings can be rebuilt, but the lives lost today can never be replaced." He faces the other leaders, many who talk in hushed whispers or wear stricken expressions. "You have seen firsthand the dangers that oppose us. These are not the delusions of a fearful leader. This is just the beginning. The time has come to stand together, or we will lose everything."

The catfolk healer steps forward. "Antadale will stand with Seascape."

The gnomes nod in unison. "As will Pruxford."

"And Wandermere," echoes the centaurs.

"The merfolk of Mistville will join your cause."

One after another, each of the leaders pledges to the cause.

King Orso turns to Kurzol. "Make sure the wounded are tended to, and then bury the dead. For the time being, I want the entirety of my kingsguard at the portal. I will speak to the people of Seascape before the night is over, but for now, we must convene a council."

The leaders climb the stairs, but I don't move. Chief Rizza, Gord, and Jira will speak for the trolls. I'm a hero, not a leader. Taryn starts to follow them, but I grab him on the shoulder.

"Aren't you coming?" asks King Orso.

I shake my head. "I made a promise to win Goldspire to your cause. It's time I make that happen."

He nods before turning around.

Limery sits on my shoulder, his body still warm from the battle.

"Do you have one more fight left in you for today?" I ask.

"Limmy is ready." He smiles.

I find Pressley at the wall, still staring into the ocean. "What was that thing?" he asks.

"Just a taste of what's coming." I look into the depths of dark energy that conceals his features. "Are you ready for new lands, gold, and glory?"

"Point the way."

Taryn retrieves his pets from the stables, and we gather around the portal. I summon a full army of horrors, ten of each, and Pressley summons nearly as many skeleton warriors.

When we step into Goldspire this time, we'll be ready.

CHAPTER 30
ONE MORE LAST TIME

I FOCUS on the rune for Goldspire and step through the swirling portal. A moment later, the sandy arena awaits. It's closer to nightfall this time, and dozens of pyres blaze around the arena.

Hundreds of people sit in the stands, and I can't help but wonder how much free time these people have on their hands.

A few battles are already underway. I spot two lizardfolk fighting a beastman with the head of a lion. A dark-skinned human battles a spotted minotaur.

"Back again?" A familiar deep voice booms nearby, drawing my attention.

Dakota, the level-thirty-three minotaur, stares in our direction. He's every bit as intimidating as I remember with broad shoulders and beautiful golden fur. His wide obsidian horns glimmer in the light of the pyres, and his nose ring glows orange with their reflection. The thick chain that killed Taryn hangs from his waist like a belt. It's weighted on one end with a ball, and the other end is tipped with a sickle that holds the weapon in place.

"Yeah, but this time, I brought a few friends."

My horrors and Pressley's skeletons spill out into the arena. Stompy snorts beside me, and Berry lets out a low growl. Ruby hides between Stompy's legs. Pressley, Taryn, and I stand beside each other, with Limery on my shoulder. If there was a way to take a screenshot of us right now, I know it would make an awesome poster.

Steam shoots out of Dakota's nose. "Then I guess I'll have to even the playing field. Mordrir!"

A level-thirty satyr runs over from the edge of the arena. The humanoid goat walks on two legs with thick hooves. He's like a leaner version of the minotaur. He's not the half-human/half-goat hybrid I'm familiar with from mythology. This one is big, strong, and powerful. His entire body is covered in light brown fur, and he wears a sash that covers his right shoulder and midsection. His left shoulder has a spaulder, similar to my own, that protects his arm down to the elbow. He wields a long spear with a ring of metal on the butt, making the weapon capable of being swung. Two sharp horns stick out of the top of his head, and a wispy goatee hangs from his chin.

You've got to be kidding me. We come here with extra backup and now we have to fight two?

I talk low enough that only Taryn and Pressley can hear me. "It's going to be okay. We're stronger and smarter than the last time we faced Dakota. We've also got Pressley and Limery. We've got this."

Pressley grunts, and Taryn nods. Hardly the confident reaction I was looking for, but it'll do for now.

"We gots this, Chods!" I can always count on Limery to be my biggest cheerleader.

"Let's hit them with everything we've got."

Pressley's skeletons and my horrors take off across the arena. There's a crackle near my ear as Limery takes flight and conjures a fireball.

Dakota and Mordrir take a fighting stance and prepare for our onslaught. As our minion army swarms them, Dakota unhooks his weapon from around his waist and winds it up like a lasso. He lets it fly, and the weighted end soars in an arc, sending bones flying as it dismembers half of Pressley's warriors.

Mordrir holds his spear at the ready, and when my horrors descend on him, he stabs his spear so fast that it moves in a blur. Perfectly-placed jabs pierce the skulls of a third of my horrors, downing them instantly.

While the beastmen are preoccupied, Taryn lands a lightning bolt on Dakota, stunning him in place. Pressley's skeletons attack the stunned minotaur, stabbing with their rusted blades. By the time the stun wears off, they've taken out ten percent of his health.

Dakota smashes his fist in the sand, and the earth explodes, rocketing the skeletons away. Meanwhile, Limery erupts a wall of fire behind Mordrir, stopping his retreat as the rest of my horrors overwhelm him.

I think we have the upper hand, but Mordrir uses his spear to vault over the horrors and create space. He then spins his weapon in an arc, killing several more horrors.

Limery tosses another fireball, but the satyr rolls to the side and it dissipates against the sand.

Pressley looks over at me. "Are we going to fight or watch them all day?"

Point taken. "Let's get in there!"

We charge into the fray as Dakota and Mordrir focus on the last of our minions. Pressley's armor clanks with each step, and his sword emanates dark energy as purple sparks trail up and down the blade.

Stompy's thunderous steps quake the earth around us, and Taryn casts Imbue on Berry, doubling his size. The two beasts run straight for the satyr.

Mordrir stabs my last horror through the eye, and then uses his spear to vault over Taryn, but Taryn is ready. He raises his sapling staff and the vines extend, wrapping around the satyr as he jumps overhead. As Stompy continues to charge, the force of the moulhaug slams Mordrir into the ground. Stompy drags him through the sand for several meters before the satyr frees himself.

As soon as Mordrir is free, Berry pounces on him, sinking his teeth into Mordrir's exposed shoulder. Blood stains the sash covering his chest.

Dakota lowers his head and charges Berry, ramming his horns into the bear's side. Mordrir quickly crawls to his feet, but we have them surrounded. Pressley, Taryn, and I form a triangle, threatening them from all sides while Limery hovers above us.

Dakota snorts. "I see you've got a few new tricks up your sleeve. Well, so do I!"

He stomps hard and the ground quakes, the earth rising like a wave as the arena floor moves like a mudslide. When the rolling sand hits us, the ground explodes, knocking me into the air. I land with a thud, and the impact knocks the air from my lungs. I crawl away on my back, gasping for air.

Limery flies down to check on me. "Is you okay, Chods?" His eyes radiate concern.

"I'm...fine," I get out between gasps.

I stumble to my feet. We've thrown just about everything we have at them, and they don't seem fazed.

Mordrir stabs Stompy in the leg, and the moulhaug bellows in pain. A new group of skeleton warriors rushes into battle and are immediately destroyed. Limery takes to the air and starts hurling fireballs, but Mordrir is too fast and Dakota barely takes any damage. He must have a pretty high fire resistance.

"Do either of you have a better plan?" I ask.

Pressley turns to me. "We need to eliminate one of them. Can you hold off the minotaur while the rest of us take on the goat?"

"I'll do my best. Limery, put a fire wall between them. We need to split them up."

A flaming wall erupts between the two beastmen. I summon a horror and toss it at Dakota, exploding it right in front of him and drawing his attention.

I point at the minotaur. "You and me, let's go."

Dakota laughs. "You think you can handle me?"

I spin Destroyer in my palm. "Try me."

He spins his chain overhead and stalks in my direction. The chain whirs loudly with each swing. When he lets it go, the weighted end flies at me like a rocket. I swing Destroyer with all I've got and hit the weighted ball perfectly. It flies back at Dakota even faster than he threw it, and he barely dodges his own weapon.

He blinks rapidly. I don't think he was expecting that.

Lightning crashes nearby, but my focus is solely on Dakota. I continuously summon horrors and send them to Pressley and Taryn.

Dakota swings his weapon again, and again, I hit it like it's batting practice. We repeat this process several times. For the moment, we're in a stalemate. His weapon's range keeps me from getting close, but I'm blocking every attack he throws at me.

I summon a horror and toss it in his direction, but he demolishes it before it gets close enough to do damage.

As long as I keep him distracted, the others might have a shot.

I chance a glance in their direction, just in time to see Taryn surround Mordrir with a ring of poisonous mushrooms. A lightning bolt comes crashing down, but the satyr vaults over the ring of fungus. The lightning crashes into the sand, releasing the mushroom's poisonous gas.

Pressley runs in, sword raised, as purple sparks trail down its edge. He swings for Mordrir, but the attack is parried. The sparks jump from Pressley's sword and crawl down Mordrir's spear. Mordrir throws his weapon in a panic before they reach him.

Now's our chance.

I'm tackled to the ground with enough force that my vision goes dark around the edges. A sledgehammer of a fist connects with my jaw and stars light the darkness. Fuck me! I should never have let my guard down.

Another fist rocks my world, and I can't see straight. I activate Berserker Rage and my vision clears. Dakota punches again, and this time, I move my head to the side. His fist only grazes my skull. As he pulls back for another punch, I rake my claws across his chest, and blood spurts all over me. Dakota grimaces in pain.

A burning ball of heat smashes into Dakota, knocking him off me, and Limery immediately returns to helping the others. I retrieve Destroyer and return to Dakota. He's already on his feet, with the sickle in one hand and the weighted end of his chain in the other.

He slings the weighted end at me and I raise my weapon to block it, but the chain wraps around Destroyer's handle. While I'm unable to wield my hammer, Dakota seizes the opportunity and stabs at me with the sickle. I'm forced to decide between fighting for my weapon or not being stabbed.

I let Destroyer go and live to fight another day.

Except Dakota has all the advantage now. He has the range and the weapons.

I equip the Halite Shield, my only defense, and wait for him to make the first move.

He laughs. "Are you going to beat me to death with a shield?" He leans his head back, roaring with laughter. "Look at your friends. It's over."

I turn to see Pressley with a spear stabbed through his side. Mordrid stands on top of him while Taryn looks on in horror.

"Taryn, run!" I yell. If we're going to lose, there's no point in him dying too.

Before Taryn has a chance to move, Pressley's hands glow a vibrant purple. He reaches forward and grabs Mordrir around the biceps. Smoke rises from inside of Pressley's armor and his health begins to rise as Mordrir's goes down.

Taryn extends the vines from his staff, preventing Mordrir's escape, and Limery flies down, pressing molten hands around the satyr's neck.

Mordrir's health drops to zero. Pressley tosses the body aside, and it collapses into the sand. He pulls the spear from his side and crawls to his feet with fifty-percent health.

Now, it's my turn to laugh. "You were saying?"

Pressley lifts both hands in front of him. A black aura forms around them, pulsing with tendrils of dark energy that grasp at the air. His health trickles down as the aura grows. The tendrils coil together, forming a ball of darkness between the death knight's hands. When the ball of energy is as large as his chest, he shoots it at Mordrir's corpse. The satyr's body absorbs the energy and his body stirs.

Dakota looks on in horror as Mordrir stands, his golden eyes now a deep purple.

Pressley picks the spear up off the ground and hands it to his new minion. "I think this belongs to you."

Mordrir takes the weapon and charges at Dakota. This is our

chance. We can finally end this. I summon three more horrors and send the Horror of Power and Horror of Finesse right behind Mordrir. I grab the Horror of Vitality by the horn and hold on to it.

Mordrir jabs with his spear, but Dakota parries it to the side. Both horrors attack the minotaur's legs. The Horror of Power jabs with its tusks while the Horror of Finesse rakes with its claws. Dakota quickly kills them, but while he's distracted, I toss my third horror at him. He stabs it through the head, but the passive slow keeps him from escaping Limery's fireball and Taryn's lightning bolt.

Through divine luck, Taryn's lightning stuns the minotaur for a second time. Mordrir stabs his spear through the minotaur's throat, and the fight is over.

A horn blares, and the crowd roars with applause. The pyres burn brighter, and a notification flashes across my vision.

Congratulations! *You have defeated a gladiator in the Goldspire Arena. You now have access to the continent.*

After a moment, the bodies of both Dakota and Mordrir fade away. For the time being, the arena is quiet and there are no battles taking place.

That's strange. I thought only heroes' bodies did that.

Pressley chugs a health potion, and Taryn casts Restoration on Stompy.

Limery lands on my shoulder. "We dids it, Chods. We wons!"

I smile. "You're right. We did it. And we couldn't have done it without all of you." I turn to Pressley. "So, what do you say, want to party up and explore what Goldspire has to offer? I need to find the castle or whatever passes for leadership around here first, but after that, nothing but adventure awaits."

Pressley waits a moment before responding. "I will be there for you when the time comes for us to band together, but for now, there are still things I must do on my own. Good luck in your travels." He extends a hand to me. "It was a pleasure to fight by your side."

He picks his sword off the arena floor and sheathes it. At the far end of the arena, one of the gates is now open. Pressley shakes Taryn's hand as he passes.

I walk over to Taryn and clap him on the shoulder. "It's been a hell of a few days, but maybe we can have a little fun before shit hits the fan again."

He smiles for the first time since nearly losing his pets. "You know, that sounds really good."

I pick up Destroyer and we are heading for the exit when a deep voice calls to me.

"You might want these back."

I turn around to see Dakota holding a small chest. His body looks good as new. There's no blood in his fur, and the hole Mordrir put in his neck is but a memory. Stranger yet, he's still level thirty-three.

Taryn looks just as confused as I am.

"How are you not dead?" I ask.

Dakota laughs. "I'm a Goldspire gladiator. We keep the lands of Goldspire free from the weak, but as long as we are on arena grounds, we never truly die. It has been a long time since heroes set foot in Goldspire, but it is tradition that should they perish and win victory on another day, all items shall be returned to them." He hands me the chest.

I open it, and inside are all the items we lost after dying the first time. Sea Scorpion, my Petrified Staff, the phoenix feather, the legendary Angel of Death Brandy, and more. It's all there.

"You are a resourceful warrior. May your adventures in Goldspire be fruitful."

With that, he turns to the portal as a new challenger appears on the platform.

We take our items from the chest, and I put mine in my satchel. Once again, I have more weapons than I know what to do with, which is fine by me. With Taryn and Limery by my side, Goldspire won't know what hit it.

Continue the adventure in Sentenced to Troll 4

Acknowledgments

Congratulations! *You have finished* Sentenced to Troll 3.
  3 of 6 completed.
  +1 stat point to distribute.
  +1 Review to leave.

Thanks for reading! I hope you had as much fun reading about Chod and his adventures as I did writing them. This adventure is just getting started. If you enjoyed the book, please consider leaving a review. Reviews and word-of-mouth are the lifeblood of indie authors. The more positive reviews I have, the more likely it is that others will take a chance on this series.

There are so many people to thank for helping make this novel a reality. If I miss someone, know that it was not intentional. I have a terrible memory and someone is bound to have slipped through the cracks.

Cindy Koepp has helped me immensely with feedback and improving my craft. She sees the drafts in their roughest forms, and I owe a great debt to the character development over these three novels.

Peezy, better known as Pressley the Death Knight, has been one of my greatest supporters. Thanks for believing.

Thank you to my beta readers: Rei S, Bryan O'Bannon, Jeremy

Cunningham, and Ryan Adams. You guys helped pick out the small details that made a big difference.

To my Bronze tier Patreon supporters and above: Tim Krason, Michael Percell, Robert Schaefer, and Frank Pisauro, I'm humbled by your generosity.

Eric Martin, you have embraced the voice of Chod, and I can't wait to see your take on book 3.

To Bella, Lawson, and Albus, my fur-babies, I'll never be able to truly articulate the impact that you three have made on my life. Ya'll are perfect in every way.

If you're looking for more books similar to my own, check out LitRPG Books.

ABOUT THE AUTHOR

S.L. Rowland is a cozy fantasy and LitRPG author known for crafting immersive worlds filled with adventure, heart, and a touch of humor. A lifelong gamer and fantasy enthusiast, he draws inspiration from tabletop RPGs, video games, and the fantastical. When he's not writing, he enjoys weightlifting, hiking with his Shiba Inu, and enduring the heartbreak of being an Atlanta sports fan.

SLRowland.com

Patreon-For signed paperbacks, advanced chapters, exclusive short stories, art, merch, and more.

Newsletter: For updates on new releases, sales, and behind the scenes content!

Email: slrowlandauthor@gmail.com

Find out more at https://linktr.ee/SLRowland

ALSO BY S.L. ROWLAND

Tales of Aedrea

Cursed Cocktails

Sword & Thistle

The Halfling's Harvest

There Be Dragons Here

Pangea Online

Pangea Online: Death and Axes

Pangea Online 2: Magic and Mayhem

Pangea Online 3: Vials and Tribulations

Sentenced to Troll 1-6

Path to Villainy: An NPC Kobold's Tale

Collected Editions

Pangea Online: The Complete Trilogy

Sentenced to Troll Compendium: Books 1-3

Sentenced to Troll Compendium 2: Books 4-6

9 781964 567068